A Choice *of* Angels

a love story
Charles Sobczak

A Choice of Angels, by Charles Sobczak
Published by: **Indigo Press LLC**
        2560 Sanibel Blvd., Sanibel Island, FL 33957
        www.indigopress.net
        Toll Free: (877) 472-8900

Printed in the United States by Whitehall Printing Company, Naples, FL

This is a second edition printing/September 2005

Hardcover edition: ISBN 0-9676199-7-1
Trade paperback: ISBN 0-9676199-9-8

Angel drawing by Shelly Castle, Castle Graphics, Inc.
Cover design by Robert Radigan & Charles Sobczak
Book design by Charles Sobczak, Kristinn Blount and Jennifer Rando

Acknowledgments

It was the summer of 2000, in the lobby of the Highlander Motel in Arlington, Virginia, when I met her. She had fair hair, a wonderful smile and, as I was soon to discover, she was a Muslim from Egypt. I was already thinking about writing this story, and when she unexpectedly came in to have a late-afternoon cup of coffee, my very first thought was that she was a godsend. She was.

We started talking. I had a hundred questions concerning Islam and she was very accommodating, answering each and every question as well as she could. Eventually, she inquired about my interest in her religion. I told her about the novel I was working on.

I told her that a close friend of mine had always wanted me to write a novel about growing up in a dysfunctional family. We would talk at length about it — his father having been institutionalized in the late 1950s — mine having drunk away his life. We had even decided on a title for the memoir: **War Babies.** It alluded to the unending wars between our respective parents.

I tried to write **War Babies** three times, with every effort ending up in the trash. The reason, I eventually discovered, was simple: the real story was about a much larger dysfunctional family — the family of man.

So I told her all this, the Egyptian girl with the beautiful eyes. I told her that I was writing a novel about the son of a Southern Baptist minister falling in love with a Muslim girl at a university in Atlanta. As I finished she started to cry.

When I asked her why she was crying she told me her parents, years ago, had sent her to England to study abroad. While at Oxford, she met and fell passionately in love with a young Anglican boy from London. She told me that my story and her story were the same. They fell in love, wanted to marry, raise a family and share their lives together.

It never happened. Her parents discouraged the marriage and his parents told him, in no uncertain terms, that they would disown him if he married her. He broke it off. She told me that she still loved him.

That's when I asked her this question: If you had to choose between being with him or being a Muslim, which would you choose?

She didn't hesitate an instant. "I would choose love," she replied.

I looked at her, tears in her eyes, and said, "That will be the title of my new novel."

"What do you mean?"

"I will call it **A Choice of Angels.**"

Because we should never have to make that choice. I believe that God would want us, His children, to choose love over the clothes we dress Him in. Be it the purple vestments of Catholicism, the burqas of Islam, or the yellow robes of the Buddhist monks, these customs belong to us. Why would God want how each and every culture chooses to worship Him keep us from loving each other? Are not all the world's religions different paths up the same mountain?

It is this Egyptian girl, whose name I cannot recall, the young woman from Cairo, that I have to thank. She was an angel. Most importantly, she was right. The world's great religions, as devout as their followers may be, still do far too much to divide than to bring us together. All this on an earth which, through the miracle of electronics, becomes smaller and smaller every day.

There are so many others to thank. I have to thank my wife Molly, who was willing to venture forth with me to Istanbul in May of 2001 — not that she objected all that much. I would like to thank Abdul 'Haq Muhammed for his excellent course on Islam, and Jay Richter for his insights into contemporary American Christianity. As Jay put it, "WWJD?"

I cannot overlook all the people who labored over the early drafts of this book, including Michael Lister, Scott Martell, John Jones, Sharon Heston, Joni Selement, and Murat Sariyildiz of Istanbul. I have to thank Jerold Roth for putting up with me while in Atlanta, and Chuck Wingo of Oglethorpe University for his assistance. I must also thank Anne Bellew and Renny Severance of the *Islander* for their diligent editing, and Mina Hemingway for her insightful suggestions. I also have to thank my hard-working assistants, Jennifer Rando and Kristinn Blount, for all their dedication and Kent Dalzell for his fine job with the galley proofs.

Not to forget Norm Zeigler, Libby Grimm, Phoebe Antonio and Bob Wimbush for their hard work copy editing the final drafts of this novel and particularly Bob Radigan, who has surpassed my expectations with the finest book cover ever. All of these wonderful people added their input and comments, and I appreciate the sincerity and dedication they showed in doing so. In my heart, they are all angels.

And last, but not least, the tens of thousands of readers who have given me so much encouragement to continue this journey. The many people who have called, written, e-mailed or spoken to me about how much they've enjoyed reading my books. I cannot tell you how much it means to me. Writing is a lonely endeavor, and your kind words of support make it all worthwhile. I can only hope you enjoy reading this love story as much as I've enjoyed writing it. Now, let's tell this tale.

Charles Sobczak
February 2003

This book is dedicated to my father,
Stanley Sobczak,
who taught me
— the hard way —
how to forgive.
(1920 – 2000)

And a woman who held a babe against
her bosom said, Speak to us of Children.
And he said:

Your children are not your children.
They are the sons and daughters of Life's
longing for itself.
They come through you but not from you,
And though they are with you yet they
belong not to you.

You may give them your love but not
your thoughts,
For they have their own thoughts.
You may house their bodies but not
their souls,
For their souls dwell in the house of tomorrow,
which you cannot visit,
not even in your dreams.
You may strive to be like them, but seek
not to make them like you.
For life goes not backward nor tarries
with yesterday.

You are the bows from which your
children as living arrows are sent forth.
The archer sees the mark upon the path
of the infinite, and He bends you with His
might that His arrows may go swift and far.
Let your bending in the archer's hand
be for gladness;
For even as He loves the arrow that flies,
so He loves the bow that is stable.

from **THE PROPHET,**
by Kahlil Gibran, 1923

A Forest of Glass

Bare trees. The winds of winter slipped down the southern slope of the Smoky Mountains and fanned out across the expansive Piedmont of Northern Georgia. Daybreak came in shades of gray. At the crest of Kennesaw Mountain, a thousand feet above the town of Marietta, a light rain began to freeze. As it settled on the bare trees — on the bitternut hickories, the black oaks and the silver maples — ice began to encase their naked branches.

The sun refused to help. It climbed the hidden staircase of that January sky in vain, unable to penetrate the dense clouds. Soon, it would become colder. The freezing rain would descend Kennesaw Mountain until every tree, every flowerless dogwood, was wrapped in ice.

By midday the forest would no longer be a forest of wood — it would be a forest of glass. An exquisite, delicate wilderness of frozen crystal. Branches perfectly sculpted, trunks held captive by a thin laminate. Later that evening, the wind would pick up sharply. Sometime after midnight, the snowfall would follow.

This was the day they would meet. A cold afternoon in one of the coldest winters Atlanta had ever known. They would exchange those first flirtatious glances across the classroom. She would smile and he, in turn, would smile back. Young lovers finding each other at a university. A story told and retold over the centuries.

She, Ayse Yalçin, from Istanbul, a vibrant, dark-eyed Muslim. He, Daniel Mark Harris, from Macon, a rebellious blue-eyed son of a Baptist preacher. Neither of their families wanting this to happen, never dreaming that it could.

When the winds picked up at dusk that day, the branches of the stalwart oaks began to break, the ice began to fall. The forest of glass, spun by the bitter cold, began to shatter. Limbs falling upon limbs, ice-encrusted branches, one after the other, shattering on the forest's floor. The fragile forest of glass came crashing down, fracturing like the families of these two young lovers. A clash of cultures unresolved.

For this is a tale of intolerance, pride and perseverance. The tale of Daniel and Ayse, as modern as it is ageless, as present as it is past.

Daniel walks across the room to speak with Ayse as the classroom is dismissed. She chooses him. He chooses her. Together, they choose love.

Istanbul, Turkey

A flock of gulls floated high above the lights of the Blue Mosque. The uncountable birds danced in and out of the powerful spotlights that shone on the six towering minarets. Their white wings contrasted sharply with the darkness that had fallen hours ago upon the ancient city. Every evening, until the lights were extinguished at midnight, the seagulls would arrive. They would come in by the hundreds from the Sea of Marmara and the rushing currents of the Bosporus.

Once over the massive dome of the mosque, they would circle and swoop in an eerie silence. Mystical and ethereal, as if riding some invisible thermal of Islam. It is a ritual of nature that remains forever unexplained.

"Allâhu akbar, Allâhu akbar, Allâhu akbar, Allâhu akbar!" More than two thousand mosques across the sprawling city began their final call to prayer. "Allâh is great," was repeated four times, followed by the ceremonial invitation to prayer that has gone unchanged for a thousand years.

But the voices of the muezzin have long since been replaced by loudspeakers. The call to prayer was electronic and amplified a dozen times louder than a man's lowly voice could call out. Adding to the timeless nature of the song was the fact that every mosque began the call to prayer within minutes of each other, never synchronized with the surrounding mosques. The chant would overlap and echo in strange, electronic harmonies.

Allâh is great, Allâh is great, Allâh is great, Allâh is great!
I testify that there is no god except Allâh,
I testify that there is no god except Allâh!
Mohammed is the messenger of Allâh,
Mohammed is the messenger of Allâh!
Come to prayer! Come to prayer!
Come to success (in this life and the Hereafter)
Come to success!
Allâh is great, Allâh is most great.
There is no god except Allâh.

The sound of a thousand prayers being heard at once, coupled with the circling gulls above the Blue Mosque, made the moment surrealistic. A mixture of modern and ancient. A mixture familiar to the people of Istanbul, sitting at the crossroads of two great cultures since the dawn of history. East meeting West. Asia and Europe, the two continents separated by a rushing river of saltwater, the Bosporus.

In her room, ten miles from the towering minarets of the old city, Ayse briefly rested her computer mouse and bowed her head in prayer.

"In the name of God the merciful, the Giver of mercy..." Ayse closed her eyes and spoke these opening words of prayer to herself. While the computer screen flashed images of links to Amazon.com and the infinite connections of the Internet, Ayse retreated into her prayers, into the salat, as she did faithfully every day at dawn, noon, mid-afternoon, sunset and now, at nightfall. In this, she mirrored the city of her birth — ancient and modern at once.

Within a few minutes, the call to prayer was over. Ayse Yalçin reopened her dark brown eyes. She moved the tiny arrow to scroll down the search bar on her computer. She was on the net, searching universities in America. She had just left the Web site of Clemson University. It was a well-designed site, she decided. It looked like a wonderful school, but it would to be too big. By now, Ayse knew her mother's objections by heart.

If she were ever going to be allowed to attend a school in the United States, it would have to be a small, private school with no religious affiliations. Elif, Ayse's mother, did not want her Muslim daughter involved with a Christian college — be it Catholic, Methodist or any denomination.

A state school, or a party school as Elif referred to them, was out of the question. Elif knew that most of the large American universities were as notorious for their beer drinking, pot smoking and drug taking as they were for their academics. If she was going to allow her daughter the latitude of attending a college in the United States, it had to be a small, quiet place. A safe place.

That's why Ayse kept searching. She had several schools in mind. There was

Clemson University in South Carolina, already saved in her list of favorites, although Ayse knew her mother would probably object. Another possibility was Susquehanna University in Pennsylvania, though the thought of spending a winter in central Pennsylvania made her think twice about making that application.

It wasn't that Ayse didn't like winter, because she did. Six years ago, she and her two older brothers, along with her mother and father, had gone skiing in the Ülüdag Mountains of Northwest Turkey. It was a delightful vacation. But a week of skiing, sledding and making snowballs was enough. It rarely snowed in Istanbul and, when it did, the snow was gone the following day. An entire winter of snow and ice, month after freezing month, was unthinkable to a young woman raised near the southern shore of the Black Sea.

It was better to search for a school in the South, thought Ayse as she scrolled down the search bar, anxious to find a college her mother would approve of. Anxious to find a world beyond the borders of Turkey.

Ayse would search past midnight. Finding an interesting school in New Orleans, checking out its Web site, reading its mission statement, and taking notes. Her college was out there, somewhere in the vast world of the Internet. She would find it.

Macon, Georgia

ell, Dad, maybe God doesn't exist. Maybe we made him up to protect ourselves from the unknown."

"Don't you dare to speak about God like that, Daniel! That's blasphemy, not only against God, but against the Holy Spirit. As it says in Matthew 12, Verses 30 through 32...

"He that is not with me is against me; and he that gathereth not with me scattereth abroad. Wherefore I say unto you, All manner of sin and blasphemy shall be forgiven unto men: but the blasphemy against the Holy Ghost shall not be forgiven unto men.

"And whosoever speaketh a word against the Son of man, it shall be forgiven him: but whosoever speaketh against the Holy Ghost, it shall not be forgiven him, neither in this world, neither in the world to come.

"You had better mind your tongue, Daniel, mind your tongue or face the harrowing consequences of eternal damnation."

"If God doesn't exist, then hell doesn't exist, Dad."

"Hell exists. Satan exists and he is slowly, insidiously taking possession of your soul, Daniel.

"Ye are of your father the devil, and the lusts of your father ye will do. He was a murderer from the beginning, and abode not in the truth, because there is no truth in him. When he speaketh a lie, he speaketh his own: for he is a liar, and the father of it. John, Chapter 8, Verse 44."

They were at it again. Rebecca could hear them from the kitchen, father and son, arguing. This time it was about the existence of God. Some evenings it would be about politics, other evenings would fall victim to accusations of racism or abortion rights, but most of the time the battle lines were drawn over religion.

Six years ago, when Daniel's older sister, Ruth Anne, was still living at home, their arguments would rarely go this far. Ruth had a way with them, Clay and Daniel. A way of keeping them at bay. A way of keeping the peace.

But now things were different. Within a few minutes, if the debate continued to heat up, Daniel would get up from the table in disgust. He would throw his cloth napkin down in a fit of anger and head upstairs to his room. Once behind a locked door, he would put on his headphones and turn the volume up on his Walkman CD player until the noise inside his brain made the noise of his father disappear.

After a half hour of listening to torturously loud music, Daniel would turn the volume down and pick up his journal. His journal had become his lifelong confidant, his story told in infinite detail to no one but himself. Because so many entries had been made over the years during the middle of the night, when he was unable to sleep, Daniel had named his personal diary *Book of Midnights*. There were twenty notebooks filled with his innermost thoughts, his secret fears. More volumes were certain to follow.

Rebecca had tried to intervene, to mediate between father and son as Ruth had done so adeptly, but to no avail. Her pleas fell upon the deaf ears of the two strong-willed men arguing in the dining room. Clayton Aaron Harris, her husband for the past thirty years, had always been resolute. From the early years, just after attending the Southern Baptist Theological Seminary, through his first congregation in rural North Carolina, Clay had been dedicated to Jesus. Clay's well-worn Bible was not open to interpretations. It wasn't a negotiable Christianity that Minister Harris preached every Sunday at the largest and newest church in Macon. His religion was, like the Ten Commandments, written in stone. Granite.

It was King James Christianity. Born again and proud of it. Rebecca had always admired Clay's resolve. Rebecca loved to sit there on Sunday morning, surrounded by one thousand of the faithful, listening to the man she had married preach the word of God with such fervor, with such conviction, that it made the Holy Book come alive. Clay could recite a parable so intensely that he made you feel as if Christ were there beside him, whispering each line into his ear. Making sure he got every phrase, every nuance, just perfect.

Rebecca loved Clay, and she loved him without reservation. She loved the deep blue of his eyes, his silver hair, his sturdy, powerful frame, but more than the physical aspects of his English good looks, Rebecca loved his passion. If there ever were a man born to proclaim the Word of God, it was Clayton Aaron Harris. His sermons could save the darkest of sinners, cast out the deepest demons. His preaching seemed as though it could raise the dead.

At home, removed from his lofty pulpit and face to face with his rebellious son, Daniel, Clay felt vulnerable. In his enormous church, he could bring two hundred people to their feet, arms waving, palms turned upward to the Lord. In his church, salvation was at hand. At home he struggled to get his boy to say grace. It was a constant battle, an unspoken war between father and son where no quarter was given.

As Rebecca submerged the greasy frying pan in the dishwater, she could hear the two of them going on and on in the dining room. Clay quoting Scripture and Daniel countering with notions of atheism, agnosticism or existentialism. She was glad to be in the kitchen, relieved that she didn't have to watch Clay's face redden with anger. His fair skin turned flush with outrage, unable to fathom where Daniel got his far-fetched notions, asking why the Lord, who had given them so much, had also given them Daniel. Given them this troublesome cross to bear.

From the safe harbor of the kitchen Rebecca heard one of them push back his chair. She knew it must be her boy. She listened in despair.

"I don't care, Dad. I'm fed up with Numbers and Deuteronomy, Corinthians and Matthew. I wish that just once, you could say something on your own. Something that didn't end in Verse 18, Chapter 20 through 23.

"But you never have and you never will. It's 'Jesus said this and Jesus said that.' Well, I'm really, really tired of it, Dad, and I'm going up to my room."

"Don't you dare talk to your father like that, Daniel. Now you listen to me..."

Rebecca heard Daniel's feet pounding up the oak-trimmed stairs. She heard his door slam and knew he was throwing the latch behind him. Clay had stopped shouting at his son when he was halfway up the stairs. Rebecca took up her dishrag and started scrubbing pieces of fried chicken off the cast iron frying pan. Tears were rolling down her face and falling into the dishwater. Her lips made the slightest of motions as they prayed in silence. She prayed for peace, as a million mothers had prayed before her. Peace between them.

In Daniel's Room

Rebecca knew her son well. After locking the door to his room, Daniel donned a pair of headphones and vanished into the sounds of Slipknot. The music was frenetic and loud, like the sound of people trying to kill each other using garbage cans. Daniel vanished inside of it, making the sound of bashing metal erase the sound of his father's voice.

With the headphones on and the music on a rampage, he picked up a book and started reading. Daniel had the ability to shut off one part of his senses while engaging another. The screaming guitars and crashing drums of Slipknot drifted off as Daniel's keen mind began focusing on the novel he was reading

It was *Siddhartha* by Herman Hesse. Knowing how his Father felt about reading books on other religions, Daniel derived a strange satisfaction from reading a book about the Buddha. It was as much about reading how Siddhartha achieved enlightenment as it was about committing a sacrilege in his father's eyes. Daniel knew how his father felt about Buddhism — the same as he did about all other religions. He lumped them all together under paganism. He felt the same about all the world's great religions: Hinduism, Buddhism, Judaism, and Islam. Lost souls the lot of them. Every believer doomed to hell.

That's why Daniel had been drawn to them, reading and studying the world's religions since the seventh grade. He knew it irritated his father and he derived a rebel's pleasure from that knowledge. To Daniel Harris, reading *Siddhartha* was like reading a dirty book. Sacred smut in his father's eyes.

Over time, it became more than that. It became a search for truth. A young man's quest to make sense of his world. As Slipknot blared and night fell, Daniel read on, trying to picture in his mind's eye what it was like in northern India two thousand, six hundred years ago. Why Siddhartha Gautama would give up everything — his princely lifestyle, his beautiful wife, his worldly possessions — to wander around the countryside for six years in austerity. And do it all in search of this thing he called Nirvana. Whatever Nirvana is.

By midnight the Slipknot CD had run through its dozen songs three times and Daniel's eyes were struggling to keep focused. It was time to call it a night. Tomorrow was Saturday and his weekend chore was to mow the expansive lawn surrounding their suburban home in North Macon.

It won't take me more than two hours on the riding mower, Daniel calculated as he set down his paperback. After that, I'll finish reading this novel.

Just before going to sleep Daniel reached under his mattress and took out his journal. It wasn't anything fancy, nothing more than an inexpensive, spiral notebook. The kind you buy at Wal-Mart.

Daniel took out his pen and opened it to the next blank page. The notebook was over half-filled with notations and occasional ink drawings. He smiled as he picked up his pen, no longer filled with the angst he felt earlier. At ease and alone, Daniel started another entry into his *Book of Midnights*.

March 27,

Dad and I had at it again during dinner. Man, he pisses me off. I can't wait to get out of this house. Then I won't have to hear him go on and on about Joshua chapter this and John chapter that. Bullshit. The Bible is a book full of bullshit.

Just like this Buddha guy. How weird can you get? He takes a little journey out of his palace at the age of twenty-nine and totally flips out because he sees a bunch of losers in the countryside. What was he thinking? I wish I could take him to downtown Macon some late Friday afternoon to see the losers down there, hanging out by the river and the train tracks. All of them drinking out of paper bags and looking like death reheated.

There were losers back then just as there are losers now. Poor people and stupid people who just don't get it. Well, screw 'em. And screw my dad while you're at it.

Because that's what I don't get about religions. There are so many gods out there, over two thousand Hindu gods alone. Not to mention all the gods we've shelved over the centuries — the Norse gods and the Greek gods, the Egyptian gods and the pantheon of Roman gods. They're all put out to pasture by the latest craze, that being my Father's born-again bullshit. My father's fundamentalist bent.

A year and a half and I'm out of here. I'll find a college that doesn't live and die religion and I'll never come back. Not to Macon and not to this hellhole. That's not all that long when you think about it — eighteen months. Now that makes me want to sit up and shout "Hallelujah."

Hallelujah!

Daniel laughed as he tucked his journal back between his mattresses and his box spring. He kept repeating the word hallelujah to himself as he pulled the warm blankets over him. He sang an old familiar hymn until he drifted off to sleep.

North Macon Baptist Church

"Hold all calls, Rose. Tell them I'm working on my sermon."

Clay lifted his finger from the intercom button on the phone and felt relieved. It had been another hectic morning at North Macon Baptist Church. He had received several calls from members of the landscaping committee, discussing the three proposals that had just come in. Between reviewing those proposals and Mrs. Edwards calling to inform him that her husband's cancer was terminal, Clay had found little time to work on Wednesday night's sermon.

So after a light lunch and a tall glass of homemade iced tea, Clay had decided to put the world on hold and spend time polishing his sermon. It was his fourth in a series of seven on the Book of Revelation. Tonight he was going to speak on the sounding of the trumpets.

The Book of Revelation had always held Clay captive. It spoke of the rapture, of the seven-headed dragon, of God and Magog and the defeat of Satan. Clay was certain we were in the end of days. The New Jerusalem had been established after the Second World War and the signs of the second coming could be witnessed everywhere.

The Holocaust was involved, as was the dropping of the two atomic bombs on Japan. Each of the seven trumpets of the Apocalypse would soon be sounded. After that, the final judgment would come. Christ would once again walk the earth to judge the quick and the dead. Clay had envisioned it all, and knew the end time was drawing near.

AIDS, ebola, pollution, nuclear devastation — they were all tied into this climactic completion of God's will. Armageddon was at hand, and Clay, as pastor, wanted to be certain his congregation was ready. Certain they would survive the seven plagues, and to know firsthand the signs of the last judgment.

Clay opened up his tattered King James Bible and began reading Revelations 8: Verse 1-12. *The fourth angel blew his trumpet and immediately a third of the sun blighted and darkened, and a third of the moon and the stars, so that the daylight was dimmed by a third, and the nighttime darkness deepened. As I watched, I saw a solitary eagle flying through the heavens crying loudly, "Woe, woe, woe to the people of the earth because of the terrible things that will soon happen when the three remaining angels blow their trumpets."*

Clay read on, how the fifth angel will open up the bottomless pit, and the locusts will arrive, stinging those men who did not have the Mark of God, not killing them, but torturing them for five months with the pain of a thousand scorpion stings. They will all want to die, but God will not grant them the relief of death.

The Destroyer has arrived.

By late afternoon Clay had finished his sermon. It was a dark, foreboding message he was going to deliver that Wednesday night. But he knew it was a message his flock needed to hear. Because the end was coming and Clay wanted his people to be among the one hundred and forty-four thousand who would endure the last days. He wanted his congregation to have the Mark. He knew his only son, Daniel, would be unmarked. He knew Daniel would perish if he continued along his blasphemous ways.

He tried not to think about his singular failure for long, knowing how far apart he and his boy had drifted these last few years. Feeling the chasm between them growing deeper and wider, like some crack in the earth threatening to swallow them both into the abyss of estrangement.

Clay prayed for Daniel before closing his Bible. Earlier on, he had planned to head home for dinner, but he didn't want to endure another heated argument with his son before the seven-o'clock service. He would have to let Rebecca know that his plans had changed. She would understand.

He had saved half of his turkey and cheese sandwich just in case. If he was still hungry at ten, he could have some leftover biscuits and gravy before going to bed. No, it was easier to take a short stroll outside, catch a glimpse of the falling sun and eat his cold sandwich on the picnic table behind the sanctuary. The thought of going home for a few hours and fighting with his boy kept him from leaving the church, just as it had the previous ten weeks.

Clay was looking forward to having Daniel head off to college in a year and a half. Long ago, he had wanted his son to attend his alma mater, the Southern Baptist Seminary in Louisville. Five months ago Clay would have settled for Baylor, or even Mercer. Daniel was impossible. At this point, unbeknownst to his wife, Clay was willing to let Daniel attend any school he wanted to. All Clay wanted was to have him out of the house.

The intercom interrupted his reflections.

"Reverend Harris, I just wanted to let you know I'm heading home for the day. Is there anything else you need before I leave?" asked Rose.

"No, but thanks for asking, Rose. I'll see you tomorrow."

"Have a good night, Reverend Harris. I pray that your sermon comes out well."

"I do too, Rose. Thank you and God bless you."

"Good evening then. I'll lock up behind me."

With Rose gone, Clay's thoughts turned to the Lord. He asked that Christ show him the way with Daniel. Clay prayed that the Holy Ghost should come down from above and fill Daniel with the spirit of the Lord, turning him away from the false prophets he studied and the evil of his ways.

The final days are upon us, thought a Christian minister in his lonely office in an empty church on a cold March afternoon in the northern suburbs of Macon. For Clayton Aaron Harris, the seven trumpets were already blowing.

Nisantasi Girls School

D id you find anything last night?" asked Fatimah.

"A few more possibilities. One school in North Carolina, another in Georgia, and two in Louisiana,"

"I don't know why you bother, Ayse. You know your mother isn't going to allow you to go. She wouldn't let either of your brothers attend school in America; why on earth would she let her only daughter go overseas?"

"My brothers gave in too easily. They knew their grades might have kept them from getting admitted to an American school, so when my mother objected, it was easy for them to decide not to bother. They didn't want to be embarrassed by not being accepted once she allowed them to go.

"My grades are very good, Fatimah, much better than either of my brothers, and my mother knows it."

Fatimah and Ayse were between classes, walking down the long, well-kept hallways of the Nisantasi Girls School. Within the next few minutes, each would be inside of her respective class, Ayse taking geography and Fatimah studying Spanish. They would take their lunch together after class, as they had for the past three years.

This year, the Turkish equivalent of their junior year in high school, they had only one class together — English. They spoke English to each other most of the time — as much to practice the language as out of habit.

English was the second language of Turkey, just as it was the second language of the world. It was the language of movies, music, business, science and the

Internet. If you wanted to succeed in Turkey, you spoke English.

From lowly cab drivers from Capadoccia to Ayse's father, Mustapha, English was the language of commerce and the upwardly mobile. Mustapha had any number of clients in America. Without his ability to communicate with them, via e-mail, fax and phone, his bottom line would be dramatically affected.

Ayse's family lived well. They had a cook, a cleaning lady, a chauffeur and a gardener. Their home sat high atop the hill in an older suburb of Istanbul overlooking the flowing Bosporus. The views were stunning and the house was spacious and well appointed. The only difference an American might note is that the windows had ornately decorated bars over them to prevent burglars.

Her father went to his office every day in a Lexus, driven by Abdul, his chauffeur. Dinner was served by Halil, a cook they hired from the Balkans when the first wave of refugees had arrived ten years ago. Ayse Yalçin had been born into money, a life not unlike any upper-class family from Germany, Japan, or the United States. Good schools, fine clothes and expensive furnishings. Merchandise purchased at malls in greater Istanbul sporting the same ubiquitous chains as every upscale mall in America.

Hand-carved antiques imported from France, fine wool rugs from the Anatolia region and a marble dining room table from Greece. Electronics from America, Korea and Japan. Cell phones, pagers and satellite televisions. Ayse's world was the same world as Daniel's. It's just that her Father drove past mosques on his way to work, while Daniel's drove past Methodist and Evangelical churches. The streets were paved with the same asphalt, the cars ran on the same fuel and the people in both cities had many of the same dreams and ambitions.

The world was becoming smaller. That's why Ayse wanted to go to college in America. Because, in a way, she felt American. Most of the movies she and her friends had grown up watching were made in Hollywood. She loved Julia Roberts's smile just as much as would a young girl in Wichita. Ayse thought Matt Damon was cute, but Johnny Depp captivating.

She had grown up with the music of U-2, Prince and N-sync. Not only could those boys sing, thought a young dark-eyed teenage girl of seventeen, they were adorable. America had always been no further away from her than the remote on her satellite television. As much as her mother tried to keep her away from her electronic connection to the rest of the world, Ayse loved it.

Later that afternoon, as Fatimah and Ayse discussed boys and music over lunch, Ayse realized she would miss her friends and her life in Turkey should her mother consent to letting her go. Hers was a good country, filled with devout Muslims who loved their nation of sixty-five million.

It had its troubles, just like America had theirs. The Kurdish minority in the east was a constant problem, and the economy was suffering through a recession. The Turkish lira had just been devalued and, as a result, her Father's business was struggling.

But things were no different in America. Ayse had read how the blacks in America were still far from being treated as equals and the Hispanics held most of the menial jobs. The U.S. economy was in a recession and businesses across the nation were laying off thousands. Every nation has its own set of problems to deal with, reasoned a mature young lady.

It was just that America had this shine to it. A glow that seemed to rise above the crowded corridors of Istanbul's grand bazaar and the constant haggling over prices in the ancient spice market. It had style.

After lunch, Ayse and Fatimah said goodbye to each other. Their afternoons were filled with different classes and, aside from passing each other in a hallway at some point, they wouldn't have any time to visit again until tomorrow's English class. Abdul would swing by to pick Ayse up at four and she would be home a half an hour later.

She planned to discuss her university choices with her mother and father at dinner tonight, despite the fact that doing so might upset them. Ayse realized she would need to start making applications to schools soon if she had any chance of getting in after her senior year. Her mother knew this and would never broach the subject of her daughter attending an American school.

❂

Abdul showed up in the Lexus promptly at four and Ayse climbed into the back seat with her backpack. There was a line of expensive automobiles stretching down the block, most chauffeur driven, to pick up daughters who belonged to the upper class.

Land Cruisers, Mercedes, Lincoln Navigators and Jaguars parked along a tree-lined boulevard beside the wrought-iron gates of the school. The girls all pouring out at once, laughing and waving to each other. Each of them dressed in a dark-blue blazer, with a long plaid skirt and a white blouse, looking not unlike the dismissal of an all-girls Catholic high school in Boston or Chicago. Most of them dark-haired, with a few having dyed their hair with an auburn henna or, if their parents allowed, a blondish tone. As blond as jet-black hair would dye.

But it wasn't a Catholic school. It was a private Muslim school. They studied the Qur'an, not the Bible. They knelt to the east and they prayed more often than did most Christians. Mohammed was the Messenger of God for Muslims, just as Christ was the Messenger of God for Christians. The rest of the courses they studied were the same. Islam has always encouraged learning, and Nisantasi Girls School believed learning was the cornerstone to a deeper understanding of the world.

Ayse said hello to Abdul in Turkish and buried herself in a textbook. Abdul was a kind man. He spoke very little English and had no need to learn it at this point. He was fifty years old, with two boys at home and a loving wife who did not work. They lived in one of the many high-rise apartment complexes just east of the old city. After his driving duties were completed for the day, Abdul would get into his Fiat and drive home to his wife and children. He rarely arrived home before seven in the evening and he never complained.

Ayse arrived at her home by four-thirty. The traffic coming up the hill from the highway along the Bosporus was steady but tolerable. Istanbul was a city with too many automobiles and too few streets. Some afternoons Abdul couldn't make it back to Bebek until after five. Everyone in Istanbul, from the chauffeurs to the cab drivers, was used to it.

After watching Ayse punch in her security code and let herself into the back-door of the house, Abdul sped off in the direction of her father's office in Taksim. When Mustapha left his office between five-thirty and six, Abdul would have the Lexus parked outside waiting for him. Abdul Güzel was dutiful to a fault.

Ayse said hello to Halil, who was preparing dinner in the kitchen, and went up the back-servants stairway to her room. Dropping her hefty backpack, she threw herself on her queen-sized bed. She executed a flawless half twist in the air and landed, as always, flat on her back. Completing the acrobatics of coming home to her room after school, Ayse grabbed the television remote with her left hand before the second bounce and flipped on MTV. It was time to unwind. Her half hour of mindless television before going down and saying hello to her mother and spreading her school work out on the kitchen table.

She watched a Jennifer Lopez video followed by a new release from the Back Street Boys. A batch of commercials pushing everything from diet colas to Honda Accords followed. Ayse never touched the mute. She found herself equally absorbed by what America was selling as what America was singing. They were interlinked with the modern mythology of consumerism. America, imagined Ayse, is a land of plenty.

Time drifted by. The half-hour became an hour and Ayse knew she had to start digging into her school work or cut her net surfing for American universities later that night.

She hit the off button and rose from the imprint her hour of downtime had left on the soft mattress. Taking off her blazer, she picked up her backpack and bounded down the front stairs. Mother was next.

Elif was in the living room reading the Qur'an. She had heard Ayse arrive, listened to her run up the back stairway, heard the television go on and go off, and listened to her footsteps coming down the front stairway. Though Elif had noted all of this, none of it had distracted her reading of the Qur'an. As Ayse approached, she continued reading.

Tell the believing men to lower their gaze and be modest. That is purer for them. Lo! God is Aware of what they do.

And tell the believing women to lower their gaze and be modest, and to display of their adornment only that which is apparent, and to draw their veils

over their bosoms, and not to reveal their adornment save to their own
husbands and Fathers... or children who know naught of women's nakedness.
And let them not stamp their feet so as to reveal what they hide of their
adornment. And turn unto God together, O believers, in order that ye may
succeed. Qur'an 24.30 -32.

Elif Yalçin was a traditional Muslim woman. She was old school. She didn't wear the full burka, as did the women of Pakistan and Arabia, but she wore the chador. It was a black cloak covering the body, head and hair, but not her face. The Qur'an and the shari'ah require that when a woman becomes of age she must cover her body from the ankles to the top of her head, extending down her arms past the elbow. To Elif, wearing the chador was a sign of prestige.

Elif was in her mid-fifties, four years younger than Mustapha, her husband of thirty-two years. Aside from offering her services to charities, Elif had never worked. Her role was that of being a mother and raising their three children, a role which Elif accepted with a devotion uncommon in the modern Western world. She loved her children beyond reproach.

She looked Muslim. Dark-skinned, dark-eyed and having beautiful black hair slightly graying beneath her chador, she personified what an American would perceive as an Islamic woman. Sitting there, on a fine leather chair, her feet resting on an ottoman, and her eyes poring over the sacred words of Mohammed, Elif could have been the model for a Turkish painting. The painting could have been done five hundred years ago as readily as today. Timeless and traditional, like an Islamic *Whistler's Mother*.

"Hello, Mother," said Ayse in Turkish.

"Hello, my daughter," responded Elif without looking up.

"I'll be in the kitchen doing my homework if you need me for anything," said Ayse.

"That is fine," said Elif.

That was all they said. Ayse went down the hallway to the kitchen and Elif kept reading her sacred text. This ritual would be repeated with little variation five out of the seven days a week. It was, in part, the polarity of their two worlds that kept their conversations to a minimum. Elif would like to see her daughter follow in her own footsteps.

To have Ayse settle down and forgo her notions to study abroad. But there were thousands of mothers like Elif in Turkey. Not understanding their children. Afraid to let them go. They felt helpless in the face of this shrinking world. Some had tried to cut their children off from the electronics of the modern world, but this proved futile.

They could not sequester their children from the deluge of beepers and cell phones, computers and radios, satellite televisions and Walkmans. If they took them away, their children would simply go to a friend's house, or stay after school to use the search engines the $17,000 annual tuition had purchased for their students. There was no escaping it. The only hope was prayer.

That was what Elif was praying for when Ayse arrived home from school and it was what Elif would be praying for until she sat down to dinner in an hour. She prayed Ayse would have a change of heart and not want to leave her native Turkey.

She prayed that Ayse would choose to attend Bosporus University overlooking the Sea of Marmar and the bridge of Fatih Sultan Mehmet spanning the mighty strait. That she would find a good husband, marry and raise her children in Istanbul. She prayed things would stay the same, and not change so dramatically in a world that thrived on change.

A little after six, Elif heard the Lexus pull in the driveway. She heard the car doors slam and knew Abdul was leaving, walking down the street to where he parked his Fiat every morning. She listened for the back door to open, for Mustapha to say hello to Halil and go kiss his daughter, studying geography at the kitchen table. Elif heard her husband's footsteps as he walked with his heavy stride down the long hallway to the living room.

He said hello to her in Turkish and came to kiss her on the lips. They spoke briefly of their day as he found a comfortable place on the sofa. He opened up the *Hürriyet* newspaper that was folded under his arm and started catching up on local events and the ceaseless charades of Turkish politics.

A half-hour passed in silence, broken by Halil's footsteps down that same tiled hallway and her announcing to them that dinner was ready. Ayse put down her studies of the peoples of Southeast Asia, Mustapha his business section, and Elif her Qur'an. They gathered together at the dinner table.

After sitting, Ayse prayed quietly to herself, *"In the name of Allâh, the Merciful, the Compassionate, O Monarch that nurtures us with His bounty! Show us the source and origin of these examples you have shown us! Draw us nigh to your seat of rule; do not let us perish in these deserts! Take us into your presence and have mercy on us! Feed us there on the delicious bounty you have caused us to taste here! Do not torment us with desperation and banishment! Do not leave your yearning, thankful and obedient subjects to their own devices, do not cause them to be annihilated. Thanks for boons and health. Amen!*

Each of her family prayed their version of this prayer silently, then they began their meal together.

Dinner was a traditional Turkish meal of roast lamb, and imam bayildi, a local dish made from eggplants stuffed with tomatoes and onions. Halil was an excellent cook. She used nothing but Halaal meats and the finest of herbs and spices. Twice a week Abdul would take Halil to the spice market to ensure the best quality of ingredients. She would walk to the nearby butcher shop that sold only Halaal, or permitted meats, in Bebek and, once a week Abdul would take her to the nearby supermarket for additional supplies and sundries.

Halil lived on the top floor of the house, in a third-floor apartment over the two empty bedrooms where the boys had once slept. She received two weeks a year off to return and visit her family in what was once Yugoslavia. Both of her sons had been killed in the war. Her husband had died decades ago in an automobile accident. All that was left were her two sisters and an aging brother. Still, she enjoyed going back home to Macedonia.

Ayse brought up the university topic first, knowing that if she didn't say anything, Mustapha and Elif would never mention it. It was her battle to win or lose.

"I found some more schools on the Internet last night that I thought you might be interested in, Mother."

"American schools?"

"Why yes, of course," said Ayse.

Elif did not respond.

"Tell me about them," interjected her father.

Ayse was anxious to discuss them, and her father's invitation to do so was a welcome relief. Elif sat and ate in silence. She would have none of this, but it was not her place to question her husband's interest in the topic. Mustapha was less inclined to be as parochial about the matter. His business had taken him to America a score of times in the past decade and would likely send him back again before the year was ended.

He had contacts for his carpets in New York, Chicago and Atlanta. He knew the world was growing smaller and felt there was no reason to try to keep Ayse from it. Still, he would respect Elif's decision not to allow her daughter's exodus if it came to that. His wife ruled the household just as he ruled his office. Their respective jurisdictions were not to be taken lightly.

Ayse dove into her latest crop of prospective universities with a childlike enthusiasm. She talked about Clemson, the strengths and weaknesses of two schools in New Orleans, and a small college in Atlanta that had caught her eye.

Halfway through Ayse's describing the merits of Tulane University, Elif interrupted.

"If we do allow you to attend a school in America, you can rest assured it will not be located in a decadent Western city like New Orleans, Ayse."

"But Mother, please let me finish."

"You are finished."

Mustapha glanced over to Ayse and nodded. They had better drop the subject or the dinner would soon turn distant and dour. Her father's nod signaled that they could continue this conversation later, when they were alone. Then they could speak at length, without Elif's opinions.

Halil brought out a fabulous dessert of baklava and everyone's eyes lit up. It was Ayse's favorite and, guiltily, she took a second serving. The three of them excused themselves and headed off to their respective corners of the spacious house. Tomorrow was Friday, the day of worship for Muslims and both Elif and

Mustapha wanted some time to prepare for the upcoming holy day.

Ayse went back to Vietnam, Cambodia and the politics of mapmaking. Halil stayed in the kitchen until well past nine o'clock cleaning up, and preparing for breakfast tomorrow. After Halil had retired to her room, Mustapha came in and sat at the kitchen table beside his daughter.

"You can tell me about the college in New Orleans now, my sweetheart."

"Thank you, Father."

Ayse abandoned her homework, anxious to discuss her plans. She told her father about the two schools in southern Louisiana. When she had completed her descriptions, Mustapha remarked, "They sound wonderful, Ayse, but your mother is right. I have been to this New Orleans and I would not want you to go to college there. It is a big city filled with troubles. The French Quarter and Bourbon Street are not what we have in mind should we allow you to go overseas to school.

"Find someplace less filled with temptation should you expect your mother to grant you permission to go away. Tell me about the school in Atlanta. Is it Emory University?"

"No, Father, it isn't Emory. I researched Emory and felt it's just too large. I am used to such a small campus, like Nisantasi.

"It is a small, private school called Oglethorpe University, which is a silly name, don't you think? It only has twelve hundred students and it's not affiliated with any religious organization."

"I've never heard of this school, Ayse, and I've been to Atlanta a dozen times in the past ten years. It's an odd name for a university, isn't it? Where is it located?"

"It's on Peachtree Street, north of the city. I'll print out some material on it if you are interested."

"That would be nice; we can look at it together over the weekend. Now get on with your studies. Atlanta would be a good choice because I have friends and contacts there. At least there would be someone to look after you should something happen."

"Thanks for being so understanding."

"We shall see. Now get back to your homework, or you'll not pass the entrance exams."

With those parting words of advice, Mustapha left the room and went upstairs to the master suite. He flipped on his television to see what was happening on Wall Street. The market was just opening and he wanted to know how his investments were doing.

A bit before eleven, Elif came and joined him in the bedroom. They both readied themselves for a night of rest, kissed and fell quickly asleep.

In Ayse's room just down the hall, her Hewlett Packard printer worked past midnight turning out Oglethorpe's Web pages in preparation for the weekend ahead. Ayse knew her father held the key to America. She wanted to have everything to be ready when he would ask to see it. It would be.

Daniel's Room

It was a moonless, windless night. In the calm, Daniel could clearly hear his Father's Ford Explorer come up the long gravel driveway. Daniel heard the garage door open as the truck approached, and in the stillness of the night, he thought he even heard the car door slam.

Clay was home. Home after delivering his apocalyptic message to nine hundred believers. Home to have a cup of tea and catch up on the news on CNN before retiring. Home to relax, knowing that Daniel had never once come down to greet him after Wednesday night's service. Nor had his boy attended that service once in the past three years.

Daniel heard the kitchen door close, and the brief, muffled conversation that followed between his parents. Rebecca had stayed home because of a headache. She never missed his Wednesday night services unless she had one of her migraines. Earlier in the day, just after Daniel had come home from school, a fierce migraine had put Rebecca flat on her back.

Earlier, Daniel had brought his mother iced tea, a blanket and her Bible. She had taken her medication around six and hadn't stirred since then, spending the last four hours alternating between drowsing off and reading passages from Psalms. Daniel kept after his homework at the kitchen table and checked in on his mother periodically. As much as he disliked his father, he loved Rebecca.

Rebecca Edwards, her maiden name, had been born and raised in Macon. Her family was well-monied. Her parents, Julian and Sarah Edwards, had made their fortune in the booming pulp industry near Tifton, Georgia. They had moved to Macon during the Great Depression because Sarah Edwards could no longer stand the smell of her husband's enormous paper mill. Her husband eventually tired of commuting and trying to run the business from a distance, so Julian sold out to a large international paper company shortly after the war.

When Julian and Sarah passed on, Rebecca and her sister inherited a considerable estate. Now the only thing they needed to do to was to hang onto their wealth, invest wisely, and let it make more of itself. Their father had put everything in place before his passing, and both Rebecca and her sister, Lila Jean, had grown accustomed to living with hardly a thought about finances.

They had never gone without and, safely nurtured by the best lawyers, accountants and investment firms in Georgia, they never would. Lila, Rebecca's older sister, had married a banker and they lived five miles away. Lila had raised two lovely daughters who were comfortably married and securely interwoven into Macon's upper crust. Lila Jean and her husband, Roger Dodd, spent most of their retirement taking luxury cruises or playing high handicap golf rounds at the Macon Country Club.

Rebecca was thin and frail. Her skin was lily white, her eyes an astonishing shade of blue. She had thinning light brown hair and a delicate, porcelain face that seemed to have been hand-carved by Tennessee Williams. She was the epitome of Southern graciousness. Well-mannered, genteel and a member of every social club and civic organization in Macon, Rebecca was the ideal wife for the most successful Baptist preacher in Bibb County. She was wealthy, subservient and discreet.

They had been married thirty years, having originally met at Macon Baptist, back when the church was still located downtown. Clay was a handsome, inviting young man. His enthusiasm for preaching had come to him honestly, his father having graduated from Campbell University in North Carolina and a respected Baptist minister in his own right. They had come to Macon just after the Second World War. Clay's mother had family in Macon. They moved after his father unexpectedly died of a heart attack while giving an intense sermon one morning at his church in Augusta.

After a few years of courtship, they were married in the same church they had met at in Macon. Rebecca, being a dutiful Southern wife, followed her husband's career through any number of small Southern towns. They lived in simple, backwoods homes provided by the various churches and were happy to do so. It was in one of those homes where Ruth, Daniel's older sister, was conceived.

Clay was offered the associate pastor's position at Macon Baptist Church soon after Ruth's birth and quickly accepted the position. It was no small coincidence that Lila, Rebecca's sister, was on the nominating committee. She wanted to have her sister back in Macon. Money has a way of influencing even the most altruistic of believers. When Clay became the associate pastor, Lila donated a substantial sum of money for a new wing onto the church's burgeoning private school. The board of directors was grateful.

Clay soon became the rising star at Macon Baptist Church. Senior Pastor Lestor Drake, with his more traditional approach to the Word of God, could not compete with the sermons being delivered by Clayton Aaron Harris. When Clay started in about fire and brimstone, the congregation could almost feel the heat coming from the pulpit. Lestor turned more and more toward the administrative functions of the church and gave Clayton free reign over the preaching.

When Lestor retired, the church council didn't even consider taking applications for the senior pastor position. Clay moved up within a fortnight of Lestor's departure and the call went out for a new associate pastor. Under Clay's preaching, Macon Baptist flourished.

Two years later, a committee was formed to begin searching for a location for a larger church and campus. Within a year they had purchased a two-hundred-acre parcel to the north of town. Soon thereafter, the architects were drawing up plans for the largest, most stunning Baptist church in Bibb County.

Daniel had been a part of it from the very beginning. He had attended school at Macon Baptist, gone to Sunday School and worshiped there up until three years ago, when he stopped going to church. That was when he and his father had first started having at it, the year he entered the eighth grade at Macon Baptist.

At first, Rebecca felt it was just a phase her son was going through. Just a part of growing up. Clay was outraged by his son's behavior from the onset, which only made matters worse.

By mid-term of the eighth grade it was obvious to everyone that something was wrong. Daniel wanted out of his father's Baptist school. He wanted to attend public school like other kids. He was rebelling against everything and anything that had to do with his religion and his upbringing. He was becoming a P.K. — a preacher's kid. The combination of the onset of puberty and inheriting his father's strong will laid the groundwork for Daniel's fiery rebellion.

The family had gone to counseling together, and Clay made Daniel see two different psychiatrists who specialized in adolescent behavioral problems, but to no avail. Eventually, Daniel sacrificed his grades to get his way. His honor roll status as a student plummeted to a C-minus by the third quarter. He became impossible. After innumerable teacher conferences and arguments that got them nowhere, Clay conceded. Daniel could leave.

Daniel finished the last quarter with a B-average, salvaging his GPA only because he knew he would enter Macon High School the following year. He was as ecstatic about changing schools as his parents were dismayed. The rift between father and son had opened up, and nothing was going to stop it from widening.

Nobody, not even Daniel, knew the reason behind his rebellion. Something within him had snapped, sheared in two without any hope of being repaired. It wasn't that Daniel stopped being religious, it was just that he was searching. He woke up one morning and knew that his father's God and his God were not the same.

There were plenty of signs that this day was coming. Disagreements between them about abortion, stem-cell research, women's rights and a host of other heated topics. But these were minor skirmishes and they alone could not have foretold of the battles to come.

Now it was different. Clay had wanted his son to attend a good Baptist college since the day he was born. Three years later, all Clay wanted was to get Daniel out of the house. He was a black sheep, an embarrassment to his father in the eyes of his congregation and his community.

As Daniel listened halfheartedly to his parents speaking, too far away to be able to make anything of their conversation, he put down his math book and took out the *Book of Midnights*. It was ten-thirty, and Daniel didn't want to stay up past eleven on a school night. He wanted to jot down some of his thoughts in his private journal before going to sleep.

March 28,

Dad just got back from church. I hate Wednesday nights. I usually get to head downstairs about now to get a bowl of ice cream, but I've learned never to risk it after Dad's returned from a Wednesday-night service. He gets too full of himself after delivering his sermon. Too pumped up on Jesus.

The last time I went downstairs after a Wednesday night service was a year ago. I'll never forget that night. He started in about me not even going to church any longer and how I was going to rot in hell for my sins. I was sick of his shit.

I told him that as far as I was concerned, I was already rotting in hell, only this particular hell was in suburban Macon, with an asshole for a father.

He told me to get out. Had Mom not intervened, I think I would have packed my bags and left that night. I don't know where I would have gone, but I was ready. In some ways, I wish Mom hadn't stepped in.

I did apologize a few days later, knowing I had gone too far. And Dad apologized to me, saying that he was just so disappointed. Why's he disappointed? I don't see why he thinks his God is the only God. The only way to get to Heaven.

That's the part that really gets to me — he's right and the rest of the world is wrong. What makes him think that his God is better than Vishnu? Better than Allâh? Better than Ra, or Thor, or Zeus, or a thousand Gods that have come before him and the thousand more to come?

Hasn't history taught us anything? How many men have died going into battle armed with nothing more than their shield, sword and a God no one even remembers today? A God just as valid as the Father, Son and Holy Spirit are to my father. It's madness — madness followed by centuries of killing.

Kill the Jews, kill the Muslims, kill the Catholics, kill the Hindi, kill the Sufi, kill the Protestants, kill, kill, kill. Why? If these Gods are so loving, so caring, so divine, why do they we go on like this? Armed to the teeth with our Bibles, our scriptures and our weapons. It just doesn't make sense.

But I can't explain this to Dad. I can't let him read this journal. Ever. This is my journey, and it's a path I have to walk alone. And that's how I feel — I feel so damn alone. Dad thinks it's just because I'm so stubborn and disobedient. And, in a way, I am.

But my refusing to go to church isn't because I'm being disobedient. It's because religion scares me. That's what Gods are to me — shadows. Shadows that whisper in our ear. Shadows that make a handful of us right, and the other handful wrong. Shadows and myths.

Dad wants to know why I don't think it's wrong to be an atheist. Shadows and myths, that's why.

Daniel put down his pen and notebook and remained motionless for the longest while. The house was silent, his mother and father gone to bed while he wrote. It was eleven-thirty when he slipped his notebook between his box spring and mattress.

He fell fast asleep, glad to not be dreaming of gods.

Eighteen Months Later

A bright red, late-model Ford Explorer cruised past the eastern edge of Hartsfield-Atlanta International Airport on one of the twelve lanes of Interstate 75. It was heading north, driven by a thin woman in her fifties. She looked delicate and refined, as one would imagine the poet Emily Dickinson might have looked. The radio was tuned into some obscure evangelical station located on the lower end of the FM band. Neither the driver nor the passenger was paying any attention to the message the evangelist inside the radio was proclaiming.

The two passengers had not talked much over the last few hours. Rebecca had tried to strike up a conversation with her son several times, but to no avail. Daniel wasn't in the mood to converse. He knew his mother wanted to have a heart-to-heart before dropping off her youngest child at college, but he avoided giving her the opening she needed to get such a conversation started.

He knew she wanted to know if he had packed his Bible. He had, but he didn't want to tell her. He knew she wanted to lecture him on the dangers of drugs and alcohol once he was away from home and his parents' supervision. He had already imbibed and had taken enough drugs to know the dangers well enough. He didn't want to talk about either topic.

All he could think of was being free.

Clayton Harris was in his office at North Macon Baptist. He had made it clear to them that he did not want to make the journey to Atlanta. He had some paperwork to catch up on and his office was where he was going to be spending his Saturday morning. When Rebecca asked what could possibly be more important than taking his only son to college, he didn't reply.

When Clay got to his office, he picked up the John Clancy novel he had started reading a week ago, put his feet up on his desk, and buried himself in a world filled with terrorists, victims and heroes. Clancy's well-scripted black-and-white was a welcome respite from the dark-gray world the Harris family had descended into.

Clay was glad it was over. Daniel was like a bad tooth that wasn't being tended to. The tiny cavity that had started five years ago was now a fully abscessed piece of his life, the pain unbearable, the only relief left was having the tooth removed.

Clay felt, like his wife, that by taking Daniel away, as though pulling out a bad tooth, she was removing this terrible source of pain from his life.

The worst was over. All that remained for Clay was to pay for the room and board, the textbooks, and the tuition for the next four years. Perhaps two years of post-graduate work if Daniel continued on with his studies. His boy wouldn't be home again except for Thanksgiving, Christmas and Easter. Clay told Rebecca to inform her son that he would pay the dormitory expenses year-round if Daniel desired. It was with the understanding that his son would find summer employment in Atlanta and not in Macon.

Rebecca talked it over with Daniel and the agreement between them was finalized. Rebecca had become the arbitrator, carrying their conversations back and forth between father and son in an attempt to keep them from arguing any more.

She was the one who told Clay about Daniel's applying to Oglethorpe. Clay reacted calmly, to the point of indifference. It wasn't a state school, which Clay had half expected after Daniel's stint at Macon High. It wasn't affiliated with any church or religious organization. That, too, was good — thinking Daniel might seek out a Catholic, or God forbid, a Jewish college.

Baylor, the seminary in Louisville, even the local Mercer University in Macon had been long since removed from Daniel's list of possibilities. At one point, Clay had still held hope for Mercer. Several of Daniel's friends were planning to attend Mercer and had asked him to join them. They tried, but Daniel wanted no part of it. Mercer was founded by Jesse Mercer, and he was a Baptist. Besides, Mercer was in Macon, and Daniel wanted out of Macon just as vehemently as he wanted out of his red-brick, white-trimmed Colonial. It was too Southern, too small and too inbred. He had narrowed his choices down to Tulane, Emory or Oglethorpe in Atlanta.

He missed the application deadline at Tulane, and didn't feel like going through the lengthy process of appealing his oversight. He liked the thought of living in New Orleans, the French Quarter, and the rolling Mississippi, but he felt it wasn't meant to be.

He had driven the car up last spring to check out both Emory and Oglethorpe and decided Emory had that big-city feel to it. He left Emory and drove the twenty miles across town on that rainy morning in April to see the campus firsthand. Oglethorpe was smaller, quieter and more focused on the liberal arts.

Daniel liked the scale of it and, as he walked through the campus, he was fascinated by the strange quotations Dr. Thornwell Jacobs had inscribed above the entrances. Those quotes and the bizarre Crypt of Civilization were the deciding factors. The Crypt, which was built into the foundation of Hearst Hall, wasn't to be reopened until the year 8113. That appealed to Daniel. He had such little faith left in mankind that the thought of going down to visit this peculiar shrine to the future was reassuring to him.

Daniel also felt a kinship to the deceased Dr. Jacobs. The enigmatic quotes above the portals reminded Daniel of something he might scribble down in his *Book of Midnights*.

As he stood by himself in the library that afternoon, he was intrigued by the words carved in the portal above him. He read them quietly to himself, pondering their meaning.

Hast thou no need of your fresh power to find anew thy holy grail —
a thing which reckless youth must do because the careful aged fail?
Uplifted to that cross, Lord God, with outstretched hand we wait the nail.
Thornwell Jacobs

This inscription spoke to him directly. He knew, somehow, it was important. Time would decipher its secret and its purpose. He read and reread the quote until he had memorized it. He picked up an admissions package. Oglethorpe was his college.

As these memories ran through Daniel's mind, his mother pulled off the interstate at West Paces Ferry. She wanted to take the slow, winding road east to Buckhead before connecting to Peachtree and continuing north. This route wasn't the shortest, but it was the loveliest. It would bring them past the governor's mansion and a host of other expensive, well-manicured estates.

She loved this part of Atlanta. Over the years, Clay and she had been inside any number of elaborate homes in Peachtree Heights West. Formal dinner parties with Atlanta's elite, enjoying pheasant under glass, fine desserts and the fellowship of other wealthy Georgians. It was Clay's fabled preaching and Rebecca's well-respected inheritance that opened the stained glass doors to their spiral stairways and crystal chandeliers. Rebecca kept trying to remember which house belonged to whom as they drove slowly east toward

Buckhead. She wished Clay had come along, he was so much better at this sort of thing — remembering the connections to money.

The intersection where the three roads meet — West Paces Ferry, Peachtree and Roswell — was busy. It was always busy. Sports bars, nightclubs, fine restaurants and new hotels seemed to keep this bustling, northern part of Atlanta constantly on the move. Rebecca considered warning Daniel about hanging out in Buckhead, known for its nightlife and moral decay, but resisted the urge to do so.

They sat through two light changes and eventually started moving north again, the last few miles to Oglethorpe. Once past the Buckhead district, traffic opened up and Rebecca and Daniel were soon pulling into the university. They took a backroad around the perimeter of the campus and parked in front of Jacobs Hall, the dorm where Daniel would be staying for the upcoming fall semester. There were station wagons, minivans and SUVs parked and double-parked all around the cul-de-sac that formed the interior courtyard of the complex.

The buildings looked tired, thought Rebecca, as she popped the rear-door latch to the Explorer. Old and tired.

There were four apartments in each of the five buildings that comprised the complex. Daniel's was on the top floor, with a shared bath and one other roommate. He didn't want his mother to see the apartment, knowing there could well be posters of Bob Marley smoking a huge spleef or pin-ups of Anna Nicole Smith already adorning the walls. Neither would go over well with Rebecca.

It was better to have her unpack his things at the curb and take them up after she departed. It would take him longer, but he had nothing to do between now and the beginning of classes on Monday.

"This is it, Mom, I'm off to college," said Daniel.

"My boy, my beautiful baby boy," she replied, coming around to hug him after closing the rear hatch.

"Say goodbye to Dad for me."

"I'm sorry he's not here to see you off. You know how stubborn he can be."

"Too stubborn, Mom. Sometimes Dad can be too stubborn. I'm going to miss you, Mom. I'll e-mail you as often as I can, and I'm still planning to be home for Thanksgiving. Until then, it'll just be readin', writin' and 'rithmatic," he said in an exaggerated Southern accent.

"Be good, Daniel. And remember, your father and I love you."

"I love you too, Mom."

She let go of her protracted hug and, teary-eyed, went around the front of the Explorer to the driver's side.

"Drive safe, Mom, and thanks for bringing me here."

"It was the least I could do for you, Daniel. Now be good."

"Bye."

Rebecca didn't say anything. Tears were running down her pale white cheeks and she was embarrassed by it. She didn't want to appear weak, even if she was. She put the car in drive and rolled away, leaving her only boy standing on a cracked sidewalk beside a pile of suitcases, trunks and backpacks. He was gone, and she was going to miss him.

The worst was over, she thought. Although Clay had tried again and again to have her choose sides, Rebecca would not. They were both wrong.

So as Clay and her son drifted further apart, she became closer to him. Daniel was proud of her for remaining strong — surprised at her fortitude. Clay would go on for hours, late into the night, trying to convince Rebecca that Daniel was a lost sheep, a poor, wretched sinner and doomed to hell unless he was to change his ways. Rebecca would have none of it.

Daniel, thought Rebecca, was just testing his father's faith. He was going through a phase. A time when we doubt our beliefs and question authority. Daniel would get through it, and would stand as tall as his parents when he did.

Clay couldn't disagree with her more, and he never relented in his attempt to sway her to his side. But he could not convince his wife that her blue-eyed boy was evil. He was perhaps lost, but he was not evil.

Rebecca kept crying as she turned back onto Peachtree. She would be back in Macon before dinner if the traffic weren't too bad.

Daniel grabbed one of his suitcases and headed toward his apartment building. He stopped at the bottom of the stairwell. He was crying. There were all the emotions of a child's first day at school colliding within him. He stood there, weeping gently to himself.

A part of him was glad to be done with it — glad to be through the arguments over homosexual rights, prayer in public schools, or evolution — glad to be away from his father's relentless self-righteousness. But he was sad as well. Sad to be leaving. Leaving Macon, his friends and his mother. Knowing he was going to miss her hush puppies and corn bread. Missing the routine of it all; his room, his sanctuary and his past.

He started walking again, and as he approached his building, a young man with a thin goatee jumped the last three stairs and landed two feet in front of him. He startled Daniel back into the present. The young man could see that he had been crying, but intentionally didn't say anything to him.

"Hey, name's Randy. Apartment 3-A, Jacobs Hall. Where ya headed?"

Daniel paused for a minute. He took a piece of paper out of his front pocket and double checked his address.

"Daniel Harris," looking down at the paper to be sure, "Apartment 3-A, Jacobs Hall."

"Cool, man, we're roommates. Can I help you with yer shit?"

Daniel smiled. It was nice to hear someone say shit so indiscriminately. To swear with a flair totally natural.

"Yeah, that'd be great."

Randy reached over, grabbed Daniel's backpack and bounded back up the stairway he had just jumped down. Five steps above him, Randy turned around, winked, and said, "We're gunna have us a ball this year."

Yes we are, thought Daniel as he smiled. Yes we are.

Hartsfield-Atlanta Airport

"Don't forget your briefcase, Father."

"I won't."

Mustapha reached into the overhead compartment of the Boeing 757 they had flown on from Heathrow and grabbed his leather briefcase. He was glad his daughter had reminded him — having been up for twenty straight hours.

Outside, it was a perfect summer day in Atlanta — warm but not hot. The sunlight was pouring through the mid-afternoon clouds, each one placed in the sky as if by a painter's studied hand. The wind was light, dashing between the sunlight and the shadows cast by the islands of clouds above. A hint of autumn, distant and obscure, was in the air.

Ayse was glad to have returned to America. This time she would be here for four years, and not just for a brief vacation. This time she would really be able to get a sense of this wondrous nation. This nation of immigrants and ingenuity.

They waited for the plane to empty.

As they walked up the ramp into the terminal, they smiled at each other. Mustapha knew how exciting this moment was for his daughter. He took note that, even through her exhaustion, her smile radiated from her youthful face. Her dark eyes held a twinkle in them as they disembarked, like a little girl unwrapping presents on her birthday — innocent and unforgettable.

Ayse and Mustapha began the long trek down the endless corridors of Hartsfield International and stood in line at customs. They got out their passports and the paperwork from the university along with Ayse's student visa. It was a tedious process, one which Mustapha was all too familiar with. His passport was covered in stamps from a dozen nations. The carpet business was no longer confined to the Grand Bazaar of Istanbul, but part of a much larger world.

Just past the final gate they saw their driver, holding up a large piece of white cardboard with the name *Yaltcin* misspelled and hand-written across it in black felt-tip pen. Mustapha had arranged to have a driver meet them at the airport. He did not feel like wrestling with Atlanta's traffic after a nine-hour flight from Heathrow. It was easier and safer to hire out and let someone who knew the local roads drive them to Oglethorpe.

After a brief introduction, the limo driver grabbed their bags and helped them to the car. When he finished loading in Ayse's suitcases full of blue jeans and silk blouses, the driver got into the Towncar and turned back to his employer.

"Where to, sir?"

"Oglethorpe University, please. We've got to get this young lady an American education."

Ayse smiled at her father's comment as the driver pulled away. Ayse could see the towering skyscrapers of downtown Atlanta in the distance. The sight of such magnificent buildings filled her with a sense of awe.

The freeways and the traffic reminded her of Istanbul. Too much traffic, she reflected. She wondered how bad it would be during the weekdays. It couldn't be as bad as Istanbul. Nothing could be that bad.

The driver took them up I-75 to the Peachtree exit. It was a slower route to take, but the driver wanted to give them a feel for Atlanta, overhearing them talk about his city in the back seat — sometimes in English, sometimes in an incomprehensible Turkish.

They soon found themselves caught up in the traffic jams of Buckhead, though no one seemed to mind. Mustapha and Ayse took turns gazing out the tinted windows and smiling at each other. This was just too exciting, thought the young Turkish girl. Too exciting to be real.

They arrived at Oglethorpe within an hour of leaving the airport. Ayse felt a little self-conscious stepping out of the limo in front of Lupton Hall. She had asked her father not to rent such a conspicuous automobile, but he had laughed in response. If his only daughter was going to attend school in America, then she was going to arrive in style. She was his princess, and he was treating her like one.

Several of the other arriving students and their parents watched as the black, polished Towncar pulled up to the cul-de-sac between Lupton and Phoebe Hearst Hall. They wondered who might be coming out from behind the darkly tinted windows of the chauffeur-driven automobile. They soon saw this trim, well-dressed Middle-Eastern-looking man step out of the driver's side of the back seat, followed by an attractive young girl, with jet black hair and a captivating smile.

Mustapha was wearing a finely tailored, dark blue suit; Ayse was dressed in blue jeans and a cotton sweatshirt. Obviously, she was here to attend college.

Obviously, noted the students and parents observing them from a distance, the family was wealthy.

Mustapha and Ayse walked over to Lupton Hall and Ayse stopped to read the inscription above the doorway. It was another of the quotes from Thornwell Jacobs. Ayse read it, curious as to what Americans might inscribe upon their buildings of higher learning:

All this I learned, that he who buildeth well is greater than the
structure that he rears, and wiser he who learns that heaven hears, than all
the wordy wisdom letters spell.

Thornwell Jacobs

She looked at, but didn't say anything to her father, uncertain of how to interpret the quote. Her father shrugged his shoulders and laughed a little as they went inside, looking for the admissions office to complete some additional paperwork and get directions to Ayse's dorm.

"It looks like a castle, doesn't it, Father."

"It certainly does, Ayse. A castle for my princess."

"Oh, Daddy, don't get started on all that nonsense."

Once inside, they found the office. After waiting their turn, they went about the business of signing in and finding out where Ayse would be living. The staff informed them she was going to be staying at Traer Hall, an all-women's dormitory just north of the library. After completing more paperwork, they were back inside the limo, winding through the narrow roads that took them to the dorm. The driver and Mustapha helped Ayse take her things upstairs to her small, but adequate, second-story apartment.

Traer Hall was a plain, modern building with a large central courtyard. It was built in the sixties, and had a nondescript feel to it. Young ladies and their families were pouring in and out of Traer Hall as it filled with freshmen and sophomores eager to get started on their upcoming year. Ayse became electrified with the youthful energy surrounding her.

She took her new key out and opened the door to her room. Her roommate, a girl named Ellen Baker, had yet to arrive. The admissions office had informed the Yalçins that Miss Baker wasn't expected in until Sunday.

Once inside, Mustapha took a look around and felt the apartment, although small, would be fine for his daughter. He knew when he returned to Istanbul in a week his wife would want all of the details, so Mustapha took a long, studied look at the small kitchen, the combination living/dining room, and the two tiny bedrooms. There was only one bathroom, shared between them, with a single shower.

Elif had decided early on not to fly to America. She thought the United States was too self-indulgent, too consumptive and pompous. She had been to America a half-dozen times with her husband when Mustapha had come on business, and once when they took their three children to New York years ago. To Elif, that was more than enough.

It had been a struggle convincing Elif to allow Ayse the privilege of attending a U.S. college, let alone trying to convince her to see her daughter off. So Elif had remained in Turkey, reading her Qur'an and tending to their household. Elif was glad to have avoided a long voyage to a county she disliked.

Over the next hour and a half, Mustapha helped his daughter carry up her things and unpack them. After a while, seeing he was being more of a nuisance than a help, she spoke up.

"Thanks, Dad, but I can do the unpacking myself. I know you want to help, but..."

"But what? You don't need your father's assistance any longer?"

"Dad," Ayse said condescendingly.

"Okay, I know when it's time to leave. But we are still on for dinner tonight, right?"

"Of course we are. I wouldn't miss it for the world."

Mustapha walked slowly over to his only daughter, gave her a hug that all but smothered her, and kissed her gently on the forehead.

"I'll be back to pick you up just after seven," said Mustapha as he went out the door.

"I'll be waiting, Dad," answered his daughter.

Mustapha walked down the flight of stairs and back to the limo. A couple of girls were standing there, talking to the driver. He was smoking a cigarette and acting the part of a chauffeur. When he saw Mustapha approaching, the driver quickly broke off his conversation with the college girls, tossed his cigarette butt down, putting it out with his highly polished shoe, and went around to open the door.

Mustapha climbed in the back seat and breathed a sigh of relief. It had been a very long day and he was looking forward to his room at the Hyatt. His plans were to catch a brief nap and head to Oglethorpe by seven. Reservations were already made at Pano's & Paul's. Tomorrow he was going to have lunch with some clients in Atlanta and catch a six o'clock flight up to New York for a few more days of business.

✹

Ayse unpacked her things, noting how much smaller her dresser and closet were than those at her home at Istanbul. She wondered what her roommate might be like. A girl named Ellen. What a funny name for a girl, she thought — Ellen.

After unpacking, Ayse lay down on her single bed for a little rest and within a few minutes fell fast asleep. She dreamed of a town along the coast of southern

Turkey she had visited once as a child. It was a town called Ephesus. She and her two brothers were running up and down the marble stairs of the open amphitheater when they saw a man standing on the stage. His feet were not touching the ground and when he spoke, all Ayse heard was an ethereal, mystical song, like the sound of a thousand flutes.

Her brothers turned to her and both said, "Look, it's Paul, the Christian." They said it in perfect unison and, as they did, the vision of St. Paul vanished.

When Ayse awoke she was unsettled by her recollection of the dream. It was just before seven and she had to get ready before her father returned.

"Perhaps it is just because I am now living in a Christian land, that I should have such a strange dream," she said quietly to herself while undressing to shower.

"Perhaps I'm a little frightened by it all, being so far away from my family for the first time."

These thoughts stayed with her all through their dinner and beyond. She was alone for the first time in her life. A young Muslim girl in the enormous city of Atlanta. She had a right to feel afraid.

Daniel's Dorm Room

So, where y'all from?"

"Macon, and you?"

"Louisville, Kentucky. Have you ever been there?"

"No, can't say I have."

"You're not missin' much. It's an old river town, boring as dog shit."

Randy Clark had just finished helping Daniel haul up his things. From his first pounce off the stairway, Daniel knew Randy was going to be a hellion for a roommate. He had that collegiate, Bohemian look to him. The thin nose, the wire-rimmed glasses and a small goatee on his narrow chin made him look like a young, Southern Marxist.

"Mind if I put on a CD?"

"No, I don't mind."

Randy opened a battered briefcase filled to overflowing with his CD collection. He rifled through the disorganized pile of CDs within it and pulled out an early Bob Dylan album. Within a minute the room was blaring with mid-sixties protest songs sung by a young man who looked not unlike Randy.

Daniel walked over to Randy's briefcase and glanced down to check out the rest of his CD collection. It held an eclectic assortment of music, none of which came as any surprise to Daniel. There was Alanis Morrissette, The Doors, U2's latest offering, some punk, some offensive rap and some ancient Joni Mitchell. Daniel laughed to himself as he took note of the music, thinking how glad he was that he brought his own tunes and a pair of headphones.

When Daniel turned around to continue to make small talk with Randy, he found his roommate sitting there, cross-legged on the bed in a makeshift lotus position, lighting a joint. Randy took a long, well-studied hit and held the reefer out to Daniel.

"Want a hit?"

"Just a small one."

Daniel took a single, perfunctory toke and continued unpacking while Randy finished the joint. He put the roach back in a small tin stash box and fell back on his bed, stretching out and floating off into the lyrics of some obscure Dylan tune that was still somehow relevant.

This is going to be fun, thought Daniel to himself as he stuffed his belongings into the cheap wooden dresser that came with the room.

Sunday Afternoon

'll be fine, Dad. Remember, doing this was my idea in the first place. I'm not your little girl any longer."

Mustapha was having a difficult time letting go. He was waiting to board his plane and decided to make one final phone call to his only daughter before leaving. He was going to miss her laugh around the house, miss her glorious smile.

"You will always be my little girl, Ayse. Do you have those telephone numbers I gave you last night?"

"Yes, Dad."

"Remember, in Atlanta you have to dial the area code as well as the local number. It has become such a big city, this Atlanta. I called Omer Sadri and Vasif Kortan this morning and told them you might be calling. I told them that whenever your schedule would allow, you would make Friday's call to prayer at the Jamaat Al Muslimeen Mosque, and they said they would be happy to escort you.

"Do you know what your class schedule is?"

"Not yet, Dad, I'll get it this afternoon at registration. I promise to call them should the need arise and I will make it to mosque as often as I am able. You and I both know the love of Allâh is within us, and not just in a mosque somewhere in Atlanta."

"This is true, Ayse. This is well spoken."

"I'm going to miss you, Dad."

Mustapha realized his daughter was trying to hang up. He looked over at the gate and could hear the loudspeaker asking for any first-class passengers. He was next, but he wanted to add one last piece of fatherly advice.

"No dating, Ayse. You remember what your mother and I talked to you about. We don't want you doing any dating or going out with American boys — Muslim or Christian. We let you attend the university only because you promised us you would go there for study and not for romance. Are we clear about this?"

"I promise, Dad, no dating of any kind. Just my studies and my new friends."

"That's good. I love you, Ayse."

"I love you too, Father. Now catch your plane and have a safe flight to New York. Say hello to mother for me when you return to Bebek and give my brothers my love."

Mustapha didn't want to say these next few words but he did so reluctantly, "Goodbye and may Allâh watch over you."

"Goodbye, Father."

With that, Mustapha Yalçin hung up the pay phone, grabbed his briefcase and dashed toward the boarding gate. They were already into coach seating by the time they double-checked his passport and ran his ticket through the automated machine. Flying had become much more difficult for him since the attacks, he thought, as the clerk took an excessive amount of time reviewing his passport.

You would think they would know better than to blame all of us for what a few madmen had done. But they don't. They see my dark skin, my brown eyes and dark hair and in it they see every Middle Eastern person from Cairo to Kabul. It is understandable in a way, conceded the frustrated Turkish businessman, as he continued down the long ramp leading to the jet. Understandable but unfair.

Book of Midnights

It was Sunday night, teetering on Monday morning. Daniel had spent the morning organizing his room and wandering around the campus. He had visited the Phillip Weltner Library, the Performing Arts Center and the Schmidt Center, which, along with the older field house, served as the gymnasium for the school.

He rambled around, taking his time while strolling the numerous wooded paths that criss-crossed the western edge of the campus. It was like having a private park right on campus, thought Daniel as he ambled through the chestnuts and oaks towering above him. A good place to get lost.

In the afternoon, like all of the other new students at Oglethorpe, he went through the tedious process of registration. Most of his freshman courses were mandatory, including Narratives of the Self, a math course, an arts course and a phys-ed requirement. Spanish was his only elective and he had no trouble getting in. That would be enough to handle for his first semester. Like half the freshmen at Oglethorpe, Daniel hadn't settled on a major. He thought he would wait and see what appealed to him before diving into a specific field of study.

After registration, he decided to have dinner in his room and not go out with his new roommate. Randy had been invited to a party up in one of the fraternity houses on Greek Row. No doubt they were already looking for prospects in the new crop of freshmen. Daniel had a hard time seeing a madman like Randy in a fraternity, but anything was possible.

When he left, Randy was as high as a kite, so Daniel figured his new roommate was going because he was bored. He had offered to share his stash with Daniel for the second time in two days, but this time, Daniel politely turned him down. He didn't feel like getting stoned.

Around eleven forty-five, with Randy still at the party, Daniel picked up his pen, grabbed his notebook and started writing.

Sunday, August 28, 11:45 p.m.

A great day! Registration went well and I had a chance to talk to several new students. Randy, my roommate, is a pothead. What else is new. Half the kids at Macon High were potheads. The shit just makes me sleepy.

I like the campus. The woods are great. Big, old trees and a little stream cutting through the forest. There's a small wooden bridge that spans the creek and a well-worn path that leads to it. It's pretty.

I stayed in last night, set up my computer and watched Mad TV. *Randy was gone. He loves to party. I can't imagine what his grades were like in high school. He must have done well enough to get accepted here, but Lord only knows how.*

He reminds me of an old hippie. He wears baggy jeans, flannel shirts and always has several strings of beads around his neck. That and his John Lennon- style glasses. But he's okay. I just wish he'd stop offering me pot, I'm not all that wild about it.

I don't miss home. Not that I thought I would. I don't miss sitting down to dinner with Mr. Baptist. It's going to be a real pleasure not to have to listen to Matthew 7, Verse 4 through 8, or Jeremiah whatever every time I ask to have the potatoes passed.

Randy hasn't mentioned God once in the past two days. I think his religion is somehow tied into the chronic use of marijuana. Maybe he's a Rastafarian. All he'd needs to do is add the dreadlocks and speak with a Jamaican accent, mon.

I'm reading another book on Buddhism. I love it. It's called The Snow Leopard, *by Peter Matthiessen. It's all about hiking around Nepal, looking for these rare mountain sheep. But it's way cool and I'm enjoying it. In a way, it's all about searching for God.*

Well, tomorrow I'm off to school and I suppose I'd better sign off. I hope Randy isn't too loud when he comes stumbling back in sometime during the middle of the night. Until again.

Daniel, the Buddhist, Harris.

Autumn at Oglethorpe

The season slipped by. The days passed into weeks, the weeks to months and the seasons changed along with the river of time that held them. By late November the trees that stood behind the Performing Arts Center were standing naked in the wintry winds. The paths Daniel loved to wander were cushioned with a carpet of fallen leaves, many the same color as the red Georgia clay they blanketed.

Thanksgiving came and went, and Daniel decided to remain on campus for the holiday. Daniel had grown accustomed to a life without argument. A life of studying late into the night, reading obscure novels in his cubby at the library and occasionally hanging out with his lunatic roommate.

Ayse found her own rhythms. Her roommate turned out to be a doctor's daughter, as Southern as Scarlet O'Hara in bell-bottomed blue jeans. Ellen spent hours every morning before heading off to class, curling her dyed-blond hair, polishing her nails, checking and re-checking her lipstick.

Ayse and Ellen discovered they had nothing in common. Ellen was not at all interested in her studies, spending the majority of her time with a covey of like-minded Southern belles, all of whom were more interested in sorority parties and senior boys. All of them looking for their MRS degree.

Ayse and her roommate quickly developed a well-defined, perfunctory relationship. They seldom spoke and, aside from the countless, endless showers Ellen took, Ayse was fine with the arrangement. She just couldn't understand Ellen's materialism and shallowness. But she never once broached her feelings with her well-coiffed, green-eyed roommate. Some things are best left unsaid.

Daniel and Ayse did take note of each other on several occasions as the summer conceded to the winds of winter. Ayse saw him several times in the student center, sitting off by himself and alone. She thought he looked interesting, with a distant, saddened look in his eyes.

To her, he looked a little like Brad Pitt, but not as movie-starrish. His hair was more blond and his chin and face less squared, but there was a clear resemblance between the two. Ayse noticed there were other girls who made note of Daniel's handsome looks.

She had become friends with two Muslim girls who were both sophomores at Oglethorpe, one from Egypt and the other from Lebanon. They both commented on how cute he was. None of them, Ayse included, even knew his name.

Ellen and her flock of belles took note of Daniel's handsome face but nothing more. The distant, introspective look in his eyes kept them at bay. They kept to the obvious — the jocks and the frat boys. Besides, Daniel was a freshman.

Daniel noticed Ayse. She looked interesting. Different. Her long, straight black hair, her dark eyes and foreign looks appealed to him. He had heard through the grapevine that she was from Turkey, but he had never gone so far as to find out her name. He was too busy with schoolwork, burying himself in his studies.

Still, across the grassy courtyard of the campus, in the hallways of Phoebe Hearst Hall or in the cafeteria, he would steal glances of Ayse, just passing observations, as though he was watching her through a large telephoto lens — distant and detached. He noted her smile, as she and her two friends would laugh and behave as girls do over lunch in the cafeteria.

He liked how differently she acted. How unique she looked. Her face slightly wider than usual, descending through the generations from the Mongol horsemen who had come to the Near East a millennium ago. He noted her brown eyes and pierced ears — adorned with two bright gold earrings, simple and elegant. He wondered what it must be like for her here in America, thousands of miles from home.

But they never met. Their circles of friends never crossed and they ended up taking no classes together. Theirs was a relationship of passing smiles and stolen glances across a crowded lunchroom. Neither felt compelled to pursue their casual flirtations. They were both too immersed in their studies and their solitude.

The semester finally dove headfirst into a flurry of final exams and the nervous anticipation of Christmas break. Both had plans to go home. Ayse was anxious to see her father and mother and Daniel knew he eventually had to make a cameo in suburban Macon. He was going home to see his mother, and that was it. He had already made a promise to himself to avoid his father at all costs. Not that it was a promise he could keep.

Christmas in Macon

The red Ford Explorer retraced its path southward to Macon. Rebecca and Daniel were sitting on the same gray leather seats as they had four months ago. I-75 was still crowded with traffic, even on a Saturday morning. Daniel was going home for Christmas. He was going home to have a disquieting Christmas dinner with his family, complete with roast turkey, mashed potatoes and the likelihood of a full-blown shouting match with his father. He dreaded the thought of it.

"So how was it?" Rebecca interrupted his apprehensions.

"It was great, Mom."

"Do you like your professors?"

"They were good. I really liked this course called Narratives of the Self. It was fascinating."

"It's an odd name for a college course, Narratives of the Self. What's it about?"

Daniel was being dragged into a conversation again. His mother knew his reluctance to discuss his world with her, though she never understood why. She felt her son must be unfairly lumping her together with his father. She was far more tolerant than Clay, and although she seldom approved of the way Daniel thought, she never let it cast a shadow on her love for him.

"It's about life," said Daniel.

"Big topic, Daniel. Could you be a little more specific?"

"We studied Homer, St. Augustine, Descartes, Shakespeare, and a Chinese religious mystic named Lao Tzu. Dad would have loved it," added Daniel sarcastically.

"Now Daniel, don't start in. Dad's not here and I'm not here to interrogate you. I just want to know what Oglethorpe was like. I haven't had much of a chance to talk to you since August and you didn't come home for Thanksgiving. I'm just trying to make pleasant conversation. That's all I'm trying to do, nothing more."

Rebecca was frustrated. She could see nothing had changed. The strained dynamics of their family's relationships were still stretched to the edge of tearing. For the moment, it looked as though they were all in for a long, ugly Christmas together.

Daniel, to Rebecca's surprise, continued. "Lao Tzu, the story goes, lived a couple of hundred years before the birth of Christ, maybe earlier, since the records of ancient China are sketchy at best. He was a sage, an ancient wise man. He wrote a collection of poems called the *Tao Te Ching*, which roughly translates to *The Way of Life*.

"But the *Tao Te Ching* isn't like the Bible. It's more philosophical. More like a long, mystical poem.

"You've probably seen the circle of yin and yang. Yin is the dark, the water and the female side of the universe, and yang is the bright, airy, male side of the world. Whereas Christianity states that there is a constant battle between good and evil, Taoism states that without evil, there cannot be good. Without darkness there cannot be light.

"Virtue isn't dictated to you in Taoism. There are no Ten Commandments. Virtue is found by becoming less and less self-important. The way to lead is by not leading, the way to act is by not acting. My favorite passage in the Tao Te Ching was, *"The greatest men who ever walked the earth left no footprints."*

Rebecca smiled, looked at her boy and said something that surprised him. "Your father would have one heck of a time preachin' that religion."

Daniel laughed. Somewhere in the heavens Lao Tzu laughed with them. They relaxed and made small talk the rest of their journey south.

✺

They arrived at the house just past noon. Daniel's stomach was in knots as they headed up the long, winding driveway. Nothing had changed. The lawn, now tinted brown, was well trimmed. The trees surrounding the house were bare except for the ground junipers and the handful of Southern pines standing behind the house.

It had only been four months, but it felt as if he had been away for a decade. As if he had been on a long, silent voyage to distant parts of the world and, like Marco Polo, was just returning.

Rebecca broached the silence, sensing her son's apprehension.

"Dad's not home. He had some work he needed to catch up on at the office. He said to send his love and he's looking forward to visiting with you tonight at dinner."

"Sure."

Rebecca pushed the remote and the garage door opened. She pulled the Explorer in until the tennis ball Clay had hung touched the front window of the truck. Daniel looked around the garage and everything was in perfect order. The hedge trimmer was hung where it was supposed to be hung. The rakes, the pruning shears, the riding lawn mower, everything was where it should be.

Daniel grabbed his bags and went inside the house, bounding up the stairs to his room. He threw his things down in the middle of the floor and pounced on his bed. He hadn't missed his family but oddly enough, he had missed his bed. It was broken in perfectly to the contours of his muscular frame and it fit him perfectly.

After a spell, Rebecca walked over to the stairwell and yelled up to him, "Lunch is ready."

He heard her call and when he did, he realized how hungry he was. The knots in his stomach had disappeared when Rebecca told him his father was at church. The comfort of his bed had reassured him that it wouldn't be all that bad. Before too long he would be back in Oglethorpe, away from the endless feuding of his home life.

"I'm coming, Mom." Daniel shouted down while still lying on his back. "I'm coming."

Clayton Harris arrived home after six. He had been catching up on some accounting all afternoon, and had intentionally delayed leaving sooner. By the time he pulled into the driveway his stomach was every bit as knotted as his son's had been earlier in the day.

As he pushed the remote and opened the garage door, Clay was hoping the Explorer wouldn't be there. He was thinking they might have had car trouble, or even a minor accident, anything that would have kept Daniel from making it back home. But nothing had happened. His boy was back, along with the demons that possessed him.

Clay walked into the kitchen and saw Rebecca preparing a pork loin for dinner. She took one look at him and knew.

"Where is he?"

"He's up in his room, on the phone. He's been calling his old high school friends all afternoon. Getting caught up on the news."

"Did you have a nice drive down?"

"Fine. We had a fine drive. Once we cleared the airport, traffic wasn't too bad."

"Well, I'm going into my den. Call me when dinner's ready."

Rebecca wanted to say something about Clay going up to welcome his boy home but she didn't.

She was nervous. Like two prize fighters in their respective locker rooms, they were both inside the arena. She wasn't looking forward to dinner. She opened the oven and uncovered her marinated pork loin. As she pulled back the foil and the hot air poured out of the four-hundred-degree oven, she hardly took note of the searing tinfoil she had grabbed without a hotpad. As she ran her fingers under some cold water, she thought about dinner.

The explosion could occur at any time, when Clay was passing the mashed potatoes or Daniel was enjoying a slice of homemade corn bread. One of them would say something that would goad the other into taking the bait. They would dive head first into a shouting match over gods, Darwin, or the ACLU. The gloves would come off and the two of them would have at it, bare-fisted and drenched in the blood, sweat and tears of their endless disagreements. The fight would end like a hundred bouts before — with Daniel throwing down his napkin in disgust, running upstairs and locking his room behind him.

All that would remain were four weeks of mutual animosity. Rancor and sarcasm, scorn and contempt from sunrise until the end of each day. Like two injured bulls in the same small enclosure — wounded and angry.

If they start in tonight, Christmas will be ruined, thought Rebecca as she put the casserole side dish filled with okra and peas into the microwave. New Year's will be anything but new.

I'm asking you, Lord, grant my family some peace over these next few weeks. If you can bring peace unto the world, which I know you can, then bring it to my home.

With her prayer still in her thoughts, Rebecca went over to the stairwell to call to her son, "Dinner's ready, Daniel, wash up and come on down."

Next she walked over to the den to find her husband's head buried in *The Macon Journal*. She just had to say something to him, hoping it might help.

"Clay, dinner's ready."

"Thanks, honey. Let me just finish up on the business section and I'll be right in."

"Clay, one more thing."

He slid his reading glasses down and looked up at her standing in front of his mahogany desk. "Yes, dear."

"Let's try to get along with Daniel these next few weeks. He's here for only a short while and we may not see him again until Easter. I don't want to ruin the holidays with you two fighting about something or other tonight. It's Christmas time, Clay. Ruth and her family will be with us in a few days, and none of us need it."

"I'll do what I can, Rebecca. But if he starts in, I'm not going to sit there and be told what's right and wrong. I've got my principles, my beliefs and the teaching of Jesus Christ, our Lord and Savior, to defend. I'll go easy if he goes easy. But if he starts in on one of his crazy notions about Buddhism or faggots, then I'm not going to sit there and take it.

"You can't ask me to do that, Rebecca. I know you want peace in this family but I'll not forgo everything I believe in just to have peace. That's not peace, that's cowardice. I'll not turn my back on Jesus, Rebecca, and you should know right up front. Jesus wasn't tolerant, Rebecca. When he saw someone sinning, he went in and overturned the tables in the temple. Don't expect me to do anything less."

Rebecca could see her husband's face flush with anger as he spoke. She could tell he was every bit as uneasy about their first dinner together as she was, and that he had been stewing over it for quite a while.

"Just do your best, and don't start in if you can avoid it. Do it for me, please." Rebecca added as she turned and went into the kitchen.

Her hand shaking, she reached in and took out the tenderloin. She grabbed the tinfoil that had burned her fingers a few minutes earlier and placed it back over the two pounds of baked pork. She could feel the heat working its way through the thick hotpad as she placed the covered dish on a trivet on the dining room table. The mashed potatoes, the okra and the corn bread followed.

Daniel appeared first, looking ever so handsome. His natural good looks and deep blue eyes made their dining room come alive again. Rebecca realized how much she had missed her son over these past months.

Clay was a few steps behind him. She paused.

"Well, Son, welcome home."

Clay, ignoring Rebecca's wishes, started quoting Scripture, "*But the father said to his servants, Bring forth the best robe, and put it on him; and put a ring on his hand, and shoes on his feet: And bring hither the fatted calf, and kill it; and let us eat, and be merry: For this my son was dead, and is alive again; he was lost, and is found. And they began to be merry.* Luke, 15, 22 through 24."

Daniel wanted to react, but didn't.

"I've been at college, Dad, and I haven't been spending your fortune on wine, women and song. I've been studying. I will take you up on the fatted calf however, and I'm looking forward to some of Mom's home cooking after months of dorm food."

They shook hands as they greeted each other, and Rebecca appreciated the fact that Daniel had refused to take the bait. The handshake was casual and distant, like a handshake between two businessmen who were meeting for the first time. Calculated and cool, wondering what they might expect from each other. Wondering what the bottom line was.

"Well then, Daniel, let's sit down and see what your mother has cooking."

Clay took his seat at the end of the table, Daniel where he had always sat, between the two, with his back to the arched opening that led to the living room and the stairway beyond. That way, should things go poorly, he could bolt for his room without having to go around either of them. The safest place to sit.

"Let's say grace, shall we."

They said grace. Daniel realized while saying it that he had not done so once since leaving home last fall. He didn't mind. He bowed his head and spoke in unison with the two of them.

"For what we are about to receive, let us be truly thankful. Amen."

Clay added. "And thank you Lord for keeping our boy, Daniel, safe and healthy these last four months as he studied hard and tried to find his calling. We're thankful our boy's back here with us for these next few weeks and we pray that this short, precious time we have to spend together will be a glorious time. A time to celebrate your birth, Jesus, and a time to have our family together again. Amen."

"Amen."

Dinner passed without incident. As the bowl full of mashed potatoes emptied and the arguments she feared never happened, Rebecca breathed a sigh of relief. They were not going to get into it, at least not tonight.

They spoke about his classes and Daniel never mentioned Lao Tzu or Taoism, knowing that doing so would only serve to enrage his father. They shied away from anything controversial. All that was left was dessert, and round one was over.

Just as Rebecca was bringing out the coconut cream pie, Clay asked Daniel something which he had never mentioned before. Not through all of his years at Macon High, nor in the summer that followed. Rebecca was surprised by her husband's interest in the subject at all.

"Any young ladies yet, Son?"

"No, no one special. I went out to a couple of fraternity parties with my roommate, Randy, and I met some girls there, but nothing ever came of it. For the moment, I'm too busy with my schoolwork to start thinking about women. I figure there will be plenty of time for girls over the next four years."

"That's mighty grown-up thinking, Daniel. I'm proud to hear you telling me that's how it is, because you're right. You're young yet, and you've got plenty of time to fall in love and settle down. Your mother and I didn't marry until I was twenty-eight and she was twenty-four. You'll turn nineteen soon, and you've got your whole life ahead of you.

"God has a woman out there for you, one that will love you and care for you, give you some fine children and be there for you through thick and thin. Taking your time can't hurt, can't hurt one bit."

"That's how I feel, Dad. I'll find her when the time comes. In the meantime, I'm up at Oglethorpe for an education, and that's what I'm focusing on – learning."

Dessert went by without incident. Compliments flowed to Rebecca for a fine meal as Clay headed off to the living room to see what was on the big-screen TV. Daniel helped his mother clean up and eventually joined his father in front of the tube.

They made small talk until late into the night. Rebecca cleaned up the kitchen and came in to join them for the ten o'clock news.

She could sense it, a tentative truce was in place. The truce Rebecca had prayed for. The next few weeks went by without incident. Daniel and Clay, by the time Rebecca packed the Explorer up to chauffeur Daniel back to Oglethorpe, appeared to be getting along better than they had for years. Perhaps absence does make the heart grow fonder, thought Rebecca.

Even his sister, Ruth, took note of the civility between the two men. College, it seemed, was helping. It was letting them both have their own fields to run in, away and free from each other.

As he drove back to Atlanta with his mother, for the first time in his life, Daniel was actually looking forward to returning home for Easter. It had been the perfect Christmas break with his family — his family rediscovered.

Returning to Istanbul

*A*yse had ample time for reflection on the long, arduous flight home. She had curled up into a ball on her comfortable, first-class leather seat, dividing her time between dozing off and thinking about the last four months of her life at Oglethorpe.

Her first semester grades were good. She had managed all A's save for biology, which was never her favorite. She didn't enjoy dissecting things, preferring to admire the wonders of the biological world from a distance and not with the aid of a microscope or scalpel. Biology, she had decided, was for men. She had only taken the course as a part of her prerequisites.

Her favorite course had ended up being Narratives of the Self. She loved the discussions, the writing and the broad perspective the course offered. Because of it, she was contemplating pursuing an English major. Having been born and raised in an Islamic nation gave her a different perspective of the world. Over the course of the first semester, it had made for some interesting discussions.

Ayse missed Istanbul. True, she reflected while curled up, looking out the window at the vast darkness of the Atlantic Ocean seven miles beneath her, the two cities had much in common. Each had too many cars and too few roads to put them on. They were vibrant and alive — Istanbul ancient and mystical, Atlanta youthful and energetic. Racially diverse, brimming with opportunity and wealth, Atlanta was the heartbeat of the twenty-first century South. Ayse found it fascinating.

Fascinating, but secular and impersonal. She knew she had succumbed to moments of alienation. The feelings of being alone and vulnerable in a foreign land. True, her two friends, Hatice from Egypt and Kasha from Lebanon, had helped, but making friends with any of the American girls had proven difficult. Ellen was without hope. She was infinitely more concerned with her curling iron than learning about the Qur'an. She was in school to find a man.

Ramadan had come and gone during the first semester. It had started on November 6, ending twenty-seven days later with the Night of Destiny, when Muslims break the fast. That night, the three of them, Hatice, Kasha and Ayse, took a cab to Buckhead and celebrated. True, they drank a bit more wine than they should have, but it was one of the best times Ayse had over the past four months and she would do it again tomorrow if she could.

Her fast had been far from perfect. She awoke each morning before dawn and grabbed a bowl of cereal, some fruit and a glass of juice and managed most days without eating or drinking anything until sundown. There were a few days, mostly during the week, when she just couldn't make it. She would quickly ask for Allâh's forgiveness and grab a snack out of one of the many vending machines around campus. With her studies, the month of fasting was sometimes more than she could endure. She prayed Allâh would understand.

But school had been a good experience and, even though she missed her friends and family back home, Ayse knew she had to return in late January and continue with her American education. She knew it was a part of her destiny, knowing early on that her life was in God's hands. That was the depth of her faith and her devotion. Allâh, the merciful One, would show her His way.

She fell back to sleep praying to God. Thanking him for giving her so much and returning her safely to Turkey. She looked forward to visiting with Fatimah and hearing all about her new boyfriend, Surat. My life is good, she thought as she drifted off to sleep. My life is good.

❁

From a dead sleep, Ayse heard the sound of the jet engines changing pitch. They had crossed the Atlantic and were approaching Orly airport in Paris. It was now mid-morning in France. From her window she could see the barren fields of western France, the rugged shoreline of the Normandy coast and the small villages and cities below.

There were a few clouds, but they were small and scattered. It was a cold, windswept winter day beneath her, sunny and holding just above the freezing mark. She was glad she wasn't going to have to leave the airport for her connecting flight. It was only going to be a matter of a short walk down through the aging terminal to the second leg of her journey home. Her next flight was on an Airbus, operated by Turkish Air.

She knew her seat would have ample room and the in-house movie would be in English and Turkish. The flight would take her up and over the Alps, across the Balkans and the former Yugoslavia and into Istanbul from the west, crossing the edge of the Aegean Sea. It would still be daylight when she landed, although the winter sun would be setting behind the plane, and the shadows of the surrounding hills long and dark.

If there were enough daylight left and the Airbus circled in from the north, Ayse knew she would get a grand view of Istanbul. The plane would come down the Bosporus, flying high over the Domabachie Palace, the medieval Hagia Sophia and the Blue Mosque. Eventually landing at Ataturk Airport, just as darkness was overtaking the city once known as Constantinople.

She had taken this flight several times before and could only hope they would come in from the north. She loved the view of her city from a mile high. From that vantage point she could clearly make out the fallen ruins of the Roman walls that had once encircled Istanbul.

How rich and steeped in history was her city. Layers of history, infused with conquest and defeat, Christianity and Islam, Greeks and Romans, all leaving their mark in stone and mortar at this crossroads to Asia. Even before recorded history, when the land bridge that had once crossed between Asia and Europe failed and the great flood waters poured through the Bosporus Valley, inundating the freshwater lake that is now the Black Sea. A flood that many scholars believe is the basis of the Biblical story of Noah and his ark.

Ayse was going home, and her heart raced as she boarded the Airbus. She looked forward to that first embrace from her parents. America was so young, thought Ayse. So young and so amazing.

❁

Mustapha and Elif were awaiting the arrival of their daughter as she walked up the ramp and into the concourse. Ayse hugged her mother, followed immediately by a warm embrace from her father. Elif was crying and Mustapha quickly produced a handkerchief for her from his black, woolen sports coat.

Abdul said hello to Ayse and promptly took her carry-on. The three walked to the car, sending Abdul in to get Ayse's suitcase when it arrived on the carrousel. Meanwhile, they squeezed together in the back seat of the dark-blue Lexus and began to converse.

There was much to talk about and much to catch up on. They spoke Turkish and Ayse found it strange. She had not spoken in Turkish for quite some time, and for the first time in her life she felt as though it was a foreign language, so familiar had she become with English.

They talked all through the hour-long ride back to Bebek. Elif asked Ayse about boys.

"And have you kept your word about dating?"

"Yes, Mother. I have not gone out with anyone, just as I promised."

"But you have found some friends, you told us in your e-mails."

"Two girls, both of them Muslim. One of them, Hatice, is from Egypt and the other girl, Kasha, is from Lebanon. Hatice has gone home to Cairo for this break, but Kasha's family could not afford to fly her home. She is still in Atlanta, working at the library over break. She is on a work-study program to help pay for her schooling. Her family could not afford to send her to school if this were not so. She is a very good student."

"She sounds like a good person."

They talked about her studies, about life in America, about all the news in Turkey and beyond. When they arrived home, Ayse went up into her room with her things and rested awhile before coming down for dinner. She was already suffering from jet lag induced by the eight-hour time change. It would take her a week to work through it. Tomorrow morning she would call her friend, Fatimah, and catch up on all the latest gossip about her fellow students from the Nisantasi Girls School. She couldn't wait.

✪

The four weeks in Istanbul passed quickly. Ayse, with her mother's permission, went out on a double date with Fatimah and a friend of Surat's. They saw a new American movie and went out to get ice cream sundaes afterward. It was a nice evening, but Ayse knew from the start that Ahmet was not her type.

It was just an evening out, fun while it lasted.

When it came time to drive her to the airport, Elif and Mustapha were both a bit heartbroken. The month together had reminded them of how empty their large house was without their lovely daughter filling it with her smile.

Ayse would have to fly back to America alone this time, as Mustapha did not have any immediate business in the States that could justify the expense of going there to deliver his daughter to Atlanta. Mustapha had given her ample cash to take a cab from the airport to school and Ayse was familiar enough with America to handle the return journey alone.

As they stood together at the drop-off area in the airport, tears and embraces mingled in the cool morning air.

"You have a safe trip, Ayse. And e-mail us upon your arrival at university."

"I will, Mother."

"You call us if you need anything, Ayse," said Mustapha, his eyes clearly laden with tears.

"I will, Father. I will call if I need anything. But don't worry, and remember, I will be back home for the summer in four months. We will have the whole summer together. We can go out to Princes Island and take out the boat. We will have a wonderful time. So don't be saddened by my leaving, it's only for a little while."

Ayse was trying to comfort them. They were growing old before her and she could see it was hard for them to give her up. Her mother, dressed in a dark brown chador that covered her graying hair, looked smaller than Ayse remembered. Mustapha, his mustache solid gray, and his shoulders not as broad and straight as she recalled, also showed the passage of time.

She hugged them one last time and headed toward the automatic doors, her carry-on rolling behind her and her coat draped over her arm. She walked fifty feet into the airport, turned and waved at her mother and father through the glass windows. Already, they seemed distant to her, as though she were waving to them from across the Atlantic.

Ayse turned and walked briskly toward security with tears streaming down her cheeks. She wondered why she had chosen to study in America and not to stay in Istanbul to attend Bosporus University. It would have been so much easier on her family.

She kept thinking about it all the way to Zurich. It was, in the end, an impossible question to answer. Staying in Istanbul was not meant to be. That was the only answer she could find....it was not meant to be.

Past Midnight

Daniel couldn't sleep. He looked over at the dark-red digital display and it read 2:31. A moment or two would pass and the display would change to 2:34. Time was slipping by, eating itself alive as he lay on his bed, staring at the empty ceiling, thinking of the last four weeks.

After ten minutes had vanished into the abyss of night, Daniel realized he wouldn't be able to get back to sleep until he had filled in a few more pages in his journal. As he opened the single drawer to his nightstand, he took out his notebook and pen.

He was dreaming about his father just before he awoke. They were playing catch in an empty field. It was summer, and Daniel was young again. The dream started Daniel thinking about how unexpectedly well the two of them had gotten along recently. How Christmas dinner was a joy, with Ruth, his sister, and her husband, Chet, there along with their boy. He wanted to write it down, capture it, before time whitewashed it into another blur of memory.

January 15,

I'm back at school. It's late. It's always late when this pen touches down. Touches down with my thoughts colliding and my eyes unable to stay closed. Anxious and restless, like I've been most of my life.

Why am I keeping this journal? It used to be my way of getting even with Clay. I've read my old notebooks and they read like hate mail. There is so much anger in them. Now, since this truce he seems to have called, I don't know why I'm going on.

Christmas was fabulous. My father started in with the Prodigal Son parable but I wouldn't let him go there. He knows how hard I've worked this first semester, completing my first four months of college with a 3.8 GPA. He knows it wasn't easy.

No, dad was good to me. They bought me a brand-new laptop for Christmas, we never fought, and I even broke down and went to Sunday services twice while I was home. Maybe it's just that they are finally seeing me as my own person — seeing me as a grownup. Two days before leaving, dad asked if I'd consider coming home for the summer, telling me he had a great part-time job lined up. How unlike him.

I hope things are finally changing. I just want to be able to make up my own mind about who and what I want to be. I don't want to be forced to go to some Bible-belt college where religion is jammed down your throat by neo-Nazi zealots. Where everyone thinks alike, dogmatically certain they've found the truth, the way and the light.

The truth is bigger than that. God is bigger than that. He's not static. He's alive and dynamic, like the world around us. He changes like the seasons. That's how I see him, though I know my father wouldn't agree with me on this one.

But I'm glad Christmas went well. I'm hoping this New Year will be a new year for dad and me. That he'll respect my decisions and allow me some latitude. That's what I pray for.

I'm excited about registration tomorrow. I've elected to take another Narratives Course, this one on Art and Culture. I really enjoyed my other Narratives Course. This one is more a study of the relationship between human art and culture. A history of art through time. It sounds great. I just hope it isn't filled by the time I get to it.

Maybe I can catch some more sleep. It's nearly three and I've got this alarm set for eight fifteen. I wish I wasn't this restless. But I am.

Daniel slipped his pen back into the spiral of his notebook, then tucked them both away in the drawer of his nightstand. He pulled the gold chain on the small lamp beside his bed and went back to staring at the blood red numbers on the digital clock. 2:56 blinked into 2:57. Somewhere after the disappearance of 3:04, Daniel fell back to sleep. He slept without dreaming.

The First Day of Classes

It was cold. The temperature was holding just below freezing but rain was still falling, darkening the sidewalks and the dead lawns of the campus. Winter had arrived, with a gray, unbroken sky empty as the bare trees that surrounded Atlanta.

High atop Kennesaw Mountain, thirty miles from Oglethorpe, the rain was freezing on the branches of the white oaks and chestnuts, spinning a forest of glass. On campus, the rain settled on the stones of Hearst and Lupton halls, making their castle-like architecture seem older, as if they were built at the same time as the crumbling walls of Istanbul.

The students were unusually sullen and withdrawn for the first day back at school. They were thickly wrapped in overcoats and scarfs, their backpacks heavy with textbooks still unread and notebooks yet to be filled. Everyone was withdrawn, as if sealed up in an attempt at hibernation. Waiting for spring. Waiting for something other than this bitter, lifeless cold.

Daniel had made it through his first two classes without incident. It was just another day at college. He had to wake Randy before heading off to his first class, knowing that if he hadn't, Randy would have missed school. Randy, his eyes bloodshot from a frat party the night before, thanked him, and ducked into shower just as Daniel closed the front door behind him.

Now, just after lunch, he was going to his first elective of the second semester. He had managed to get a slot in Core Curriculum 104, Art and Culture, and he was looking forward to finding out what the course was about. The class was in Hearst Hall, Room 214. Hearst Hall was his favorite — it housed the Crypt of Civilization.

He had wondered what Dr. Jacobs was thinking when he commissioned the Crypt to be constructed and sealed in 1940. In it, Dr. Jacobs had placed an assortment of books, artifacts and objects which best depicted life in America at the time. It was not to be opened until the year 8113. That was over six-thousand years from now. That was exactly twice as long as all recorded history to date, Dr. Jacobs had meticulously calculated. Still, a strange date to choose, reflected Daniel.

He was thinking about the enigma of the Crypt as he entered the classroom. Half a dozen students were already seated, only one of whom he recognized. The professor, Professor Lathcombe, came in behind Daniel. The next person to walk into the room was Ayse.

She was wearing a full-length, dark-brown woolen coat. She had a long, black cotton scarf covering her head, falling down and across the coat. The scarf was wrapped in the fashion of the chador. Ayse had draped it that way intentionally. The cold reminded her of winter in Istanbul and she knew a chador would keep her warm.

Daniel's eyes followed her across the room. He had observed her many times on campus during the first semester. On several occasions he had positioned himself in the lunchroom to be able to better watch her. She fascinated him. She was so withdrawn, timid and cautious, just like the dark-eyed doe he had seen once in the forest behind the school.

This was the closest he had ever been to her, and he now realized how beautiful she was. As she passed, she glanced toward Daniel and, for an instant, their eyes met. She smiled. Her smile fell like a shaft of sunlight that cut through the dull gray clouds. Daniel smiled back, shyly, realizing his hand had been caught in the cookie jar.

Ayse sat three seats over, in the first row of chairs that were arranged in a semi-circle around Lathcombe's desk. A few more students filtered in. Deciding it was time, the professor walked over and closed the classroom door. It was five minutes past one.

"Good afternoon, students. My name is David Lathcombe, and I'll be your instructor this semester. This course, in case you are lost, is Narratives of the Self 104, Art and Culture. Is anyone here in the wrong classroom?"

Two students checked their schedules, smiled sheepishly, picked up their bags and made for the door. Professor Lathcombe chuckled to himself as they closed the door and scurried off. They were obviously in the wrong class, and Professor Lathcombe, who had always marveled at the ways of college students, had learned to ask that question every time he started a new semester. There was always someone who had gotten their course numbers or room numbers flipped around. *Dyslexia academia*, he liked to call it.

Ayse smiled at the incident and slipped out from beneath her woolen coat. Below it, she was wearing blue jeans and a light-blue knit sweater. Daniel couldn't take his eyes off her, and he quickly noted how small and delicate her shoulders were. She was smaller than he had remembered, but then he had never been this close to her.

The professor continued, "Now that we've got that cleared up, let's talk about what this course is going to cover. The primary focus of study these next four months will be the relationship between art and the culture that helps to shape that art. We will look at..."

The professor's voice faded away into background noise as Daniel drifted off into watching Ayse. She was fascinating. Although she had taken off her coat, she had left her scarf on, covering her dark, almost auburn hair beneath it. The chador made her look more exotic. He wondered what country she was from, knowing she was a foreign student from the first moment he saw her.

She must be Islamic, he thought, noting the way she had wrapped her cotton scarf. She's always with those two other girls, and I know one of them is from Egypt. Maybe she's from Egypt? I wonder what it is like to be raised as a Muslim?

Her family must have money, sending her to a private school in America. Or maybe Oglethorpe has student aid for foreign students. Either way, it must be difficult for her and her friends, so far from their homeland and customs. It must be lonely.

"...And, as we shall see, the relationship between art and culture sometimes determines both the subject matter and the aesthetic direction of that art. A prime example of this relationship can be found in the study of Islamic art.

"When the Arab and Middle Eastern world turned to the teachings of the Qur'an, all depictions of Allâh or the face of the Prophet Mohammed were strictly forbidden. Statues or paintings depicting God were seen as a form of idolatry. With this in mind, we will compare and contrast the architecture of the Middle Ages, where, on the other hand, we have the great cathedrals of France adorned with thousands of statues of saints, martyrs and images of God. To the east, we have the great mosques filled only with sunlight and the arabesque tile work of Isnik and Morocco."

Daniel watched as Ayse took in the lecture. He saw her stir as Professor Lathcombe began talking about Islam. This was going to be an interesting class, he thought, especially with her in it.

After a half-hour lecture, Professor Lathcombe told the students which textbooks they would need for the course and gave them their reading assignments for Friday's class. As Daniel jotted down his notes, Ayse returned his glance with a smile. They were flirting.

Not the overt, open kind of flirting her roommate Ellen might do at a party, but a subtle, sweet flirtation. One that spoke of innocence and curiosity — like two children wanting to play together but unsure of what to say or how to bridge the gap of introduction. Curious yet cautious.

"Do you have any further questions?" Professor Lathcombe surveyed the classroom only to realize his students looked as they always do the first day of class, bored and disoriented, as if they were in college by some kind of clerical error.

No one said a thing. "Well, then, until Friday, same time, same place. Class is dismissed."

The rumbling of twenty students filled the room. Ayse did not rush out, since her final course of the day was not scheduled until three-thirty.

Daniel was through for the day, so he, too, took his time getting his things together. He watched and waited as the students with a two-thirty class hurried out. The professor left, anxious to get back to the solitude of his office. Within a minute, Daniel realized only the two of them remained.

He glanced over toward Ayse, only to find her eyes were already upon him. It was an awkward moment and Daniel knew he had to say something — he had to break the ice.

"Hello, I'm Daniel," he said. It was a stupid thing to say, he thought, a second after saying it. Totally stupid.

"I'm Ayse."

She had replied. What should I say next? What do I do now?

"I'm from Macon, Georgia, where are you from?"

"Istanbul."

"That's not in Georgia, is it?"

Ayse laughed. Her laughter helped. Her laugh disarmed Daniel, setting his nervous fears aside in a way nothing else could have. He knew, as he looked into her dark-brown eyes, that she didn't mind his advances. She had watched him many times over the past four months, noting he wasn't like the other boys, always eating lunch together, or being loud and crazy between classes in the courtyard.

No, this boy was different. Withdrawn and quiet for the most part. She had even taken note of his favorite cubby in the library, seeing him there on several occasions while she herself enjoyed the solitude of the library. He was good looking, almost as good looking as a movie star, she thought.

She put away her smile for a second and answered his question. "No, Istanbul is in Turkey, a few thousand miles east of Georgia."

Daniel didn't know what to say next. Talking to girls was never one of his strong suits, especially pretty ones. But he didn't want the conversation to end, so he said the first thing that came into his mind.

"Do you want to see the Crypt of Civilization?"

"The what?"

"You know, the Crypt, downstairs by the bookstore. The one Thornwell Jacobs put there in the forties. It's one of my favorite places here on campus. It's too weird."

Ayse had not been to the Crypt. She had heard something about it, but thought it was some kind of cemetery. Although she was curious, she had no inclination to search it out.

"Where is it, this tomb?"

"It's not a tomb. There's no one buried in it. Unless someone was left in there by accident when they sealed it. It's here in Phoebe Hearst Hall. It's down the basement, just opposite the bookstore. When you get to the bottom of the stairway, take a left. It's just down the hallway on the right."

Ayse gave Daniel a curious look. She thought it an odd thing to be asking someone you just met to go to look at a crypt together, but he was so handsome and intriguing that the thought of saying no never entered her mind.

"It sounds interesting. I'll go."

Daniel felt the weight of the world lifting off his shoulders as he stood up and walked over to her. What if she had said no? He couldn't dare think of it.

"Can I carry your coat?"

"That would be nice. It's heavy. I rarely wear it but it was so cold this morning.

Do you think it is going to snow?"

"They're saying it'll probably snow this evening. Does it snow in Istanbul, Georgia?"

She handed Daniel her woolen coat, smiled again, and knew he was teasing her. She didn't mind, since she had grown up with two older brothers who had teased her for years. She answered his question.

"Rarely, only when the winds sweep down from the north, blowing across the Black Sea and bringing the winter storms with it. When it does, it melts quickly."

They made small talk as they walked down the stairwell together. It was two flights to the basement, and by the time they hit the last floor, Daniel wished Hearst Hall was a hundred stories tall.

When they got to the bottom, Daniel pointed left. "It's this way."

They took a few steps and came upon the massive, stainless steel door that sealed the Crypt. It was then that Ayse took off her scarf. As she did, Daniel watched her long, flowing reddish-brown hair fall along her shoulders. It seemed to him to be like a dark, auburn-tinted waterfall, silky and liquid. She ran her long, thin fingers through it several times to comb it, then shook her head gently, letting it fall where it may.

"Is this it?" she asked.

"Yes, it's the Crypt of Civilization. Dr. Jacobs was the president of Oglethorpe back then. He decided to put it here as one of the first time capsules ever created."

Ayse looked at Daniel in disbelief. "What's a time capsule?" she asked, speaking with a charming foreign accent.

"Don't you have time capsules in Turkey?"

"No. Should we?"

"I don't know. I guess I thought everyone knew what time capsules were. But I've never been abroad, so maybe they're more American than I thought.

"Anyway, this Crypt, which was put here in 1940, has a bunch of stuff in it that tells who we are, and who we've been up to this point in time. Here, read this plaque."

They stood there together, silently reading the engraved plaque above the large metal door that had been sealed shut over sixty years ago.

THE CRYPT
CONTAINS MEMORIALS OF THE CIVILIZATION WHICH EXISTED IN THE UNITED STATES AND IN THE WORLD AT LARGE DURING THE FIRST HALF OF THE TWENTIETH CENTURY IN RECEPTACLES OF STAINLESS STEEL IN WHICH THE AIR HAS BEEN REPLACED BY INERT GASES ARE ENCYCLOPEDIAS, HISTORIES, SCIENTIFIC WORKS, SPECIAL EDITIONS OF NEWSPAPERS, TRAVELOGUES, TRAVEL TALKS, CINEMA REELS, MODELS, PHONOGRAPH

RECORDS AND SIMILAR MATERIALS FROM WHICH AN ADEQUATE IDEA OF THE STATE AND NATURE OF THE CIVILIZATION OF 4000BC TO 1940AD CAN BE ASCERTAINED. NO JEWELS OR PRECIOUS METALS ARE INCLUDED.

WE DEPEND UPON THE LAWS OF THE COUNTY OF DEKALB, THE STATE OF GEORGIA AND THE GOVERNMENT OF THE UNITED STATES, AND OF THEIR HEIRS, ASSIGNS AND SUCCESSORS AND UPON THE SENSE OF SPORTSMANSHIP OF POSTERITY FOR THE CONTINUED PRESERVATION OF THIS VAULT UNTIL THE YEAR 8113, AT WHICH TIME WE DIRECT THAT IT SHALL BE OPENED BY AUTHORITIES REPRESENTING THE ABOVE GOVERNMENTAL AGENCIES AND THE ADMINISTRATION OF OGLETHORPE UNIVERSITY. UNTIL THAT TIME, WE BEG OF ALL PERSONS THAT THIS SEALED DOOR AND THE CONTENTS OF THE CRYPT WITHIN MAY REMAIN INVIOLATE.

OGLETHORPE UNIVERSITY
BY THORNWELL JACOBS, PRESIDENT

FRANKLIN DELANO ROOSEVELT
PRESIDENT OF THE UNITED STATES

EUGENE TALMADGE   ANNO DOMINI, 1936 AB
GOVERNOR OF GEORGIA   UNIVERSITATE RECONDITA
ANNO VICESIMO TERTIO

"Eight thousand thirteen seems like a long time from now. Do you really think this school will be here, or this building still standing six thousand years from now?" asked Ayse.

"Probably not."

"What exactly is in it?"

"Lots of stuff. Old seventy-eight phonograph records, a can of beer, some silverware, a set of encyclopedias, books, photographs and film. Even some toys, like a set of Lincoln logs, a pinball game and a toy pistol. I've got a pamphlet that lists everything that's in it."

"Why did he make this crypt?"

"I guess Dr. Jacobs wanted to put an assortment of all the things that made up civilization on the date he sealed it, May 28, 1940, just before the war."

Daniel continued. "He was an odd duck, this Dr. Jacobs. He wrote books about the cosmos, awarded honorary degrees to presidents and women and inscribed all those quotes above the doorways."

"Yes, I've read several, but I don't understand them. I thought they must have something to do with the Bible."

"In a way they do, but in another way they don't. You're not Christian, are you?"

"No, I'm Muslim."

"Well, they do sound Christian. Do you want to hear my favorite?"

"You've memorized them?" Ayse looked at Daniel curiously.

"Only one. I memorized it because I think it means something, although I'm not at all sure what. *Hast Thou no need of young fresh power to find anew thy holy grail — a thing which reckless youth must do because the careful aged fail? Uplifted to that cross Lord God with outstretched hand we wait Thy nail.*

"What do you think?" Daniel said to Ayse, who was looking perplexed.

"I'll have to give it some thought. Don't you have any idea what it means?"

"Not really, but it's important. It's somehow connected, but I don't know how."

There was an awkward pause. Daniel knew it was time to say goodbye. He couldn't place why such a feeling had overcome him, but it had. The pause grew longer, as though time itself was being stretched, when Daniel broke the silence.

"Well, we'll talk again. I've got to get running now to get some reading in before dinner. I'll see you Friday in class, right?"

"Yes, I like the class so far. It was nice to hear something about my culture for a change."

"He seems like an interesting teacher, Professor Lathcombe, doesn't he?"

"Yes, he does."

"Well, until again, nice meeting you, Ayse."

"It was nice meeting you, Daniel. Goodbye." She smiled one last time and went into the bookstore. Daniel raced up the stairwell they had just descended. His feet seemed a thousand times lighter than they were when the two were coming down, as though he had been released from the laws of gravity.

He walked outside and noticed the first few flakes of snow appearing out of the seamless gray sky hanging over the city. It was cold. High atop Kennesaw Mountain, the winds were picking up. Chunks of ice were falling, shattering a forest of glass.

Love was born on that cold, wintry afternoon in Georgia.

Near Midnight

Something had happened. Daniel tried not to think about her the entire afternoon. The harder he tried to put Ayse out of his thoughts, the more present she became. It was a feeling unfamiliar to him, disconcerting in a pleasant way.

It was her last glance, just after he had handed back her woolen coat, when she turned around and walked down the hallway toward the bookstore. Her long, reddish black hair falling past her shoulders, her youthful, slender body moving down the hallway. The well-sculpted body of a young woman dressed in worn blue jeans and a light-blue sweater. Not voluptuous, but thin and athletic, with the graceful movements of a panther.

He couldn't stop thinking about her. He had scrambled up the stairway and dashed to the library as though he weighed half his normal weight. A helium of unknown origin left him light-headed and weightless, as though the campus had been mysteriously transported to the moon's field of gravity.

But it hadn't. The day became darker and the snow kept falling. Daniel stayed at his favorite study station on the second floor of the library reading pages of a textbook that seemed disjointed, as if someone had taken each page from a different novel and bound them together into one incomprehensible manuscript. His eyes pored over the words but they made little sense, meanings lost in the hieroglyphics of distraction.

All he could think of was her smile. Her smile had captured him. Her smile that came unexpectedly, and left him in this state of euphoric uncertainty. Daniel had not experienced anything quite like this before.

As the clock in the library approached six, he realized he had to stop reading whatever it was he'd been reading and return to the cafeteria before dinner was stopped being served. He wasn't hungry, but he told himself he was. He was going there to try to catch a glimpse of Ayse.

Daniel had promised himself that, even should he find her, he wouldn't speak to her. It might make him appear to be too forward. She was from another country and he had no way of knowing how to behave, what their customs were like. No, it was better to err on the side of caution, he reasoned. If she's there, I'll just say hello, or wave, or smile at her and sit off in the distance where I can watch her. That's my plan. After all, I'll be sitting near her on Friday again. After class, maybe we'll go down and see the Crypt again, or, if it's nice out, take a stroll through the courtyard.

Daniel kept daydreaming, playing out a thousand different scenarios as he left the library and walked the short distance to Emerson Student Center. He left the library without wearing his jacket, but on his way to the student center, he stopped and put it back on. It was bitterly cold and the wind was howling. The snowfall, which was light but falling steady, swirled in the gusts. He found himself shivering. This was the coldest winter he had ever experienced, much colder than any he could remember in Macon.

Once in the cafeteria, he grabbed a tray, some silverware and went through the serving line. Meatloaf with mashed potatoes and gravy. Peas and carrots. Everything lifeless. He grabbed a salad and an apple before flashing the elderly woman at the cash register his meal ticket. She wrote down his number and let him pass, their eyes never making contact.

He walked into the cafeteria and looked around. She wasn't there. Randy was off in a corner hanging out with a gang of expatriate wannabes. He wasn't in the mood for Randy, or his collection of alienated college students. Daniel picked out an empty table in the corner and dined alone.

After dinner he put his jacket back on and went to his dorm. A standard mixture of television, laptop time, coffee and textbooks swallowed the next few hours. He kept thinking of her. He tried to get to bed early, remembering his eight-thirty math class tomorrow, but Randy came in and woke him just after eleven. Randy made himself a peanut-butter-and-jelly sandwich to rid himself of the munchies and, in his typical style, produced the maximum amount of clinging and clanging possible. After inhaling the sandwich, Randy went into his bedroom and crashed. Crashed without washing up or brushing his teeth. Randy at his finest.

Daniel stared at the blank ceiling for half an hour, then turned on his night light, picked up his spiral notebook and wrote a poem.

Wednesday, Jan 17

She steals the meanings right out of my dictionary

Her smile has left me dangling here
On this stage I've never known.
Suspended like some marionette in
This comedy, alone.

Where all my lines are upside down,
My script in disarray.
I dance and sing unwittingly,
Not knowing what to say.

Who is this girl, this innocent?
Who's stolen this, my script?
And left me quoting gibberish
In what language I have left.

Whose hair cascades like music
Played in canyons of my heart.
Whose eyes invite me inward
To a world that stands apart.

She steals away these meanings,
These adjectives and verbs.
And replaces them with muted songs
In a language I've not heard.

In a language made of gemstones
Hanging silently in skies.
Where the moon looks on with envy
At the midnight in her eyes.

Daniel Mark Harris

Daniel put down his pen and laid the notebook on his chest. Except for the rhythmic motion of his breathing, and the barely discernable pounding of his heartbeat, he stayed motionless. But within, his emotional heart was racing. His thoughts ran up and down flights of stairs a thousand times taller than the Eiffel Tower.

Up and down, up and down a hundred times a minute, with naught but the vision of her face before him. In this, his outward calm belied the havoc within. They were unconnected, like the polarity of two massive magnets. He felt as if he might explode.

After a while, he picked up the poem and read it back to himself. It was silly, he thought. He was half-tempted to tear it out and throw it in the garbage. He didn't.

He closed the notebook, stuck his pen into the spiral, and turned out his lamp. He went back to staring at the same blank ceiling.

The poem isn't silly, he reflected. I've never written a love poem before and it's just because I feel stupid for writing one now. That's the problem. It's not the poem's fault, it's my fault. My fault for feeling this way about a girl I hardly know. A girl I just met. A girl from Istanbul who probably thinks I'm the biggest dork since Carrot Top. Not that she'd know who Carrot Top is.

Daniel kept staring at the ceiling, his thoughts caught up in a meaningless battle within. He stared until his eyes became too sleepy to keep open. He fell asleep just after one o'clock, and dreamt of Ayse all the night.

Ayse's Room

Ayse could hear Ellen on the telephone in the living room. She had been on the phone for the past two hours. The girls had decided not to go out tonight. In lieu of going out they were doing phone.

"Oh, can you believe Sandra Lee has Jason in her math class? He's just too cute to believe. Don't you think he looks like Nick Carter from The Backstreet Boys? I sure do.

"Who's in your class?"

After asking that, Ellen would remain silent while the Southern belle on the other end of the line gave Ellen the lowdown on a boy in her chemistry class, or the jocks in Algebra 102. They seldom discussed boys like Daniel Harris. Singular, introspective kids with good grades and brains that functioned. They focused on basketball stars and popularity contests. Colleges, for girls like Ellen, were what they have been called for decades — high schools with ashtrays.

Ayse didn't mention her afternoon encounter with Daniel to her roommate. Even if Ellen found it mildly interesting, she would only be feigning concern. She had accepted the fact that she ended up rooming with this strange Muslim girl and, by this time, paid no attention to Ayse. Her assigned roommate was just another fixture, like a cupboard or the kitchen sink. Something she was stuck with through her freshman year. Next year, if Ellen's plans went well, she would be living in a sorority house. Ayse and her prayer rug would be relegated to something that had happened. Something unfortunate.

But Daniel was foremost on Ayse's mind. She kept seeing his blue eyes and hearing him trying to explain the Crypt of Civilization. It was the color of his eyes that enticed her. She had always been surrounded by men and women with brown eyes. Turkish eyes, some in shades as light as hazel, but most as dark as the bark on the trees of winter. Never blue.

She had finished her last class of the day at four twenty-five and decided not to have dinner at the cafeteria. She had been told the meatloaf they were serving had pork in it, a meat expressly forbidden by the Qur'an. The meatloaf, the gravy, all of it was unacceptable to Ayse, Hatice and Kasha. They decided to grab a small salad and dine together in Kasha's room.

Ayse had not mentioned Daniel to her friends either. She didn't want to say anything that might start them thinking she had a boyfriend. All three of them had promised their families they would not date while attending college. It was a condition between them and their parents to allow them the privilege of attending a college in America. Besides, thought Ayse as they chatted and ate their salads together, Daniel and I may never speak to each other again.

Of course, Ayse didn't believe that. She was already anticipating her Art and Culture class on Friday. Throughout the entire first semester, he was one of a few boys on campus who had caught her eye. He was so good-looking and intriguing. Always off by himself, thoughtful and withdrawn, like an artist.

Ayse was getting tired. She had been reading *Don Quixote* for one of her language classes. It was a difficult read, written in a style of English foreign to her. She decided to call it an early night and prepared for bed. She brushed her hair, washed her face and brushed her teeth quietly while Ellen continued running her telephone marathon.

Ayse fell asleep contemplating the Crypt of Civilization. It seemed such an odd thing to do, to save all these things from the present for someone to look at six thousand years from now. But, in a way, it wasn't unlike Istanbul, where they had saved many, many things from the past. Things like the Serpentine Column near the Blue Mosque, which was cast from the weapons of the defeated Persians in 479 B.C. Or the crumbled ruins of the old tower and fortresses that once encircled the city. In Istanbul, antiquity was ever present.

The city itself was a time capsule. Maybe Dr. Jacobs invented the time capsule because America loves everything new — new and disposable. Perhaps that's why he built the crypt — to save a piece of history before it became lost to progress.

With her thoughts tumbling between the crypt and the boy who told her about it, Ayse fell fast asleep.

Friday's Class

Ayse was the first student to arrive in class that afternoon. She didn't look up as the students dribbled in, not wanting to appear anxious. She buried herself in *Don Quixote*, amused by his misadventures and those of his squire, Sancho Panza. Ayse had become more accustomed to Cervantes's style of writing over the past few days, and she found herself enjoying his classic tale of misguided chivalry.

When Daniel came in, he took note of Ayse. She was there, and his heart fluttered the instant he saw her.

She was wearing a heavy, colorful sweater. It was knit in a style similar to Peruvian alpaca sweaters, with intricate patterns and bright, floral colors. Her thick, dark hair was pulled back into a single ponytail. Her pants looked to be the same pair of threadbare blue jeans, but these were flared at the bottom. She had on the same pair of leather boots she had worn on Wednesday. Expensive boots, but of a different style than the other girls at school wore. European-looking, with high, thick heels and a dull, jet-black sheen.

Daniel tried not to stare, but did. Ayse tried hard not to look up from her book until the professor started speaking, and managed to refrain from looking at Daniel. Five minutes into class, with the professor rambling on about the paleolithic paintings of the Lascaux Caves in south-central France, and the rock paintings of the Australian Aboriginals, she returned one of Daniel's glances with a simple, understated smile.

As she did, Daniel's heart leapt off the edge of the world. He knew. It was only a glance, followed by a smile. But in the language of lovers, it was more than that. It was her consent. It was yes. It was what women have done since the time of those cave paintings and untold centuries before. It was the look of lovers.

The professor continued with his lecture on primitive art, citing American

Indian stone carvings and pictographs discovered across the furthest reaches of the prehistoric world. He spoke of the commonality of the drawings and the creatures they depicted. Monstrous bulls dueling in some primordial world where language was young and writing unknown. Where people worshiped sun gods and rain gods and demon gods whose once powerful reigns have long since been lost.

"It was a time of brutal tribalism and human sacrifice. An ugly, survivalistic world countered only by the splendid beauty of these fourteen-thousand-year old cave drawings, etched in charcoal and ochre on canvases of stone."

Professor Lathcombe continued, "The dawn of recorded human history did not begin with writing, it began with drawing. It began when man, for reasons known only to those who made these prehistoric sketches, took up the burnt, charcoal tips of his hunting spears and drew. He drew what he knew, a menacing world of saber tooth tigers, wolly mammoths and aurochs. All of them now extinct. Relegated to bones and paleolithic drawings. In time he included stick figures of himself in these drawings.

"Simplistic scenes of men hunting, subduing and conquering the beasts that surrounded them. Over the centuries, he discovered copper, bronze, then iron and the tools that were fashioned from these metals. Metals that made civilization possible.

"Next week we'll move to early Egypt and the culture of Mesopotamia in what is now modern-day Iran. We'll study the neolithic world of the Bronze Age, the cradles of civilization along with the art those cultures produced. Read pages twenty-nine through thirty-seven of your text by Monday."

Almost as an afterthought, Professor Lathcombe added, "And have a nice weekend. Class dismissed."

The professor went behind his desk and sat down and gathered his notes while his students poured through the same door they had come in an hour earlier. All but two students.

Taking note of them, he lingered longer than usual at his desk, curious as to why these two students had stayed behind. He had watched them exchanging glances the first two classes and suspected the usual. The usual being the boy-meets-girl story. Adorable in a way.

"Hi," said Daniel as he approached Ayse.

"Hi."

There was an awkward silence. After what seemed like a thin slice of eternity, Daniel broke the silence. "Want to go for a walk?"

"Sure."

Professor Lathcombe smiled to himself while idly shuffling his paperwork. He knew. Every bit as lovely as a painting by Monet.

Daniel and Ayse walked out of the classroom. As soon as they reached the doorway, Ayse turned around and spoke to Professor Lathcombe, "I'm enjoying your class, Professor Lathcombe. I'll see you Monday."

Daniel noted her comment. He pondered for a minute and realized he never heard a student say anything as thoughtful to a teacher at Oglethorpe.

"So, how've you been?"

"Fine. I'm glad it's getting warm. It was so cold last Wednesday."

"Yes. It never gets this cold down in Macon."

"Where's Macon?"

Daniel laughed. As they headed to the courtyard Daniel explained where Macon was. He told her about his hometown, about the Georgia Music Hall of Fame, the Cannonball House and the fact that Macon was spared Sherman's torch during the Civil War. Small talk, odds and ends about each other's lives that never mean much beyond the pleasure of hearing each other's voices.

They walked west past the theater where the Shakespeare Festival was held each year, and into the small woods that lay between the campus and Greek Row further up the hill. The sunlight shone brightly, unhampered by the naked limbs of the trees. It warmed their shoulders as they walked. Ayse talked about what it was like to grow up in Istanbul and Daniel about fishing for catfish in the Ocmulgee River that cut through Macon.

A half-hour slipped away when Ayse looked at her watch and told Daniel she had to get going to her next class.

"So soon?" asked Daniel.

"We can talk again after class on Monday. But I really have to be going now, I don't like being late."

"I can tell. You must have been the first person in class today."

"I was. It is how my father taught me to be — to be prompt. It has become a bad habit."

"No. It's a good habit. Hurry on now, though I can hardly wait 'til Monday."

"Oh, don't be silly."

"I'm not being silly."

With that, Ayse turned and walked down the path they had just taken. The sunlight splashed across her hair, making the reddish hues come alive. She walked directly, never looking back until she reached the paved pathway a hundred yards away. Then she turned briskly, her hair whipping round as she did, and waved a goodby to Daniel. He waved back as his heart pounded harder than he thought it possibly could.

Time Goes By

Weeks passed. Some afternoons, when the north wind was wailing and the weather inhospitable, they would stay in Hearst Hall. The two of them might walk to the bookstore together for Ayse to purchase a new pen, or Daniel a new notebook for his journal. On those occasions, they made a point of walking together over to the Crypt of Civilization. Daniel had obtained the list of items contained in the Crypt, and he enjoyed reading it to Ayse as they sat beside the steel door.

She never understood the reasoning behind the crypt, deciding it was something only Americans would do. A ceramic-lined room full of cigarette holders, Schick electric razors and fish hooks, to mention but a few of the items Daniel read off to her. She laughed when he came upon a particularly odd piece, like the time he told her about the set of dentures — uppers only.

Some afternoons they sat comfortably on the couch in front of the fireplace on the main floor of Hearst Hall. There, they would discuss what Professor Lathcombe had just lectured on — the Temple of Dionysus, or the Acropolis, Roman architecture, Mayan pyramids or the Great Wall of China. They rarely discussed religion, or the differences between Islam and Christianity. For the moment, it didn't matter.

On sunlit, warm afternoons, they would go for a stroll. They would wander out to the wooden bridge that spanned a creek that never held water. Both happy to be spending time with each other, smiling, joking, talking about the world.

Hatice and Kasha saw what was happening, but they didn't interfere. They knew nothing serious would come of it, understanding the cultural and religious differences between Ayse and Daniel would eventually end their relationship. When the semester ended, so would this passing flirtation.

Daniel's roommate, Randy, also noted the glint in Daniel's eye. He had seen the two together on several occasions — never holding hands, or kissing, but walking along, smiling and laughing. He teased Daniel about it, but Daniel dismissed it with his standard response, "We're just friends, Randy. Nothing more than that. We're just friends." As if by repeating it enough times to his roommate he might be convinced of it himself.

But in his heart, he knew. So did she. His world was changing. His thoughts drifted more and more toward the shoreline of her dark-brown eyes and enchanting smile. He looked forward to every Monday, Wednesday and Friday with a passion once foreign to him.

One late night, three weeks after meeting Ayse, Daniel awoke from a restless dream. Without so much as thinking about it, he wrote the following.

Friday, Feb. 9, 2:30 a.m.

She is a gift. This beautiful young woman from the Near East. A gift that came unexpectedly, like a package in the mail. A wonderful package filled with her smile, her voice, her presence.

I've never felt like this before. I feel myself wanting all the time in between —

the long, tedious Tuesdays and insipid Thursdays — to go away. To disappear into some black hole of time so I can get to my seat across from her and listen to Lathcombe lecture for an hour while we exchange glances.

After class comes our time. Our half-hour together, three times a week. Our conversations about America, about Turkey, about anything at all so long as I'm with her. It doesn't matter where we go or what we do, at least not to me. All that matters is to be with her.

I know this isn't good. I can't imagine what my father would say if he knew I was spending time with a Muslim. I've listened to him at dinner going on and on about the Islamic menace. If he found out that I was, I mean, if he found out I am...

That's what's happening, isn't it? I am falling in love. I don't want to admit it, I don't even want to write this into my journal. It's because I know it's an impossible dream, for us to be together. She with her family in Turkey and my father the epitome of intolerance. It would be easier to fly to the moon, or to walk on water than it will be to have Ayse for my own.

Still, my heart longs for her. I count the hours until I can spend those minutes again beside her. I think of her constantly, like some tape loop that plays and replays itself in my thoughts. Her dark, Mediterranean skin, her adorable accent, but mostly, her soul. Her priceless, tender soul.

I'm thinking about asking her out but I'm not sure how to handle it. She's told me about the promise she's made with her parents and it doesn't leave me many options. Maybe we could go to a museum, or somewhere that could tie into our art history class? I could ask Randy if I could use his Honda for an afternoon and we could spend some time together away from Oglethorpe. I'm not sure what she'd say, but I'm tempted to ask her.

Enough for now. I'll see her again today and take it from there. My heart races at the very thought of it. If love is a virus, I've got a fatal case. And worse still, I don't care.

Daniel wrote nothing more. He slipped his pen in the wire of his notebook and turned off his bedside lamp. He didn't want to think about what he had just written. He didn't want to acknowledge that it might be true. But it was.

Friday's Class

"Theirs was an empire unprecedented in the history of the world. Their architectural achievements have never been duplicated or surpassed, not even with today's technology. The Colosseum, the Parthenon, the Theater of

Marcellus, the roads they constructed, the aqueducts, all speak of the Romans' skills in engineering and design. They were the empire builders.

"Steeped in Greek tradition, and borrowing most of their gods from the Greeks, the Romans dominated the entirety of the Western world from the British isles to the Middle East.

"But like all great civilizations, it wasn't to last. With the Edict of Constantine in the year three hundred and thirteen, and the proclamation of Christianity as the official religion of Rome, the world would soon be slipping into the abyss of the Dark Ages. The great works of Aristotle, Socrates and Plato would be burned by the papal hierarchy of the Roman Catholic Church. For the next five hundred years, the Western world would march backward into the darkness of medieval Europe.

"On Monday, we will begin studying Christian art and the Byzantine art of the Middle East. Please read pages one hundred ten through one hundred and forty-four of your text. We'll see all of you here Monday at one-thirty. Have a nice weekend. Class dismissed."

The room filled with the sound of closing textbooks and the shuffle of backpacks. Ayse looked over at Daniel and smiled. She too had come to look forward to their time together.

They got up and went into the hallway. It was a typical Friday afternoon between classes — students frantically trying to make their two-thirty class, teachers standing in the doorway, discussing some obscure detail of their lecture, or a student trying to explain why his paper was late. The student coming up with a new twist on the age-old standards of implausible excuses. The professor shaking his head in disbelief.

Ayse and Daniel strolled calmly through all of this. Ayse had her next class in an hour and she knew the next half-hour or more belonged to them.

"Let's get some coffee in that little café in Goodman Hall. I didn't sleep well last night and I could use a cup of joe to pick me up. Do you want to?" asked Daniel.

"That sounds fine. But I'd rather have a Diet Coke," replied Ayse.

"Great, I'm buying."

They walked out of Hearst Hall and headed west toward the small café located in the front of Goodman Hall. It was a typical college coffee shop, serving an assortment of pastries, hot dogs and hamburgers. Nothing out of the ordinary.

"One large coffee with cream and one Diet Coke please," said Daniel to the woman working behind the counter.

"That'll be two dollars even," she said while turning around and pouring the two drinks.

Daniel paid while Ayse waited beside him. They took their drinks and went back outside. The weather was gray and cool, a typical winter afternoon in Atlanta. The temperature was hanging stubbornly in the mid-fifties. The sky overcast and dull.

They found a bench on the fringe of the courtyard and sat down. Daniel tore off a piece of plastic allowing him to sip his hot coffee and Ayse poked a straw through the center of the can lid into her Coke. They didn't say anything for quite some time, satisfied with the knowledge they were together again.

After a few minutes, Daniel broke the silence.

"Ayse, would you like to do something together over the weekend? Maybe go to the High Museum? I've heard they have a great exhibit on Matisse."

Ayse didn't respond. She hadn't anticipated Daniel ever asking her to go out, thinking their friendship would never leave the well-defined parameters of these afternoon meetings. She hadn't thought about it because she didn't want to allow herself that luxury.

She knew her parents would not approve, even as a friendship. For her to be spending time with a Christian boy would be cause enough for concern, but for that boy to be the son of a minister? No, it would never work. They had made it clear to her she was not to do any dating while at college, and this seemed like a date.

"Daniel, you know I've promised my parents not to date while I'm here in America. We've talked about this before," said Ayse.

"Oh, this isn't a date or anything. It's just that I thought it might be a nice way to kill some time over the weekend. Randy, my roommate, said I could use his car any time I wanted to, so getting there wouldn't be a problem.

"The museum closes at five and we could be back on campus before six at the latest. My parents are patrons and admission is free. It would be like a field trip for Professor Lathcombe's class."

Ayse said nothing. She looked over at him, the straw still in her mouth, her head slightly tilted and her brown eyes looking up at him sheepishly. She smiled, took the straw out, and repeated his comments, "It wouldn't be a date. It would be a study trip for school, right?"

She was searching for a way to say yes. A way to allow herself the joy of spending some time with Daniel without breaking her promise. If it was a field trip, something they might do for extra credit or research, then it wasn't a date. It was a part of her education.

"Yes, it's strictly educational," said Daniel, a little too excitedly. He quickly added, "before the semester's over we'll be studying modern art, Impressionism and Post-Impressionism and I'm sure Matisse's paintings will come up.

"Here, let me check."

Daniel flipped to the back of his text and rifled through the index. He knew Matisse's paintings were in there, because he had already looked for them at lunch. He wanted to show her that it was okay, that they weren't going on a date or anything resembling a date. They were going to the High Museum for academic purposes only.

"Here it is, on page four hundred and forty-six, Henri Matisse — Fauvism and the avant-garde movements of the early twentieth century. See?"

Daniel showed her a large, full-color painting by Matisse. Ayse smiled a smile that could tame a savage lion. It was a yes.

"Maybe they'll have this painting in the show."

"We'll be back by six?" she asked firmly.

"I promise."

"Then I'll go."

Daniel's heart exploded. The very thought of spending an entire afternoon with Ayse sent his emotions soaring. Inside himself, he was somewhere in the stratosphere, high above the sprawling metropolis of Atlanta. High enough for him to see both cities, the ancient Istanbul, at the crossroads of the East, and Atlanta, at the crossroads of the new South.

Outwardly, he remained calm, not wanting to make it appear like it was anything more than doing a homework assignment with a friend.

Ayse's heart, though more cautious, was also flying. It was to be their first date together, and she knew it. A rose by any other name is still a rose. Tomorrow couldn't come soon enough.

The High Museum of Art

The old Honda sputtered into the parking lot at the museum with an unusual amount of fanfare. Randy had warned Daniel about the muffler being rusted through but assured him the problem wasn't dangerous.

"Just keep the windows down and don't put the fan on re-circulate and y'all be fine," he had said earlier that morning before giving the car keys to his roommate.

Daniel heeded his advice. The Honda sounded like it needed work. It had several rust spots, more than a few scratches and dents and it shifted funny. But the newly installed Sony CD player sounded fabulous. For Randy, it was always about priorities.

Ayse walked to Daniel's quad just after lunch. He didn't ask her in, fearing the worst should Ayse see the disheveled interior of their apartment, so he met her outside by the disheveled exterior of Randy's rusting Honda.

They parked the car, glad to have silenced the backfiring engine, and walked to the entrance of the museum. It was another lifeless, colorless day in Atlanta. A dull-brown earth spread beneath a cement-colored sky. Winter in the South.

Once inside, Daniel produced his student ID and, after the attendant checked out the patron status of his parents, Mr. and Mrs. Clayton Harris from Macon, he and Ayse were admitted free of charge.

"It comes in handy from time to time, to have parents with money," remarked Daniel.

"Yes, if my parents didn't have money, I wouldn't be here."

"Nor would I. There's no way I could afford the tuition at Oglethorpe if it wasn't for my mother's inheritance. Her father came from South Georgia. He made his fortune in the paper business, and sold his mill just after World War II.

"That's when they moved to Macon, where my mom eventually met my father."

"Oh," responded Ayse, unsure of what to say.

They proceeded down the well-lit hallways of the gallery. The brilliant halogen lights of the museum made up for the dismal gray that saturated the world beyond. It was as if the inside had become the outside.

They found their way to the Matisse exhibit and started viewing the prints and paintings on display. They looked at *Blue Nude IV,* painted in 1952, near the end of the artist's life. They chatted and compared it with his *Dahlias,* with its flat, dimensionless canvas and bright-red flowers.

They stood before Matisse's line drawing, *La Fleur,* and both of them were taken by it.

"Look how simple it is, Ayse."

"Simple, but beautiful."

Like her, Daniel thought to himself. Like Ayse. As she looked at the drawing, Daniel took a few steps back and looked at her looking at the drawing. They were sisters, this woman who had posed for *La Fleur* and this Turkish woman now studying it. Both with broad faces, clean, well-defined features, and dark, inviting eyes.

"She could be your sister," Daniel commented.

"I don't have a sister, but if I did, she would be the ideal sister. She looks a little like me, doesn't she?"

"Yes, she does. Only you're far more beautiful."

Ayse looked over her shoulder at Daniel, smiling and blushing at once. She was embarrassed by his compliment, but loved hearing it.

"I thought this was supposed to be an educational field trip," she said sternly after gathering her composure.

"Ooops," he said. "I got carried away by all of these heavenly works of art, and somehow you were included. Will you please forgive me?"

"Never," said Ayse, smiling as she did.

They were flirting. Surrounded by a gallery full of colorful paintings by a French master, it was as though they were drawn into the canvases. It was as if they had joined hands with the festive members of *The Dance.* Circling hand in hand on a blue-and-green canvas in a celebration that knew nothing of the differences between them. They continued strolling through the exhibit.

Standing in front of *Still Life with Magnolia,* Daniel spoke. "We have a magnolia in our back yard in Macon. They have the most striking flowers. The way they are framed against the dark green, waxy leaves of the magnolia tree makes them all the more glorious.

"Do you have any magnolias in Istanbul?"

"No, not that I know of."

"Do you mind being away from home? From Istanbul and your family?"

"Not when I'm with you."

Daniel beamed. He felt, right then and there, like going over and hugging her. Taking this delicate young woman into his arms and smothering her in his embrace. But it wasn't time yet. In his thoughts he held her, kissed her, even made love with her, but in the well-lit corridors of the High Museum of Art on a Saturday afternoon in Atlanta he did nothing of the sort. He smiled coyly and went on.

They finished viewing the Matisse exhibit and looked passingly at some of the other exhibits. Before long, Daniel suggested they should get a cup of coffee from a nearby Starbucks and return to campus.

"Why the hurry?" Ayse asked.

"Because I think we should make these other exhibits, the one on folk art and the photography galleries, as part of another field trip. Don't you agree?"

"Why certainly. I can hear Professor Lathcombe now, telling us that we must never rush the study of fine art."

They winked at each other and Daniel knew he had found a way to see her every weekend. After the High Museum's visit there could be a field trip to the Fernwood Museum of Natural History. After that he knew he would be able to find other galleries and exhibits scattered across Atlanta. The possibilities were endless.

If Randy wouldn't let him take the car, they could ride the bus, or take a cab. Anything to be with her. Anything.

They arrived back on campus just before six. Daniel wanted to kiss her goodbye, and secretly, in his heart, he did. Outwardly, he politely walked Ayse back to her dorm room and said goodbye without so much as taking her hand. He didn't want to frighten her away. She was, like Professor Lathcombe had lectured on at art class, a work of rare beauty.

"We must never rush the study of fine art," the professor would remind his class repeatedly.

In Daniel's eyes, Ayse was Botticelli's *Venus* and Da Vinci's *Mona Lisa* fused. He was willing to take a lifetime studying her.

Spring

The dogwoods blossomed beneath the canopy of hardwoods and southern pines that covered the eastern slope of Kennesaw Mountain. In places, the innumerable white blooms made it appear as if, sometime during the previous night, it had snowed flowers. The scent of the dogwoods mingled with the intoxicating aromas of spring as Daniel and Ayse backpacked up the long, steep foot trail to the summit.

"Not an easy trail, is it?" asked Daniel rhetorically as he glanced back at Ayse thirty feet behind him.

"No," replied Ayse, trying to catch her breath.

"Do you want to take a break?"

"That would be nice."

"There's a fallen tree trunk up ahead. Just hang in there a few more minutes."

"I'll be fine, you go on up ahead."

The climb had been steep and steady and Ayse was getting tired. They were over half-way to the top of the mountain, and Daniel could see it was time for them to take a breather.

He made it to the fallen tree, sat down and took off his backpack. As Ayse climbed the last hundred feet behind him, Daniel took out a bottle of ice water and took a long drink. Even though it was the perfect afternoon for such a hike, cool, clear and windless, he too was tired and thirsty.

"Going down will be a lot easier," he yelled to Ayse as she slowly ascended the trail.

"I hope so," she said softly.

She finally caught up to him and, taking off her backpack, sat beside him and took out her own bottle of water. She took a long, refreshing drink.

Daniel watched her as she did. He could see the beads of sweat on her forehead and neck. The beads ran down the sides of her cheeks and fell to the forest floor. She was wearing a light T-shirt and he couldn't help but notice that beneath it, her small breasts were lifting up and down in harmony with her heavy breathing. Her hair was back in a ponytail, but several strands had worked free and were hanging down along the sides of her face, wet with perspiration.

This is how she would look were we to make love, Daniel thought. Were we ever to go beyond this friendship and spend the night together, this is how my Ayse would appear, like a dark panther after the hunt. A young woman after an hour of lovemaking, sensual and winded.

It was difficult for Daniel not to think about their friendship becoming something more. They had spent most of the last dozen Saturday afternoons together and every excursion had been a joy. Most of their trips had been to museums, all under the guise of field trips and extra credit. Even Professor Lathcombe had joined in their conspiracy of romance. Daniel had mentioned to the professor that Ayse and he had seen the Matisse exhibit and enjoyed it.

He was pleased to find students who were willing to go the extra mile and said, "If you want to, you could each do written reports on your field trips and if I like what you've written, I'll give both of you extra credit."

Daniel was delighted. Ayse had no reason to doubt that these weren't dates, but an official part of her curriculum at Oglethorpe. She began mentioning her field trips in her e-mails to her parents in Istanbul. Of course she left out the fact that the class making these trips consisted of two students — one being a handsome, blue-eyed Southern boy from Macon, Georgia, and the other being a beautiful Muslim girl from Turkey. It was an error of omission.

Everyone on campus knew what was happening. Randy laughed aloud some mornings as he handed the keys to his Honda over to Daniel.

"You're going where?" he would ask a second time, as if to double-check his hearing.

"We're going to the Historic Oakland Cemetery. You know, the burial site of Bobby Jones, the famous golfer, six governors, soldiers, a bunch of mayors. Even Margaret Mitchell, who wrote *Gone With the Wind,* is buried there. You can't get any more historical than that."

"Well," said Randy sarcastically, "I suppose you two lovebirds are running out of legitimate museums by now. You're down to graveyards and...where was it last week, the papermaking museum? Lucky the semester's over soon. You two would be going door to door along West Pace's Ferry looking for houses full of antique furniture."

"Cut it out, you jerk. We went to the Robert C. Williams American Museum of Papermaking because I wanted to show Ayse how my grandfather had made his money. It was a nice museum, with displays tracing Egyptian papyrus-making all the way through modern manufacturing techniques."

"Professor Lathcombe commended both of us on our reports about the museum."

"Daniel, don't you think the good Professor Lathcombe sees through your charade? Ayse's parents won't let her go out with anyone while she's here, so you two have come up with this tour of every obscure museum or historical site in Atlanta as a way of beating the system.

"Let's see, it was Stone Mountain two weeks ago, the Jewish Heritage Museum a few weeks before that and what's coming up, the something or other Nest Museum?"

"The Wren's Nest House Museum. That's where Joel Harris wrote his famous Uncle Remus tales, you know, the story of Br'er Rabbit and his friends. For all I know Joel and I are related. We've got the same last name." Daniel was having fun verbally sparring with Randy. "Just give me the keys, and I'll be on my way."

"Bring her back full," requested Randy.

"I always do."

That had become the arrangement. Ever since the High Museum, Daniel brought the Honda back filled. Every week, Randy and his party-loving friends would run it down to fumes. Every Saturday, Daniel would return it filled. It was fair. Daniel had taken the car to Midas shop a month ago to have the muffler fixed.

Randy didn't even notice.

As winter waned and spring invaded the campus, students took note of Daniel and Ayse. As they strolled across the dandelion-cluttered courtyard they radiated an unseen light. Hatice and Kasha sat beside them at dinner, basking in the invisible aura they emanated. Absorbing some of the gamma rays of their ever-increasing love. Everyone saw it but them.

They wouldn't let themselves see it. Theirs was just a friendship, an extended field trip to Fernwood, Stone Mountain or the Museum of Aviation Flight and Technology. It didn't matter where they were going on any given Saturday afternoon, all that mattered was they were going there together.

❂

"Well, shall we continue on?" suggested Daniel to his classmate.

"Just one more minute. I love sitting here like this. The air smells fresh and alive. Look at the sky. Have you ever seen it so blue?"

Daniel and Ayse gazed up. By this time the leaves had unfurled from their buds, though they still held that light-green, waxy tint. The mint green contrasted sharply with the infinite blue sky beyond. The birds of spring were returning, their songs filling the air beneath the emerald canopy. It was a day hand-carved by God for young lovers.

Within a few minutes their eyes had drifted down from the sky and they found themselves looking at each other. When their eyes met, each knew what the other was thinking. They were in trouble.

"Let's go," Daniel insisted, needing to break the spell.

"Okay. Onward and upward."

They started hiking, heading up the well-trodden dirt path to the top of the mountain. Originally, they were going to see the furnishings at Rhodes Hall, but had decided before leaving Oglethorpe that it was too fabulous a day to spend it inside. They could wait for a rainy day to take in that Romanesque-style mansion. Today had to be spent outdoors.

So they decided to visit the site of the battle for Atlanta. A site where the Confederate army had made one final, valiant stand against Sherman's overwhelming forces.

Neither Daniel nor Ayse held any pretense this excursion had any actual relevance to Lathcombe's curriculum. Neither Daniel nor Ayse planned to write a paper on this expedition. This choice was theirs alone and they knew it.

They had taken their backpacks, loaded them with sandwiches, candy bars and water and driven north to Kennesaw State Park. The windows on the Honda were wide open and they were thrilled at the thought of having a picnic together on so perfect an afternoon.

They were a little more than a quarter-mile from the top, keeping a steady stride up the hill. After crossing the road, they made for the last stretch of path before the summit. They could have easily taken the bus up, but the hike was more inviting.

As they neared the top of Kennesaw Mountain, they started to see some of the old fortifications. Places where the cannons once stood, pointing downward toward Sherman's advancing armies. There was one site that still had two war cannons in it, though they had not been fired in over a century.

Once they made the top, they looked out over the bluff facing west, and found a clearing just off the path.

"Let's have our picnic here," said Ayse, pointing to the small patch of grass near the summit.

"Looks good."

They hiked over and took their backpacks off. They threw them down near the edge of the clearing, which was shaded somewhat by towering chestnuts and hickories. Although it was still early spring, the Georgia sun was gathering momentum, and after the long hike uphill, the shade felt cool and comfortable.

Daniel sat with his back against a tree trunk and watched as Ayse unfolded a red plaid tablecloth and spread it across the grass. She went over and opened Daniel's backpack, taking out the sandwiches, chips and two new, unopened bottles of water, placing them on the tablecloth.

"Looks like quite a spread," said Daniel, smiling at her as he spoke.

"I'm hungry," she said.

"Me, too. Let's eat."

Daniel sat on the ground beside her. They made small talk while enjoying their sandwiches. It was a scene from a romance novel set in Georgia. Two sweethearts having a picnic on the top of a mountain on an ideal spring day beneath a sky as blue as the Hope diamond.

When they were through, they laid beside each other and stared up at the infinity above. They were both intoxicated with the knowledge that they were alone together in this forest. Tired, full and drunk on the champagne of being beside one another on such a glorious day. Lovers at rest.

Daniel felt it was the perfect moment to ask Ayse about some things which they had never spoken of before.

"Tell me about Islam," he said.

"Why do you ask me about Islam, Daniel? In all these months, we have never once talked about religion. Why do you want to do so today?"

"Maybe because it's so clear, so perfect a day that I think God can see us both lying here and that He wants me to better understand you. I think He wants us to find each other. Provided, of course, that there is a God."

Daniel continued on, as though he were talking to himself.

"Because religion is difficult for me, Ayse. My father has always been so intense, so adamant about Jesus and his teachings that I've grown fearful of churches and mosques, temples and prayers. I know that someday we're going to have to talk about it, and today seems like the day."

Ayse could hear it in his voice. She could hear the tenderness, the sound of all young men who find themselves defenseless against their own feelings toward the woman by whom they've been taken. Afraid, yet unafraid. The curious chemistry of passion and vulnerability.

"Don't ever be afraid of God," Ayse began. "The word Islam means 'surrender' in Arabic. We, as Muslims, must surrender to the will of Allâh, the one and only God.

"You must know that Allâh is the God of Abraham, of Moses and of Christ. Mohammed was the last prophet, revealing God's message to the world through the Qur'an, which is not unlike your Bible in some ways. The Qur'an was revealed to Mohammed by the Archangel Gabriel, the same Archangel that had been sent to tell the Virgin Mary she was to give birth to the Christ Child.

"We are not so different, you and I. It is just that the ways of men keep us from understanding how much alike we are, not the will of God, the will of Allâh."

Daniel listened. Ayse's words spoke of truth, and he didn't mind the unbroken silence that surrounded them. The filtered sun falling through the fresh, green leaves above them, the smell of dogwood blossoms and the sound of a thousand thrushes, wrens and mockingbirds in the forest surrounding them more than filled the silence. A moment unforgettable — sacred and serene.

"Have you ever been to Mecca?"

"No, but my mother's been there twice. My father only once. It is a great thing, to go on a pilgrimage to the Ka'ba. To see the Holy City of Mecca and circle God's sacred site is one of the greatest moments in the life of a Muslim.

"My father said that as the crowd pushed against him, walking in a large circle counter-clockwise around the Ka'ba, he felt as though he was no longer a single person, but a small part of a larger world. He said it was the most spiritual experience of his life.

"I hope to go to Mecca someday. To see the Great Mosque and circle the Ka'ba seven times. But it is not necessary to make a pilgrimage to Mecca to see the Ka'ba. The Sufi Muslims say the true Ka'ba is within the heart of the seeker," said Ayse as she stared into the deep-blue sky.

After another long silence, Daniel responded, "It's like visiting the Vatican for a Catholic, or a journey to Jerusalem for a Jewish person in a way, isn't it?"

"Yes, but it's more than that for a Muslim. It is one of the great pillars of our religion."

"Tell me about them, these pillars of your faith."

"There are five. The acceptance of only one God, Allâh, and the acknowledgment that Mohammed was his messenger, that is the first and greatest pillar. To say prayer, or salat, five times daily is the second pillar. It is best if you can be in a mosque, or that you are facing east when you pray, but it is not necessary.

"The third pillar is the zakat, or the offering of alms. It is where we must give one-fortieth of our wealth each year to the poor and needy. In doing so, we make the money we have earned that year, the money we keep for our own needs, pure. The fourth pillar is fasting during the month of Ramadan, which is similar to your Christian tradition of Lent.

"During Ramadan, we must fast for thirty days, eating only a small meal at sunrise, no food nor water during the day, and another meal after the sun goes down. Nothing else is allowed, and when the month of fasting is over, we have two traditional celebrations. The *Night of Destiny* and the *Breaking of the Fast.* These are, in some ways, similar to your tradition of Christmas.

"The final pillar is the pilgrimage to Mecca, or what we call the hajj, and I have already told you about that."

The silence returned. The breeze had picked up and the leaves high above them were fluttering in the wind. The mockingbird's song could be heard above all the others from the forest that engulfed them. It sounded heavenly.

After a long time had passed, long enough for a person to note the shadows had moved, Daniel broke the tranquility with his whispered voice. "I wish today didn't have to end. I wish we could both lie here forever, listening to the song-birds and watching the sunlight dance between the leaves. That we could be together like this forever, and the world around us wasn't divided by nations, colors or creeds. That we were all just people. That's what I wish for."

Without saying a word, Ayse moved closer to Daniel. As he lay there, spellbound by the color of the sky, he was suddenly aware that her face was before him. She had undone her ponytail and her strands of reddish brown hair filtered the sunlight like the leaves beyond. Her eyes were filled with tears.

Slowly, as if floating, she came closer and closer to him. Then, for the first time, their lips met. They kissed in a mystic silence so overwhelming that it made the mockingbirds hush. They melted into one, and Daniel knew, without question, Ayse loved him. It was the kiss of an angel.

Time stopped. For the next hour they said nothing. They embraced, they smiled, they kissed and kissed again. Their hands played together in that game of hands all young lovers know. They rolled across the tablecloth in a passionate silence. Sometimes Daniel would block the sunlight, sometimes Ayse.

The shadows lengthened and the blue above took on shades of gold, hinting at sunset. They embraced and said nothing. Six o'clock came and went and Ayse made no protest. She did not want to return to her dorm. Ever.

As darkness nudged at the canopy above, and the sunlight made the shadows long and lonely, Daniel broke the spell.

"Ayse, we have to get going."

"No, I want to stay."

"I know what you want, because I want it, too. But we have to go back to campus. It isn't time yet."

was lying beside him. Her breathing deep and passionate, her breasts now
in the same rhythms they were earlier, when they had stopped to rest
iking up the mountain. Beads of sweat were on her forehead and her eyes
housand surrenders. Daniel knew she wanted him to make love to her. And
ted nothing more than to make love to her. But it was not time.

se," said the young, electrified woman lying beside him.
"

el was stronger than her. She did not ask him again.
picked up their things and packed them hurriedly, suddenly realizing they
to make it down the hill before the park closed and the gate locked. The
day was failing and soon the path would be difficult to follow.
in the hour they were back in the Honda, making their way through traffic
Oglethorpe. Ayse had retreated into herself and remained quiet for the
de. Daniel had turned on Randy's CD player to find Bob Marley inside
ging "One Love" as if on a cue.
it came on, Ayse looked at Daniel and in her smile said thank you. Thank
knowing what passion never knows. That it was not time.

Night

l couldn't sleep. He found himself lying in bed, thinking of her. Thinking
hat had happened on the mountaintop. Thinking of the taste of her lips,
of her well-sculpted body against his. Thinking of love.
is thoughts only added coal to the fire. It would never work. Neither his
or his mother would approve of their son having a relationship with an
girl. Even if Rebecca, the more tolerant of the two, could be convinced
ight work, his father would never, ever consent to it.
sister Ruth, the peacemaker, would also have a difficult time
nding how her brother had let himself get into this mess. Dating a
? Falling in love with an Islamic girl? Unthinkable in the narrow hallways
thern Baptist family. Unthinkable and unacceptable.
l knew it. He knew it as he recalled the interplay of their hands. The touch
ality as they lay in silence beneath a sky spread above them like a
satin sheet. Her long, thin fingers dancing and intertwining with his
ong hands. The electricity, as though their fingers were filled with the
f some undiscovered energy.
ndered the nature of Islam. He asked himself why Islam was the fastest
religion in the world, and thought how his father would never accept that
r. But it was true, and Daniel could show his father the evidence to prove
e was such a thing as a race for men's souls, then for the time being, as

hard as the Christian world was running, Islam was winning.

Winning in Africa, Central and Southeast Asia. Converting Hindus and Christians, Buddhists and pagans. Bringing them closer to God, closer to Allâh, in a manner far more egalitarian and devout than his father's narrow beliefs. Praying to God five times a day, prostrating themselves on the ground, bowing before the Almighty. Fasting, sharing, making a pilgrimage across continents just to be near the Ka'ba and the holy cities of Mecca and Medina.

Daniel tried to imagine his father with his face on the floor, humbling himself before God thirty-five times a week. He chuckled aloud at the thought of seeing his father kneeling on a prayer rug. He would look so silly, in his well-pressed sports coat and woolen slacks. So out of context.

No, Daniel couldn't see it. He could see his father behind his desk at the office, a tall glass of iced tea in one hand and his King James Bible in the other. Reading a section of scripture about Jesus' love for the poor; then, in the same service, announcing the upcoming Mediterranean cruise to the Holy Land, complete with six-course dinners and Bible studies on the forecastle. A safe, distant Christianity far removed from the slums of Bombay or Cairo and the realities of a larger, far more complicated world. A world of hunger and hopelessness, immeasurably distant from the suburbs of North Macon.

With these armies of conflicting thoughts battling within him, Daniel turned on his bedside lamp, reached into the top drawer of his nightstand and took out his notebook. He needed to release these anxieties. He started writing.

Sunday morning, 1:15 a.m.

We kissed. We were lying atop Kennesaw Mountain together, watching the leaves and the sky above when she appeared above me, tears in her eyes, and kissed me. If she were anyone other than who she is, this would have been the happiest moment of my life.

But her name is Ayse Yalçin, and she's a Muslim from Istanbul and I would have to be the world's biggest fool to think my family, especially my father, is going to approve of our romance. Our truce from Christmas will be shattered the instant I tell him about her. It was the best day of my life on that mountaintop yesterday and, at the same moment, it was the worst.

I cannot tell Ayse. No doubt she already knows this relationship is not a good idea. Her mother made her promise not to date while in college, so it's clear that they must be as hard-line about Islam as my father is about being Baptist. We could make quite a stir.

I'm certain if Ayse's mother knew we were falling in love on the other side of the world, she would pull her out of Oglethorpe tomorrow. Ayse, like me, must remain silent about our feelings or run the risk of her being grounded in Turkey — never allowed to return to America.

How did this happen? What should I do? I can't stop thinking about her. Her smile, her dark-liquid hair, her fabulous body. Oh, there I go again, playing those wonderful tape loops in my head. Wanting nothing more than to watch them over and over until I can be with her again, shooting more film for my imagination.

While driving home from Kennesaw this afternoon, I thought of a poem. It sort of explains what happened, why we've come together like we have. It doesn't resolve anything, because only time will resolve it. This is it.

When Love Occurs

Like two lonely planets we have accidently
Fallen into each other's field of gravity.
Now, caught in a dance of cosmic design,
We wait.

In this soul of myself,
In the molten core of my earth, I feel both
The power and the fear of this newfound attraction.
An invisible magnetism whose origin
Lies in the color of your eyes,
The invitation of your smile.

What should I do?
Should I draw closer to you, pulled in by
The cadence of your voice, the warmth of your skin.
Knowing that in doing so we will have to
Someday endure their disapproval.
The anger to follow.

No, instead, I will wait.
The closer we become, the more we risk
Collision. The catastrophe of two cultures
Impacting in a maelstrom of disfavor.
My father's anger certain to appear,
Her family's disappointment.

But to draw apart may prove impossible.
Both of us caught in this gravitational pull of hearts
This enslaving orbit neither sought.
Neither understands.

For no one knows when love occurs.
No one knows why, or how, or who the lonely planets will be.

In the course of a lifetime we pass by tens of thousands of people.
Only a handful will ever come to know us.
And of the few that do,
That alter the speed of our rotation, or change the course

Of our lives through this space of being,
Only one may hold the singular gravity of love.

So I wait.
I wait for the phase of the moon.
I wait for something to happen,
For a meteor to pass by, somehow pulling us apart.
Sparing us from drawing closer.

I wait for eternity if need be.
I wait to find out if you can feel this pull.
This force unseen that draws me toward you
In this galaxy of love we've fallen into.

Daniel Mark Harris

Daniel closed his notebook, tucked it away and turned off the light. Sleep still denied him. His thoughts splashed within his head like a sea churned wild by a tempest. It was worse than a tempest, it was a hurricane, and Ayse and he were in the eye of it. A calm, they knew, could never last.

Monday, After Class

Professor Lathcombe packed his briefcase slowly, looking over his reading glasses on more than one occasion to observe them. They were whispering, but there was no way he could hear what they were discussing.

Something was wrong. The chemistry of their relationship had changed and the professor sensed it the moment they'd entered his classroom. This time, unlike the dozen Mondays prior, neither had turned in a paper describing Saturday's museum. Perhaps they are splitting up, he pondered. Perhaps they didn't go out this weekend.

Professor Lathcombe didn't say anything as he closed his briefcase and pushed in the latches, making a loud mechanical click in the empty classroom. Daniel and Ayse didn't hear the noise. They stood together, backs turned toward him, and continued their muted conversation. Professor Lathcombe left the classroom.

"I shouldn't have done what I did. I'm sorry," said Ayse to Daniel, her face not more than a few inches from his.

"No, don't blame yourself. I should have stopped you, before we kept going. But it felt so wonderful, so sensual. I don't know whether I would be able to find the strength to say no to you next time."

"What are we going to do?" Ayse asked, a look of anguish in her eyes.

"We're going to wait. But I don't think it's a good idea for us to go on a field trip this Saturday. If something like this happens again, I won't be able to stop.

"We had better keep our visits to our after-class meetings, otherwise there's no telling where our hearts may take us. Let's be honest with each other, Ayse, taking this relationship any further is major trouble for both of us.

"What would your parents think if they knew you had been seeing the son of a Christian preacher?"

Ayse didn't answer Daniel. She took one look at him, rolled her dark brown eyes, then took her index finger and ran it straight across her throat. Her pantomime described it best.

She knew they could steal her back to Turkey immediately. Ayse had made a promise to her mother and breaking that promise meant her tenure in America, her studies, would be terminated. That was their agreement, and nothing would make Elif amend it.

If they continued seeing each other, their hearts would win over. The will is strong, but the flesh is weak, recalled Daniel, as he and Ayse got up and headed outside.

In the courtyard, spring was consuming the campus of Oglethorpe. The dogwoods were in full blossom in the woodlands to the west, the persistent dandelions were sprinkling the greening lawns with patches of bright yellow. The birds singing melodies of the mating season, and the sun smothering the world with a warm, renewing light. It was impossible not to feel it.

Trying not to touch each other, Daniel and Ayse walked to their favorite bench and sat down. She had pulled up her scarf, covering her head in the fashion of a chador. She was using it as a shield, not wanting to entice Daniel in any way.

It didn't help. In his imagination, Daniel could still see her thick, dark hair falling beneath it. He looked at her outward distance and saw only the beads of sweat that had gathered on her face and neck on Saturday as they made out atop Kennesaw Mountain.

They had crossed the line that afternoon and there was no turning back. Ayse sat beside him, cool and reserved outwardly, but wanting nothing more than for him to take up her hand and start the dance of fingers once again. To pick up where they had left off, tangoing their hands together, fingers sliding and dashing across the ballroom floor, held close and sexual.

Minutes passed in silence. Spring kept throwing its barrage of amorous beauty at them. The fragrance of a million blossoms, the warmth of a returning sun, the laughter of the students passing by, invigorated by the energy of this April afternoon.

Daniel turned to say something and, as he did, his right hand accidently brushed against her left hand. When it did, a charge of a thousand volts of electricity jumped between them. Ayse withdrew her hand instantly, as if she had just touched the handle of a searing pan.

"I'm sorry. I didn't mean to touch you."

"No, it's okay. It's just that..." Ayse didn't finish her sentence. She really had no idea as to what she was going to say. Her knowledge of English lost in this newfound language of tenderness.

"Ayse, what are we going to do?"

"I don't know."

"All I want to do is to hold you again, no, even more than that, I want to make love to you. And that doesn't work for either of us."

"Daniel," Ayse's voice had a tone to it he had never heard before, "you must know I have never been with a man before. And last Saturday, I wanted to be with you.

"Had you not stopped me, I would have let you make love to me right there and then, atop Kennesaw Mountain."

"I know."

It was just as Daniel spoke these words that he reached over and took Ayse's hand. She welcomed his grasp and, this time, surrendered to it. She didn't care if any of the passing students took note as they walked by, nor did she care if her mother sensed it, or if his father filled with anger because of it. She knew only what her heart was telling her.

She was in love with him, and Daniel with her. Nothing would ever be the same.

The Last Day of School

"I would like to personally thank all of you for signing up for this course and I hope that you have learned something over this past semester. We have covered a lot of ground these past four months, from cave paintings to the impassioned canvases of Jackson Pollock and, throughout our journey, we have seen time and time again the intimate relationship between the artist's vision and the culture that surrounded him.

"For those of you pursuing an art degree or, if you are looking for additional core credits, you should consider taking a follow-up course I will be teaching next fall. The course description can be found in your annual bulletins. The course number is Art 251: Special Topics in Art History.

"In Art 251 we take much longer, studied looks at specific periods in the history of art that have had special significance and a lasting impact on our world. Periods such as the golden age of Greece, the Byzantine period and the influence of the Eastern world on Western art and the European Renaissance. Many of you who have enjoyed Art and Culture, which is a prerequisite for taking Art 251, by the way, will probably want to take this course as well.

"Have a great summer, and it's been fun sharing these last four months with all of you."

With that, Professor David Lathcombe flipped the two open sides of the six-hundred-and-forty-two-page textbook together in a loud and ritualistic fashion, as though signifying to the twenty students in his classroom that it was officially over. They let go a small, but enthusiastic round of applause. The consensus among them was that Lathcombe had been a good teacher and that this had been a good course.

Near the end of his summation, when the professor was giving his synopsis of next year's course, he looked directly at both Daniel and Ayse. Earlier, he had wanted to make it perfectly clear to them that he wanted to see them taking Art 251 next fall. They had proven to be outstanding students and he knew they would have as much to gain by taking the course as well as they would by offering something to it.

But he knew something had gone wrong. Although he had no way of knowing what it was, he wanted to help. They had been distant for the past few weeks. Ayse's generous smiles had disappeared and a number of times they left his class separately, not even speaking with each other before leaving.

As the students walked up and thanked him, shaking his hand and saying how much they'd enjoyed his class, Professor Lathcombe kept an eye on Ayse, who was still seated at her desk. He mentally noted that Daniel had not left the room either, sifting through his paperwork as if stalling. The professor wondered if they would leave together, on this final day of classes. If they didn't, then his suspicions were correct.

The last few students said their goodbyes and, as they did, Professor Lathcombe gathered his notes and textbooks and packed them carefully into his satchel. Daniel and Ayse were still in the room, though they had not spoken a word to each other. As he walked out the door, heading back to his office, Daniel spoke up.

"Thanks for the great class, Professor Lathcombe."

"Thanks for all of your excellent reports, Daniel." Looking over to Ayse, who was still sitting quietly, her head bowed as though in prayer, Professor Lathcombe added, "and thanks for all of your input and observations on Islamic art and culture, Ayse. I hope to see both of you this fall. There have to be a few more museums out there for the two of you to conquer."

With that, the professor vanished into the hallways of Hearst Hall, leaving them alone. The silence grew heavier. It gained weight and significance as the second hand on the large clock behind the professor's desk ticked off every passing second. They remained seated, knowing that sooner or later one of them would have to break the silence. One of them would have to say something, anything to remove the tonnage of time that kept falling on them.

After five minutes crawled by, Daniel looked toward Ayse and said, "I'm going to miss you."

Ayse didn't respond. Two weeks ago she had decided to stop seeing Daniel. She told him two weeks ago it was over. She had talked it over with Hatice and Kasha and they both agreed with her. It was the only thing to do.

Her friends knew the custom in Islam was for the religion to follow the man. That it was acceptable for an Islamic man to marry a Christian, but never the other way around. Ayse's parents would not and, by tradition, could not condone her relationship with a Christian. Knowing their romance had no future, and despite Ayse's intense feelings toward Daniel, she decided it was better to end it. End it before the summer break. Before her return to Oglethorpe in the fall.

Daniel, at first angry and resentful of her decision, was resigned to it. He knew that pursuing this any further would never work. He couldn't imagine his mother and father approving of their relationship and, like Ayse, saw no future in their feelings for each other. They were trapped in the confines of their respective religious backgrounds. There was no tomorrow for their love. No release from the prisons of culture.

"Don't say anything, Daniel," Ayse responded in a sullen, tearful reply. "Of course I'll miss you, but we've been through all this before. We both know it's the right thing to do."

"I know, but it won't stop me from missing you."

"No, I suppose it won't."

Daniel rose from his chair, swinging his heavy backpack across his right shoulder. He walked toward her and stood before her. With her head bowed and tears streaming down her cheeks, Daniel bent over and kissed her hair.

With that, he turned and walked out the classroom doorway, never looking back.

Ayse remained in her chair. Seeing he had left the room, she folded her arms together on the desk and let her head rest on top of them. The tears flowed like a river searching for an ocean they would never reach.

She cried until she ran out of tears, and still she wept. As the clock approached three-thirty, Ayse got up, picked up her book bag, and walked to the final class of the second semester. She prayed to Allâh that she would not cross paths with Daniel before her flight home tomorrow afternoon.

She kept her head down, staring at the terrazzo floor of the hallway and trying to keep anyone from seeing her tearful eyes. Her heart was broken. She wanted nothing more than for the world to go away. It wouldn't.

Summer in Macon

Just after Daniel's Christmas visit, his father had arranged a part-time summer job for his son. It was with The Robert James Paint Company. They had painted the new church a few years back and Clay had become friends with Bob James, the owner. He was also a member of the church and was, as Clay phrased it, a genuine Baptist.

The Monday after Daniel and his mother made their return journey to Macon, Daniel started working for the paint company, using the family's Ford Explorer to get to and from the various job sites. It was the ideal summer job, mindless and paying Clay's boy an inflated hourly wage. Robert James was ensuring that when it was time to repaint North Macon Baptist Church, his firm would get the contract. A genuine Baptist.

Daniel dove into his painting job with an unanticipated enthusiasm. He was up early and home late. Although it was only supposed to be a part-time position, some weeks he would end up putting in forty, fifty, even sixty hours a week. Only Daniel knew why he had become such a model employee.

The balance of his time was divided between doing household chores and hanging out in his room, reading. He seldom called or went out with his old friends, many of whom were back in town from colleges across the country. He couldn't think of dating.

All he could think of was Ayse. Her voice, her smile, her tenderness, her laugh, her graceful movements, her delicate hands, her hair, her eyes, the richness of her skin, her touch, simply her. She was everywhere in his every thought and the more he tried to not think of Ayse, the more he did. Love had captured him and, by mid-summer, he had surrendered to it, losing all desire to free himself from its amorous grasp.

His mother, Rebecca, had noted Daniel's preoccupation from the moment he sat beside her in the Explorer on the drive home. She didn't know what the matter was, but she knew her son well enough to sense something was going on behind his facade of business as usual. She kept trying to pry it out of him. A mother's intuition is a powerful instinct, and she was determined to find out what her boy was thinking before their drive north to Oglethorpe in late summer.

The truce between Daniel and his father was holding. Daniel had dedicated his summer reading to the study of Islam, Hinduism and Buddhism. He was careful never to discuss this with his father, nor leave the books anywhere visible. They were all hidden in his room, hidden as another boy his age might hide a *Penthouse* or a *Playboy* from his father.

The difference being that *The Tibetan Book of the Dead* or the *Bhagada Vita* were far more profane and degenerate in his father's eyes than was the playmate of the month. These books, from Clay's perspective, were the handiwork of Satan, with the devil as their author. Daniel kept them carefully guarded from his father.

Midway through July, on a steamy Saturday morning before Daniel was to start the riding mower, Rebecca began a conversation with her boy with the sole intention of finding out what was going on. Daniel had just finished some of his mom's blueberry pancakes when the conversation began. Clay was at church, leaving them alone.

"Danny," as she often referred to him in casual conversation, "did you enjoy the pancakes?"

"Loved 'em, Mom."

"What's on your schedule today?"

"With all this rain, it looks to me like the lawn needs a haircut."

"That's nice of you to keep the lawn mowed for us, Son. Dad just doesn't have the time these days and we both appreciate all the chores you've been doing. It won't be long before you're back in college.

"Tell me, Danny, do you miss school?"

"Yeah, I guess I do."

"Do you have many friends up at Oglethorpe? You've hardly talked about them if you do."

"A few friends. I like Randy, my roommate, and we've hung out a bit. But to be honest, Mom, studying takes up most of my time."

"What about girls, have you met anyone special at school?"

Daniel hesitated. It wasn't a long pause, but it was a sufficient break in the conversation to lead Rebecca to believe love might play a hand in his aloofness.

"Oh, a few."

"You haven't mentioned anyone in particular to me. Is there anyone special?"

Daniel was in a quandary. Yes, there was someone special, someone unbelievably special, but how could he tell his mother about her? Daniel knew neither of his parents would approve. Still, he wanted to share what he was feeling for Ayse with his mother, hoping that, by some miracle, she might understand. He thought he might carefully test the waters, just to see what her reaction might be.

"Well, there was this one girl I went out with a few times."

"And who might that be?" asked Rebecca, knowing she was in.

"She's a foreign student. Her name is Ayse."

"That's a funny name. Is it a Spanish name? It sounds a little Spanish, doesn't it? How do you pronounce it again?"

"Ayse. It's like saying 'eye' and 'shaw' together, only shorter. No, she's not Spanish. She's from Turkey. She was born and raised in Istanbul."

"Oh, that sounds interesting. Our neighbors, the Wilsons, just got back from a cruise that stopped in Istanbul. They said it was a fascinating city, full of history and culture.

"I didn't think there were many Christians in Istanbul. But, of course, there must be a few, since it's not far from Ephesus. You know, that's where Paul preached during the early years of Christianity."

"She's not a Christian, Mom, she's a Muslim."

Now it was Rebecca's turn to hesitate. She smiled at her son slowly, almost mechanically, searching for her next sentence.

"Well, it's nothing serious, of course."

"No, she broke it off before heading back to Istanbul for the summer."

Rebecca didn't like the sound of this. "Broke it off," sounded too much like there was something there to break off.

"That sounds like the sensible thing to do. These modern, mixed-religion relationships never work. I don't think that I need to tell you how your father feels about those Muslim people, do I?"

"No, you don't, Mom. But I would appreciate it if you didn't sound so condescending when you're describing 'those Muslim people.' They're not all that different from 'us Christian people.' Ayse's a very nice girl and I'm kind of sorry she doesn't want to see me any longer."

The plot was thickening, and far too quickly for Rebecca's liking. He was lovesick, she thought. Oh, my God, he's been in this daze because he's thinking about her, about this Islamic girl. Clay will have an absolute fit when he hears about this. She went on.

"Well, Danny, don't be disappointed. You and I both know full well that your father thinks they're all terrorists of one kind or another. He wouldn't be very happy to hear you've been going out with one."

"We weren't dating, Mom. We went to a few museums together to earn extra credit for one of our classes. We're just friends, that's all."

"Well why did you say she broke it off a minute ago. Friends don't exactly break up, do they?"

"I didn't mean it that way."

"How did you mean it?"

Daniel felt the walls closing in, the snare tightening.

"Look, let's just drop it, Mom. I need to get started on the lawn, if you don't mind."

"That's fine, son. We can talk about it some other time."

Daniel burst out the kitchen door into the sweltering heat of mid-summer Macon. He was angry with himself for ever mentioning Ayse to his mother. It was useless.

Ayse might well have been black, he thought as he turned the key to the John Deere. Yes, as far as my family's concerned, dating a black girl would be easier. As long as she was a black Southern Baptist I might stand a chance. But a Muslim? Impossible.

He tried not to think about it as he maneuvered the mower up and down the expansive lawn. He tried to think about something above the bullshit that surrounded him. So he thought of that late afternoon atop Kennesaw Mountain — the scent of spring, the setting sun. Things that brought joy to his heart.

He had never known it was possible to miss someone as much as he missed Ayse. Riding that mower across the grass, recalling her every move, her grace, her laughter. He missed her more than rain.

Istanbul

He looks a little bit like Brad Pitt, only his face is thinner and his eyes bluer. He has light brown, almost blond hair and a beautiful smile."

"Is he tall, like most Americans?"

"No, but he's tall enough."

"Oh Ayse, you're in love."

"I am not in love, Fatimah. You had asked me about Daniel and I am simply telling you about him. Nothing will come of this. Just before school let out, I told him I never wanted to go out with him again.

"We met at our special place on a bench along the courtyard at Oglethorpe and I told him it would never work for us, because of our cultural differences, and there was no reason for us to continue seeing each other when college resumed in the fall."

Fatimah giggled on the other end of the line. That girlish, perceptive giggle that makes fun of someone whom you know is fooling herself, but not her best friend. They had been on the phone for an hour. After a long flight and a restless night, Ayse had called Fatimah the following morning.

Still drowsy and disoriented with jet lag, she had promised her friend a week ago via e-mail that she would fill her in on her first year in America as soon as she felt recovered from her journey. The eight-hour time change was never easy.

"Don't try to fool me, Ayse. You will see him within a day of getting back to America. You have a huge crush on this boy and you know it."

"I did have a crush on him, but it's over."

"Please, Ayse. Don't even go there. Tell me this, though, before you have to run. Is he a good kisser?"

"Fatimah, how could you ask me such a question?"

"Well, is he?"

"I don't know. I've never kissed him."

"This is worse than I imagined."

"What do you mean, Fatimah?"

"Now you're lying to me. You must have kissed him at least once if you went to all those museums together. Just a little stolen kiss somewhere along the way?"

Ayse couldn't continue. She couldn't lie to her best friend. But she didn't want to admit to the fact that she had instigated it. Fatimah needn't know everything.

"He kissed me once," admitted Ayse.

"When? Where were you when he did it?"

"I can't tell you now, not over the phone like this. My mother might accidently pick up the other line. Let's get together and go to the mall in Üsküdar tomorrow. We can talk about it then."

"What time?"

"We can take a cab to the ferries around noon, how does that sound?"

"It sounds fun. You call the cab and have him swing by my house along the way. Once we get to Üsküdar we can hop on a minibus and take it to the mall.

"We'll eat lunch at Kentucky Fried Chicken, just like when you were back in America. Then I can tell you all about Omer, the boy I met at Istanbul University this year. He is the sweetest man I have ever known."

"So you, too, have fallen in love, Fatimah."

"I have not. He is very good to me. His father runs a small trucking business and his family is very nice."

"Then you've already met your future in-laws?"

"Stop being silly, Ayse. We'll talk more about this tomorrow."

"Yes, tomorrow."

"Goodbye, Fatimah."

"Goodbye."

Ayse put down the receiver and flopped down on her comfortable bed. It was odd to be back home, back in her room, decorated as if for the beautiful young princess her father always felt she was.

It all seemed distant to her — the canopy bed, the doll collection on the shelf beside the bathroom door. So very distant, as if this were the bedroom of a young girl she no longer knew. She was just going to be staying in this child's room for the summer while the young girl was away. Then, when Ayse returned to America in the fall, the little girl who really lived here would return, and everything would be as it was.

✦

The next day's ride on the ferry to Üsküdar was delightful. The sunlight played whimsically on the blue waters of the Bosporus as the old, rusty ferryboat took another load of passengers to Asia. The thirty-minute ride vanished in time as the two pretty girls in the corner made small talk and giggled. They were ten years old again, telling secrets to each other, as little girls are prone to do.

By the time they boarded the minibus and waited for it to fill, Fatimah knew everything she wanted to know. Almost. There was something wrong with Ayse's story, and as the minibus pulled into the busy streets of Asia, Fatimah, speaking in English among a busload of Turks, continued her friendly inquisition.

"I don't know, Ayse. There's something wrong with your story."

"There's nothing wrong with my story, Fatimah. That's exactly as it happened. We were up on the very top of this mountain, Kennesaw Mountain, and I was just lying there, then Daniel turned and started kissing me."

"But all those weeks before, all those trips to the museums. In the parking lots, in some corner of one of the galleries, he never once tried to kiss you before that day? It doesn't make sense to me. Are you sure it was he who kissed you that day on the mountaintop?"

Ayse was mad. That was the trouble with Fatimah, she knew her too well. Ayse knew her friend wouldn't let go of this until she confessed.

"Okay, Fatimah. But you have to promise not to tell anyone, ever, about what I'm going to tell you. Is it a promise?"

"I promise."

"Daniel had just finished talking to me about how he felt about God and how wonderful it was for the two of us to be up there, on top of this mountain. He started telling me he disliked religion because it seemed to tear people apart more than it did to bring them together.

"It was his voice, so soft, so sincere. The sun was setting, the leaves were rustling in the wind and the sound of the birds..."

Fatimah's eyes were starting to water. Ayse was telling her story so well that Fatimah could see herself there, with this handsome American prince on the pinnacle of a distant Georgia mountain.

"Well, I started to cry. It was hard not to cry. I knew what he was saying was right, that our religious and cultural differences were keeping us apart. I was sad because of it.

"The tears kept coming, and Daniel kept talking, both of us gazing at the sky above us. I felt so sad for us, for everyone in a way, that I knew I had to do something. So, without thinking, I sat up, turned, and leaned over him, my tears falling, and kissed him."

Fatimah was looking out the window. She had intentionally sat by the window when they had gotten on the minibus and she was glad for it now. Tears were streaming down her cheeks as Ayse told her lover's tale. Fatimah felt foolish to be crying in such a public place, but she couldn't stop.

Without looking at her friend she said, "That is such a beautiful story, Ayse. I would have done the same. I would have kissed him, too. There are times when men need tenderness, and yours was such a time."

Ayse went on, "After that, he returned my kiss. Then we both started embracing, crying, kissing and holding hands. For the next hour we were trying to do all the things we had both wanted to do during the months before. It was very passionate.

"As the sun set, and it started getting dark, I asked him to make love to me. Right there, on that grassy knoll just off the main path. I don't know what had come over me, but at the moment, it felt perfectly natural. I felt it was the right thing to do."

"You didn't! You didn't make love to him there, did you?" Fatimah's tears had stopped in disbelief. Neither of them had been with a man and Fatimah wanted to know if Ayse had been the first of them to know what it was like to make love.

"No, but not because I didn't want to. I did. I wanted to and I would have. I could just feel him inside of me and nothing else mattered. I have never felt like that before in my life.

"But Daniel said, 'No, not now, the time isn't right.' We stopped soon after that and hiked back down the mountain."

The minibus they were riding on kept lumbering up the hill toward the mall. It stopped and sputtered, honked and bounced along the crowded streets of Asia. It was filled to overflowing with the people of greater Istanbul. Traditional Islamic women wearing the chador and carrying cloth shopping bags filled with vegetables and dried fruits. Old Turkish men with long, salt-and-pepper beards, thick moustaches and bad teeth. Their huge grins illuminating the interior as the bus shook and rattled.

Near the back, two pretty young girls were still talking. Sharing a day together, not unlike a million other young girls in the world. Talking about boys, about love, about growing up in the world.

An early-summer afternoon in Istanbul. Cloudless and infinite, as it always has been.

A Week Away

Something was wrong. It was three-thirty in the morning and Daniel was wide awake, wrestling the army of demons he had struggled with a thousand midnights before. Unconquerable armies, full of ill-defined fears and unresolved angst. This particular battle had been brought on by suspicion.

The pattern in their suburban home had been broken. Daniel was too astute not to have noticed it. He had awakened from one nightmare only to find himself in another. Anxiety was overwhelming him, causing him to reach for his notebook in yet another attempt to exorcize those demons. At three-forty-six a.m. Daniel started writing in his *Book of Midnights*.

Thursday, August 18

Something's up. Mom told me yesterday she won't be driving me to school next week. She said Dad wants to take me to Oglethorpe this year. That's a problem.

Neither of them have said anything to me about my conversation with Mom concerning Ayse, and I can't help but think it's somehow tied into the sudden change in drivers. Mom and Dad have probably been talking about it in private and no doubt Dad wants to have one of his heart-to-hearts with me. One of those father-and-son moments where he climbs his pulpit to lecture me on how to behave like a good, obedient Baptist.

It's not going to be a pleasant ride. Not if he starts in. Not when he puts on his preacher's hat and starts quoting the Bible as though he were the only authorized interpreter on the planet. It'll be horrible.

But that's not what's keeping me up, although it sure as hell doesn't help. The real issue is Ayse. I keep wondering what to do. All summer long I've thought of little else but her.

Like yesterday, while painting that house on Adams Street, not more than a block from Mercer, I kept thinking about that afternoon. That spectacular afternoon on the mountaintop when she leaned over and kissed me. It was the most wondrous moment of my life. As I sat there on the frontporch steps, stirring the five-gallon can of paint with an electric mixer, I kept wondering about us, about what's going to happen.

As I brushed on the paint, my thoughts wandered back to the coming semester. Will she take Lathcombe's class this fall? Will she be there on the first day of class? Will she be sitting across from me, smiling, her eyes shining and her hair tumbling down across her shoulders? If she isn't there, what will I do?

What if we don't share any classes next semester? What if she doesn't come back to Oglethorpe for her sophomore year? The thought of never seeing her again weighs upon me like the weight of the moon. I don't know if I could bear it.

I know that she and I have ended it, but I cannot help but feel it hasn't ended. We need more time to sort through this. That our relationship came so unexpected, so unanticipated to either of us; that our feelings took us by surprise, as if we were ambushed by our hearts...

I thought about this all through dinner and I wanted to write a poem about it. Something that would explain it...

What I didn't know.

I can still hear your voice in the empty hallway
Of the High Museum
That first day we were free.

I can hear you speaking of Matisse,

No, it doesn't work. I'm tired and I know I've got to get back downtown to finish the trim. Just one more week of smelling latex and I'm back at Oglethorpe studying Byzantine mosaics. I know I'll take Lathcombe's class. I'll take it and pray that she'll take it, too.

I need her more than air.

The Princes Islands

*T*he horse-drawn carriage slowed as it ascended the long, winding road that led to Isatepe, the northernmost hill on the island. It would be another twenty minutes before they climbed to the top and Ayse was glad for it. Once beyond the small town center of Buyuk Ada, there was little to observe other than passing pines and cistus shrubs. The solitude appealed to her. The clicking of the horses' hooves against the paved road, the sound of wind rushing through the pines, were all Ayse wanted to hear.

Everything else was noise. The noise of Istanbul, filled with fifteen million people. The rumbling and honking of cars and trucks vying for position on the crowded thoroughfares. The noise of her mother, constantly reminding her to be on her best behavior during her sophomore year. Lecturing Ayse again and again, telling her to remember to e-mail, to write, to study hard and, most importantly, never to date or be out with a man after six. As if six p.m. were the witching hour for a Turkish princess. Even the noise of her best friend, Fatimah, had worn on her, advising Ayse as to what she should do upon her return.

One week Fatimah would insist that the best thing to do would be to let him go. Remain stalwart and unbending in her commitment never to see Daniel again. Then, the following week, noting how forlorn and despondent Ayse had become, telling her to get back together with him as soon as she reached Atlanta. After months of advice that seemed to change as often as the breezes, Fatimah's counsel had become noise.

Now, as the summer clouds suspended themselves lower in the sky, and the first faint traces of fall danced on the breath of the wind, all Ayse wanted was to be left alone. Alone with the rhythmic clopping of horse hooves and the sounds of the approaching fall.

"Look at the view, beautiful view. Don't you think it is so beautiful," said the Turkish operator of the horse-drawn buggy to his passenger. He spoke in Turkish, and he smiled a toothless grin as he did. Her driver was a native of Buyuk Ada, the largest of the five Princes Islands. Ayse could not recall ever renting his rickety buggy before, but then again, over the decade her family had owned a summer place on the island, she realized she probably had ridden in his carriage before.

There were no cars on Buyuk Ada, just as there were no cars on any of the Princes Islands. Just brightly painted, horse-drawn carriages. The carriage she was riding in was covered by a long, flat canopy made from a Mediterranean-blue canvas. Long white fringes hung along the outside edge. The four wheels of the cart were handmade, as were the two opposing wooden seats. They had been carved out of the local pine and painted in a colorful and intricate style not unlike a circus wagon — charming in a Gypsy-like fashion.

The driver, sitting in front and above the canopy on a high buckboard, was exposed to the elements. When it rained, he got wet. As wet as the pair of old, swaybacked horses that were straining and snorting loudly as the hill rose steadily before them. The tempo of their eight hooves hitting the ragged asphalt methodically slowed as the climb steepened. Ayse was glad she was alone, thinking about how much harder it must be when the carriage was filled with tourists.

But the tourists were gone by now. The shadows of the pines were growing long and the touch of fall in the air would soon be deepening. In another month, the islands would be returned to the natives. Their enchanting carriages would revert to the business of picking up the local islanders for a quarter of the fare they were presently charging. Carrying loads of friends and relatives up and down these hills, ferrying with them pieces of furniture, goats and groceries. By then, Ayse would be back in the world of noise. The noise of Atlanta.

But today, the last full day she would have at their summer place, Ayse wanted some time alone. She had hired this carriage to take her to the small coffee shop at the end of the road. From there she would walk the final kilometer to the walls of the old Christian monastery at the summit. She would do so alone, with neither Fatimah's nor her mother's ceaseless monologue of advice.

"Here we are," said the driver as he pulled back the reins and brought his two panting horses to a halt. "I will wait for you here."

The driver, with his gray woolen cap and big grin, jumped down from the buckboard and came around to the side of the carriage to help his sole passenger down. He took Ayse's young, smooth hand, noting how much softer it was than his wife's rough hand.

"I'll be about an hour; are you sure you want to wait that long?" asked Ayse of her driver.

"I'll just have a cup of coffee here, no problem."

"Thank you."

The driver, with his short, graying beard and tattered sweater, turned and walked toward the coffee shop, hailing some of his fellow drivers as he approached. They knew the end of the summer season was near. Fares would plummet and the coffee shop would close for the winter. The oldest of them, a hunched and aged Turk now running a donkey-ride business beside the coffee shop, yelled over to the driver as he walked up the wooden stairway that led to the shop.

"Good afternoon, Halil. You have the prettiest cargo of the day."

"Yes, this is true, Ahmet. She is much prettier than all of your donkeys put together."

The old Turk laughed. Indeed, Ahmet and all the other carriage drivers in the coffee shop were keenly aware of that.

It was impossible for them not to take note of her, exiting Halil's carriage like a young queen in some Middle Eastern fairy tale, her dark eyes and richly toned skin, like the color of sand blowing across the open deserts of Arabia.

Ayse overheard the men and their comments, but did not turn around to acknowledge them. She knew they meant no harm. They were just behaving like men. Men are all alike, she reflected, as she began her trek. All alike.

The path leading to the monastery was wide enough for Halil's horse and carriage to have continued. But it was understood by all the carriage drivers for hire on Bayuk Ada that the trail was only to be used for supply wagons and not for those tourists or visitors who wanted to see the ancient monastery of Christ, built in 1547. Those visitors would have to make the final ascent on foot, a personal pilgrimage to a locally renowned Christian shrine.

The pilgrims who made the journey up to the monastery would tie pieces of white cloth on the gum cistus shrubs along the path. It was said that by doing so it would bring them good fortune and bestow God's favor upon them.

Ayse admired a few of the heavily adorned shrubs along the way, noting that from a distance, the countless white pieces of fabric attached to them made it appear as if they were in bloom. Like Turkish dogwoods, thought Ayse as she walked steadily up the long hill. The dogwoods of pilgrimage.

Near the top, the pines were crooked and bent from the ceaseless wind. They soon thinned away to nothing. On a barren outcropping of rock near the pinnacle lay the foundation for the hand-hewn stones that formed the outer walls of the monastery.

The large wooden doors leading into the monastery were closed. The last tour of the day had finished an hour ago. Ayse had never intended to see the small museum inside, or the medieval relics it held. She had come to overlook the Sea of Marmar and think about Daniel.

What should I do? Ayse pondered while staring out across the wind-ruffled sea one thousand feet beneath her. It has been a difficult summer for me, unable to talk to him, e-mail or write him, but equally unable to forget about him.

I long to hear his voice. Listen to him talk about a Monet painting at the High Museum or just making small talk while we walk into the woods behind the Performing Arts Center. Seeing him look at me with those blue eyes, look at me with love in his heart.

But I shouldn't see him again. I should let him go. My mother and father would never forgive me if I go on with this relationship. They don't know anything about it. Only Fatimah knows, and she has promised never to say a word to them.

Should I take Professor Lathcombe's class this fall? Will he take it? Yes, he will. He will take it and hope that I will take the course because he knows it may be the only way he can see me this fall. He will sit near me and he will look at me with that tenderness in his eyes. If he does, I do not think I will be able to continue. I will surrender my heart and soul to him and forget about my promise to my family.

I shouldn't take Lathcombe's course. I should not sign up for his class next week. I should stop this beating heart of mine. If only I could.

The autumnal wind kept up its relentless march toward the south as Ayse sat on a piece of exposed granite high atop Buyuk Ada. A few monks in the monastery noticed her from their windows high above the outer wall of this Greek Orthodox retreat. Sensing the anguish in her soul, they prayed for her.

Ayse was in need of their prayers. She needed the prayers of a thousand angels in helping her to make the right decision. Choosing between her culture and her heart. She recalled longingly that romantic afternoon atop Kennesaw Mountain. Even the memory of it could make her breath race and her heart stir. She had never known a love as deep as the love she felt for Daniel.

She missed him more than she would this air that blew her dark hair back and brought tears to her eyes while she gazed, eyes wide open, into the steady breeze.

But there would be no decision made that afternoon, high above the Sea of Marmar. She prayed to Allâh for guidance. A flock of Turkish crows flew by, riding the steady wind from the north as they did. Their gray heads and dark bodies contrasted sharply with the broken blue sky and white clouds above. The sound of their caws grew louder, crescendoed, then faded as they flew off.

Life can be so complicated at times, thought the lonely young woman atop the highest hill on the Sea of Marmar. Do I choose my family, my traditions, my religion...or do I choose love?

The Ride to Atlanta

It was quiet in the Ford Explorer. Clay had put on his favorite Grand Old Opry tape and listened while the SUV rolled north along I-75 at sixty miles an hour. It was still summer in the deep South, and the morning clouds had yet to begin their daily climb to the towering thunderheads they would be by late afternoon.

Dad always drives slowly, thought Daniel as he listened to Minnie Pearl tell another of her corny jokes followed by June Carter and Johnny Cash singing a folksy love ballad. Dad drives slowly and listens to cassettes that have to be a hundred years old. Funny he doesn't have an eight-track system custom built to fit in the dash, thought Daniel, smiling softly.

The tape kept playing and the Explorer kept heading north. It rolled past the little towns of central Georgia that amount to no more than two gas stations, a grocery store and, if you're lucky, a restaurant. Towns named Popes Ferry, Forsyth, Locust Grove and Blacksville. Southern and rural, complete with trailer homes perched on cinder blocks and two good-lookin' peach trees in the front yard. Poor blacks and poor whites living in the same small town, equally happy and unhappy, all of them owning pick-up trucks with bad wiring. Towns whose only fame came from being just large enough to merit putting their name on the exit sign along the interstate.

Daniel took no note of these towns as they rolled by, the cruise control stuck mercilessly at sixty miles per hour and his father humming along with a Tennessee Ernie Ford song. A tune sung heartfelt and deep about the misfortunes of coal mining. Daniel didn't care about rural towns or coal mines, he was thinking about Ayse. He knew before he was dropped off, his father was certain to give him "the talk." He had known it a week ago.

So before the other foot fell, Daniel had decided to focus his thoughts on the mysterious Islamic girl from Istanbul. Focus on her.

Would she take Lathcombe's course? Daniel doubted it. If she did, would she even speak to me? Daniel's thoughts were lost in this debate when Clay leaned over and unexpectedly silenced Loretta Lynn mid-song. He sat up straight and started his inevitable lecture.

"Well, Son, looks like you're in for another year of college."

"I'm looking forward to it, Dad."

"Mom and I sure miss you, boy. The house has never been so quiet, now that both you and Ruth Ann have flown the coop."

Daniel hated this vacant warm-up. His father and he were at it like cats and dogs before he left for college last year. His mother might have missed him. If his father did miss him, it was because he hated mowing the lawn himself.

"Well, Dad, it's all part of growin' up."

"Y'all got that right, Son. It's all part of learning 'bout life, just like when I was off preachin' in the hills of North Carolina before I met your mother. Just part of stretchin' your wings and gettin' your footings, so to speak.

"God has a plan for all of us, Daniel. And it sometimes takes us a while to discover what that plan might be."

Here it comes, thought Daniel. When he heard the word God come into the conversation he knew trouble was just around the corner. His father went on.

"But I'll be the first to tell you, Daniel, you have to be careful in today's world. Things aren't the same as when I was a boy. We didn't have this thing called the Internet. Heck, all the television stations were in black and white and news didn't travel on satellites at the speed of light. No, things moved slower back then and because of it, I don't think young men made as many mistakes as they do today.

"It's because the devil uses technology to turn this new generation away from Jesus. Nothing scares me more than seeing a young man or young woman at our church surfing the net like they love to do. Satan hides in those Web sites like some evil spider, just waiting for some God-fearing Christian to land on one of his Web pages.

"Why the pornography, the anti-Americanism, the attacks on good Christian values seem to be the rule and not the exception on the Internet. It's a crying shame such a beneficial technology has fallen into the hands of Lucifer."

Daniel didn't respond to his father's diatribe. What could he possibly add to such a shortsighted perspective, he pondered? The Internet had a million Christian sites, just as it had a million porn sites. It was an invention that tied the family of man together in an unprecedented fashion. Everyone with a telephone line and a modem was linked together in this fabric of fiber optics and digitized images.

Why did his father think of the Internet as an instrument of Satan? Daniel didn't want to engage Clay, certain there was more to follow.

"What really bothers me most was how these terrorists have been using their computers to send messages back and forth to each other. If they were writing letters, or using radios, we could pick up their messages and avert the terrible incidents like the destruction of the World Trade Center and the cowardly attack on the Pentagon.

"But the children of Satan, the Muslims, they know how to work with the Devil. They've been working with him since the day Mohammed was born. Satan himself probably invented the Internet to help his followers continue their jihad against the Christian world. Their holy war against the teachings of our Lord."

So that's where he's heading, thought Daniel. Mom must have said something about my seeing the Islamic girl and Dad's taken it from there. I should have known. But I won't put up with it, it's not fair of my father to throw Ayse, a girl he's never met, into the same fiery pit he throws the militants who attacked America. Ayse's hardly a terrorist. Daniel spoke up.

"Not every Muslim's a terrorist, Dad."

Clay took a long, deep breath and shook his head. Rebecca was right, Daniel had fallen for this young woman and thus had fallen into Satan's snare. Clay took it upon himself to set his son straight, before Daniel's soul was condemned to eternal damnation.

"No, they're not all bomb-throwing, gun-wielding terrorists like the Palestinians. But like everything, there are different degrees of terrorism. And while some Muslim people might seem like good people, might behave and act like decent people, underneath that lamb's wool lies the heart of a heathen wolf.

"Whatever you think about them, bear in mind there are only three things the Islamic people want in this world."

"And what are these three things?"

"Number one is the annexation of Jerusalem and the total annihilation of the Jews. Number two is the obliteration of Christianity. And number three, as prophesied in the Book of Revelation, the conquest of all nations. The Muslim people will not stop until they have accomplished these things, and woe to any God-fearing Christian who gets in their way.

"As it says in my King James Bible, *"Beware of false prophets, which come to you in sheep's clothing, but inwardly they are ravening wolves.*

"Ye shall know them by their fruits. Do men gather grapes of thorns, or figs of thistles? Even so every good tree bringeth forth good fruit; but a corrupt tree bringeth forth evil fruit." Matthew 7, 15 through 17."

Daniel joined the debate. "It's not fair to use the actions of a few radicals to judge an entire religion. Christians have done terrible things to each other as well. We don't judge all Christians by the actions of a few. Look at that man who shot the abortion doctor in Buffalo, New York, a few years ago. You can't call every Christian a murderer just because one of them has committed murder.

"Look at Nazi Germany, Dad. Hitler and his fascists sprang from a nation that was almost entirely Lutheran. With their so-called God guiding them, they managed to gas over six million people — Jews, Gypsies, political opponents — whoever stood in their way. Islam, Judaism, Christianity, we've all had our fair share of terror."

They were into it now. They were approaching the southern edge of Atlanta, and they could see the large airplanes coming in to land a few miles ahead. Watch them cross all twelve lanes of I-75 as they descended, soaring low and loud before smoking their giant tires on the hot runways.

"But the scripture goes on, Daniel. And this is the important part of Christ's message. *"Every tree that bringeth not forth good fruit is hewn down, and cast into the fire.*

"Wherefore by their fruits ye shall know them." Matthew 7, Verses 19 and 20.

"Those terrorists are the fruits of Islam. There are many good people who aren't aware of being a part of that unholy tree. But they cannot say that they are not aware of the fruit their religion produces. The tree of Islam, planted by the false prophet Mohammed, bears the fruit of hatred and terror. It bears the fruit of evil and destruction.

"For Jesus said it all when he spoke in John, Chapter 14, Verses 6 through 7, *"Jesus saith unto him, I am the way, the truth, and the life. No man cometh unto the father but by me.*

"If ye had known me, ye should have known my father also: and from henceforth ye know him, and have seen him."

"This is the cornerstone of our faith, Daniel. Our faith is based on the fact that Jesus Christ, our Savior, was the son of God become man. That he died for our sins and rose again from the dead to forgive us and show us the way to eternal life.

"The Muslims refuse to acknowledge this. They reduce Christ to being a mere prophet. Then, as if that isn't blasphemy enough, they declare Mohammed to be the final, what they call the seal of all prophets. They claim Mohammed, not Christ, to be the greatest of all prophets.

"As Paul said in second Corinthians 11, Verses 13 and 14, *"For such are false apostles, deceitful workers, transforming themselves into the apostles of Christ.*

"And no marvel: for Satan himself is transformed into an angel of light."

"That was Paul speaking to the Corinthians, warning them to be watchful for those whose intentions seem forthright and honorable but whose messages come from the lips of Lucifer.

"There's another verse that I think you need to hear, Son. And from what your mother's told me, this one hits close to home. *"Be ye not unequally yoked together with unbelievers: for what fellowship hath righteousness with unrighteousness? and what communion hath light with darkness?"*

"And what concord hath Christ with Be'lial? or what part hath he that

believeth with an infidel?"

"That's 2 Corinthians, Chapter 6, Verses 14 and 15."

Daniel didn't respond. There was no use in trying to change his father's opinions. They were made of hardened steel, unbending and unalterable. Arguing would accomplish nothing more than making himself angry. Clayton's God was the righteous God. All others were wrong. There was only one passage through the narrow gates of Heaven and his father held the key. The only key.

Daniel knew his dad's intention was to get him to discuss his relationship with Ayse. He knew that's why he'd offered to take him to Oglethorpe. But Daniel wasn't going to give him the pleasure of dragging Ayse into this. She wasn't involved with these acts of terrorism nor, in Daniel's mind, could she be held accountable for the actions of others. In Daniel's eyes, Ayse was an angel, with a heart as tender as an angel's feathers and a soul as white as their wings. He would not let his father drag her into his embittered world. Daniel's silence held.

When his father realized his son would no longer engage him, he punched the play button on the tape and listened to Loretta Lynn finish her ballad. Clay stared straight ahead, satisfied with the heartfelt sermon he had just delivered to his son.

By this time, they weren't far from Oglethorpe. Anger started flowing through Daniel's veins like thick, black bile. Hell wasn't buried deep in the earth, scorching hot and filled with the wretched clamoring of a billion damned souls. It was here, sitting next to your father in a Ford Explorer exiting I-75 onto West Pace's Ferry. Hell would last twenty more minutes.

Daniel's blood thickened with every stoplight and traffic jam. Eternity didn't drive this slow. Loretta Lynn's liquid voice sounded as if it were screaming, joining the chorus of the damned. Daniel wanted to explode. He felt as if his heart were pumping more blood through his body than his veins could handle. His body was about to burst in place, splattering the leather interior of the truck with his seething wrath. He was filled with rage.

Outwardly nothing changed. His father kept the SUV in the right lane of Peachtree Road, driving mercilessly slow. He used the brake incessantly and had no idea that the young man next to him was boiling inside. Minnie Pearl was back on the cassette. Clay thought she was funny.

"Take a left up there, Dad, that's the main entrance to the school."

"Thanks, Danny. I almost drove right past it, didn't I?"

"Yeah."

Clay pulled off Peachtree and into the small circular drive that cut between Lupton and Hearst Hall. There was one other car dropping off a young girl.

"Well, Dad, thanks for the ride," said Daniel tersely.

"Where's your dorm room, son? Wouldn't it be easier to drop all your things off in front of your dorm?"

"Not really, there's probably a ton of cars up there and it could take all day. I'll just make a couple of trips and carry it up."

"Suit yourself."

"Besides, Dad, I know you want to get heading back."

"Yes, I do. But I hope you understood what I was trying to tell you earlier."

"I heard you, Dad. I heard you loud and clear."

"Praise God, Daniel. Praise the Father Almighty."

"Sure."

Daniel walked around the truck and opened the back hatch. He took out his four bags and one large trunk and threw them on the curb beside the driveway. The sooner he could see his father driving south on Peachtree the better, he thought, as he lifted the heavy trunk, realizing that carrying it all the way to his dorm was going to be a struggle.

I'd carry a thousand of these if it would get me one less second with that asshole, he thought to himself as he set down the heavy trunk.

He placed two of the bags on the trunk and walked to the passenger's window.

"Bye, Dad."

"God bless you, Son."

Clay pressed the electric button on the driver's side and the window in front of Daniel slowly closed. It was heavily tinted and Clay all but disappeared from Daniel's view as it smoothly rolled up. From where he was standing, Daniel could now see his reflection as well as his father's image beyond the tinted glass. He was amazed to see that, outwardly, he looked fine. His light brown hair was a disheveled from handling the luggage, but his dark-blue polo shirt was clean and well pressed. He looked through his reflection and took one last glance at his father.

Clay was wearing his driving glasses. His hair was thinning, but his white hair still radiated an air of distinction. His face was drawn tight and his lips were thin, held firmly together, as though clamped. He was wearing a long-sleeve pinstripe shirt with a button-down collar. He wore a pair of navy blue slacks that held a permanent crease. Though he could not see them, Daniel knew he had on his burgundy penny loafers. He knew because Clay never left the house without them.

But oddly, Daniel didn't see a Baptist minister through the dark window of the Ford Explorer. He saw an old man. Any old man. Any old man dropping off his college-age son at a small private school on the outskirts of Atlanta.

His blood was thinning. He was letting go of the anger. Releasing it. He watched as the Explorer pulled onto Peachtree to begin its journey south. As it sped away, Daniel was relieved.

Someday my rage will tear through my skin. Someday Dad will go too far, Daniel thought, as he reached down to pick up one of his two suitcases. I don't look forward to the day that happens, but I know it will.

He lifted the large suitcase and tossed it on his right shoulder and, leaving the rest of his stuff on the curb, started the long climb to his dorm. It felt good to be carrying such a heavy object. His pace up the hill was strong and steady, fueled by pent-up anger.

Tomorrow was Sunday, he remembered, as he trekked toward his dorm room. I wonder if I'll see her? I wonder how her summer was? I miss her, he thought, as he shouldered the heavy burden of his suitcase. I miss her dearly.

Tuesday Night

Daniel couldn't sleep. He had seen her twice thus far. She hadn't even waved. She was wearing her head scarf like a Muslim woman, and she kept her head bowed while she was walking. Her lovely face shrouded deep within the cotton scarf. It was over.

Tomorrow was the first day of Professor Lathcombe's sophomore class, Special Topics in Art History, and Daniel knew she wouldn't be there. He was certain of it.

He kept staring at the digital clock beside his bed, watching the minutes tick by in a silence that shouted. His roommate, Randy, had not yet returned from some fraternity party he and Daniel had been invited to. Randy knew all along that attending frat parties wasn't Daniel's style, so it came as no surprise when Daniel declined.

But now, late into the night, the red, changing numbers kept ticking by as the silence grew denser, almost swallowing itself in the darkness. At 1:32 a.m. Daniel flipped on his bedside lamp and took out his *Book of Midnights*. It was a new notebook, with only a handful of pages filled. His old one from the summer had been filled with the poetry of a lonely heart and page upon page of the anger he harbored toward his father. It was retired. Placed beside his collection of completed notebooks and stored in a locked box beneath his bed in Macon. His emotional life's history reduced to twenty-odd dimestore notebooks and the ink of a few dozen pens.

He opened the green spiral notebook to an empty page and began writing.

To Ayse, My Gift

It races on a track of satin,
Uninvited, restless, sharp.
It came quite out of nowhere
This photo-finish of the heart.

I never did quite see it for
I was sleeping, though awake.
And though the dust has settled some,
It's not easy to forsake.

It's not easy to release you
From the pleasure of our run.
For I would just as soon release,
The stars, the moon, the sun.

Your gift goes without saying
While mute symphonies perform
And a chorus of lost seraphim
Singing hymns before the storm.

For love is all the gift there was
Between us, that sweet spring.
But our lives cannot unwrap it
And that, such sadness brings.

But not all we feel can fit within
These moments known hereof.
Least of all that soul of yours
My pleasure was, to love.

Daniel Mark Harris

Daniel tore the page from his notebook. He had never torn a page from any of his notebooks and, as he ripped it away, he felt as though he were committing a kind of sacrilege. He had never shared a word of his *Book of Midnights* with anyone. Not his mother, nor his sister Ruth, not even his roommate Randy. His notebooks were his and his alone. A tale told by a lonely writer to himself.

For the first time in his life he felt compelled to tear out a piece of himself and give it to her. Give it to her the next morning, should she come to class. It was more than a poem written on a piece of paper he would be handing her. It was a piece of his soul, and the thought of handing her that page filled him with dread. His hands shaking slightly from the magnitude of his decision, he folded the page neatly into a small, pocket-sized note.

If Ayse has decided to take Lathcombe's class, I will give this to her. If she doesn't show up, I'll throw it in the garbage. God, I hope she shows.

Professor Lathcombe's Class

Daniel arrived early on the second floor of Hearst Hall. Lathcombe's course was being held on the same floor of the building but not in the same classroom. It was three doors down, on the other side of the hall, facing away from the campus, toward the northeast. The morning sun was still slicing through the windows when Daniel took his seat.

The seats were arranged in a straight row, not in the semi-circle they were last spring when he first met her. He chose a seat where he might have sat last year, but the different arrangement of the chairs served to remind him it would never be the same.

One other student was seated in the classroom when Daniel arrived. He recognized him from last year's course. They smiled at each other, acknowledging the commonality of recognition but never spoke. It was enough.

Several other students scurried in as the clock above the doorway edged toward ten a.m., the scheduled start of the course. Daniel recognized a handful of other students, most from last year's Art and Culture Class, others from math classes, or from the other core curriculum course Professor Lathcombe taught.

Her face was not amongst them.

Professor Lathcombe came in at one minute after ten. Daniel's heart had been sinking with the arrival of every student. He looked around him and noted there were only four empty chairs left when the professor came in, closing the classroom door behind him. She wasn't coming, and the thought of not seeing her, not being able to hand her his note, broke his heart. The chemistry of his blood was changing again.

It wasn't turning dark with rage as it did on Saturday during his father's lecture. It was turning gray. It was as if the pure, sunlit sky outside was fast becoming cloudy. The endless blue replaced by a blanket of thick, impenetrable clouds. Clouds of winter, bare trees and a sense of hopelessness.

Daniel felt an overwhelming urge to get up, walk to the door, and leave. He wanted the world to go away. He wanted to be left alone with his sorrow, to walk out of Hearst Hall on that magnificent sunlit morning and keep walking. Walking north, toward the ice fields inside of him. Walking for weeks and weeks on end, heading nowhere.

He resisted the urge, knowing it wouldn't help. He sat and felt his heart pump rivers of frozen blood through his veins — lifeless and cold.

Professor Lathcombe started his introduction.

"Hello, and welcome back to Oglethorpe. My name is David Lathcombe and this course is titled Art 251, Special Topics in Art History. If any of you are in the wrong room, now's the time to leave and find the room you're supposed to be in."

Amidst a handful of chuckles and an overzealous smile from the professor, two students rose, gathered their things and headed toward the door. They were embarrassed, and one of them, the young lady, was flush from blushing. As they worked their way through the rows of chairs, the professor continued.

"It happens every fall. Don't be embarrassed by going to the wrong room, after all, that's why you're all going to college. To learn something," he said in a dry, sarcastic tone.

Just as the blushing girl was closing the door behind her, another student's hand took the open door from her. Daniel watched it closely, still hoping. The hand was young and small, with skin the color of sand dunes. It was Ayse.

She came in, still wearing her head scarf, and found a seat. Professor Lathcombe smiled at her. She looked at him and apologized.

"Sorry for being late, Professor. I went to last year's classroom by mistake."

"It's okay, Ayse. No doubt one of the students who just left is taking your seat right now. It's a ritual I'm all too familiar with."

Daniel's blood thawed. The ice jam that made him want to disinherit the world broke free. The gray skies of an endless winter were swept away in a single heartbeat.

The professor sat at the edge of his small desk and began speaking. He was wearing a long-sleeved, button-down shirt and a pair of dark-brown, cotton slacks with a braided leather belt. He looked the part of a college professor.

He started telling his students what the course was going to be about, handing each of them a four-page syllabus as he did. He talked about the two textbooks they would be using and covered the material outlined in the syllabus as the minutes slipped by.

Daniel heard him, taking notes along the edge of the syllabus. Daniel realized he was pretending to be just another college student in just another classroom on just another first day at just another university on just another fall morning in America. But he was none of these. He was a young man wildly in love with a girl sitting twenty feet away. Everything else was irrelevant.

Daniel was unexpectedly dragged back into reality when Professor Lathcombe concluded his lecture.

"And for those of you interested in gaining some extra credit this semester, there is a new exhibit on display this fall at the High Museum of Art. Last year," continued Professor Lathcombe while looking at Daniel, "I had some students in my class who did some excellent reports on several of the area's museums and I would like to encourage all of you to consider doing the same this coming semester.

"The new exhibit at the High is *The Paintings of the Renaissance*. The collection includes works by Giotto and Raphael. It will be there through October and I've already seen the exhibit. I can assure you, the works displayed are extraordinary, and since we will be looking in depth at the influence these painters had on the future of art, this is something all of you should consider taking in before it moves to the West Coast.

"Does anyone have any questions?"

As several students raised their hands and a volley of questions and answers went back and forth across the room, Daniel looked toward Ayse. She had heard Professor Lathcombe's advice and she, too, knew he was talking about Daniel and her. They had gone to nine museums together, and several historic sites. They had hiked Stone Mountain, admiring the massive bas-relief carved in its face.

They had climbed to the top of Kennesaw Mountain together in the spring, falling in love with every step. They had gone to cemeteries, historic houses and they had discovered a truth that never changes as they did — that love is God.

Ayse could sense Daniel's stare, but she still didn't look over at him.

Professor Lathcombe answered the last question, reiterated his first assignment and dismissed his class. Ayse remained in her seat. So did Daniel.

She knew he would be coming over to her in a moment and was, in her heart, glad for it. It was something she had thought about for four long months — seeing him again.

Professor Lathcombe lingered behind his desk, taking more time than needed. He wanted to see what the two of them were going to do, knowing they'd parted ways prior to the summer break. He had wondered why they had split up, seeing how much they enjoyed each other, but had never asked either of them.

He had made a special point of mentioning his extra-credit policy. Professor Lathcombe liked them both. He felt they made a nice couple and, despite their different religious backgrounds, hoped they could make their relationship work. As he fumbled with his paperwork and stalled, he watched as Daniel got up, reach into his pocket for something, and walk over to Ayse.

He was too far away to hear what was said.

"Hello, Ayse."

"Hi, Daniel."

Ayse looked up at him. His eyes shone the color of the Sea of Marmar. His handsome face took hold of her.

"I have something for you. It's a poem I wrote last night."

As Daniel stretched out his right hand to give her the folded poem, Ayse reached up with her right hand to take it from him. For a brief second, their fingers touched, and the electricity they had felt atop the mountain flashed across their skin in a tiny shock of passion. Nothing had changed.

Without saying a word, Ayse unfolded the page of Daniel's *Book of Midnights* and started reading the poem. Every word, every sentence, every stanza walked through the walls she had tried to build around herself as if they were made of mist. It was no use pretending.

As she read on, her hair covered by a light-brown cotton scarf, her head bent over, Daniel stood before her, unable to detect her reaction.

Professor Lathcombe, seeing they were involved, folded up his satchel and headed out the doorway, coughing loudly once in the hallway, intentionally letting them know he was gone. Time hung in the air like a solitary white feather, drifting idly back to earth.

Daniel noticed a tear fall on the poem. A second tear followed, soaking into the paper and discoloring the blue ink as it did. He could hear her sobbing, but he still could not see her face.

A moment later she looked up at him. She looked deep into his eyes and saw, once again, the Mediterranean sapphire of his gaze. She saw how hurt he was, how alone and vulnerable. There were only three words left in the world for her to say, and with the courage of a solitary warrior facing a hundred thousand, her eyes welled with tears, she looked at him and said, "I love you."

The feather landed. It had fallen from an angel.

The High Museum

Daniel and Ayse stood before a large canvas of Sandro Botticelli, called *Spring*. It was a masterpiece of the Italian Renaissance, on loan from the Uffizi Museum in Florence. The seven characters in the painting were celebrating the coming of spring in a clearing amidst the forest behind them. The three graces were dancing together, their sheer gowns barely covering their voluptuous bodies.

On the right, the zephyr wind could be seen, blowing warmth back into the world. Above the woodland ritual, a solitary cherub, in the form of a cupid, aimed his bow at the young man on the far left of the painting, mysteriously pointing the arrow upward.

"I think that same Cupid shot us both last spring. I know I was fatally wounded that evening atop Kennesaw Mountain. Not that I mind," said Daniel.

Ayse looked at Daniel and smiled. She chuckled a bit, knowing it wasn't Cupid's doing at all. It was one of her arrows that had pierced him, delivered by a kiss. They squeezed each other's hands and moved down the gallery.

"She looks so peaceful," remarked Ayse.

"She's glad to have the Christ child in her arms. It's typical of these paintings of the early Renaissance, to focus on religious themes. Coming out of a thousand years of theocracy, it was difficult for them to let go."

"Who is that man to the left of her?"

"I'm not sure. I think it's John the Baptist."

"Is he the founder of your religion, the Southern Baptists?"

"No, not really."

They were standing before Giovanni Bellini's painting, *Madonna and Saints,* painted in 1470 in Venice. The painting depicted three figures sitting on a windowsill. Behind them, in the distance, stood a medieval village, with a pale blue summer sky above it.

"Do you know who the woman to the right of Mary is?"

"No, I don't, but she must be a saint. Catholics are more into saints than Baptists. I'm not very helpful when it comes to knowing which saint is which."

"Nor am I. We have no saints in Islam. Not even the prophet Mohammed is a saint. We don't have paintings, stained-glass windows or sculptures depicting gods. In the Qur'an, Mohammed specifically condemns all of these things as forms of idolatry."

"We don't have any paintings or sculptures in my father's church either. We do have a large cross behind the pulpit. It would be hard to imagine a Baptist church without a cross. We also have a huge baptismal behind the pulpit. It's large enough to baptize adults in.

"My father loves to do baptisms every Sunday morning, wading waist deep in the water and dunking the converted in. All of them adorned in fine white gowns."

"It seems kind of strange to me," said Ayse.

"There are a thousand differences between our two religions, Ayse. But the fact remains that, had the early Christians not gone on the Crusades, the Western world might still be locked in the intellectual prison of the Dark Ages. The crusaders, when they returned from the Holy Land, came back with copies of works by Aristotle, Socrates and many ancient scholars.

"In the West, all of those books had either been destroyed as works of heresy, or kept safely guarded in monasteries and the private collections of the Holy Roman Church. To the papal hierarchy, knowledge was evil. It was up to the papacy to protect their flock from the falsehoods of the pagan, ancient world. They believed those manuscripts were the work of Satan.

"But during that same time period, Islam embraced knowledge. From my reading this summer I learned that the eleventh and twelfth centuries were times of great learning in Persia and Syria. It was only after the invasion of the mongol tribes that the great Islamic civilization collapsed.

"Because of the Crusades, the Islamic world taught us Arabic numbers and returned many of our own ancient texts to us. In large part, we have only Islam to thank for our Renaissance."

"Not many people know that, and I'm duly impressed. I didn't know I was dating a scholar.

"It says in the Hadith of Ibn Majah, *'The search for knowledge is an obligation laid on every Muslim.'*"

"I'm hardly a scholar, Ayse. It's just that I had a lot of time this summer. When I wasn't stirring paint, or mowing the lawn, I took up reading books about religion. Not just Islam, but all the great religions, ancient and modern.

"It was funny at times. I would come down for dinner thinking about the

Egyptian sun god, Ra, or the Buddhist vision of Nirvana, only to find my dad quoting another passage of scripture and saying grace over collard greens and fried chicken. It seemed strange to me, stranger than baptism."

"Did you ever discuss any of your books with your father?"

"Oh, Ayse, you have no idea what my dad is like. As he loves to put it, *'For God so loved the world, that he gave his only begotten Son, that whosoever believeth in him should not perish, but have everlasting life.'*

"There is no room for inaccuracy in my father's view of the world. A person either accepts Jesus Christ as his or her personal Lord and Savior or faces eternal damnation in the fires of hell. Neither Mahatma Gandhi nor Mother Teresa, who happens to have been Catholic, is allowed into Clay's Heaven. There are no Buddhists or Muslims, no matter how good, living in my father's version of heaven. You either believe, or you don't believe. There is not one millimeter of flexibility in Clay's perception of the Christian religion.

"If he knew I was reading a book about Zoroaster or Jainism, he would disapprove vehemently and warn me that such behavior is the work of Satan. That there is only one truth, one Bible and one way. That's my father."

Ayse stood silent. Talking about religion only served to remind her how foolish both of them were for behaving the way they were: holding hands, walking down the galleries of the High Museum, looking at the great paintings of the Renaissance and being in love. It was all an illusion. A fool's paradise.

Afterward, they were planning to go out to dinner and, Ayse knew she was directly disobeying her mother's six o'clock curfew. With every tender kiss, every embrace, every hour they spent together they fell further into the trap of love.

"What would your father say about us?" asked Ayse as they walked down the hall.

"Let's not talk about it. We know our parents won't understand or approve. We've known that all along. Let's just enjoy the afternoon and take it one day at a time.

"Maybe we'll both get hit by a car on the way home and never have to deal with what they're going to say to us when we tell them."

"That's a morbid thought, Daniel."

"It is, but it proves the point that we never know what the future holds. All we have is the moment, Ayse. This time together. That's called living in the here and now — not worrying about tomorrow. For tomorrow may never come. It's the Buddhist way of looking at the world."

Ayse smiled. He was right. It served no purpose to worry about their future. They had Randy's battered Honda until tomorrow, reservations at a restaurant in Buckhead and, for the moment, each other. Nothing else mattered.

Fall Semester

The semester passed in a euphoric mist of young love. Long walks through the forest behind the school, watching the seasons change. Watching the lush green leaves of summer bleach to a brilliant orange in the backwash of the advancing north winds. Feeling the air transforming itself, losing the thick, humid weight of a Georgia summer to find a crisp, invigorating edge, sharp and welcome after the heat.

Ayse and Daniel spent every Saturday together and, on some weekends, when their study load was manageable, Sundays as well. They visited all the museums again. They even returned to the Museum of Paper Manufacturing, where the docent remembered them. He took two hours of his time to walk them through the museum. The docent was charming. They patiently learned the nuances of the paper-manufacturing process for a second time within a year. They were too embarrassed to write a report on it for Professor Lathcombe.

They ate lunch together every day, and spent long hours after dinner sitting in the student center talking. Ayse introduced Daniel to Hatice and Kasha and they could see why Ayse had become so enamored of this good-looking American boy. He was a catch.

As the winter break approached and the semester, amid a flurry of midnight cramming sessions and two-hour exams, neared its close, Daniel and Ayse grew troubled. Ayse had broken her promise to her mother and Daniel had ignored his father's warning. Their hearts had taken them where their heads knew they should not have gone.

The fantasy of the last four months was drawing to a close and, as if in unison with their apprehension, the trees atop Kennesaw Mountain were bare, stripped of their leaves by the tilt of a lonely blue planet revolving around a sun. The winter sky had returned, repainting itself a sullen gray as it laid siege on Atlanta.

Ayse and Daniel knew they needed to talk. There were decisions that had to be made. With three days remaining before Ayse's flight to Istanbul and the arrival of Daniel's mother to pick him up for Christmas break, their fairytale romance was soon to meet its first dragon.

One afternoon, on a Wednesday before having dinner together at the student center, Ayse had arranged to have Daniel meet her at the Crypt of Civilization. The weather outside had turned ugly and, whenever that happened, they would stay indoors. Sometimes they would have coffee in the small cafeteria in Goodman Hall, other times kick back on the couch in front of the fireplace in Hearst Hall, telling stories about their past, but they had not met in front of the Crypt since last spring.

Daniel thought it unusual for Ayse to ask him to meet at the Crypt, but in the back of his mind, he knew. Neither had said anything to their families. Professor

Lathcombe, Randy, Hatice and Kasha and half the students and faculty at Oglethorpe University knew what was happening, but not the people who mattered.

As Daniel walked down the staircase to the bottom floor of Hearst Hall, he sensed the gravity of their meeting. At the bottom of the stairwell, he turned to the left and saw Ayse sitting down in front of the large stainless steel door. Her knees up, her head resting on them and her arms wrapped around both her legs. She looked so small, he thought, so fragile.

She was crying. He walked over to her, took off his backpack and tossed it on the floor without saying a word. He sat beside her, taking her into his arms and letting her head rest upon his chest, like a parent comforting an injured child.

Ayse's tears rolled down her cheeks, falling silently on Daniel's black cotton jacket. He could hear her sobbing and he knew why. He knew she would have to tell her parents when she arrived in Istanbul. Ayse could not go on misleading them another semester. She didn't have the heart to lie.

A handful of students glanced at them as they went into the bookstore. They said nothing. They could see this was a private moment and, though they wondered, hearing her sobs and seeing the look on Daniel's face, they did not intrude. Perhaps it's a quarrel. Maybe they're breaking up, thought a few of them as they walked up the stairway on their way to class.

They didn't stare or cross the unmarked boundary that surrounded these young lovers. The girls who observed them saw the strong, concerned look on Daniel's face and wished for a moment they were the woman being held in his arms. They saw themselves sitting there in Ayse's place, wishing they had someone's shoulder to cry on. Someone who cared for them as much as he cared for her.

The young men would see them and wish it was he who held this beautiful girl in his arms. Her auburn hair cascading over Daniel's chest. Her skin, foreign and captivating in its rich tones. A princess from a distant land, what great joy it would be to be her prince.

Still, they knew not to trespass this unseen barrier that encircled Daniel and Ayse. They continued into the bookstore, looking to sell back some textbooks they no longer needed.

After a long time, Ayse spoke.

"Will it really be here six thousand years from now?" she said in a whimper.

"You mean the Crypt?"

"Yes, Daniel. Do you think any of this will be here centuries from now?"

"I don't know."

"It makes me so incredibly sad. To think of all the misunderstanding and hatred in this world. Everyone judging everyone else because of the color of their skin, or their upbringing, or the gods they believe in and, all the while, stockpiling weapons to defend their judgments.

"I don't know what Dr. Jacobs was thinking when he put all those things in there, those relics. Did he really believe there would be anyone around six thousand years from now to reopen it?"

Daniel, wanting to make her smile, answered her question with another question.

"Of course they'll open it. Why wouldn't some future generation want those two mannequins, a bunch of old Atlanta newspapers and a Bridgeomatic game? They'll be just dying to play a round of Bridgeomatic."

Ayse laughed. She looked up at him and gave him the smile he had hoped to see. Her eyes were still filled with tears but they lay in juxtaposition to her laugh. He squeezed her hard enough to take her breath away. It felt good. Reassuring.

"What is it, Ayse? I know you didn't ask me to meet you here because you were worried about Thornwell Jacob's crazy Crypt."

"No, it's about us."

"I know."

"I have to tell them, Daniel. It's not fair of me to go on like this. They need to know how I feel about you, and I'm so afraid of what they're going to say. My father might be a bit more understanding. He likes America and he has a lot of business in the States. He will not like it, but he probably won't get too upset.

"But my mother, Elif, she's old school. She's repeatedly warned me not to get involved with anyone while I was away at university and look at me now — I'm sitting here in the basement of Hearst Hall in the arms of Daniel Harris, the son of a Southern Baptist minister.

"I have no idea what my mother is going to say, Daniel, but I can tell you my visit back to Istanbul will not be good."

Daniel took her little hand and squeezed it so tightly it hurt. He knew they had been avoiding this conversation for weeks. They had not wanted to think about their future together, instead allowing themselves the luxury of basking in a wondrous present.

"My trip home won't be any easier than yours, Ayse."

"Are you going to tell your father?"

"Yes, I have to. I've never felt so apprehensive about anything in my life. I know what my father's reaction will be and trust me, Ayse, I dread the day I break the news to him.

"My mother, Rebecca, like your father, won't be as mad. But she won't oppose my father. She is the perfect wife in that regard and always has been. Even if she thinks it's okay for us to be dating, she won't say anything to Clay. She loves my father immensely and she has learned to be obedient to him. Obedient to a fault."

"What will happen?"

"I don't know. I don't know any more than I know whether or not someone will be here to cut through these stainless-steel welds sixty centuries from now. Whether this crypt will endure, or melt in a nuclear holocaust because some self-righteous lunatic like my father couldn't keep his finger off the trigger.

"That's the trouble, Ayse. My father would just as soon pull that trigger than see the world work things out. His favorite passages of the Bible come from the Book of Revelation.

"I don't know how he's going to react when I tell him we've been dating. In a way, I don't care. He's not me and no matter what he says, I want to be with you when we return to school in January. Do you understand?"

"That's if I return."

"Don't even think that, Ayse. I love you and that's all that matters."

"I love you too, Daniel."

That was all they said. They sat there for a while longer, holding each other as if they were both on a ship sinking in a cold, deep ocean. They knew this might be one of the last times they would ever be together. That Ayse's mother might pull her from Oglethorpe for breaking her vow, and that Daniel's father might do the same.

Their glorious fall had led them into the chill of winter. Three days left. Time has a ruthless heart.

The Flight Home

*T*he Boeing 747 Ayse was on felt as if it weren't moving. It was hanging in the air above the Atlantic as if it were facing a five-hundred-mile-per-hour headwind. The jet was stationary, suspended in time, taking an eternity to cross the dark, angry waters of the North Atlantic. Minutes passed in multiples of a hundred. Hours became days.

Ayse couldn't sleep. She knew she must, that it would be mid-day when she landed in Istanbul and she needed to rest, but it was of no use. She was too nervous to sleep. She was trying to think of how to break the news to them. Where to break the news to them. When to break the news.

Her apprehensions kept swimming around in her thoughts like sharks in a feeding frenzy. The sharks were hungry beyond reason. Her fears, her worries, were consuming her alive.

"Can I get you anything?"

A Delta flight attendant, checking the aisle of sleeping passengers, leaned over and spoke to Ayse in a polite whisper. Ayse was startled by her unexpected appearance.

"No. No, thank you."

The attendant, seeing the young lady was troubled, asked a second question.

"Are you afraid of flying?"

"No, I like to fly. I mean, it doesn't frighten me."

"But you look worried. Is anything the matter?"

Ayse looked up at the tall, lovely woman and started to say something, but couldn't. Unable to stop herself, she began sobbing. As she did, Ayse took both of her hands and covered her face, embarrassed at losing her composure. Her face buried, she was unable to stop the flow of tears.

The attendant, knowing that every passenger on the plane except this young woman was asleep, and seeing the empty seat beside Ayse, took a minute to sit beside her. She put her arms around the girl, not unlike the way Daniel had held her three days before in the basement of Hearst Hall.

"Do you want to talk about it?" asked the attendant as Ayse's sobbing subsided.

Ayse looked up and, in the dim light of the airplane cabin, saw that the woman holding her was a good woman. She had long, light brown hair that hung just past her shoulders and brown eyes that had a distinctive sparkle to them, even in the dimly lit interior of the airliner.

Ayse's instincts told her it would be good to talk. No one else would hear what was being said, and, because it was late, the flight attendant had no one else's needs to tend to.

"Would you mind?" asked Ayse.

"No, that's why I'm here. I want to know what's troubling you."

Ayse wiped her tears on the sleeve of her blouse and took several deep breaths to regain her composure. She had so wanted to talk to someone, anyone, to ask them what she should do when the plane landed at Ataturk Airport later that same day. So Ayse began her story.

"You see, I fell in love with a boy at college. His name is Daniel, Daniel Mark Harris. I cannot tell you how much I love him because I love him more than I could ever explain. But it was an accident, falling in love like we have, it really was an accident.

"Last spring we started going to museums together for extra credit in an art course we were taking and, as the weeks went by, we became closer and closer.

"He is the sweetest, kindest man I have ever known. I don't know what our future holds, but if there is a future for us, I pray we will be with each other forever."

The attendant looked perplexed. Surely this couldn't be the reason for her tears.

"But love is a wondrous thing. Why are you crying?"

"I'm from Istanbul. When we land in England, I catch a connecting flight that takes me home to Turkey. My father, my mother and my two brothers are Islamic. We are Muslims, who believe in the teachings of the Qur'an and the prophet Mohammed. Daniel is from America. He is a Christian. He is the son of a Baptist imam. No, that's not how you say it. I mean a Baptist minister.

"My mother made me promise that when I went to a university in America I wouldn't date or become involved with anyone, even if he were Muslim. I wasn't supposed to be dating while I was in the United States.

"Now I'm going home for the winter break and I am in love with an American boy. I must tell her."

"You must tell your mother?" asked the woman, confused by Ayse's last statement.

"Yes, my mother, Elif."

"She will understand."

"No, you don't know my mother. She is a devout Muslim. She does not like Americans and she has learned not to trust Christians. Our families' roots go back a thousand years in Turkey.

"In her heart, my mother's still fighting the crusaders. She still remembers the time when we were called infidels. When we were the unbelievers who desecrated the Holy Land and held Jerusalem captive. Her dislike of the West runs deep and I don't think she will understand my feelings toward Daniel at all."

The stewardess paused a minute, as though reflecting, then spoke. "Your mother is first and foremost a woman. She may be a Muslim. She may dislike the West and have good reason to. She may be angry and disappointed in you for breaking your promise, but she is still a woman.

"When she looks into your eyes, and sees the love that lies within your heart, she will forgive you. You did not go to America to find the love of this young man. Love found you. No matter how hard a woman's heart, it cannot stand in the way of genuine love.

"Tell your mother the truth and give her some time. Let her work through the disappointment and the anger she will feel at first. But it is important that you not falter or waver, even for an instant, in keeping your affections for Daniel.

"When your mother knows your feelings run deep, she will come back to you, and she will hold you in her arms like she did when you were a child. She will bless you and set you free to discover the beauty of your feelings. It is what mothers must do when they know their child has left the nest and found her own path. These are truths that never change."

Ayse looked in the flight attendant's eyes and found solace in her gaze. The fears and apprehensions that had overwhelmed her flowed out. Ayse felt a calmness settling upon her troubled seas. The sharks vanished, disappearing into an immeasurable, elusive blue.

"Will she forgive me?"

"Yes, she will do more than forgive you. She will give your love her blessing and send you back to America with it. All she wants is for you to find happiness. She will see that happiness unfolding in your heart and, after time, she will know you have chosen well."

"Oh, thank you so much. I needed someone to talk to, and I'm so glad you found me."

"Rest now, we still have hours before we land in England, and you need your sleep. This will be a long day for you, and remember always, Ayse, God is with you every step of your journey."

With that, the thin, graceful attendant rose from her seat.

"Can I get you a blanket and a pillow?"

"Yes, if you would be so kind," answered Ayse.

The woman, dressed in her blue Delta blazer, reached up into the overhead bin and took out a blanket and two pillows and handed them to Ayse.

"Sleep well, my princess."

Ayse smiled and took the pillows, placing them between herself and the bulkhead of the plane. She covered her body with the dark-blue blanket and within minutes, fell fast asleep.

The flight attendant continued toward the aft of the plane. She walked slowly down the aisle of the 747, checking on the passengers and making certain everyone had all the pillows and blankets they needed.

✪

The change in the pitch of the jet engines awoke Ayse. The pilot got on the loudspeaker and said they would be landing at Heathrow in twenty minutes. It was daylight, although most of the cabin windows were closed and the interior of the airplane still dark.

Ayse uncovered herself and got up to go to the restroom. She remembered the flight attendant that came to her during her endless night and, as she headed to the back of the plane, she looked for her. Ayse wanted to thank her.

There was a waiting line to the restroom, and as she waited, Ayse turned to another attendant to ask where the tall, brown-haired stewardess might be found. Ayse felt a little foolish for not having asked her name the night before.

"Hello. Could you please tell me where I might find the other flight attendant, the one who was on duty last night?"

"Certainly, do you remember her name?"

"No, I'm sorry, I forgot to ask her. But she was tall, with long, brown hair, brown eyes and the kindest voice, surely you would know her."

"Are you certain this happened last night?"

"Why yes, around two-thirty in the morning. I wasn't able to sleep and she came and talked to me. She was so reassuring."

The flight attendant looked at Ayse in disbelief. This girl must be mistaken. It was dark last night, dark and late. It would have been easy for a tired passenger to become confused.

"We don't have an attendant on board that fits your description. You must have been dreaming, or mistaken."

"No, I was wide awake. I couldn't sleep and she came to comfort me."

"I'm sorry, but whoever it was that comforted you, she's not on this airplane."

Ayse hesitated, noting the patronizing look this woman was giving her.

"Perhaps I was dreaming," said Ayse, not wanting to press the issue. But Ayse knew she was not mistaken. There was a woman who spoke with her last night, who gave her two pillows and a blanket and continued down the aisle of the airliner. The woman was tall and graceful, and said the kindest, most reassuring things to her.

"Yes, it was late. I must have been mistaken," Ayse reiterated to the flight attendant as she went into the small bathroom.

The plane landed in England fifteen minutes later. The flight attendant who had spoken to Ayse during the night never reappeared.

Perhaps I really was mistaken, wondered Ayse as she disembarked. Perhaps I had fallen asleep without knowing it and I was dreaming. But it seemed so real to me, her long brown hair, her beautiful voice and the kind words she said. I hope it was real.

No, she even said my name, though I never told it to her, recalled the young girl from Istanbul as she walked onto the concourse. She was real.

The Ride to Macon

ebecca Harris arrived on time, which came as no surprise to Daniel. It was a cold, unforgiving afternoon in Atlanta, with the color of the winter sky identical to the color of the pavement of I-75 — confederate gray.

Daniel was waiting outside his apartment when the Explorer pulled in. He didn't mind standing in the cold, damp wind. Even though the gusts flushed his cheeks and made his fingers hurt, he found a comfort in the pain. He knew it was only physical. It would pass. In the next few days, the pain would be far worse and would not pass as quickly.

Rebecca smiled at her son as she pulled up to the curb. He had packed one small backpack. He knew he still had plenty of clothes in his closet at home and, unlike last summer, winter break was only four weeks long. He had all he needed in his single bag.

Daniel ran around to the back of the truck, opened the door and threw in his backpack. He came back around to take the passenger seat beside his mother. He winked at her as they pulled away. Daniel remembered their last conversation. A heart to heart which resulted in his father's stern lecture on this same journey north. He climbed in and began a carefully guarded conversation.

"Hi, Mom. Thanks for coming to pick me up."

"Anytime, Daniel. I'm not like your father. I'll use any excuse to spend some time on the highway. Take in some different scenery. How was school?"

"Great."

"And your grades?"

"Good, Mom. Four A's. One B."

"Not bad, Daniel. Your father will be proud."

Daniel reached over and turned on the radio. He knew it would be tuned to some Christian FM station. It would be some preacher from Tennessee or Mississippi telling their airwave congregation that the end days are on hand and now is the time to repent. Now is the time to turn to Jesus. A time for salvation.

Daniel smiled, amused by the fact he had guessed correctly.

Rebecca knew her son didn't like these stations and took his gesture as a signal that he didn't want to talk. She had listened to the station all the way to Oglethorpe, turning it off a few blocks before pulling into the university. She agreed with the preacher, knowing from her husband's sermons that we were in the final days. The Jewish people had returned to Israel. Nuclear war was inevitable, and the marked one was amongst us, turning those without faith into instruments of the devil.

The thought of being here when it happened, when the Book of Revelation became flesh, thrilled and excited Rebecca and Clay. The signs were everywhere. The troubles in the Middle East, the rampant homosexuality in America, the moral decay of nations, everything pointed to the beginning of the end.

Daniel would have none of it. He had studied enough religious history to know Christians had been preoccupied with the Judgment Day since the hour of the crucifixion. He knew the apostles believed the Last Judgment would come within their lifetime.

After it failed to happen, it became one sign after another that led the Holy Mother Church to think the return of Christ was always a few years away. Daniel had learned that thousands had panicked in the year 999, believing without question Christ would return the morning of the new millennium to battle Lucifer in the final war between good and evil.

Every generation thereafter had its list of irrefutable signs: the bubonic plague, the Crusades, the sighting of comets, meteor showers, volcanic eruptions, assassinations, the appearance of Mother Mary at Lourdes, miracles, invasions, solar eclipses — all had served as indisputable evidence of the second coming of the Lord. The prophesied return of Christ to pass God's final judgment on the quick and the dead. The truth being that each event was followed by a disappointing no-show.

No, the fool on the radio, so convinced that we were in the final days, was the same fool in the pulpit a thousand years ago predicting the same impending doom. History had proven all these Christian soothsayers wrong. Daniel knew the Book of Revelation had been added to the Bible hundreds of years after Christ's death. The way Daniel saw it, the Book of Revelation was a liturgical typo.

As he listened to the man at the microphone expounding with hysterical fervor about anthrax and pestilence, Daniel laughed. It was a new twist on an old tale.

The odds favored it would end as yet another, anticlimactic no-show. History has a great sense of humor.

Aside from filling the SUV once at a gas station near Locust Grove, the ride to Macon was uneventful. Both Rebecca and Daniel had left the radio on the entire trip and, after awhile, the preacher's voice became unimportant.

"The world is ending soon," he would say in an impassioned proclamation that went as unnoticed as the sound of the radials hitting the highway. Road noise. The end of days became road noise.

Daniel wondered where and when he would tell his father about his relationship with Ayse. He was not afraid. He knew his father would disapprove and had resigned himself to dealing with that disapproval when it came. Daniel realized he would have to endure a series of lectures on why it was wrong for the son of a Christian Minister to be seeing a Muslim. Daniel was ready. He loved Ayse enough to withstand a thousand lectures.

He had already donned his rusted armor weeks ago, knowing full well this battle was inevitable. He recalled his father's diatribe last summer on the evils of Islam. His father had never mentioned her name, but the meaning of that lecture had come through loud and clear.

Daniel must cease and desist. He must not continue on with this madness. Islam is the religion of the great Satan and its founder, Mohammed, is a false prophet. Nothing good could come of seeing this infidel, whoever she might be. His father would think it, but never say it, stopping just short of calling his girlfriend what many a Southerner called the people of the Middle East — sand-niggers.

Daniel had ignored his father's lecture just as he had every lecture his father had given him since he was thirteen. They were, in Daniel's mind, all bullshit.

The upcoming confrontation was going to be just another nail in the coffin of a relationship that was already dead. His father was always right. Daniel was always wrong.

When they pulled into the driveway, Daniel noticed the trees were bare again. The trees were trapped in this cycle of life and death, growth and dormancy, spring and fall. Daniel smiled as he took his backpack out of the back of the car and walked toward the front door of his house.

We're like the trees, he thought, but we just don't realize it. We too are caught in this cycle of life and death. The wind was still cold and his fingers returned to feeling the pain they had earlier. Daniel didn't mind. He remembered what the Buddha had said — life is pain.

Christmas Eve

The smell of fresh-cut pine filled the house. Daniel had come downstairs to have a glass of milk to settle his churning stomach. The Christmas tree lights had accidently been left on, giving the living room a warm, colorful glow at two-twenty in the morning.

The ornaments and tinsel danced on the Scotch pine, their motion a result of the hot air furnace running non-stop. It was cold outside. Cold enough to snow, but the snow wouldn't make it this far south. It would fall on the Blue Ridge Mountains two hundred miles to the north and stop there. The only winter to arrive in Macon was the bitter wind.

Daniel came down the stairs, walking past the stockings hanging on the stone fireplace, and on into the kitchen. He opened the refrigerator and poured himself a tall glass of milk. He took a long, steady drink from the glass and immediately felt better. Calmer.

The last week at home had not been easy. Clay and Rebecca had made several attempts to pry some information out of him about his relationship with the Muslim girl, but to no avail. He kept avoiding specifics and carefully steering around their inquiries. He had decided he was going to tell all of them: Ruth, her husband Chet, Clay and Rebecca, on Christmas day. He reasoned that the joyous occasion of the birth of Christ might help to keep tempers from flaring, their reactions from spiraling out of control.

Just before finishing off the milk he went over and raided the cookie jar. Rebecca had been baking all week in preparation for tomorrow's Christmas dinner, and the contents of that jar on Christmas Eve was a treasure trove of Mexican wedding cakes, gingerbread men, and ornately decorated sugar cookies. He smiled as he chomped off the head of one of the gingerbread men. Tomorrow my father will probably want to do the same thing to me, he thought as he finished his milk.

He put the lid back on the cookie jar and rinsed his glass in the kitchen sink. The sink, like the rest of the kitchen, was spotless. His mother would notice his midnight glass of milk and the three missing cookies. Everything in her kitchen was inventoried and exactly where it should be. She prided herself on the cleanliness and orderliness of her kitchen.

Daniel headed upstairs, turning off the tree lights before he did. The room lost its charm in the darkness. It suddenly seemed colder inside.

He headed into his bedroom and took out his notebook. Until the milk and cookies made him sleepy, he would take a few minutes for another entry into his journal. He opened his notebook. He was a mere forty pages beyond the only page he had ever shared with another living soul. The page he had given to Ayse.

His writing had tapered off with every passing week. For the past four months of his life, he had been happy. Gloriously happy. There were a handful of love poems and a dozen pages of diary entries, explaining in great detail how much he loved her, or detailing what they had done together that day.

Tonight was different. Tonight he was returning to his book of angst, his long, unbroken soliloquy about a family divided by religion. A family hanging together by tattered, gossamer threads that resembled a broken cobweb. He was about to try to break free of that web and he was frightened to death about the repercussions.

December 25, 3:00 a.m.

I can't sleep. It's all rushing back to me, like the tireless north wind outside, all the uneasiness, the anger. I know what he'll say. He'll tell me to end it. To walk away and forget about her. That it won't work.

He'll charge right into it, quoting scripture left and right. He'll drag up passages from every book in his well-studied Bible proving, beyond doubt, that Islam is a false religion. Proving Ayse is an infidel, sent by the devil to drive a wedge into the very heart of our good, Christian family.

God, I hate him. I hate his attitude. I hate his preaching. I hate his pretentiousness, his smugness and his singular phone line to God. What makes him so self-righteous?

I believe in God. I believe in the teachings of Jesus Christ, but I don't have to go around condemning everyone who happens to view the world differently. I don't have to be in the business of trying to save souls every hour of my waking day, especially when the souls don't want or need to be saved.

What's so wrong with calling God Allâh? What's so wrong about praying five times a day, fasting for a month each year and making a pilgrimage to a holy city once in your lifetime? Is it so different from saying grace at every meal, the Lord's Prayer before going to bed and making sacrifices during Lent? What's the difference between Mecca and the Crystal Cathedral, or the Vatican, or Lourdes, or the thousands of country churches across the South?

Why do we hold them in judgment when Christ himself told us not to do so? Not to judge.

What's the use? I know it won't go well and I can't expect it to. It's Christmas. It's Christmas and I'm wide awake at three-fifteen in the morning and the wind outside won't stop blowing.

I wish I hadn't been born a PK. Sometimes I wish I hadn't been born at all.

Christmas Dinner

Ruth, her husband, and their boy showed up at two in the afternoon. The house was awash in the milieu of Christmas — the aroma of a baking turkey, the scent of pine, the sound of Perry Como's Christmas Album on Clay's ancient phonograph and the colorful decorations appointed throughout the house. Festive and traditional.

His sister and her family walked in carrying an armload of presents and two freshly baked pumpkin pies. Their child, Jason, immediately dashed off to the living room, rifling through the unopened gifts beneath the tree. Searching frantically for those with his name on them.

The television blared a football game between two college teams. Daniel was in the living room, feet resting on an ottoman, hands holding a mug of warm cider. He smiled as he watched young Jason darting for his presents, recalling how he and Ruth would do the same years ago. Some things never change.

Rebecca was in the kitchen, her apron wrapped around her waist, food scattered across the countertops in varying stages of preparation. Her famous okra dish, cranberry sauce, collard greens, turkey dressing and a tray of Christmas cookies that would turn the head of Martha Stewart.

A Southern Christmas, differing only from a Northern Christmas in the lack of snow outside and the aroma of okra cooking.

Chet sat down next to Clay on the sofa and immediately began opining on one of the quarterbacks.

"I can't believe they let Adams start, after the hit he took last week against Oklahoma."

"They said it was just a sprain, I figured they'd start him," said Clay, showing his one-upmanship over his son-in-law.

"Still, their backup quarterback is every bit as good as Adams. I was hoping he'd get the nod. What's the score?"

"Sixteen to twelve. It's still the first half, but the two-minute warning's due any time. I still think LSU will take it. They've got one heck of a defense this year and they're not giving those good-ol' boys from Alabama much of a chance. They've shut down their running game."

"Yeah."

Daniel didn't participate. He didn't care who won or who lost. Georgia hadn't made the playoffs this year and even if they had, Daniel didn't care. Every Christmas, every Thanksgiving, his father would consume most of the holiday watching husky men bang against each other in some over-hyped contest that ultimately meant nothing. Daniel was no more interested in the game in front of him than was the chair he was sitting on.

His thoughts were elsewhere. He had thought he would mention it after dinner.

Everyone would retire to the living room, where the television would have evolved to a Lions versus Bucs game, and make ready for dessert. That dessert being pumpkin pie with whipped cream, home-cooked by Ruth, who had now joined her mother in the battlefield of a holiday kitchen.

Jason, just turning four and adorable, had taken out some plastic cars he had received earlier and was pretending to be running a NASCAR race around the perimeter of the dining room table. Round and round and round went his supercharged Grand-Am. Ruth and Rebecca dodged his laps while setting the table.

"Dinner's ready in twenty minutes, boys!" shouted Ruth over to the three men whose eyes were affixed to the tube. "Hope y'all are hungry."

They were hungry. They had all skipped breakfast and were ready to begin carving into that nineteen-pound bird browning in the oven. They would have to miss the ending of the LSU game, but with Georgia knocked out of the bowls, it wasn't important. Had Georgia made it, dinner would wait.

❂

At quarter of four, the Harris family gathered around the dining room table. The banquet set before them exquisite in every detail. The turkey, golden brown and overstuffed with homemade dressing, was the centerpiece. The gravy, rich and creamy, sat ready to be ladled over a steaming bowl of mashed potatoes. The cranberry sauce, the okra casserole, everything cooked to perfection.

Clay began with his customary grace, adding to it like he loved to do during these holiday meals, "For what we are about to receive, let us be truly thankful. And Lord, let this meal be blessed just as you have blessed this family. Blessed us with a loving daughter, Ruth Anne, who has given us a wonderful grandchild. Blessed us with a son who studies hard and brings home grades that make a mother and father proud.

"Thank you Lord for this day, a celebration of your birth centuries ago. This special day when you were brought into the light of the world as our Savior and Redeemer, in Christ's name, on his birthday, we pray. Praise be the Lord!"

"Praise be the Lord!" responded all four adults sitting at the dining room table. Jason, still in his high chair beside his mother, made an attempt at saying the response but it came out sounding like, "Pwaze be the Lard." Clay chuckled and remarked, "We've got another preacher in the family, Ruth. You just be sure to keep him going to Sunday school and he'll be after my job in no time."

"He'll have some big shoes to fill, Dad," added Ruth.

"I believe he could fill them just fine. Now let's enjoy this dinner your mother has spent all day preparing. Please pass me that bird so I can practice my carving skills."

Small talk and the rattle of plates, silverware, serving platters and glasses filled the dining room. The football game played on in the distance, although the volume of the television had been turned down to the point where it vanished beneath the Tammy Wynette album that had been stacked above Perry Como.

Daniel remained distant. He shared in the feast like a stranger invited to someone else's family holiday. His mind wasn't on the game or the sights and sounds of this celebration in a Southern suburban home, but six thousand miles to the east. She would be sleeping by now, past midnight in Istanbul.

Christmas would have come and gone without notice. December twenty-fifth for her and her family held no more meaning than December twenty-seventh. Ramadan ended three weeks ago and the months afterward would pass without notice of Christmas, Ash Wednesday, or Easter. None of these Christian holy days meant anything to Ayse and her family. Daniel found it strange, almost sad in a way, realizing how much these days meant to him.

After dinner was over and before dessert was served, the conversation took on a heavier tone. Clay had brought up some problems they were having at the school. One of the science teachers had been asked his personal opinion about evolution versus creationism by a tenth grade student. The instructor said he didn't find the concepts incompatible.

"Of course, it didn't take long for Mr. Fonda's comment to find its way back to my office. A few of the parents have asked for his resignation since the incident and the entire matter comes up before the board two days after classes restart in January."

"What do you think will happen?" asked Ruth.

"It's not what I think will happen, Ruth. It's what I know will happen. Mr. Fonda will be dismissed."

"Why?" Daniel interjected.

"Why? Because the two are not compatible. Every good Christian knows there is no truth to the theory that we evolved from monkeys. The explanation of man's origins is laid out word for word in the Book of Genesis, Daniel. We will not tolerate any teacher who thinks otherwise."

"Apes, Dad. Not monkeys, we evolved from apelike creatures."

"Daniel, let's not get started," warned Ruth. "We're having a lovely dinner on a fine afternoon and I don't think this is the time or place to have one of those conversations."

"Well I do. In ten days a perfectly good teacher is going to lose his job because he's teaching the truth. There's overwhelming evidence that the theory of evolution is real. There are billions of carbon-dated fossils out there that verify Darwin's theory and no evidence whatsoever to prove the theory of creationism. Why should he be fired for telling the truth?"

"There is no truth but the word of God, Daniel. If there is one lesson I've learned in my life, it's that the Bible is His word, and, fossils or no fossils, we are to accept His Bible word for word, without any reservations. Mr. Fonda's opinion is only going to expose the young, impressionable minds of our ninth and tenth grade students to a world of lies and deceptions. That's not what North Baptist School of Macon is about."

Ruth sensed it coming. Rebecca didn't want to enter into the fray. Ruth's husband, Chet, had secretly never believed in creationism, but wouldn't dare voice his opinions around Clay. Daniel was on his own.

"What is it with you, Dad? Why can't you appreciate the bigger picture? Think of how magnificent all of God's creations are. How wondrous and glorious is He who designed the dinosaurs, the galaxies, the whales and the peoples of the world. What's wrong with seeing everything that is laid out before us, and not just what happens to be spelled out in the King James version of the Bible?"

Ruth rolled her eyes and waited. Rebecca pulled back her chair.

"I think it's time to head to the kitchen and start fixing up the whipped cream for our pie. Would you like to join me, Ruth?"

"Yes I would, Mama."

Rebecca and Ruth got up and removed themselves from the dining room. They wanted out. They saw the two of them playing with dynamite and they wanted to find a bunker to hide in before the first stick blew. The kitchen was the safest place in the house.

Chet stayed. He reached over and unstrapped Jason from his high chair and sent him into the other room to play with his trucks. Then he went back to his seat.

"I want pie, Daddy," said Jason as he set him on the floor.

"In a minute, Son. Now run along."

The stage was set. Everyone who might get bloodied by the approaching discourse had been cleared out of the room. Chet enjoyed it. He held a great respect for Daniel. He had always admired the way his brother-in-law had stood up to his father. He wasn't about to miss the next engagement. It was far more entertaining than a bowl game by a couple of marginal football teams, and a hell of a lot more violent.

"Daniel, I'm disappointed in you. I knew I shouldn't have sent you off to some liberal college in Atlanta. But I knew there was no place for a boy like you at Baylor or Mercer. You're just too clever for your own good.

"And I feel sorry for you, Son. I feel sorry because if you continue down the terrible path you are on, there will be no turning you away from the gates of hell. This isn't a game we're playing, Daniel. This is a battle.

"It's a struggle for your soul and the soul of every living person on God's good earth. I haven't dedicated my life to the teachings of Jesus Christ for nothing. I can set the record straight for those young kids attending our school by making sure that Mr. Fonda, and his theory of EVILution, are never mentioned at our good Christian school again."

It was time. Daniel knew it was time. Ayse, six thousand miles to the east, stirred restlessly in her sleep, somehow sensing what was about to be said.

"It's EVOLUTION, not EVILution, Dad. And as long as we're on the topic of Christians, I think it's time I tell you something."

The tone of the day darkened. Outside, the north wind howled beneath a clear, sunlit sky. Inside, shadows and abyss took hold of the dining room.

"And what might that be, Daniel?" asked Clayton Harris in a voice so condescending it could freeze a beating heart.

"I'm seeing an Islamic girl at school."

The doors and windows of the house disappeared. A wind more wicked than winter could produce swept through the room and sent shivers down Chet's spine. Clay's eyes lit up as though he were preaching a sermon to Satan himself.

"What did you just say?"

"I'm dating an Islamic girl at Oglethorpe. Her name is Ayse. We've been seeing each other for months. I think I might be in love with her."

The icy gale was so overwhelming that the safe haven of the kitchen was no longer protected. A gust swirled down the hallway and blew into the kitchen. Ruth's hands grew cold and the hair on her arm stood up. Rebecca felt faint and chilled, as though she'd just been immersed in a frigid pond.

Chet knew this battle had overstepped its boundaries. This was not going to be another Clayton vs. Daniel argument about abortion, evolution or a school prayer. Those were theoretical debates. Heated, even vehement at times, but always distant, and safe in that distance.

This was not. This was the son of a well-respected Baptist minister telling his father, face to face on Christmas day, that he was involved with an infidel. Nothing, no knock down, blown out argument the two of them had ever had in the past could hold a candle to this. This was a raging fire, an inferno of a proclamation that could not end well. Chet felt the heat rising as the doors and windows of the house had been resealed and the cold wind replaced by a blistering fire.

"Why are you doing this to me?"

"It has nothing to do with you, Dad. We fell in love last spring. Neither of us wanted this to happen. Ayse tried to cut it off just before school let out last May. But we couldn't. When I saw her again this fall, we started going out. She's not an infidel, Dad. She's a beautiful young girl from Turkey. And I think I love her."

Clayton Harris silently called upon the Almighty to come to his assistance. This was a great test, and Clay was determined to meet the beast head on.

"You must stop seeing her," decreed Clay.

"I won't."

"You will and you shall. If you do not, there will be grim consequences for you, Daniel. As grim and bleak as anything you've ever experienced."

"Don't threaten me, Dad."

"It's not a threat, Daniel. As God is my witness, it is a promise."

Scripture followed. Clay quoted his Bible ruthlessly for the next two hours, proving beyond doubt that Daniel was lost to the devil's ways. Book, chapter and verse were fired at him in a ceaseless barrage.

Daniel was devoured. Clay was fast upon him, tearing at his sinful ways with his hunger. Setting his boy on the straight and righteous, saving him from the grip of the great corruptor — Satan. Ruth and Rebecca soon finished in the kitchen and joined in, quoting from the various tracts they had read about Islam.

"How can those people believe in a polygamist like Mohammed?" asked Ruth, raising the issue of his multiple wives.

"They believe in the Jihad, a holy war against the Christians. They will stop at nothing to destroy us," commented Rebecca.

Daniel fought back. He quoted Matthew 5, Verse 44 from the NIV, the New International Version of the Bible, which Daniel preferred over his father's King James version, *"But I say, Love your enemies. Pray for those who persecute you. In that way you will be acting as true sons of your Father in Heaven."*

Daniel argued there was nothing wrong in loving a person who didn't believe as he did. It didn't make the person inherently evil, just because they professed to another faith. But Clay would have none of it, rebutting his son with yet another quote.

"For false Christs and false prophets shall rise, and shall sew signs and wonders, to seduce, if it were possible, even the elect.

"But take ye heed: behold, I have foretold you all things." Mark 13, Verses 22 and 23. Make note of God's words Daniel. Stop this foolishness now."

The debate continued. The sun had vanished into the long night of winter and still they feasted upon him, eating Daniel alive. They swallowed him with their religious fervor, glad to redeem him from his sin — his sin of falling in love.

Just before seven o'clock, Daniel gave in, exhausted and worn thin by their relentlessness.

"I'll try to break it off," conceded Daniel.

"You will break it off!" commanded his father.

"Nothing good can come of it, Daniel. It will only serve to embarrass your family. Mixed marriages don't work. Whites should marry whites, blacks marry blacks, Christians marry Christians and Jews marry Jews. It is the way it's meant to be," added Ruth.

"None of us could bless a marriage between you and a Muslim woman. Without a family's blessing, a marriage is doomed. No doubt her family feels the same way we do. So just let it go, Daniel. Forget about this foreign girl and start dating a good Christian girl. Even a Catholic would be a better choice than this," commented Ruth.

Daniel, exhausted and spent, knew they were right. He was a fool to think anything else could have happened. His father would not allow it. There would be too much explaining to do — to Rebecca's family, to his congregation, to his God. With marriage out of the question, why continue on with their relationship?

Tired from being bludgeoned with his father's Bible, Daniel went up to his room at seven thirty. His heart was heavy with the knowledge that he would have to end his relationship with Ayse. They had won. Daniel was completely drained.

The rest of his holiday was cold and lifeless. The sun shone out of habit. The freezing winds echoed his mood. The bare trees reached to embrace him. Daniel welcomed them into his empty, open arms.

In Istanbul

*W*ithin a half an hour of landing, Ayse was confessing her love for Daniel to her parents. Abdul couldn't help but overhear their conversation. Mustapha had chosen to sit in back, beside his daughter, while Elif sat beside Abdul in the front seat of the Lexus.

"Thank you for coming to pick me up. I cannot tell you how much it means to me," said Ayse as the car sped away from the airport.

"You are our only daughter, Ayse. The house is empty without you. The thought of not meeting you here has never crossed our minds.

"Your father just returned from a business trip in Zurich. He was thrilled to be back in Istanbul for your arrival. Your time with us is short, with only this month of winter break, so both of us wanted to meet you at the airport. We are glad to see you are well, and looking as lovely as ever."

"I am happy, Mama. But I fear that what I'm going to tell you will make you disappointed with me. You must understand it was never my intention. It was something that happened, something unforeseen, like an accident."

Elif turned her around to look at her daughter. What was this announcement that placed such a look of consternation on her daughter? Where had her smile fled?

"What is it, my dear? Did you not do well at university this semester?"

"No, I did very well. I have my grades with me and they are nothing that I would be ashamed of. But I am ashamed."

"What of?" asked her father, curious as to where his daughter's comments were leading.

"I have failed you both, and I have broken my promise to you."

Elif did not like the sound of this. "What is it, Ayse? What is it you feel you must tell us, so soon after your arrival home?" inquired Elif, wanting to discover the story behind her daughter's worried face.

"I fell in love with a young man in America. I never expected this to happen, nor did I think it would. But it has happened and I can no longer go on without confessing this love I have for him to the two of you."

Mustapha and Elif looked at each other in disbelief. This was not something they had anticipated. This was something falling from the sky, like a huge stone, striking them without warning.

"Who is it that you love?" asked her father.

"His name is Daniel, Daniel Mark Harris. He is from a small city just south of Atlanta. A town called Macon. He is a wonderful man, Mother. He is so kind and considerate. You will think dearly of him when the time comes for you to meet him."

"But is he not a Christian, with a name like that?" asked Elif.

"Yes, he is a Christian. His father is a minister in Macon. They belong to a church called Southern Baptists, and, like us, they are very devout.

"But we have talked about this at great length, and Daniel is more open to Islam than is his family. He has promised me he would discuss our relationship with his parents over the winter break as well."

"Surely he has not asked for your hand in marriage?" said Elif in a tone that spoke of disapproval.

"No, he has not. We talked about it before the semester was over, and both of us decided we would discuss our love for each other with our families before we decided what to do next."

A long silence followed. Elif turned around and stared forward. She recalled a passage from the Qur'an 22.46; *It is not the eyes that are blind, but blind are the hearts within the breasts.* Ayse was blinded by love.

Mustapha reached over and took his daughter's hand, squeezing it gently. Nothing was said.

The Lexus wound its way through the labyrinth of traffic that never ceases in this city by the Bosporus. Horns blared, tires screeched and Abdul changed lanes a dozen times with deliberate skill as tears flowed down the cheeks of Elif Yalçin.

Ayse didn't know what to say. She had been thinking of what might happen, what could happen since changing planes in England. She had played out a thousand different scenarios in her mind, only guessing which one might actually occur once the three of them were united. Once her story was told.

After the car crossed the Galata bridge that spans the Golden Horn, Elif broke the uneasy quiet. Her words came between the sounds of weeping.

"Ayse, I have never been so disappointed in you. How could you have done this to us? After the promise you had made to me that you would not date when you were in America? We had even discussed dating Muslim men, and both of us had agreed it was not a good idea. Not when you were so far away from your brothers and your family. Why did you do this to us?"

Elif's words were spoken as the flight attendant had prophesied. She had warned Ayse that her mother would be angry and disappointed. Now, upon hearing her mother's voice from the front seat of the car, Ayse knew the flight attendant was right. Her mother would not understand. Not at first.

"I didn't do anything, Mother. Daniel and I met last spring, while doing extra credit for an art class. I didn't expect to fall in love. Sometimes, love isn't something you find. It finds you.

"This fall, when I returned to school, we saw each other for the first time in a class we both were attending, and we knew that it was of no use. We could not stop each other."

"Have you had relations with him, Ayse?" asked Elif, switching to a distant, calculated voice.

"No. We have decided it would be the worst thing to do. We have kissed and we have embraced, but we have not made love. This I swear to you."

"What were you thinking, Ayse? You know how both of us feel about Christians. You cannot think we will somehow approve of such a relationship. What if you were to continue on, becoming husband and wife, how could you possibly deal with the children. Would they be raised Muslim, or Christian?" asked Mustapha.

"I think not Muslim, Ayse. The religion always follows the man. His family, especially if his father is an Imam, would never tolerate raising his grandchildren as Muslims. There is simply nowhere for this love of yours to go, Ayse. Not in this world," added Mustapha.

"Oh, Father."

Ayse burst into tears. She collapsed into her father's arms and sobbed like a child who has done something wrong. A great and ponderous silence fell over the family riding in that dark-blue Lexus. Abdul listened but did not speak. He felt the intensity of the moment but could do nothing to relieve the tension that filled the car.

He wanted to keep driving. To pass by their luxurious house in Bebek and continue northward to the Black Sea. Once there, he would drive the car off one of the cliffs into the dark, foreboding waters. He felt it would be a better end than what lay ahead.

They arrived home. Elif as silent and hardened as the limestone beneath Turkey. Ayse still crying. Mustapha holding his daughter tightly as they went into their home in silence. Ayse knew this was going to be a terrible four weeks together. Terrible and unforgiving.

Book of Midnights

*D*ec. 26, 3:35 a.m.

I should have known they would have reacted the way they did. Even Ruth was quick to take sides with Mom and Dad. Quick to condemn me.

But what have I done? I met a sweet, attractive woman at college and fell for her. What harm can come of that? Do all the rules change because she practices a different religion? It's not that she's some sort of devil worshiper, which is what my father would have me believe.

It's the same God we believe in. The God of Abraham, the God of Moses and the God of Christ. Mohammed never claimed to be divine. He was just a prophet. Why has there been so much blood spilled between our peoples since the writing of the Qur'an? Will it ever end?

Haven't the last fourteen centuries of distrust and violence taught us anything? Will the crusades ever be over? Will my father put down his sword and his rhetoric and embrace Islam as a different path up the same mountain? A path leading to the same God, the same Heaven.

But I'm caught, unsure of what's next. I suppose everything will depend on what happens between Ayse and her parents. If they don't send her back to Oglethorpe for spring semester my problems are over. I can't afford to rescue her from within the walls of Istanbul, like Ulysses did Helen of Troy ages ago.

We'll stay in touch for a while. We promised to e-mail each other should her parents forbid her to return, but that's all that's left us. A cyberspace affair destined to fade into fewer and fewer e-mails over time. Destined to perish.

Should she be allowed to come back to the U.S., I doubt I will be able to stop seeing her, despite my commitments after dinner last night. I'd rather take my chances with Mom and Dad than live without her. I don't think Dad would really follow through on his threats. He was just trying to scare me into breaking up with her. The worst he would do is pull the plug on my college funding.

I could get a job in Atlanta, strike out on my own and take a year or two off from school. That wouldn't be all that bad. At least I could be with her.

It's late and I'm getting tired. There are just too many variables for me to guess as to what's going to happen next. Maybe we should break it off. Maybe Dad's right, there being too many differences between us. Maybe not.

The House in Bebek

"It's been horrible, Fatimah."

"Your mother will come around, Ayse. Just give her some time."

"They still haven't said whether or not I'm going to be allowed to return to the United States. Even my Father's been avoiding me."

"You need to talk to her. You need to tell her how you feel."

"She won't talk to me."

"Then all you can do is pray. Pray to Allâh. Pray they will let you be together, as it was meant to be."

"Is it meant to be?"

"Yes, Ayse, you know it is."

"Perhaps you're right. Perhaps you're wrong. But thanks for calling me."

"I just thought you could use some cheering up. Are we still having lunch tomorrow at the Sultan's Café? One o'clock, as planned?"

"Yes, I'll see you then. Goodbye."

Ayse hung up the phone and looked around. She had spent too many hours in her room the past three weeks. Hours brooding, agonizing over her situation. Wondering what the final outcome was going to be. She had retreated to the security of her room amidst the uncertainty of her future. It felt safe there, tucked away with her aging dolls and new computer. Safe and familiar.

After hanging up the phone, Ayse picked up a romance novel, written in Turkish, and began reading it. It was escapism, pure and simple. The two lead characters were beset with their own heartbreak, and it was comforting for Ayse to lose herself in their troubles. Far more comforting than tormenting over her own.

After reading a half-dozen pages into the novel, Ayse heard a knock on her door. She wasn't expecting anyone, so the knock took her by surprise.

"Come in," she yelled, thinking it must be Halil, their maid.

The door opened and Elif walked into Ayse's bedroom. She had a serious, reflective look on her face that spoke of the conversation to come. Ayse was nervous. She had hoped her mother would eventually come to speak with her, but seeing Elif enter and sit on the end of her queen-sized bed made Ayse uneasy. Still, Ayse knew it was time.

"Ayse," began her mother. "We must talk about Daniel."

"I know."

"You have been very foolish, becoming involved with this American. Very foolish indeed. Do you truly love this boy?"

"Yes, Mother, more than I can find words to tell you."

"When did you first know this?"

"It was last spring. We had gone to visit a Civil War battlefield just north of Atlanta. We were on top of this mountain, a site where the battle for Atlanta was fought during the time of Lincoln in the War between the States," Ayse paused, looking to her mother to see if she should continue.

"Yes, and then?"

"The sun was setting. We were together in a small grassy area a few feet from the summit. We had just had a picnic. Daniel was lying on his back, talking about his life as the son of a minister, about growing up in the South and how he felt about the world.

"It was a glorious day. The birds were singing, the sky was clear and the dogwoods were blooming beneath a green canopy. I felt an overwhelming urge to kiss him.

"Never once, at all the museums we visited, had Daniel made any attempts to kiss or embrace me. He knew of our agreement, Mother, and he respected it. We were always home by six and he was a perfect gentleman.

"But this afternoon, we'd forgotten about time. It was magical, Mother, unlike any afternoon I have ever known. I couldn't stop myself, so beautiful was the moment, that I leaned over and kissed him. When we kissed, it was as though the world dissolved and disappeared. Once we began, we found it hard to stop.

"I must be honest with you Mother, I asked him to make love to me that same afternoon. Right there, on top of that mountain where all of those soldiers had fought to save Atlanta."

Elif interrupted, "Did you make love, my daughter?"

"No, we didn't. I wanted to, Mother, but he refused. He said it wasn't time. That it would be wrong for us to go down that path, and that we would know when it was time."

"He was right, Ayse. It would have been wrong for you to have made love that day. We know what it says about such things in the Koran. *'Those who abstain from sex, except with those joined to them in the marriage bond...But those whose desires exceed those limits are transgressors...These will be the heirs who will inherit Paradise.'"*

Ayse smiled at her mother, who so seldom quoted the Qur'an, and continued, "After that, realizing I had broken my promise to you, I told him the next week that we must stop seeing each other. That our relationship must end because there is nowhere for it to go. I told him my parents would never approve and his family, especially his father, would never consent to our relationship.

"Just before coming home last summer, I broke it off with him. I knew that is what you would have wanted me to do. We did not see each other again that spring."

"That explains it."

"Explains what?" asked Ayse, intrigued by her mother's comment.

"That explains your mood last summer. I wondered what was keeping you so distant. Why you were always wandering off by yourself on the Princes Islands. You were thinking about him, weren't you?"

"I couldn't help myself. He's such a kind and thoughtful man."

"What happened next, when you returned to college in the fall?"

"He didn't call me, or try to see me or anything. But we did end up being in a class together, and after our first class, he gave me this poem."

Ayse reached into the front pocket of her weathered blue jeans and pulled out the worn and folded copy of Daniel's poem. Elif read the poem to herself. She read it slowly, hoping to find fault with it. But as she read each and every line she could find no fault. Like her daughter, Daniel's words brought tears to her eyes.

The last two stanzas seemed to pierce Elif's hardened heart, leaving her defenseless.

For love is all the gift there was
Between us, that sweet spring.
But our lives cannot unwrap it
And that, such sadness brings.

But not all we feel can fit within
These moments known hereof.
Least of all that soul of yours
My pleasure was, to love.

"He writes very well, this young man."

"He keeps a notebook which he calls his *Book of Midnights*. He told me I was the first person to ever read from it. Look at the edge of the paper, Mother, and you can see where it has been torn out of the notebook he wrote it in. He was sharing a piece of his heart with me.

"And now, you are the second person in this world to read it. It was the kindest thing anyone has ever written to me. When he finished it, I looked up at him, knowing he was prepared to say goodbye, and I told him that I loved him.

"I do love him. If you could only meet him, spend some time with him, you would love him too, Mother."

Elif turned away from her daughter. She did not want Ayse to see the tears rolling down her cheeks.

"It will be a difficult path for you to walk, my Princess," said Elif while looking away from Ayse.

"I know."

"No, you don't know, Ayse. We're not welcome in the West. We do not recognize Christ as the Son of God and they hate us because of it. They have always hated us, from the days before Mohammed's vision they disliked us — the people of the desert.

"Our skin is dark, our beliefs are different. We have different customs, traditions and cultures. If you choose to continue with Daniel, you will feel their malice. There will always be people wanting to break you apart. His father will never approve, especially because he is an imam. His church will not let him.

"It will be a hard and perilous journey you will undertake. Nothing will be easy for you, and your love will be tested a thousand times."

Ayse waited for the words she so had longed to hear. She could tell they were forthcoming by the tenderness embedded in her mother's words of warning. It came, not from anger or disappointment any longer, but from love. Her mother continued.

"But if you love him, then Allâh will find a way for you to have a life together. I disapprove of this relationship because I know how hard it will be. But I cannot disapprove of your love."

"Oh, Mother!"

Ayse threw her arms around Elif, and hugged her like a child again, finding comfort in her mother's strength and compassion.

Elif started to weep, as did her daughter, now wrapped in her arms. Their tears fell on the white blankets covering Ayse's bed. They fell and darkened the blankets, mixing and blending together as they did.

The Drive Back to Oglethorpe

T he radio blared another revival show from some obscure FM station. An aging Southerner was preaching loud and clear as the tires on the Ford Explorer gripped the cold asphalt of I-75.

"It's comin'. Lord knows the day is comin'! And y'all better be ready for it when it comes, 'cause if you're not all ready today, there won't be time fer it tomorrah.'"

Rebecca stared straight ahead. She studied the traffic ascending the next long, rolling hill a mile in front of her. Soon she would be heading up that hill, then down the following grade, up the one after that and on and on as if driving upon an ocean of massive swells. An ocean of red Georgia clay.

Rebecca was hypnotized by the highway, oblivious to the doomsday message of the FM preacher. Not paying any attention to her son sitting beside her. She was driving, absorbed in the rhythms of the highway.

Daniel had wanted to change stations but knew that by doing so he might awaken his mother from her trance. He'd decided not to touch the radio. He tuned out the sound of the preacher's voice just as the evangelist, working from a rundown radio station on the outskirts of Athens, Georgia, started asking the listeners to send him money.

"But savin' souls don't come easy, folks, and it don't come cheaply, either. We need your support to continue on with our mission here at 89.9 FM. We need your dollars to keep the Lord's message on the airwaves. To give the good people of this Earth an alternative to the kind of decadence and moral decay that seems ta permeate this society.

"So I'm askin' you to sit down, take out your checkbook and help us out today..."

The preacher continued on with his solicitation — 89.9 FM needed money. Daniel thought about it and realized he couldn't tell the difference between this evangelist's message and his father's sermon on New Year's Day. They both needed money. Money to continue on with their ministry of saving souls.

Saving them from what? asked Daniel. Saving them from not being allowed to see the girl they love? Is that what Christ had in mind two thousand years ago?

That's what my father thinks. He's forbidden me to see her again. I don't know if I can. And why should I? Why is it more important to obey my father than it is to obey my heart? I'm going to be twenty-one in four weeks. I'm my own person now and I don't need their money or their opinions. All I need is Ayse.

The Ford drew closer to Atlanta. The signs along the highway became more frequent as the chain restaurants and gas stations beside the off ramps sprang up thicker than the Southern pines. Atlanta was twenty minutes out, Oglethorpe a half-hour beyond. It was Rebecca who first broke the silence.

"Daniel, I hope you're going to respect your father's instructions when you get back to Oglethorpe."

Daniel didn't respond. He knew from past experience that there was more lecturing to come. He would wait.

"Your daddy doesn't want to see you make a mess of your life. This crush you have on this Turkish girl, you'll get over it. I can remember my first real boyfriend back in college, long before I met Clay. I thought that I'd simply die if we broke up.

"But I didn't die. He and I just grew apart after a spell and I hardly ever think of him any longer. It's just an infatuation, Daniel. Following your heart from this point forward won't accomplish anything. I'm sure her family feels the same."

"They don't feel the same," said Daniel.

"You mean they approve of you seeing each other? I can't believe that."

"Ayse e-mailed me two days ago and told me her parents disapprove of the relationship but will not stand in her way if she loves me."

"What is this world coming to? Why on earth would they do such a thing? Don't they realize that we, as God-fearing Christians, would never allow our boy to continue on with a woman whose religion denies the fact that Jesus is Lord? A faith whose roots are in the devil's hands.

"Well, I hope you did the right thing. I hope you e-mailed her back and said that your family would have none of it. That it was over, plain and simple."

"No, Mom, I didn't."

"Don't you remember what your father said before we left this morning?"

"Yes, how could I forget."

"He swore that if you continue on seeing this girl the consequences will be grim. He means it, Daniel. Don't test those waters, Son, you're likely to find them deeper than you think."

"I e-mailed Ayse back and said we're going to have to talk about it."

"That's better. It'll be more gentlemanly of you to ease her out of it. Let her know how we feel and how we've decided that it's better to end this recklessness, before it gets out of hand."

"How you've decided to end it for me, you mean."

Rebecca didn't respond to her son's cynical comment. She knew it would only lead to more of the same. She could tell by his tone that Daniel was sitting on the brink of yet another of his senseless rebellions.

Just like the long, ugly battle he had fought with his father over permission to go to a non-denominational university. She remembered how they used to have at it every other day until Clay, exhausted, decided to give in and allow him to attend Oglethorpe.

There had been other battles joined. His haircuts in junior high, his clothes, the books he read, the movies he rented, the list seemed endless. This relationship with the Turkish girl was another link in a bad chain.

As they approached West Pace's Ferry and exited the freeway, Rebecca resigned herself to the fact that Daniel would probably disobey his father. She knew he would continue seeing this Muslim girl. She was so sure of it she would have been surprised if anything else were to happen. Daniel was as stubborn as was his father, and she could tell by his comments this morning he was not about to break it off.

Clay would have stood a better chance of making Daniel break up with her had he insisted they become engaged, thought Rebecca to herself as she approached the crowded intersections near Buckhead. Saying "yes" would have ended it, but saying "no" made Daniel more determined than ever.

Fifteen minutes later, Daniel was unpacking his things from the back of the Explorer. He said farewell to his mother and promised to write, though he never did. He looked down the street and saw Randy's beat-up Honda. He was glad to know Randy was back.

Per their last e-mail, he was to meet Ayse at the Crypt tomorrow, Sunday, at noon. He couldn't wait to speak to Randy about what had transpired over the break. Daniel needed someone sane to talk to, even if that sanity was questionable.

Sunday at Noon

Daniel woke Sunday morning after a troubled sleep. At four in the morning he was tempted to make an entry into *Book of Midnights*. For reasons unknown, he decided not to. Instead, he lay awake and stared at the ceiling. This wasn't the first time he had neglected his midnight journal, nor would it be the last.

Even though sleep eluded him, he wasn't in the mood to write. He had filled twenty-four pages of his notebook over Christmas break and, whatever demons were haunting him this particular Sunday morning, he didn't feel like immortalizing them. All he wanted was to get back to sleep.

In large part, it was their planned rendezvous that caused his restlessness. The last four weeks had gone by as slowly as one galaxy passing another in the vacuum of space. He had missed Ayse tremendously. The thought of seeing her, holding her, gave him butterflies as he finished his bowl of Frosted Flakes.

After eating, Daniel brushed his teeth and slipped on his light, denim jacket. It was fifty degrees outside — sunny, windy and cold. Atlanta in January.

Daniel hollered a loud goodbye to his roommate, went out the door and bounded down the stairs. Randy didn't hear him, having arrived home stoned and inebriated at three in the morning from some makeshift spring semester kick-off party. At this point, a lightning storm wouldn't have stirred Randy.

Daniel walked the concrete path past the student center, the library and on toward Hearst Hall. The Crypt was the ideal place to meet her. It had become their curious refuge in a world filled with adversity. The large, welded stainless steel door was like the mysterious black meteor inside the Ka'ba in Mecca. The Crypt of Civilization had become their personal shrine, their place of pilgrimage.

As Daniel's foot hit the terrazzo floor in the basement of Hearst Hall he immediately looked toward the Crypt to see if she was there. She was.

She was sitting there on the cold terrazzo floor, her back against the shiny, metallic door with a smile on her face that could cut though that steel in a heartbeat. Daniel, his hair windblown, his face flush from the cold, smiled back as he approached her.

As he neared, Ayse jumped to her feet. They threw their arms around each other and embraced so tightly that their ribs might break. It was a hug that makes the cover of *Life* magazine, when a weary soldier returns to his girlfriend after fighting a long and dreadful war.

"Ayse, I've missed you," said Daniel, whispering into her ear as they embraced.

"I've missed you too, Daniel," she responded. "We've so much to talk about, but all I want to do is to hug you. Hug you until your bones break. Hug you to death."

Then they kissed. They kissed a kiss that spins on the axis of the earth and melts the polar ice caps in a flurry of tongues and lips. A kiss of synergy — whose forces meld and become greater than the forces of each of them alone. A kiss of waves smashing against the rocky, North Pacific shoreline. A kiss of comets.

In time, Daniel pulled away from his Turkish princess and took another, long intoxicating gaze at her. She was everything he had remembered and more. There was no way his memory could possibly have painted a portrait as lovely as that which stood before him. He was enraptured by her beauty, enchanted and willing to surrender everything to the armies of her dark eyes and olive skin. Love had conquered him.

"Let's go for a walk," he suggested.

"Yes, let's."

They walked up the stairwell and through the side door of Hearst Hall. A few straggling students, checking out where their spring classes would be held, or heading to the bookstore, quickly moved out of their way as they strolled toward the doorway. The look of love emanated from them like the beacon of a lighthouse on a stormy night. The students looked at the two of them with envy, hoping they, too, might someday find a love so radiant.

"It's wonderful to be with you again, Ayse," said Daniel as they walked outside and inhaled the cold, dry air of winter.

"Thank you, Daniel."

"We're going to have the best spring of our lives. I can hardly wait for the dogwoods to bloom. Maybe we can take a trip back up to the top of Kennesaw Mountain. Or better still, maybe we can borrow Randy's car and do some camping in the Smoky Mountains. We could take a drive along the Blue Ridge Parkway, camp and just hang out in the park for a few days."

"Daniel," said Ayse in a stern, motherly tone. "I'm not sure you could keep your hands off of me if we were alone in a tent together."

"We could take separate sleeping bags," asserted Daniel. "Then I wouldn't be able to get hold of you."

Ayse laughed aloud. She was neither dumb nor foolish. If they went camping together, they would have to take separate tents.

They soon approached the woods and the red clay path that led to their bridge. Once under the canopy of the bare trees, their conversation took on a heavier tone.

"What about your father?" asked Ayse, knowing Daniel probably didn't want to talk about it.

"To hell with my father!"

"Don't ever say that, Daniel! I don't like it when you speak about your parents that way. Your father loves you. All he wants is what's right for you."

"If he truly loved me, Ayse, he would let me love you. He loves his church, his parishioners and his position. He doesn't want my life to interfere with them. He can't handle the thought of me going out with a Muslim.

"If you could hear the things he says about your religion, Ayse, it would break your heart. He blames you for all of it. The terrorism, the subjugation of women, the unending trouble in the Middle East. It's all because of the evils of Islam.

"It's not about you, Ayse. It's about the stereotypes that exist in his perception of your religion. He hears the words Jihad, Hes Bulah, al-Qaida and he's convinced that every believer of Islam is in some holy war hellbent to destroy the

Christian world. Clay's convinced himself that an army of sword-wielding Muslims is about to ride over the next hill on horseback and kill everyone in his church some unsuspecting Sunday.

"You can't reason with him. God knows I've tried. Mom tends to be more understanding, but she would never, ever oppose my father. Clay talks about the Islamic subjugation of women but trust me, Ayse, my mother wears her own veil. She wouldn't dare speak out against him, nor would most of the women speak out against their husbands in our church. As a dutiful Southern Baptist wife, it's not permitted. It's all about looking pretty and being a good, submissive wife. You're a thousand times more liberated than most of the women who meet at the church guild every Tuesday night."

Ayse listened attentively. They were leaning on the bridge rail, looking down at the empty gully beneath them. The only time either of them had seen water flowing down this creek was during a heavy summer thunderstorm, or when there was a sudden snow melt after a rare snowfall. Most of the time it lay barren and dry, looking like an arroyo carved out of red Georgia clay.

"Your father has asked you to break up with me, has he not?"

"Yes. He's ordered me to stop seeing you, or face what he calls grim consequences."

"Then we must end it, Daniel. You must do as your father wishes. It is the right thing to do."

"No. I won't break up with you for his sake. Even if you refuse to see me, I will go on loving you, Ayse. I will go on loving you until the day I die. My father's wrong to meddle with my life. He has no right to tell me who I can and cannot love. I refuse to obey him.

"I love you and I want to be with you, Ayse. Whatever the consequences, I am willing to face them a million times more than I am willing to face a future without you."

"But he is your father. You must obey him, Daniel."

"Not when he asks me to stop seeing the woman I love. The only reason he wants us to part is because he doesn't want to tell his congregation that his only son, Daniel Mark Harris, has become involved with a Muslim. There would be too much shame and embarrassment for him to deal with. There would be too much talk.

"I won't live my life to save my father's sense of pride. He can do whatever he likes — pull my tuition, my college funding, cut me out of the will, whatever he decides to do, but he cannot make me stop seeing you. This is my life, Ayse, not his. These are our times, not theirs."

"If we do this, ours will be a difficult journey, Daniel. Do you have the strength to travel it?" asked Ayse, looking straight into Daniel's eyes.

"With you at my side, I have the strength for anything."

"As I wrote in my e-mail last week, my mother does not approve, but she will not stand in the way of our love. She's told me it will be very, very difficult for us. That we will have many trials and tribulations, with only our love to carry us through. I'm not sure I can do it, Daniel.

"My father, like your mother, is less troubled by us seeing each other. He has always loved America, and he feels I am old enough to make my own decisions. I am lucky to have such a father."

"He sounds like a nice man."

"He is, but he is also afraid for what lies ahead. Will we make it, Daniel?"

"We will if God wants us to make it. If we really love each other."

They embraced and kissed again beneath the bare trees of a Southern winter. The wind kicked up some dead leaves along the dry gully and the sun fell behind a passing cloud. There would be no turning back.

Months Later

"Are you coming home for Easter?"

"No, I've got some really tough classes, Mom, and I've decided to stay up here at Oglethorpe. With everyone home for the week, I'll have the library to myself. That'll give me a chance to catch up."

Rebecca grew suspicious. She never knew her son to be quite such a serious student. She was thinking it was something other than her son's GPA that was keeping him away. She decided to confront him about it.

"You're not still seeing her, that Turkish girl, are you?"

Daniel hesitated. It wasn't in his nature to lie. He would rather engage his father in a heated debate over a particular issue than hedge, or lie about his opinion. But under the circumstances, he had to come up with something.

"We're study partners. That's all. We help each other out from time to time with homework. We proof each other's essays and assignments."

"You're not romantically involved with her, are you, Daniel?"

Rebecca was giving her son the third degree. She suspected the worst. Daniel was stubborn, just like his father. She had doubted the day she dropped him off that he would break up with this girl.

"No, just study partners, Mom. She's just someone to do my homework with."

"Well, remember what your father said. We talked about it a few nights ago over dinner. He's dead serious, son. If he discovers you're still dating her, he'll pull the plug on your college tuition the same day, and you can't come back to me later and say I didn't warn you."

"You warned me, Mom. But remember, this isn't your life and it isn't your world any longer. It's a different time and the world has changed," Daniel said to his mother, attempting to justify his decision to keep seeing Ayse. Rebecca sighed as he continued.

"We can't keep thinking we're always right and they're always wrong. The world's become too small for that. Everyone's kind of right and everyone's kind of wrong. It's like we're a bunch of alley cats that have suddenly all been thrown into a small room together. The Internet, cell phones and mass media, they've drawn us closer. We've got to stop clawing at each other or we'll all end up getting hurt."

Rebecca listened at the other end of the line and realized her son Daniel was still in love. She could hear it in his voice, a voice familiar enough for a mother's intuition to know. This was not going to end well, and all of Daniel's philosophizing wouldn't mean a thing to Clay. All that there was left to do was to pray for her boy to come to his senses. Pray and wait.

"Well, Daniel, I'm not sure I understand what it is you're trying to say, but I can tell you this. If you don't break it off with her, you'll be the one who ends up getting hurt. Just keep that in mind the next time the two of you are studying together.

"If I were you, I'd find another study partner. The Lord says it's best to avoid temptation, and being near that young woman has to be very tempting for you."

Daniel realized his mother knew. She wouldn't say anything to his father but, since she already knew, he added his final request.

"Don't tell Dad I'm studying with Ayse, okay?"

"I won't. But promise me you'll try to break it off before summer?"

"I'll try."

"Goodbye Daniel, I'll see you in May."

"Bye Mom."

Daniel set down the receiver and felt disappointed in himself. He didn't like being deceitful to his mother. It was out of character.

But he knew under the circumstances that he couldn't tell his mother the truth. He couldn't tell her that their studies included long, luxurious kisses and impassioned evenings on the tattered sofa in the living room of his apartment. He couldn't mention that he was studying the young, delightful body of a twenty-year-old princess from Istanbul. He had memorized every contour of that body over the past few months. He knew the soft curves of her shoulders, the smooth skin of her long, graceful neck where his uncountable kisses fell. He knew the firmness of her breasts beneath his hands, her legs wrapped around him as they moved ever closer toward that inevitable night when they would go too far.

The night they would not be able to break it off and stop each other from doing what they both wanted to do — to make love. To be inside of her, lost within her soul and in doing so, to complete the circle.

Daniel had been studying Ayse all spring. He studied the sound of her tired voice past midnight talking about Jesus, Mohammed and God. He studied her motions, the way she threw back her long, dark hair and the way she smiled.

He studied the landscape of her heart, sensitive and warm, feminine and nurturing.

Ayse, in turn, had enjoyed herself as much as Daniel had. She loved working herself up into a deep sweat beneath his long kisses and powerful hands. She longed for the day he would take away the last vestige of her childhood and make her a woman.

In truth, neither of them were going to spend Easter break in the library. They had booked a campsite in Cades Cove, in the Smoky Mountain National Park. Daniel had managed, using a fifty-dollar bill, to send his roommate home without his car for the week. He thanked the overpaying Robert James Paint Company for his bribery money as he handed Randy the cash. Together, he and Ayse had borrowed a tent and two sleeping bags from some fellow students.

They would leave on Wednesday and return on Sunday. Ayse had made Daniel swear to her that he would not try to seduce her while they stayed in their tent under a cold spring sky in the mountains. But secretly, Ayse hoped Daniel wouldn't keep his oath. She knew she had promised her mother not to have relations with this boy until they were wed, but her promise was fast losing ground to her youthful passions.

Ayse was excited about this camping trip. Excited and afraid.

✪

The rusted Honda pulled away late Wednesday afternoon, heading north along Highway 19 toward North Carolina. It rolled through Roswell and Cumming, hitting the foothills of the Appalachians at Dahlonega. After driving through that small country town, the highway climbed steadily, running by DeSoto Falls and Blairsville.

Soon they were in the high country. The sights and scents of a mountain spring were everywhere. They drove straight through, stopping to refill in Bryson City. Their campsite was reserved beginning Thursday night, so they had planned all along to spend the first night of their journey in a motel near Cherokee. After filling up, they decided to stay on Highway 19. That route took them through the tiny town of Ela and along the valley cut by the Cherokee River.

On the outskirts of Cherokee they pulled into a small, inexpensive motel. It was called the Bluebird Motel, complete with a classic neon sign and a cracked swimming pool devoid of water. The motel sat beside the river and, though rundown and tired, it still had a charming location.

It was getting dark and they were road-weary from the long drive. Daniel parked the car beside the motel office and they went inside to book a room.

The old neon sign had read *vacancy* and a hand-drawn, red-and-white poster below the sign advertised: ALL ROOMS, $29.95. It was a price that appealed to two college kids on a weekend junket.

Daniel winked at Ayse as he opened the door for her. This was going to be the first time they would spend the night together. They had stayed up late many evenings before this but Daniel had always ended up walking Ayse home. Evenings that meant walking her home at two, sometimes three in the morning.

Tonight would be different. Tonight they wouldn't have to think about Randy bursting in on them, or Daniel's mother calling unexpectedly. Tonight they would be alone under a rising moon on the edge of a river fresh with the spring snow melt. Alone beneath a blackening sky filled with the sounds of returning whippoorwills.

Daniel rang the desk bell and waited for the motel clerk to come out of the back room, which also served as the living quarters. They waited longer than they should have.

After ringing the bell a second time the clerk came out of his apartment and left the door cracked just enough to hear the sounds of the game show, *Wheel of Fortune*, blaring on a big-screen TV. The clerk looked unkempt and unshaven.

"Can I help y'all?"

"We'd like a room, please. Non-smoking, twin beds."

The motel clerk turned around and studied his key board. There were a dozen keys still hanging on it. He turned around and said, "I've only got one non-smoking room left, but it's only got a double bed in it. If you want a room with twins, you'll have to take one of our smoking rooms."

The clerk wondered what was going on. To him, the young girl looked to be an Indian. Probably from the reservation up the way, he thought. But if she was an Indian trying to pick up some extra cash it didn't make sense to him, with the young kid asking for a room with twin beds in it. Strange, he thought.

Maybe they were lovers. They look like lovers, but if they were, why the twin beds? Just another variation on his motel mantra, "I've seen it all."

Daniel turned to Ayse for a quick conference. The double bed would make a difficult situation worse. He wondered if the smoking room might not prove safer for them in the long run.

"Which would you prefer?" he asked Ayse.

"The single bed," said Ayse, smiling her delicious smile.

"We'll take the non-smoking room with the one bed in it, please."

"That's room number twenty six. That'll be thirty-two seventy-five with the tax. Would you like to pay now or square up with me in the mornin'?"

"We'll pay now."

As Daniel pulled out his wallet and handed the man two twenties, the clerk went back to studying the young, attractive girl. Her accent wasn't Cherokee. He looked her over once again, this time more carefully.

Ayse was wearing a pair of threadbare blue jeans, Nike running shoes and a dark blue Oglethorpe University sweatshirt. Her hair was hanging down along her shoulders in a waterfall of auburn, and her eyes sparkled — even in the poor light of the lobby.

She must be from Europe or somethin', reasoned the clerk. Her accent ain't American, that's fer sure. The clerk took the forty dollars, placed it in the cash drawer and handed the change back to Daniel along with the room key.

"You'll have to fill out this here form before you go get yourself comfortable. I didn't catch your name?"

"Daniel and Ayse Harris."

"Well, just complete this registration and then you can move right in. It'll be a right cool evening tonight. If you leave your window cracked a might y'all can hear the sound of the river. Puts me to sleep every time."

Daniel filled out the registration after sending Ayse out to check the number on the Honda's license plate. The clerk remained confused by this pairing. Why would a young man, who says he's married to this girl, not want to sleep in the same bed with her? And why would he have to send her out to find their own plate number?

That's what the motel clerk loved about the motel business — the weirdos you meet and the stories they concoct. From hookers to homosexuals, drunks to underage kids on prom night, every one of them paying $29.95 — plus tax.

"Have a good one," said the disheveled clerk as they headed out the front door.

"We will," replied Daniel.

❂

Daniel unlocked the door of the motel room and looked inside. It looked as he had expected it might. The walls were covered in dark brown paneling, the only artwork was a cheaply framed print of an autumnal landscape hanging above the bed.

The nineteen-inch television sat on a brown Formica chest of drawers. There was a remote control sitting on top of the TV set with black electrical tape wrapped around the batteries. The single luggage rack stood beside the one mismatched chair.

The room had a funny, musty smell to it, and when Daniel looked into the bathroom, he could see traces of mold growing along the edge of the shower. Still, it was okay for the price and the mattress was firm and comfortable. It would have to do.

Ayse came in behind him, carrying a small overnight bag and a sleeping bag for herself. Daniel laughed when she threw it on the bed.

"What's with the sleeping bag?"

"It's my personal protection device," replied Ayse. She continued. "If you think I'm going to get under those covers without having my own sleeping bag then you are dumber than you look, Daniel Mark Harris."

He laughed out loud and as he did he sprang at Ayse, knocking both of them onto the double bed. Once there, he quickly wrapped his arms around her and started kissing her.

"I'll scream!" she announced.

Daniel stopped. He had only been feigning his attack and Ayse knew it. The real test would come later, after dark.

"So you think your sleeping bag will protect you from these hungry hands?"

"Daniel, don't start in. You know our arrangement. I've made a promise to my mother and I'm not about to break it."

Daniel climbed off his princess and went back out to the car to get the rest of their things. He left his sleeping bag in the trunk of the Honda.

While he was out getting his belongings Ayse took a change of clothes and went into the small bathroom.

"Want to go into Cherokee for dinner tonight?" yelled Daniel through the thin bathroom door.

"Sounds good, just wait until I shower and clean up a bit."

"Need any help in there?"

"NO!"

Girls, thought Daniel — they love to shower. Daniel grabbed the remote and threw himself on the bed, hitting the on button while still bouncing. He raced through the cable stations looking for something worth watching. He could hear the shower starting and couldn't help but think about being in that shower with her.

He couldn't help but imagine himself soaping her back or helping her wash her thick, dark hair. Although they had spent many an evening on the couch together, he had yet to see her naked. Soon, he comforted himself with that thought as he surfed the cable channels. Soon.

They had dinner in town at a local Denny's. It was a nondescript meal with the only outstanding quality being the price. They took a quick drive around town, heading up past the casino, then drove to their motel room under a thick canopy of darkness.

When they got back to the motel, they parked the car and decided to go for a stroll along the river. The Cherokee was flowing fast, running up near the top edge of the bank. It was the spring freshet. There were no rapids near this section of the river but the sound of the rushing current against the rocky shoals was impressive.

"This is perfect, Daniel," said Ayse as she sat on a small plain bench the motel had placed a few feet off the river.

"Yes, this is what I love about the mountains."

They embraced. Ayse lay her head on Daniel's sturdy shoulder and they fell into a trance, a hypnosis induced by the roar of the cascading stream. The moon rose in the east and the night sky wrapped around them like a black, star-studded blanket.

After awhile, Daniel took his left hand, placing a single finger on Ayse's chin and lifted her head up to be kissed. She had no willpower to resist, so perfect was this moment. As she kissed him, the distant scent of dogwoods and blossoms filled the air. The sound of the river grew louder, making the rest of the world disappear.

They stayed on that bench for an hour, kissing, holding hands and talking about nothing in particular. They were timeless. It might have been now, it might have been ten thousand years ago, as two Cherokee lovers embraced beside this same river, on this same moonlit night.

In time, the night air grew cool and damp. Ayse told Daniel she was chilled and wanted to go back to their room. Daniel agreed.

Once into the motel room Ayse took her pajamas out of her bag and went into the bathroom to put them on. Daniel burst with laughter when Ayse walked out of the bathroom. She looked absurd, wearing full-length flannel pajamas that covered more of her than the clothes she had worn earlier.

"I'm to assume your pajamas are yet another line of defense," said Daniel.

"They certainly are," responded Ayse while crawling into her sleeping bag on top of the covers.

"We'll see about that."

Daniel unabashedly took off his pants and shirt right before Ayse. He had on plaid boxers and a plain white T-shirt. He grabbed the worn remote and crawled under the blankets beside his girlfriend. After flipping through a dozen stations, he hit the off button and reached for Ayse.

"No," she said.

"No what?" he answered.

"You're not going to touch me tonight. Remember, you promised."

"Please," he begged.

"No begging either, it's not becoming."

Daniel rolled over and started to pout. He hoped it might work. Within five minutes he started to feel Ayse's lips kissing the back of his neck. He didn't say a thing. Her kisses felt so incredibly wondrous.

Daniel had listened to the instructions of the motel clerk and cracked the window facing the river. With the television off, the room soon filled with the sound of the rushing water and the elusive fragrances of a mountain spring.

Daniel rolled back over and met Ayse's lips. With the blankets and sleeping bag still between them they started in. They were soon kicking away bedspread, blanket and sleeping bag layers as they tried to get closer to one another.

Ayse's hands slipped beneath Daniel's T-shirt. Daniel responded in kind, his hands slipping beneath her flannel pajamas. Soon his T-shirt and her pajama top were lying on the floor beside the pile of blankets and sheets.

The moonlight, as if by design, poured through the open window and drenched the room in a pale, misty hue. The two lovers were now entangled in a dance that could only end in the coda of a *pas de deux.*

In a whispered voice, mixed with her breathlessness, Ayse spoke softly into Daniel's ear. "We have to stop."

Daniel, knowing it might come to this, answered Ayse in his own regretful whisper, "No, we can't."

"Daniel," Ayse continued, her body sweating and her breathing heavy from their passion, "I cannot let you make love to me. I know you want to, and believe me, I know I want you to. More than anything else in the world I want you to be inside of me. I want to make love to you until the sun follows the moon in the east. But we must not do this."

Daniel rolled off her and sighed. She was right. Ayse continued:

"I have already broken one promise to my family and I cannot do this if it means breaking another. I have never been with a man. And when I decide to give myself to a man, I want him to be you. But if I don't keep my promise, then I will think badly of both of us, and our feelings toward each other will never be the same."

Daniel laid back in the bed, still panting from the last half-hour of foreplay. He stared blankly at the off-white popcorn ceiling above them. The moonlight filled the room with a milky glow, the river sang its spring freshet song and the scents of night blooms wafted in from the open window. He looked to Ayse, lying beside him half undressed, her breasts rising and falling with every breath, and spoke without thinking.

"Let's get married tomorrow."

Ayse's eyes widened. She was caught unaware, as was Daniel.

"Are you proposing to me?"

"Yes, I guess I am. We can drive over Newfound Gap and get married in one of those wedding chapels in Gatlinburg. Then we can go to our campsite and have the best honeymoon in the world.

"A honeymoon in a tent. What could be better?"

"But I have to ask my family."

"Why? You know what they'll say – they'll disapprove. Just as my family will disapprove if I ask them. You're still a Muslim and I'm still a Christian. But Ayse, what difference does that really make?"

Ayse cuddled up to Daniel's bare chest and wrapped her long, slender arms around him. He was right. Elif and Mustapha would never allow it. They would want her to fly back to Istanbul to discuss it and once there, do everything in their power to dissuade her. If they did grant her permission, it would only come after months of pleading. And Daniel's father, thought Ayse to herself as she lay in his arms, would never allow them to marry. He would sooner disown his son than give his blessings to a marriage between his child and a Muslim.

"Yes," she whispered in her lover's ear. "Yes, I'll marry you."

They didn't make love that night. They lay awake beside each other until late, late into the darkness thinking about what would happen tomorrow, and what would happen beyond. They were young lovers, doing what lovers have always done – throwing caution to the wind. Believing their love could weather the storm that gathered before them. Praying to God, to Allâh, to watch over them once they set sail across those turbulent seas. Praying until the peace of sleep overcame them.

Their Wedding Day

Spring saturated the morning. The sun rose in the east, seeming to be an hour ahead of schedule and anxious to chase the dew off the lime-green buds. The bluebirds, mockingbirds and returning robins joined in a chorus of song as daylight sliced through the cool mountain air. The trout in the Cherokee rose and fed ravenously on the first hatch of insects, fighting against the rushing currents as they did.

"Happy is the bride upon whom the sun shines," whispered Daniel into his lover's ear beside him. Ayse stirred. She turned herself toward him, her body safe and warm in her sleeping bag. Then she smiled. Ayse didn't have to say anything, her smile said it for her.

"Time to rise and shine," said Daniel, this time a little bit louder. "It's a fabulous morning out there and we've got quite a day ahead of us. It's our wedding day."

Ayse got out of her sleeping bag, still wearing her flannel pajamas, and grabbed some clothes out of her small suitcase. As she did, she couldn't help but wonder what she was going to wear on her wedding day. In a way, she didn't care, but in another way, a woman's way, she did.

She went into the shower as Daniel rolled up her sleeping bag and packed their things in the Honda. Ayse came out of the bathroom fifteen minutes later, looking luminous.

Daniel walked back into the room, took one long, savoring look at his bride to be and felt himself the luckiest man in the world. Ayse could see the look in his eyes and knew they were meant for each other. Despite the thousands of miles and centuries of religious contention between their respective tribes, they were a match made in Heaven.

"You look stunning, Ayse."

"Thank you," replied Ayse. "I do have one problem, Daniel."

"And that is?"

"What am I going to wear?"

Daniel laughed. He looked at his bride to be and realized that she was standing there, on her wedding day, wearing a pair of khaki slacks, a short-sleeve light-blue denim blouse and a pair of hiking boots. She looked wonderful, but not exactly bridelike.

"We'll have to buy something in Gatlinburg. They've got a dozen wedding chapels there, they must have a few stores that cater to them."

In the back of Daniel's mind, the thought suddenly occurred to him as to how on earth he was going to pay for all this. He had his father's emergency credit card, but charging any part of this wedding was certainly going to alert his father to the marriage. Ayse and he had decided that, although they would marry, they would keep their marriage a secret until the semester at Oglethorpe was over. That way, reasoned Daniel, should his father pull the plug, he would at least have completed two years of college.

Ayse agreed. She could return briefly to Istanbul to tell her parents in person, gather her things, and return to be with Daniel in Atlanta. He had over twenty thousand dollars his grandmother had left him in a trust fund and they planned to use that money to get started. While Ayse was away, Daniel would find them an apartment near the college. He knew he would have to drop out of Oglethorpe for a year or two, but for his Ayse, he would have dropped out of Harvard.

I'll do a cash advance, thought Daniel to himself as he stepped into the shower. If my father says anything I'll tell him Randy and I went camping up in the mountains and Randy's car broke down. I'll think of something.

After showering, Daniel and Ayse hopped into the car and drove along the river valley into Cherokee. They pulled through a McDonald's and grabbed some fast-food breakfast. They were anxious to cross over the Smokies and get into Gatlinburg before noon.

They stayed on Highway 441 and started the long, meandering climb toward Newfound Gap. They were in a state of euphoria.

"Look at these views. Aren't they wonderful," said Daniel as they wound their way toward the high divide.

"I've never seen anything so beautiful, Daniel."

Every corner, every turn, unveiled another glorious panorama. Soft white clouds of morning fog still laid in the ravines, while the rich greens of unfolding leaves contrasted sharply with the dark colors of the pines and hemlocks. The dogwoods smothered the understory in a display of brilliant white while the sun climbed above the panorama.

At the crest, they pulled off at the scenic view area to take in one more intoxicating view of the park before descending into Tennessee.

"It reminds me of our afternoon on Kennesaw," said Daniel.

"Better than that, Daniel. Because today is the day we become one."

Daniel took her into his arms, and despite the crowd of onlookers that surrounded them, kissed her long and deep. It was a wedding kiss, and he didn't care if the entire world was standing beside them.

A few adults rolled their eyes and some nearby children laughed as they witnessed these two lovers kissing. Daniel and Ayse took no notice. They were soaring high above the world of parking lots and sightseers. Soaring on the wings of a kiss.

✪

Three miles beyond the park boundary, the town of Gatlinburg, Tennessee, jumped out at them like a honky-tonk in paradise. As they drove down Parkway Drive, they were yanked from a world of sublime beauty to a ceaseless array of motels, Ripley's Believe It or Not, aquariums, tourist traps and souvenir shops. The contrast between the serenity of the park and the mayhem of Gatlinburg was overwhelming.

"Well, what do you think?" asked Daniel of his bride to be.

"I don't like it."

"No, it's not exactly where I would have wanted us to be wed, but we'll be back inside the park before dark, and Cades Cove is one of my favorite places in the world."

"It's so tacky," remarked Ayse.

"Massive tacky, hemorrhaging tacky," said Daniel in agreement.

They found a place to park near the northern edge of the strip. Amid the bumper-to-bumper traffic, the overweight tourists eating ice cream at eleven in the morning, the ceaseless rock shops, T-shirt joints and buffet restaurants, they managed to locate a store that specialized in Gatlinburg weddings. Weddings not unlike those performed in Las Vegas. Quick, inexpensive marriages that seldom last.

Hurried elopements that end a year later in trailer parks and unwanted pregnancies. Dimestore marriages, witnessed by strangers working for eight dollars an hour with ceremonies performed by licensed ministers feigning affections to couples they met an hour ago. Ministers or justices of the peace thinking about their next scheduled marriage, and what's on TV tonight.

Daniel and Ayse picked out simple but affordable clothes for their wedding. Ayse purchased a white dress with lace applique. The applique had seed pearls scattered across the bodice of the gown. The cut of the dress kept tight to her youthful body, and with her dark skin, it made Ayse appear more resplendent than the sunlight that washed over southern Tennessee.

Daniel picked up a simple black sports coat with a white shirt, black tie and matching pants. They stood in front of the full-length mirrors at Harriet's Wedding Shop and looked at each other longingly. Bride and groom to be, all for under four hundred dollars.

They asked one of Harriet's employees where the least expensive wedding chapels were and what they had to do to be married before the end of the day. She told them about a place called Cloud Nine Weddings. She had one of their brochures behind the counter and handed it to Daniel. He read it aloud to Ayse.

"You bring us your angel, and we'll provide the cloud. Wedding performed for sixty dollars."

"Well, what do you think, Ayse?"

She didn't respond. She smiled at him in agreement. She remembered her older brother's wedding five years ago. The banquet the night before, the lengthy Turkish ceremony and the celebration that followed. She realized she would have none of this. But her thoughts served to remind her she was marrying a Christian and her parents would never throw such a celebration for this marriage. They wouldn't invite all of the distant relatives from Ankara or Izmir. She would never have such a wedding and, understanding that, she didn't want to dwell on it.

"Sounds perfect, Daniel."

They changed back into their camping clothes and, after making two trips to the cash machine, settled up with the store. Their next stop was to the Gatlinburg Shilling Center for the marriage license.

First they had to go back and get the car. After telling the attendant they were getting married, he volunteered to allow them to come back in and park at no additional charge.

"Congratulations!" the attendant added as they walked toward their car.

The clerk behind the counter at the Shilling Center was perfunctory and detached. She was an older woman, nearing sixty, who had seen too many ecstatic couples to take note of the pair presently standing at her counter.

"Here's the form, please fill everything out and then I'll need to see some kind of IDs. You're both over eighteen, aren't you?"

Ayse looked at Daniel and smiled — they were over eighteen and crazy in love.

"Yes, I'm twenty-one. Ayse's twenty."

"Well, I'm still going to need to see some kind of ID," said the matronly county employee.

Daniel reached for his wallet and took out his Georgia driver's license while Ayse rummaged through her handbag looking for her passport. They handed them to the woman behind the counter.

"Ayse Yalçin? Is that how you pronounce it?"

"Yalçin, like yell sin."

"You're from Turkey, right?"

"Yes, I'm from Istanbul."

"I had an uncle who was stationed in Turkey back in the sixties. He said it was a real nice place. He used to spy on the Russians from some little town along the Black Sea, a place called Sinop, if I recall. Said the people there were right friendly. Y'all ever been to Sinop?"

"No, but I know where it is," answered Ayse.

"Well, he liked it over there, that's all I know. Now, I'll go and make a photocopy of your IDs and you two can fill out the paperwork."

The woman hobbled off to the back office while Daniel and Ayse stood at the counter and filled out their marriage license application. When the clerk returned, she handed them their IDs, carefully purveyed the paperwork and said, "Looks good, that'll be thirty-six dollars, cash or check."

Daniel took out his wallet and gave her two twenties. She made change from a small cash drawer under the counter and handed them a copy of the license.

"Congratulations," said the woman as the two of them headed out. "And remember, it's valid for only thirty days."

✪

Daniel and Ayse climbed back into the Honda and drove the short distance into town. They parked in the same lot and the attendant winked at them as they drove in. After parking, they walked to the Parkway and headed toward traffic light number six, their wedding clothes folded neatly in their shopping bags.

"There it is, right across from the aquarium," said Daniel, pointing to the small wedding chapel where they were about to be married.

Above the shop's entrance, there was a small sign that read, *YOU BRING YOUR ANGEL AND WE'LL PROVIDE THE CLOUD.* As they walked through the door, Daniel felt ecstatic, knowing he'd found his angel.

"May I help you?" asked the woman behind the counter.

"Yes. We'd like to get married."

"Did you have an appointment?"

"No, we just arrived this morning. Do we need an appointment?"

"No, we're not all that busy today. If you had come last Saturday, you would have needed one. On a good Saturday we'll do ten, sometimes twenty marriages a day. If you don't have an appointment, you can end up waiting for quite a spell.

"Do you have your marriage license with you?"

"Yes, it's right here," said Daniel as he pulled it out of his shopping bag and handed it to the woman behind the counter.

She looked it over and said, "Everything looks fine. Just give me a couple of minutes and I'll find someone to cover for me."

"You're going to marry us?" asked Ayse.

"Sure, I'm a minister."

"Are you a Baptist?" questioned Daniel, curious as to her faith.

"No, I'm a minister in the Universal Life Church. We're nondenominational."

"Oh, I'm not familiar with them. Is there somewhere for us to get into our wedding clothes?"

"There's a changing room down the hallway. The men's room is on the right and the ladies' on the left. When you're finished, come back out here and I'll take you over to the chapel area."

"Thanks, we'll be a few minutes."

Daniel and Ayse walked down the hallway together and kissed before going into their respective dressing rooms. As Ayse was putting on her gown, the reality of what she was doing took hold of her.

She shivered as she took off her camping clothes and put on her long, pure-white wedding dress. She shivered because she was frightened, not because she was cold. She realized she was making a commitment to a person that would last her entire life. There was no one for her to confide in, no one to ask if she was doing the right thing. Doubt began to overwhelm her. She looked at herself in the dressing room mirror and began to cry.

Daniel finished before Ayse and waited outside her dressing room. As if sensing her apprehensions, he knocked quietly on her door.

"Ayse, are you all right in there?"

"No," she said in a quivering voice.

"Can I come in?"

"Yes."

Daniel went in. He saw her standing there, weeping gently in her long, lovely gown and immediately wrapped his arms around her, smothering her in tenderness.

"We don't have to go through with this, Ayse, not if you're not sure. I don't want to see you unhappy."

The strength of his arms and the sound of his voice reassured her. The angel in the white dress felt safe again, comforted by the knowledge that he was willing to release her if she so desired. Ayse was consoled by the knowledge that Daniel loved her enough to set her free. She confided in him, "Daniel, I'm scared."

"So am I, Ayse, so am I. Here, I have something for you."

"What?"

Daniel reached into his pocket and pulled out a small, black plastic film canister. He handed it to her, then looked at her and said, "Look inside, it's for you."

Ayse took the plastic lid off the film canister. Inside, she found it filled with a wad of white cotton. She handed the empty canister back to Daniel and carefully unfolded the cotton. In an instant, she found the ring. Upon finding it, her doubts vanished.

"Where, how did you..."

Daniel saw her face fill with delight as she took the ring in her delicate fingers.

"It's so incredibly beautiful, Daniel. It looks old. Did you buy it this morning?"

"It's my grandmother's wedding ring. My mother gave it to me two years ago when I left home for Oglethorpe. She said my grandmother wanted me to have it. My grandmother told my mother that, when I found my bride, my angel, I could give it to her.

"You are my angel, Ayse. You are the most lovely, most beautiful princess in the world. I want you to have this ring. Go ahead, try it on."

Ayse looked at her husband to be, dressed in his black sports coat and white shirt, and her eyes sparkled like a galaxy. With her hands shaking slightly, she took the antique diamond wedding ring and slipped it on the ring finger of her left hand. It fit as though a jeweler had spent his morning hammering the platinum setting to the exact size.

"It fits perfectly, doesn't it?"

"Yes, but how did you know?"

"I just knew."

There were two women at the counter when Daniel and Ayse returned from the dressing rooms. The minister and a young, urbanized girl with dyed, purple-black hair and two silver nose rings.

"Why, don't you two look fabulous!" exclaimed the minister.

"Thanks," said Daniel.

"By the way, my name's Sharon, Sharon Keller."

"I'm Daniel Harris and this is Ayse Yalçin."

"I already know your names. Remember, I read the marriage license. Shall we head over to the chapel and get started?"

"Yes, sounds great," answered Daniel.

The three of them walked down a hallway with small rooms off either side. One of the rooms was decorated like an old Western saloon, and another looked like a turn of the century parlor. During the week, when the wedding business was slow, the shop doubled as a photography studio catering to the tourist trade. Couples and families would come in, dress up in cowboy outfits or turn of the century costumes and have their portraits taken. Businesses typical of tourist towns like Gatlinburg and Dollywood, which was just up the highway a half-hour.

At the end of the hallway they entered a small room. Inside was a white, slatted trellis covered in showers of red silk roses. A large, photographic mural depicting a mountain scene, complete with a waterfall, stood behind the trellis. The cloud itself was an old, electric fog machine that never quite worked. Some weddings had delicate, ankle-deep clouds beneath them, some weddings went without clouds and, sometimes, the couple had to evacuate the room amidst a cloud that reduced visibility to zero. A new machine was on order.

Sharon pressed the button that operated the cloud machine when the three of them entered the chapel room and said a silent prayer to herself, hoping this couple wouldn't be blindly feeling their way out of the fog bank in three minutes' time like the Japanese couple last week. That pair was eventually married in the saloon, dressed like an Asian version of Matt Dillon and Kitty. A goofy Japanese-*Gunsmoke* wedding.

To Sharon's delight, the cloud machine worked. This was a marriage meant to be, she decided.

"Perhaps the two of you could stand right here. Do you have rings?"

"Only one," answered Daniel, handing Sharon his grandmother's filigree wedding ring.

"What's that ring on your right hand?"

"That's my class ring, from Macon High," said Daniel.

"Well, we'll use that one. Maybe you can buy a wedding band this afternoon at one of the local jewelers. If you show them our card, you will receive an additional ten percent off."

Daniel slipped off his class ring and handed it to Sharon. She turned to Ayse, and seeing the nervous look on her face, tried to relax her before they got started.

"I noticed you're from Istanbul, is that right?"

"Yes, have you been to Istanbul?"

"No, but I'd love to go there someday. Are you Muslim?"

"Yes, how did you know?"

"I just guessed. I've married Muslim couples before. In fact, over the years I've been doing this, I've married just about every mix of couples imaginable.

"I've married Jewish couples, black couples, the list is endless."

"Yes, but Daniel's not Islamic. He's a Southern Baptist."

"Oh, that doesn't matter. I've married Hindu girls to Jewish guys, black women marrying white men, American Indians to Vietnamese, Jehovah's Witnesses to Buddhists, you name it. Practically any combination you might imagine, and I've probably stood here, over the past fifteen years, and pronounced them all man and wife.

"Believe me when I tell you, love is color-blind and nondenominational. Love is bigger than the way most of us see the world, always dividing it up by who's black, who's white, who believes in that God and who follows this God. It's silly when you stop and think about it. We're all just people, trying to find happiness in a world filled with troubles.

"That's what I like about my ministry, the Universal Life Church. It's large enough for everyone to belong to, like it states right off, it's universal. If you two love each other, and your love runs deep and true, then that's all that matters. The only thing I've learned over the years is this — with love, anything is possible."

Ayse smiled, knowing the woman who was about to marry them was right — with love, anything is possible.

The ceremony went flawlessly. The cloud machine produced the finest, purest white cloud Sharon had ever seen. Sharon had Daniel and Ayse read their vows from a standard script and the ring exchange was magical. She took a single, black-and-white photo of them as they kissed, at an additional charge of ten dollars.

They walked back to the front counter, where Sharon signed and notarized their wedding certificate, keeping two forms she needed to send to the state of Tennessee within the next three days.

Daniel and Ayse didn't bother to change before leaving. They decided to stay in their wedding clothes for a while, walking down the Parkway beaming with joy.

They were two angels, euphorically in love, walking to a jewelry store to purchase a ninety-nine dollar wedding band. With the discount, it would come to ninety-five dollars, tax included.

As tourists congratulated them and cars honked, they walked down the Parkway. A Gatlinburg marriage made in Heaven. A marriage between a Muslim girl and a Christian boy – until death do they part.

In the Tent

Ayse looked at the open sky through the mosquito netting at the top of the tent's dome. The starlight filtered through the netting in irregular patterns, leaving her the impression they were sleeping outside. Normally the nylon rain fly would have covered the dome of the tent, but when they made camp later that same afternoon, Daniel had decided that rain was unlikely. On their honeymoon night, they would let the starlight shine on them.

Ayse could hear the crackling of their campfire, whose orange glow was intensified through the red nylon fabric. She looked at her bare arm in the dim light and it looked as though her skin were the color of burgundy.

Daniel had gone to the car to bring in a bottle of inexpensive Champagne and two plastic glasses. In the distance she could hear him above the sound of the campfire, opening the front door of the Honda and flipping the trunk latch, hearing the sound of the ice rattling in the cooler.

She hurriedly unzipped the sleeping bags and spread them on the plastic floor of the tent. One bag became a thin mattress over the sandy base of the tent pad and the other she saved for a blanket, keeping away the chilled air of a spring evening.

"Ayse, could you unzip the tent please, my hands are full."

"Of course, my husband," said Ayse, getting up from under the thick blanket.

Daniel liked the sound of her words. A surge of pride ran through him as he sat beside his new bride. Without saying anything, he unwrapped the wire mesh holding the cork of Champagne and opened the bottle. The loud pop momentarily disrupted the quiet of the night.

As Ayse held out the plastic glasses, Daniel poured the bubbly liquid into them. In the dim light of the campfire, Ayse could see the look of delight on her husband's face. She remembered the words of the minister who married them earlier that day, "With love, anything is possible." This night was possible.

"Here's to us," said Daniel, setting the bottle down in a corner and holding his plastic glass to his bride. They took their arms and wrapped them around each other as they sipped the Champagne.

"It tastes funny."

"It tastes like Champagne, Ayse. It tastes like it's supposed to taste."

"I've never had Champagne before. I've had white wine, but it doesn't have the bubbles."

"Yeah, it's easy for me to forget that you don't drink very much. Everyone in America drinks, even those who say they don't. A friend of mine told me a good joke about that."

"Tell it to me, please."

"I will, but I doubt you'll get it."

"I'll try."

"All right. How do you tell the difference between a Baptist and a Methodist?"

"I don't know," answered Ayse.

"A Methodist will say hello to you in a liquor store."

Ayse looked at her husband and laughed. "I don't get it," she said.

"I knew you wouldn't, you beautiful Muslim."

"Why wouldn't a Baptist say hello to you in a liquor store?"

"Because Baptists aren't supposed to be in liquor stores. They don't drink. The irony being, almost all of them do."

"Oh," said Ayse.

"Do your mother and father drink?"

"Once in a great while they have a glass of wine, and my father keeps a few bottles of beer in the refrigerator, but he rarely opens one."

"Do you dance?"

"We love to dance."

"Then tonight, let's dance."

Daniel took a second, long drink of his Champagne and set his empty glass next to the bottle. Ayse took one more small sip and handed her half-filled glass to Daniel. The Champagne was his idea. He wanted to have some kind of celebration and, on their meager budget, a bottle of Spanish Freixenet was all he could afford.

Ayse said she would celebrate with him, but the taste of Champagne didn't appeal to her. Daniel finished her drink and set her empty glass inside his. He then leaned over and kissed his bride. Unlike the taste of Champagne, the taste of Daniel's lips upon hers appealed to Ayse. The dance had begun.

The night unfolded in a symphony of skin. The sound of the unreplenished campfire faded as the stars paraded past the skylight above the young lovers. They unwrapped each other like children unwrapping gifts on their first Christmas. Soon, they were both naked beneath the warm flannel of the sleeping bag.

By midnight, Ayse was no longer a girl, but a woman. A woman in a red tent, in a mountain valley in a foreign land with a man she loved more than she thought was possible.

A husband and wife awoke at dawn. As the red nylon turned the interior of the tent to a thousand shades of pink, they made love again. Everything had changed and everything was flawless in the cold, mountain air of dawn.

The next three days, hiking, spotting wild deer and turkeys along the ten-mile drive through the valley, were the best days Ayse had ever known. She was not Turkish, or Muslim, or anything except a young, sparkling bride enjoying her honeymoon with a spirited young man from south Georgia.

The sun shone without a reprieve for the three days they camped in the Smokies. God knew the clouds would arrive soon enough.

Three A.M. Tuesday

Book of Midnights

It felt so strange, taking off my wedding band as Ayse and I drove into Oglethorpe. I've had it on less than a week, and it seems wrong to be removing it so soon. But it makes sense, and both Ayse and I agree that it's the right thing to do.

Until the semester is over, we've decided to keep our marriage a secret. Even Randy, who asked me yesterday afternoon how the camping trip went, doesn't suspect we're no longer merely seeing each other, but married. Without my wedding band on, or my grandmother's ring on Ayse's finger, who's to know?

That's the beauty of Gatlinburg weddings. They have an aura of anonymity. That and their budget pricing. Even with our shopping spree, our entire wedding cost less than six hundred dollars. I can remember my mother and father discussing Ruth's wedding five years ago. Her wedding costs exceeded the twenty-four thousand dollar budget my parents had established.

Still, I'm worried about the VISA bill. Mom pores over them every month and those two cash advances are going to be hard to miss. I don't know what I'll say. She might not call me, seeing that school is out in two and half weeks. Maybe she'll wait until I come home.

Ayse and I have decided we'll go home for a few weeks this summer, tell our parents we've eloped, collect our things, then return to Atlanta mid-June to find an apartment. I can't wait to be living with her. If my Dad does pull my tuition, and I have to drop out of college. I'll have to find work in Atlanta and enter the real world.

Funny, I've never been in the real world. It's always been Mom and Dad's world. First high school, then off to college with all of my expenses paid. All my summer jobs have been because of Dad's influence at church. The painting job last summer, the lawn mowing jobs in high school, even that part-time job I had at Hal's Supermarket. Every one of them because of North Macon Baptist Church and my father's position as senior minister.

It will be strange to be finally cutting out on my own. I've got some money, the twenty grand my grandma left me that's still tied up in a mutual fund Dad picked out. I suppose there might be some kind of penalty for pulling the money out early, but the cash will come in handy for our rent deposits and a used car.

Ayse thinks she can convince her parents to help pay the rent, so long as she remains in school. That would help, and I want her to keep attending Oglethorpe if they let her. She loves learning and she's thinking about going on and getting her master's degree in education. She'd make a great teacher.

I'm tired now, it's almost four in the morning and I've got a full load of classes tomorrow. It's funny in a way. I'm up in the middle of the night, in my dorm room with Randy snoring away, writing in my journal and all the while I'm married. I'm the same but I'm not the same. It's a strange feeling. Strange but wonderful.

Two Phone Calls

"Hello," Daniel answered the phone on the fourth ring, having just come out of the shower.

"Daniel, is that you?"

"Yes, Mom, could you hold on a minute? I just walked out of the shower when I heard the phone ringing. I'm dripping wet."

"I'll wait."

Daniel set the portable receiver down and went into the bathroom to dry himself. He hurried, not wanting to keep his mother on hold.

"I'm back, Mom."

"Sorry to call you this early, but I know it's hard to reach you once you head off to class."

"It's not a problem, Mom. Why the call?"

Daniel suspected, even anticipated this phone call, but thought he would act innocent.

"It's about this month's VISA bill. You know, the VISA card we gave you for any emergencies that might come up at school.

"Well, I just received April's statement and it had an unauthorized charge on it. Do you know where your card is? Was it stolen?"

"No, it wasn't stolen. What's the unauthorized charge?"

"There are two cash advances for three hundred each that took place over Easter weekend in Gatlinburg, Tennessee. Now I recall from our last conversation that you were studying at school, so I thought maybe someone had stolen your card or had gotten your credit card number and I just wanted to touch base with you before canceling the account.

"When I call VISA, they'll automatically freeze your account. I felt you should know just in case you try to use the card next week before you come back home for the summer."

Daniel was caught. If there was an investigation by VISA into the incident, chances were they would discover it was Daniel who made the withdrawals. Every cash machine has a camera beside it that takes a photo of the person taking the cash advance, and the machine he withdrew the money from in Gatlinburg would have Daniel's photograph on it twice. When they sent the photo to his mother to see if she knew the person, and Daniel lied to her about not being there, she would find him out.

Still, he was planning on telling her in a week and lying about it would hold water until then. He would reimburse his parents the money out of his inheritance within a month. He didn't know what to say in the meantime. He decided to return to his original cover.

"It was me, Mom. I made those two advances."

"Why on earth would you be in Gatlinburg during Easter?"

"Randy, my roommate, and I got tired of studying and drove up to the Smoky Mountains for a few nights of camping. While we were there, he had some problems with his Honda. We had to take it to a local garage. They wouldn't take anything but cash. The brakes were shot."

Red flags were flying up at every turn of Daniel's story. Rebecca knew her son well, and his explanation for the cash advances didn't sit well with her. Like a skilled detective, she was determined to get to the truth.

"It seems like an expensive repair. Are you sure this garage was legitimate, Daniel?

"If you could give me the name of the garage, I'll have your father call them and go over the bill. For six hundred dollars, it seems as if you could replace the entire brake system. I know your father will want to have a chat with those mechanics. What did you say the name of that garage was?"

Daniel stood silent. He should have, but he hadn't anticipated his mother's third degree. Lying was never one of his strong suits, and now he was at a crossroads. He could either fabricate some obscure garage on the outskirts of

Gatlinburg, Tennessee, or simply come clean and inform his mother that he and Ayse were married. With only ten days left before he was to tell them in person, he decided to tell his mother the truth.

"There's no garage, Mother."

"I'm getting a bit confused here, Daniel. First you tell me you're staying up at your dorm to catch up on your studies, then you tell me you've gone camping with Randy and that you needed the six hundred dollars to repair his Honda, and now you're telling me the garage that did the repairs doesn't exist.

"What is going on, Daniel? Are you in some kind of trouble?"

"We got married, Mom. Ayse and I are married."

The impact of Daniel's announcement carved a crater a mile wide in Rebecca's heart. She was still reeling from the catastrophe as she continued.

"Please tell me you're joking, Daniel. Please."

"It's not a joke. Ayse and I went camping in Cade's Cove over Easter weekend and we decided to elope. The six hundred dollars went for wedding clothes, a wedding band, a marriage license and the ceremony at the Cloud Nine Wedding Chapel.

"I was going to tell you in ten days when I came home to pick up my things. But I can't go on lying to you about the broken Honda. I've never been good at lying, so I might as well tell you what happened."

Rebecca's mouth went dry, her voice grew strained and lifeless. She was devastated, and worse, she dreaded the thought of telling any of this to Clay.

"My mother's ring?"

"Yes, I gave it to Ayse."

"Oh, Daniel, have you any idea what your father's going to say?"

"I don't think the word 'congratulations, Daniel' will be the first thing out of his mouth, do you?"

"Don't get cute with me, Daniel. This isn't like one of your silly arguments over Buddhism or abortions. You've decided to spend your entire life married to a Muslim girl. How are you going to raise the children?

"How's your father going to explain your behavior to his congregation? The repercussions of your actions are overwhelming. How could you do such a crazy thing? Maybe there's a way we can have the marriage annulled?"

"I don't want to have my marriage annulled, Mom. I don't give a damn what Dad says to his flock. They're all a bunch of hypocrites. They keep that school open just to make sure none of their kids have to go to public schools and sit next to blacks or Hispanics. Half of the congregation drinks while the other half commits adultery. Don't lay this 'holier than thou' stuff on me, Mom. I've been around the assembly of North Macon Baptist Church way too long for that.

"Ayse's a wonderful woman. She's kind, she studies hard and she's very devout in her faith. She didn't drive an airplane into any skyscraper and never would. You can't go around judging every Muslim by the actions of a few radicals.

When you meet her, you'll see why I'm in love with her. Besides, when did falling in love with someone become such a transgression?"

"When you fall in love with an infidel, Daniel. That's how your father's going to look at it. He's already warned you to break it off, and now, for goodness sake, you've not only failed to break if off, you've married her. This is terrible.

"What do her parents think?"

"She hasn't said anything to them yet. We took our rings off when we got back to campus. We didn't want to draw attention to our marriage just yet. You're the first person to know. Ayse plans to tell her family when she flies home. Then, after spending a couple of weeks in Turkey, she's coming back to Atlanta. We're going to find an apartment.

"I'll use the money Grandma left me to get started. I know I'll have to get a job. We plan on living in Atlanta."

Rebecca remained silent on the other end of the line. She had nothing to say.

"Look, Mom, I have to get to class. I'm already running late. We can talk more about this later. I should be back in my dorm around eight tonight. Maybe you can give me a call then?"

"We'll see. Daniel, I love you."

"Love you too, Mom. Bye."

"Goodbye."

Daniel hung up the phone and gathered his backpack and books for school. Rebecca put the phone back on the receiver and stood beside the kitchen desk. She was in shock. She absolutely hated making the next call, but knew she must. Within ten minutes she had her husband on the telephone. It was anything but pleasant.

✪

The dorm room telephone rang at eight-fifteen that evening. Daniel picked it up after the first ring. His father's voice was on the other end of the line. Although his father was an ordained minister of God, for Daniel Mark Harris, this was the phone call from hell.

"Daniel?"

"Yes, it's me, Dad."

His father wasted no time. "Do you know what you've done?"

"Yes, I've married a wonderful woman," replied Daniel in a sarcastic tone.

"Don't get flippant with me, Daniel. This is far more serious than you think."

Daniel took a long, deep breath and sat down on the threadbare sofa. He knew what was coming. Clay continued.

"You've embarrassed your mother and me, and you've disobeyed me. I cannot let a sin like the one you have just committed go unpunished, Daniel, and I know you'll understand."

"I understand that you don't own me, Dad. I'm twenty-one and I can do what I want. I can marry whom I wish to marry and I don't need to obey you if I decide not to," spoke Daniel to his father in an equally stern tone.

"Don't you dare talk to me like that! I've given you everything over the years; the clothes on your back, money for school, we've kept a roof over your head and raised you in the ways of Jesus Christ, our Lord and Savior, and this is our thanks. Then you take off, on Easter weekend, the very celebration of the Resurrection of Christ, and marry a woman who doesn't even believe that Christ is the Son of God.

"A woman whose people have been on a Jihad against Christianity since the day Mohammed was born. A woman who's in the grip of Satan." Clay's voice was growing louder. His face was flushed, and his skin contrasted sharply with his bone-white hair.

"Don't get started, Dad. Ayse's not in the grip of Satan. You've never even met her. She's a good person. Just because she doesn't believe the way we do doesn't mean she's a terrorist. She's never tried to convert me to Islam, and I don't want to change her beliefs. We're just two people in love. Religion isn't everything."

"You're dead wrong, Daniel, because religion is everything. By thinking and saying the things I'm hearing from you, I know that what I'm about to do is the right thing. It is better to cut off the hand that steals, pluck out the eye that sins than to face eternal damnation.

"Because that's where you're headed, Daniel. You are on a treacherous course that leads straight to the hell fires. I don't think there's anything I can do to save you at this point. You wanted your freedom, your brave new world where you can marry an infidel and raise your children in some kind of mixed-up Christian, Islamic mess, and now you can have it."

"What are you saying, Dad?"

"Tomorrow morning I'm going to disown you, Daniel. You're no longer my son. I'm going to see a lawyer with Mom at nine-thirty and we're going to do all the paperwork."

"Why would you do such a thing, Dad?"

"You know damn well why," said Clay emphatically, cursing in anger.

Daniel started to cry. He tried to hold back his tears but they forced their way through his watery eyes and rolled, as silent as freezing rain, down his cheeks.

"And that's not all, Daniel. I'm freezing your bank account, I've already closed your VISA account, and I'm placing a protection order on you. You're no longer welcome in this house. I've agreed to let Mom pack your things and ship them to you, but don't think for a minute that I didn't object.

"Your tuition, your room and board are canceled immediately. It's a crying shame I've already paid the balance of this semester, knowing you've been seeing her against my instructions, but there's nothing I can do about that. If you even set foot on our yard, I'll have you arrested for violating the protection order.

You know that Sheriff McCoy is a friend of mine and a fine, outstanding member of our congregation. Don't think for one minute he won't enforce my protection order, because he will.

"So now you have what you want, your Islamic maiden and your freedom. I hope the two of you spend an eternity together — an eternity in HELL!

"And one last thing, Daniel."

"Yes, Dad," said his only son while sobbing on the tattered couch.

"I don't ever want to hear your voice again."

With that, Clayton Aaron Harris slammed down the receiver. He slammed it down so hard it nearly cracked his phone in half. For Clay, it was over. He no longer had a son named Daniel. He had died. Worse than death, he had done something so unforgivable that death would have been easier. Quicker.

Daniel heard the crash of the phone smashing against the receiver. He had wanted to say something, anything, to keep his father from going ahead with his spiteful agenda but it was too late. Everything was too late. His plan to use his grandmother's inheritance was too late, recalling that his father had co-signed with him on the investment fund. His dreams were too late.

Heading down to Macon at the end of the semester was too late. Having an apartment to live in, buying a used car, beginning a new life with his Turkish princess, everything was too late.

He didn't bother getting up to return the portable phone to its receiver. He turned it off and let it fall beside the couch. Taking both of his hands and covering his tortured face, he cried.

While he wept without restraint, Daniel wondered about God. He wondered what sort of God would do this. What kind of God would make a father turn against his son for falling in love? What kind of God splits the world into ten thousand sects, then turns each sect against the others in this global centrifuge of mistrust?

Daniel started hating God that night. He blamed God for his father's actions just as he blamed God for allowing him to fall in love with Ayse. A storm within Daniel began brewing. A storm as dark and foreboding as any that have formed within the tormented heart of a young man.

In time, the storm would overpower him. The winds would take him into its swirling arms and pull him into the abyss, taking him away from the world of light.

He thought about Ayse. How was he going to tell her? How was she going to react? What were they going to do next?

He had a little more than one hundred dollars to his name, three suitcases full of clothes, some old books and an Islamic bride. He had purchased his freedom though he never thought it would come at such a cost.

The Conversation

Daniel didn't tell Ayse about his father's call the following day, or the day after. He had decided to pretend everything was fine until they had some time together during the last weekend before finals. That was when they had the conversation.

They had both been studying in the library on a windy afternoon. Ayse had noticed the change in her husband's mood immediately but had intentionally refrained from asking him what was going on. She waited for Daniel to confide in her.

"Let's go for some coffee," said Daniel to his wife, who was sitting directly across the library table from him. "I'm falling asleep."

"Yes, coffee would help," concurred Ayse.

They left their books and notes scattered across the oak table and went out the front door toward the small café in Goodman Hall. A brisk wind was whipping through the central square of the campus, making the trees arch and the leaves of summer rustle. The days were growing longer and a sense of the approaching heat was in the air.

Daniel took Ayse's small hand and squeezed it tightly. She looked over to him and tossed one of her smiles at her new husband. He had to tell her.

"Ayse, I've got bad news."

She had waited to hear what laid so heavily upon his soul and she was glad to know he was willing to tell her.

"What is it?"

"It's my father. He called three nights ago."

"Does he know about us? Is he angry?"

"He's beyond anger. He's trying to destroy us, Ayse."

Ayse didn't respond, knowing it was Daniel's time to speak. They stopped and sat on a bench along the courtyard, the same bench they sat on after Professor Lathcombe's class.

"He's going to make it difficult for us. He's done everything he could to ruin my future, I mean our future together."

"Tell me what he's done?"

"He's disowned me, Ayse. A few days ago he and Mom met with an attorney. They've cut me out of their will. He told me it would have been better had I died than had I married you. Oglethorpe is through for me. Unless I can plead hardship with financial aid to receive some kind of grant or student loan next year, I won't be able to afford school in the fall.

"My father's pulled my tuition, closed my VISA account and worse, he won't allow me access to my grandmother's money."

"Can he do such a thing?"

"I was very young when my grandmother died and left me that money. Because I was still a minor, we set the account up in such a way that my father would have to co-sign for any withdrawals or changes in the account. I didn't think he'd go this far, but he's refusing to allow me access to the funds.

"He won't even let me in the house to collect my things. My mother's going to ship them to school. I don't know what we're going to do to get started, Ayse. I'm sorry to have let you down like this. I'm so sorry."

Daniel surrendered, collapsing into his wife's arms. He had wanted to be strong for her, but he wasn't. He had wanted to be the provider, to rent a place for them while she was in Istanbul, but that was now impossible. He had looked forward to buying a car, setting up housekeeping with used furniture from Goodwill and pots and pans from Wal-Mart, but none of it was going to happen.

After five minutes had passed, his blue eyes tinted red from tears, he looked up at his dark, Islamic bride and said, "Maybe we should have our marriage annulled, Ayse. Maybe it's not worth it."

"No, Daniel. Love is worth it. God will provide for us. You must never think like that, or doubt our love. Not even for an instant. You must remain strong and not allow your father to take what we have away from us.

"We have not sinned, Daniel. Loving each other isn't a sin, it's a gift. Just like your poem, it's a gift we've been given, and no one, not my family nor your family will ever take that gift from us. You wanted to provide for me, then provide me with your love, Daniel. The rest is only sand and stones."

Daniel listened to his bride. He found a safe harbor in her wisdom. She was right, the rest is sand and stones. He realized how unfaltering her love was and how lucky he had been in finding this strong, Middle Eastern woman. They sat together on that bench, watching the wind bend and twist the leaves of summer, and said no more.

The Plane Ride East

*A*yse's eyes were tired. They had walked their own trail of tears at the airport with her new husband, and Ayse knew her return home and the announcement of her marriage to her family would not be easy. It was going to be a long, lonely flight.

Daniel's immediate problems had been resolved. Professor Lathcombe, in whom they had confided about their marriage, had helped to intervene on Daniel's behalf. The professor had made special arrangements with the school, allowing Daniel to stay at the dorm for five dollars a night until he could find suitable accommodations. Randy had loaned him two hundred dollars and Professor Lathcombe, feeling somewhat responsible for their marriage in the first place, had given Daniel and Ayse a one-hundred dollar bill as their belated wedding gift.

Ayse gave Daniel every penny she had at the airport and, all combined, he now had just over five hundred dollars to their name. His clothes and personal belongings had arrived via UPS two days before Ayse's departure. Daniel was worried. He was about to venture into an uncertain future with five-hundred dollars and three boxes of possessions. He had promised Ayse that by the time of her return he would have a job and, hopefully, an apartment for them.

In turn, Ayse promised him she would not only tell her parents that she was a married woman, but ask her parents for money to help them get started in America. She told Daniel at the airport that although her mother would be very distraught by her decision to marry a Christian, they would probably be willing to help. They would never understand the actions of Daniel's father, and Ayse felt confident she would return within a month's time with enough of a dowry to get them established in the huge metropolis of Atlanta.

That was their tearful plan that late afternoon at the airport. There were countless fissures in their plan. Doubt filled every crack.

Ayse secretly wondered if her family might not behave as had Daniel's. Or worse, that her mother might steal away her passport and try to have the marriage annulled. Daniel wondered if and when he would find a job and how he would manage to get back and forth to work once he did. A thousand dead-end scenarios played out in each of their thoughts as they stood together in the sterile concourse.

Stood there, alone together, in a hallway filled with people pulling carry-on bags, camera kits, briefcases and purses. Strangers passing strangers in the endless rush of airports. People passing without pause, wondering why this handsome couple had such a troubled look. Why were they crying? What stories lie behind their tears?

That is how they parted. Now it was becoming dark high above the choppy waters of the Atlantic. Ayse, exhausted from days of stress, would have no trouble sleeping on this longest journey into night. She had not slept well since her conversation with Daniel on that bench a week ago.

By midnight Ayse was fast asleep. She dreamed she was riding a large winged horse over the deserts of Arabia. As the horse flew higher and higher, she looked down and saw the black cube of the Ka'ba sitting alone. It looked strange and isolated, surrounded by a sea of camel-colored sand, far from the crowds of pilgrims and worshipers it was accustomed to.

Once directly over the Ka'ba, the white horse descended to it. Ayse grew afraid as the winged horse swooped nearer and nearer the roof of this holiest of shrines. She clutched the thick mane of the horse and prayed to Allâh for forgiveness. As the horse's large hooves touched the roof of the sacred, black-draped cube of Islam, the tires of the Airbus touched the cement runway at Heathrow.

Ayse woke. She had slept so deeply that she did not even rouse for the descent into the United Kingdom. She would be at Heathrow for an hour before boarding a Turkish Airlines plane to Istanbul. She would be home soon.

As the plane taxied to the gate, she realized Istanbul wasn't her home any longer. Her home was with Daniel. Her home was a dorm room where, should she not be able to get the money from her family, she wouldn't be allowed to stay. She grew sad at the thought of it, but there were no more tears left to be shed.

She fought off the sadness and imagined a glorious future together. A future with children, a nice home in Atlanta and a world a thousand times more tolerant than the one she lived in. She prayed to Allâh that her dreams would someday come true.

The Wedding Ring

As the Turkish plane banked around the Sea of Marmar in its final approach to Ataturk Airport, Ayse looked down at her ring and grew nervous. She knew her mother would see it. She had no idea as to how her mother would react once she discovered her daughter had become a woman — a married woman.

Chills ran down Ayse's back as the plane drew near its boarding gate. The sound of the front door opening, the chimes ringing — telling the passengers it was safe to unbuckle their seatbelts and gather their personal items from the overhead compartment — all served to unnerve her. In a few minutes, Ayse would be embracing her parents. But it would never be the same. She would no longer be their daughter, but a married woman, belonging no longer to them, but to him.

She looked down at her ring one last time as she walked up the jet way. It shone brilliantly beneath the Turkish sunlight filtering through the plastic windows. It was an exquisite diamond, sharp and clear, set in shining platinum. Elif, Ayse thought, would see it at once.

Ayse noticed her parents standing just beyond security. Elif had on a dark-blue head scarf and a long, black dress. Mustapha was wearing a well-tailored pinstripe suit, looking, as he always did, as though he had just come out of a board meeting. They were smiling, thrilled to have their daughter back home for the summer.

As Ayse approached, they waved, making certain she had seen them. She walked up to them, dropped her backpack, and threw her arms around her father.

"My little princess," whispered Mustapha in Ayse's ear as he squeezed her tightly.

"I've missed you, Daddy."

She turned and hugged her mother, though not as intensely. Ayse had always been more reserved with Elif, and on this particular afternoon, she had reason for that reserve.

Abdul went down to baggage and waited for Ayse's single bag. Elif hadn't noticed the ring yet, but she was wondering why Ayse had returned home with only a single bag and her carry-on.

"Where are the rest of your things?" asked her mother after Ayse had picked up her bag and started walking toward the car.

"They're still in Atlanta, Mother."

Elif grew suspect. She studied her daughter carefully. That's when she saw it.

They piled into the back seat of the Lexus as Abdul, their chauffeur, welcomed Ayse home. She thanked him and said it was great to be back. As they got under way, driving through the heavy traffic of cabs, buses and cars that perpetually clog the roads of the sprawling city, Elif confronted her daughter.

"What is this ring on your finger?"

Ayse turned ice cold, frozen in time and afraid to answer. Elif pressed on.

"Ayse, do you have something to tell us?"

"Yes, Mother."

"What have you done, Ayse?" asked Mustapha, knowing that something had happened.

"I've married Daniel."

A screaming silence settled upon the passengers in the car. It smothered the sounds of the radio, playing Turkish pop tunes, and the noise of the crowded highway. All that was left were the sounds of their heartbeats: internal, reflective and afraid.

Mustapha didn't know what to say. Elif broke into a sweat, even though the air conditioning was turned up high and blowing icy cold.

Ayse, who was sitting between her parents, started crying.

"I'm sorry," she said between sobs. "I'm so very, very sorry."

The silence continued. It thickened like a cold, dense fog from which no one could hope to find their way out. The silence grew louder and louder, like standing in a chilling rain beside a thousand sirens. The silence was roaring.

"Why, Ayse? Why?"

"Because I love him, Mother. That is the only reason, the only explanation I can give you."

"But you could have called, told us, you could have said something," added Mustapha, clearly distraught.

"No I couldn't have. You would have only tried to talk me out of it. I knew from our conversations in December that neither of you would consent to our marriage. Calling you would have only made things worse.

"Daniel's family felt the same. We had no choice but to marry the way we did, at a wedding chapel in the mountains. We hadn't planned to do it, but in the end, it was meant to be."

The silence came back. The Lexus rolled across the Old Galata Bridge, winding around the edge of the Bosporus, then up the long, steep hill that led to Bebek. No one broke the truce of silence that had descended upon all four of them — no one dared.

Upon getting Ayse's bag and carry-on out of the trunk, Abdul, with his head bent over and buried in the trunk of the big car, looked back at Ayse and said, "Congratulations, Ayse. May you have years of blessings and may Allâh's love and mercy be upon you!

"There is great truth in what the Sufi poet, al-Sana-ie of Ghazni wrote long ago, *"At the gates of Paradise no one asks who is Christian and who is Muslim."*

When he handed Ayse her carry-on, she let it drop to the ground and threw her arms around Abdul. She was so thrilled by his words of encouragement that she couldn't stop herself from hugging him. She thanked him for coming to her rescue.

Mustapha and Elif had already walked into the house. Ayse followed, with Abdul carrying her suitcase. They carried their relentless silence into the house with them, allowing it to overwhelm the home as it had the Lexus.

Ayse went to her room, threw herself on her bed, and cried without mercy. She was home again and she was so alone. She wished tomorrow would never come.

The Congregation

And Abraham said, My son, God will provide himself a lamb for a burnt offering: so they went both of them together.

"And they came to the place which God had told him of; and Abraham built an altar there, and laid the wood in order, and bound Isaac his son, and laid him on the altar upon the wood.

"And Abraham stretched forth his hand, and took the knife to slay his son.

"And the angel of the Lord called unto him out of Heaven and said, Abraham, Abraham: and he said, Here am I.

"And he said, Lay not thine hand upon the lad, neither do thou any thing unto him: for now I know that thou fearest God, seeing thou has not withheld thy son, thine only son from me.

"And Abraham lifted up his eyes, and looked, and behold, behind him a ram caught in a thicket by his horns: and Abraham went and took the ram, and offered him up for a burnt offering in the stead of his son."

Clayton Aaron Harris cleared his throat momentarily before continuing.

"And Abraham called the name of that place Jehovah-jireh: as it is said to this day. In the mount of the Lord it shall be seen.

"And the angel of the Lord called unto Abraham out of Heaven the second time,

"And said, By myself have I sworn, saith the Lord, for because thou hast done this thing, and hast not withheld thy son, thine only son.

"That in blessing I will bless thee, and in multiplying I will multiply thy seed

as the stars of the Heaven, and as the sand which is upon the sea shore; and thy
seed shall possess the gate of his enemies;

"Genesis, twenty-two, Verses eight through seventeen."

Clayton Harris, dressed in a fine, long white robe and standing before a church filled to overflowing, stopped reading from his Bible and looked long and somberly over his flock. They were quiet. A quiet broken only by a passing cough or the cry of a closely-held infant. Nearly a minute passed before Clay resumed his sermon, but for the sinners beneath him, it felt like an eternity.

"There are times when God asks more of us than we are willing to give. There are times when only the ultimate sacrifice, the sacrifice of a child, or the willingness to commit such an act, will satisfy Jehovah."

A few of the faithful answered Clay's testimony with a scattering of "Amens" and "Hallelujahs." A dozen hands were waving above the crowd, palms outstretched and ready to accept the will of God. Clay, becoming more and more enraptured with his own self-importance, continued.

"Two weeks ago, on one of the most difficult days of my life, the Lord asked me to do what Abraham had been asked to do, to sacrifice my only son, Daniel. This was a dark day for me, a dark day indeed. The storm clouds were gathering and the wind was blowing a terrible fury. God had chosen to test my resolve by asking me to choose. To choose between the Lord and my only son, Daniel Mark Harris."

"Whom did I choose?" asked Reverend Harris of the one thousand two hundred and fifty-one of the faithful fanned out beneath him.

"Choose the Lord!" "Choose Jesus!" "Praise Jesus!" Resounded voices from amid the crowded church. "Choose God the Almighty!" shouted a believer in the back.

"For myself, there was no question. I called my son that same night. I told him if he chose to marry a heathen, an infidel, a Muslim, he was no longer my son. That I had to sacrifice him on that alter built high atop the mountain called Jehovah-jireh."

Clay paused to let the multitudes reaffirm his decision. A broken chorus of "Amen," "Hallelujah," "Praise God," filled the pause. They were behind him. They approved.

"And I drew up my knife, and I cut that boy away from my life like a festering tumor. Like a bad piece of flesh that if left unsevered, would eat away at my soul like a cancer from hell. And I knew what I had taken the path of righteousness and glory. *"And if thy right eye offend thee, pluck it out, and cast if from thee: for it is profitable for thee that one of thy members should perish and not that thy whole body should be cast into hell.* Matthew Chapter five, Verse twenty-nine.

"And if your children turn to sin, it is better to cut them away from you than allow them to pull you down in the abyss with them."

Clay was on fire now. Untouchable. He was no longer standing on the pulpit, but rising above it on a cloud of his own creation. The words of his sermon leapt from his mouth on tongues of fire and brimstone. He was delivering one of the finest, most powerful sermons of his life.

"For God asks all of us to be as Abraham. To be brave, strong and righteous. To be prepared to sacrifice your children should God ask it. Because the love of God Almighty is the greatest love. Greater than this mortal flesh we dwell in. Greater than my boy, Daniel, and far, far greater that his wayward wife. Greater than the teachings of the false prophet, Mohammed.

"A prophet who has already brought too much suffering, too many suicide bombers and murderers here in our midst. I stand here today a son-less father. I no longer have a boy named Daniel Mark Harris. He has made his bed, chosen his Islamic bride, and now, he alone must sleep in it.

"And I stand before you today asking you to stand with me. If you happen to see him, ignore him. Cast him out of your lives like bad fruit. For allowing bad fruit to stay in our midst will only assure us that the rest of the harvest will rot. Be rid of him and his evil ways. *GET THEE BEHIND ME, SATAN!*

"We must stand together in this sacrifice of Abraham. We must raise up our knives and be willing to cut away the evil. We must be strong for Jesus.

"Are you willing to make this sacrifice with me? Raise up your hands to testify to the Lord. Raise up your hands to make the ultimate sacrifice. Raise up your hands for JESUS!"

A thousand hands shot skyward as the congregation became delirious with Clay's passion. A hundred voices spoke out, overlapping and shouting, "We're willing." "Hallelujah." "God's willing." "Amen."

Clay was inebriated with himself. He was no longer Clayton Aaron Harris. He was Abraham reincarnate, standing over his son, Isaac, ready to offer him up to God. Ready to plunge the knife into his son's heart for the love of Jehovah.

"So I say unto you, my fellow God-fearing members of North Macon Baptist Church, that Daniel has died. We stand together as a family disowning him, shunning him and rejecting him for what he has chosen to do. Because a man must be held responsible for his own actions. Each of us must be held accountable for our actions.

"Daniel has sinned. Make no mistake about it, Daniel has sinned and sinned most grievously. When he slipped that wedding ring upon his Muslim bride, he might as well have stolen that ring from the Lord Himself.

"There are those of you who might say it isn't fair. That times have changed and we've got to be more understanding, more tolerant in today's world.

"But I don't want to hear that sort of talk. Not today, not ever. Because God doesn't change. Today's God is the same Jehovah Moses knew three thousand years ago. The Jehovah that smote down the Egyptians who worshiped their pagan deities and the same God who burned the evil cities of Sodom and Gomorrah.

"Let's not look back, for fear that we shall be turned to salt like Lot's wife. Let us not tempt fate, or stand in the way of God's fearful righteousness. Stand with me now and sing this hymn of praise, and when you leave this church today, be willing to sacrifice anyone, even those you love the most, who come between you and your eternity. Amen."

Clay was finished. His face flushed with the power and the glory. His wife, Rebecca, looked up at him proudly. Though she admired his sermon, she had cause for reservation. She did not want Clay to deliver this sermon. She did not want her husband disavowing his son publicly.

Rebecca felt it was a private matter, and didn't feel the whole congregation needed to be sharing in it. But Clay persisted. He felt Daniel's decision was a test of his father's faith and because of that, everyone must share in the wisdom gathered from such a test.

So it was done. Clay had disowned his son legally and publicly. Daniel was legally and morally dead. They now had only one child, their daughter Ruth. She and her husband Chet had sat beside Rebecca during the sermon.

Everyone knew Clay was going to deliver this particular sermon this Sunday morning. That's why the church was filled to standing room only. As the congregation poured out the back of the church and lingered in the foyer and the fresh morning air outside, the reaction to Clay's message was forthright.

"It was his best," said one woman to her friends.

"I loved it, he is so brave," said a man holding a Bible.

"Beautiful, simply beautiful," agreed a young lady in her off-white Sunday dress.

Clay retreated to his office, drunk on the wine of his own importance. He had no regrets, and never second-guessed his testimony. God had been good to him despite the death of Daniel. God was wondrous, felt the old man reclining in his leather chair in his empty office. Wondrous indeed.

Friday, After Mosque

S he hasn't said a word to me since I've arrived."

"Not even at Mosque?" asked Fatimah.

"No. Abdul drove us and then he went in to worship with Father, while Mom and I prayed side by side in silence."

"This isn't good, Ayse. What are you going to do?"

"I don't know what to do, Fatimah. I promised Daniel I would return to America within a month. I will keep that promise, but then there is the question of money. We need at least a few thousand dollars U.S. to get started in Atlanta.

"I know my father could easily afford to lend us the money, but if he doesn't speak to me, how can I ask him for his help? Maybe I was wrong. Maybe it was a mistake for us to be married."

"No, don't think that. You love him and you have every right to marry the man you love. Just give it some more time. Like last summer, your parents will come around. They are just shocked at your impetuous behavior. It is so out of character. They never expected this of you. Nor did I."

It felt good for Ayse to be talking to her best friend. There was no one else for her to talk to in Istanbul. The word of her marriage had quickly made the rounds of the social elite of Bebek and most who heard of it were quick to distance themselves from Ayse.

In Turkey, as in all the countries that practice Islam, it is acceptable for the man to marry outside of the religion, but not for a woman. The religion went with the man, and most felt Ayse would soon be converting to Christianity should the marriage endure. Either way, they didn't want to be part of it, or condone such behavior. They had daughters of their own to think about, longstanding traditions to uphold.

Only Abdul, the family driver, and Fatimah had supported Ayse in her decision, though neither of them could claim to know Daniel Mark Harris. Ayse had shown both of them her wedding photo — a grainy black-and-white taken at the chapel. That photograph and her ring were all she could offer as evidence to the wonderful man she had married.

The rest was in her eyes. Every time Ayse spoke of him, her eyes seemed to come alive with an expression that was hard to deny. Her voice raised a pitch and there was an electricity that seemed to shine from her as she described her blue-eyed husband. That was all Abdul and Fatimah needed to be convinced of her sincerity and conviction. Whoever this American boy was, he had a wife who loved him more than the world itself.

"You must approach your parents about it, Ayse. You must confront your father and explain what has happened to Daniel and his inheritance from his grandmother. Mustapha will surely understand."

"I hope so. But Mother will take longer. I doubt she will ever come around and approve of the marriage. She doesn't like Americans, and she has never trusted Christians. To suddenly have both for a son-in-law is hard for her. I doubt we will ever speak to each other again, Fatimah."

"She will speak to you, but maybe not this summer. I know your mother, and she can be very cold when she wants to be. I wouldn't advise you to approach her while you are here in Istanbul. Try to make amends with your father instead. He adores you and he is far more comfortable with Americans. I have never heard him speak badly of them."

Fatimah was right. Although most Americans were Christians, which was a bit of a disappointment to Mustapha, he admired them nonetheless. Americans were so enthusiastic, so refreshing and alive that Mustapha Yalçin had always overlooked their shortcomings. Mustapha enjoyed their company and their astute sense of business.

"I will try to talk with him, Fatimah. I think your advice is good. I will call you tomorrow morning, maybe we can go to the Grand Bazaar and spend some time together tomorrow afternoon."

"That would be nice, Ayse. I still need to get you a wedding present."

"Don't be silly, Fatimah. Your friendship is gift enough."

"Tomorrow then, my Ayse."

"Goodbye."

"Goodbye."

Ayse flipped the cover closed on her cell phone. She looked around her room and still felt disconnected. Pulling the blankets up to her face, Ayse started sobbing. She was afraid.

She knew she would have to break the uneasy quiet that had shrouded the household for the past four days, and that to do so would take every ounce of courage she could find. She was more than afraid, she was terrified.

Book of Midnights

*F*riday night, 11:30 p.m.
    Andrew Bragg called me last night and told me about my father's sermon. What an asshole I have for a father! It isn't enough for him to disown me, keep me from my inheritance and place a protection order on me. No, he has to take it one step farther. He has to take it to his congregation and ask that they disown me, too.

Andrew said Dad's sermon received a rousing applause. The nerve of my father to compare my being disowned to Abraham's sacrifice. Who the hell does Clay think he is, a modern day Moses?

He's just another pompous Southern preacher, thinking it's my way or the highway. Well, Dad, I just want to let you know my plans are to take the highway. The highway that leads a million miles from your bullshit.

I don't need your money, and I know damn well you'll never let me get to my grandmother's money, so I'll go out and find some of my own. I've already talked to a lawyer about the inheritance and, even if he can get it wrestled out of your hands, the lawyer would take a third and he told me it would take better than a year. It's best for me to just drop out of school and find a job.

Randy has set me up to interview as an apprentice bartender at a pub he hangs out at down in Buckhead. The pay isn't all that great, but once you get trained in as a full-time bartender, the tips can be awesome.

I've looked into some other things, including an advertising position I read about in the Atlanta Journal, but they want someone with a B.A. I don't want to take a job at some 7/11 or work the trades like I did at that painting job last summer. Painting was boring, and without dad's contacts, the pay sucks.

The bartending job sounds good. I'm supposed to check it out tomorrow afternoon. I think it's ironic that the son of a Baptist preacher should end up tending bar in Buckhead. My father certainly wouldn't approve, and that's why I'm looking forward to getting the job.

A Conversation

*T*he ice storm that had frozen Ayse's family in place showed little signs of letting up. Elif remained as distant as the nearest star, and Mustapha held fast beside her. The silence had become so prevalent that, like some black hole, even Ayse's parents had become drawn into it. It was a vacuum of disappointment.

By Monday, a week since her homecoming, Ayse was determined to break the silence. Her time was drawing short, and she knew she had to call the airline and change her return flight soon. She had, at best, three weeks to pack, plan and bid farewell to her estranged family.

If they will not break this silence, thought this lonely Turkish girl in the solitude of her bedroom, then I will. She had elected to approach her father first, knowing he would be more likely to lend her a sympathetic ear. Elif, reasoned Ayse, may never accept the marriage.

Ayse waited. Waited and prayed. Prayed to Allâh her father would grant her an audience, allow her an hour to explain how much she loved this American boy from Macon. Show Mustapha her love and her pain. The pain of appearing to lose the love of her family for the love of her husband. The pain of their intolerance toward a person, a Christian they had never met.

At six-thirty that night, after hearing her father walk in the front door, Ayse said one last prayer and descended the stairway. She was acting like a girl of seven after misbehaving. She was coming downstairs after a week-long time out. Apprehensive and submissive, her dark eyes perched on the edge of tears.

Mustapha was sitting in the living room, reclining on his favorite chair, reading the evening edition of the *Hürriyet*. The news was more of the same. The Kurds were demanding a private state in western Turkey, the Israelis and Palestinians were blowing each other up with suicide bombers and American-made tanks and there was a letter to the editor about allowing women to wear head scarves while in public office. Mustapha read the paper as if from a distance, glancing at the printed words as if they were written in a foreign language. His heart was heavy, and the news of a troubled world did little to comfort him.

"Father," said Ayse from the edge of the living room.

Mustapha slid the newspaper down and peered over the top of it at this young lady standing in his house. He was filled with anger.

"Yes, Ayse."

"I have to go back to America soon."

"Yes."

Ayse could feel the wall. It was thick and cold, like the stone walls that surrounded the old city. It was high and formidable, appearing insurmountable. Ayse stood beside it for a minute and began to weep. Mustapha remained aloof.

Then she turned away and started retracing her footsteps back to her room. It was of no use. She would have to find another way to raise the money, she would have to quit school and join her husband in the world.

Halfway up the stairs she heard her father's voice.

"Ayse."

She looked down at him, seeing he had rested the newspaper on his lap, and noting that tears were welling in his dark eyes.

"Yes, Father."

"I love you, Ayse."

"Oh, Father..." Ayse bounded from the stairs and ran into her father's arms. She did so without thinking how he might react. It didn't matter. She needed to hold him, to be held, and everything else in the world — the politics, the theologies, the corruption and the scandals — fell away as father and daughter embraced.

Their tears flowed as steadily as the Bosporus. Hearts melded into one as they held each other for the longest while. Nothing was said, as if words would only serve to reopen the chasm neither of them wanted to face. It was quiet, but the silence was different this time. It was warm and inviting, loving and gentle.

"I'm sorry, Father."

"Don't be sorry, Ayse. You fell in love and followed your heart. Why is that so terrible? I'm sorry too, Ayse. It is so hard for your mother and me to accept it. To face the fact that you're a married woman. To accept the knowledge that you must return to America, not for two more years of school, but forever. Lose you not only as a daughter, but as a Muslim. Knowing that he is Christian and you, out of respect for your husband, must turn to his religion.

"It is such a shock that we don't know how to deal with it. We have lost a daughter but we have not gained a son. It's been a sad week in the Yalçin household."

Ayse listened attentively. She needed to understand how they felt.

"You would love him too, Father. He's not like most Americans. He's sweet and sensitive, and very tolerant of Islam. We have talked about it at length, and he's not asked me to convert. He admires my devotion and my faith. There are times when he has even prayed beside me. He has told me that he thinks all of America should get down on their hands and knees five times a day to thank God for all they have. But Daniel says Americans are too proud and too vain to ever consider doing such a thing.

"Daniel's father is a Christian minister, an Imam. He is the complete opposite of Daniel. He is unwilling to be open to new ideas and unwilling to meet me. Please tell me you're willing to meet Daniel someday, Father."

"Someday, but not now."

"In a few days I must call the airline and change my return flight. I need to know what Mother and you are going to do. Are you going to allow me to continue with my studies at Oglethorpe? I cannot stay in the dorm any longer. I will need to pack most of my things before returning to America, and they will have to be shipped to Atlanta after I leave. There is so much to talk about and so much to do that I could not stand this silence another day."

"Yes, it's best the silence is broken."

"I love you, Father."

They embraced again and with their hug the river of tears began anew. There was much to discuss before Ayse's departure, and now they could talk again. Allâh had answered Ayse's prayers.

The Buckhead Saloon

aniel walked into the darkness of the Buckhead Saloon from the midday sunlight of a June afternoon. His eyes took a minute to adjust while he surveyed his surroundings. The saloon reeked of stale beer and cigarette smoke, odors that mixed acridly with the cleaning supplies used to clean the place every morning. The neon lights behind the bar seemed to inhale their own light, and at one-thirty on a Tuesday afternoon, did little to entice Daniel into having a Coors or a Budweiser.

The manager was waiting for Daniel's arrival. He looked at the oversized clock above the bar and noted that the kid was on time. It was a good sign. The last interviewee was twenty-eight minutes late. The kid before that never even showed. Good help was hard to find.

"You're Daniel?" asked the overweight manager.

"Yes, I'm a roommate of Randy's. Randy Clark — he's the one who told me to call you about the bartending job. We go to school together up at Oglethorpe."

The manager looked the boy over carefully. He was damn good-looking. That never hurt, especially when the college girls came in to shoot a round of pool. He was clean enough. Almost too clean, he thought, but that was probably a better characteristic than the asshole he'd just fired. That kid didn't know what a shower looked like. The manager continued with his interview.

"Ever work in a bar before?"

"No."

"That's good, then you ain't got any bad habits. Ever do any drugs?"

"No."

"Good, 'cause I don't tolerate no stoned-out bartenders who get screwed up all night. They pour their drinks too strong and can't make change. I don't give a shit if you get stoned, 'cause everybody 'round here gets stoned, but if I catch you being high behind my bar, you're out the door. Got it?"

"Got it."

Daniel started wondering if he shouldn't turn around and head back out the front door immediately. Walk out into the daylight of Georgia. He perused the manager carefully. He was wearing a stained, yellowed T-shirt, a pair of loose-fitting jeans that had to have a waist size in the mid-forties. He was shaven, but poorly, and he looked to be in his late thirties, maybe older. His face was heavily pockmarked and his teeth untended to. He looked rough.

Before Daniel could decide whether or not to continue with the interview, the burly manager looked him in the eye and said, "You're hired."

Then he went behind the bar and dug out a legal-sized file folder with a rubber band around it. Pulling out a couple pieces of paper and grabbing the pen stuck behind his ear, he handed them to Daniel.

"You'd better take a seat; there's some paperwork you'll have to fill out for the God-damned government. I don't give a shit if you declare all your tips or not, but you have to declare a few bucks every night just to keep the feds off your ass — and my ass, too, for that matter.

"Since you're new and still learning, you won't be doing but one late night shift a week, probably Mondays since it's our slowest night. After a month or two, y'all have to pull two late-nighters a week — and I mean staying here 'til three-thirty in the morning or later, so start thinking 'bout it now.

"Y'all be training with Jimmy Boy, sometimes Hardy and whoever else wants to show you the ropes. Jimmy Boy mostly. He's been tending bar for ten years and he's damn good at it.

"Y'all start at seven-fifty an hour, since you will be slow as molasses in January to start. If you work out, and hang in there a couple of months, you'll eventually get up to nine bucks an hour. With tips, that can make for a decent wage.

"Are you still gonna be going to Oglethorpe?"

"Not this year."

"Good. You can probably pull another late shift or two once you learn how to mix a drink. You'll get to like the joint after a while. We've got a good crew of regulars, including that buddy of yours, Randy. It's a nice place, really. My name's Steve by the way, Steve DeLany, and I'm the general manager. Welcome aboard."

Steve reached over and shook hands with Daniel. His handshake was firm and solid. Daniel wondered as he shook his hands how many times this large paw had collided with some drunkard's jaw over the course of years.

The answer was uncountable.

Daniel had a job.

Returning Home

Save for Abdul and Ayse, the Lexus was empty. It was a Saturday morning, just shy of three weeks since Ayse's arrival. The two of them, with little said, were on their way back to Ataturk Airport. Ayse was returning home.

Ayse reflected on the past few weeks in Bebek. It had been a difficult time, and in a way, it went as she had expected — badly. Elif, even upon her departure that morning, had still not said a word to her daughter. Not one word during the nineteen days she had been home. Aside from their comments that first day, Elif had never let down her wall of icy silence.

Mustapha, after that afternoon in the living room, allowed himself to speak with Ayse, but had remained distant and restrained, not wanting to give his daughter the impression he approved of her elopement. It killed him to behave like he did, but he could feel Elif's eyes upon him. He knew if he showed signs of sympathy toward his daughter, he would have hell to pay when Ayse left. He walked the tightrope between the two women with a studied caution. Falling to either side would be painful.

Mustapha did not lend Ayse the five thousand dollars she and Daniel would need to get their lives started in Atlanta, he gave her eight thousand. He told her he would be willing to do the same for her the following year, should she need the money. Being a businessman, he appreciated the fact that it was less than the cost of her room and board at the dorm. The only condition attached to the gift was that Ayse would remain in school until graduation, and he would continue to cover her entire tuition. A condition Ayse was more than willing to accept.

Ayse had told Mustapha what Daniel's father had done to him and, instinctively, Mustapha knew he must not do the same to his daughter. He loved her more than that. He thought it ironic. Ironic that a Christian minister would behave so badly toward his only son. Typical though, thought a Muslim who was born in a city that had witnessed the shortcomings of a million Christians over the centuries. Very typical.

Ayse had ample time to pack her things and ship them to the university. There were three large boxes to be shipped. They contained mostly clothes, but held some personal items and belongings as well. Her old dolls, keepsakes and gifts, all packed carefully for transit to America.

They would arrive in a month via freighter, and by then, Ayse presumed, they would have found an apartment to store them in. An apartment of their own.

Daniel had e-mailed her a week ago about his job. He told her he was enjoying bartending. It was a dramatic change from his cloistered existence at Oglethorpe. He loved the fact that the joint was frequented by all sorts of fascinating characters: drunkards, scholars, writers, co-eds and locals all sharing a drink or two before disappearing again into the vastness of Atlanta. And the tips, he wrote, were better than expected.

Ayse was heading home. Home being no longer the plush suburban life of a Turkish princess. Home no longer being a chauffeur-driven Lexus, a maid, a gardener and a cook. Home, for the moment, was going to be a one-bedroom flat in a sprawling apartment complex. Home was doing her own dishes, continuing with her studies and waiting for Daniel to return home at four in the morning, smelling of smoke, whiskey and spilled ale. Crawling into their double bed beside her, making love at dawn.

Home for her was a blue-eyed, fair-haired Christian boy with a Southern accent and a heart of gold. It was all the home she had ever wanted.

The Atlanta Airport

Daniel waited patiently just beyond the last set of security gates. Ayse's flight from France was running late. It had been held up at Orly because of mechanical problems and it was touching down ninety minutes later than originally scheduled.

As he stood there with a single, wilting rose in his hand, he kept wondering how much longer he would have to wait before he could catch a glimpse of her coming down the corridor before him. Any minute, he hoped, I'll see her again any minute.

Daniel was exhausted. The last three weeks had been frenzied and stressful.

He had searched for apartments, bought some tattered furniture, a used mattress and some dishes from a Salvation Army store, and started working forty hours a week as a bar back in the Buckhead Saloon. He had little time for sleep.

Last night, despite Daniel's objections, his boss had made him pull the late shift. Jimmy Boy, just before closing, decided to show Daniel how to mix a few specialty drinks. Daniel found himself, sleep deprived and dumb-witted, learning how to make white Russians, fuzzy navels and rum runners at two in the morning in an empty bar in Buckhead. A learning curve made treacherously steep by the fact that Jimmy Boy insisted they taste each and every cocktail for quality control before going on to the next one.

Daniel was drunk by two-thirty, just as Jimmy Boy was showing him how to splash a one hundred and fifty-one proof floater on top of a rum runner.

"Gives it that extra kick, don't 'cha think?" he asked the PK wobbling beside him.

"I guess," replied Daniel, no longer sober enough to taste the difference.

When he got off at three, he should not have crawled behind the wheel of Randy's Honda and he knew it. But the arrangement to keep the car overnight to pick up Ayse had already been struck and Daniel could ill afford a cab to and from the airport. So Daniel drove slowly and carefully back to the dorm room he was still staying in and prayed he would not get pulled over. A DUI, driving under the influence, at this juncture, would devastate them.

He made it home just before four and passed out on the dorm bed. How he had managed to get up at noon was beyond him. Ayse's flight was scheduled to arrive at one, so he hurriedly showered and sped south to make it in time.

After parking the car in a lot that was costing him seven dollars an hour, he checked the electronic arrival board to see if her flight was on time. It wasn't. He could ill-afford the twenty-dollar parking fee and hoped Ayse had some extra cash on her.

Just then, while he was thinking about the fourteen dollars in his wallet, he saw her walking down the hallway, her single carry-on rolling behind her. She was more beautiful than he had remembered.

"Ayse!" he called out to her.

"Daniel!" she replied, seeing him standing there with his solitary red rose just past security.

She went through customs and walked to her husband, a smile on her face and a tear in her eye. They embraced.

They held each other for the longest time. It was an embrace that spoke of how difficult these last three weeks had been for each of them. Both frightened, fearful they had made the wrong decision. Three weeks filled with uncertainty, apprehensions and anticipation. People passing by might have thought these two hadn't seen each other in a decade, so impassioned was their embrace.

"How was it?" asked Daniel, finally pulling away.

"It was terrible," answered his wife. "Simply terrible."

Tears began to well up in Daniel's eyes. He knew about the troubles with her mother from their e-mails. Seeing her now, and noting how tired and bloodshot Ayse's eyes appeared, made the problem even more real to him. It was not going to be easy.

"Don't worry, Ayse. We're together again and that's all that matters."

"I hope so, Daniel."

Nothing more was said. Daniel took her carry-on and they went downstairs to the carousel to collect her bags. The joy they had felt a few weeks ago in Gatlinburg was quickly fading. Fading into the reality of how these two lovers were going to have to face their future alone, without the support or approval of either of their families. Fading into Georgia Power Company deposits, midnight work schedules and the escapist chemistry of a well-mixed tequila sunrise.

Once in the car, Daniel broke the silence. "Ayse, do you have any extra cash? I'm sure the parking bill will be over twenty dollars and all I have on me is fourteen bucks."

"Yes, I've got a twenty."

She opened her small purse and pulled out her wallet. As she handed the twenty to Daniel, she noticed how bloodshot his eyes were.

"Have you been crying, Daniel?"

"No. Well...a little, I guess."

"Your eyes are so bloodshot."

"That's from drinking. Last night Jimmy Boy decided to start teaching me the science of making specialty cocktails. He insisted we taste each and every drink as a quality control."

"How many drinks did you taste?"

"Who knows? I lost count. I'm just glad I didn't get pulled over when I was heading home. I was wasted."

"Maybe your bartending job isn't such a good idea."

"I'll be fine, Ayse. It's fun in a way. Once I learn how to mix all the drinks things will settle down. I like the bar biz. It's a real kick."

Ayse was unsure. Daniel had never really been involved with a seedy crowd like this before and she was worried it might change him. She knew, deep down, he was still bitter about his father and wondered if hanging out with the nightlife-loving gang at Buckhead might prove to be a bad influence on her husband. She looked over at him, seeing his bloodshot eyes and unshaven face, and worried about their future. She had a right to worry.

"You were in late last night, Daniel," said Ayse after letting herself in the front door and walking into their bedroom.

"I'm in late every night."

"Not as late as five."

"I worked later than usual."

"But the bar closes at three, how could you work much later than that?"

Daniel rolled over, burying his head in the blankets. He hadn't expected Ayse to come home for lunch and her interrogation was annoying him. Three o'clock, four o'clock, the crack of dawn — at that time in the morning what difference does it make? Daniel had to bartend at the saloon again tonight and he needed his sleep.

"You didn't go to Jimmy's place after work again, did you?" asked his wife, not wanting to release him from her questioning just yet.

"And if I did?" replied Daniel through the blankets in an angry tone.

He waited for her reply, and when it failed to arrive, he threw the sheets off and sat up, looking at his bride. "What difference would it make, Ayse? I come home exhausted four nights a week, you're studying all the time, my family doesn't give a shit if I'm dead or alive and so what if I went over to Jimmy's house after work to play some poker and have some fun. Where else can I blow off some steam?"

Ayse stood in the doorway of their bedroom and started crying. She looked over to her husband and tried to see beyond the bloodshot eyes, the tired, harried look that had settled over him these past few months. She didn't want to see the long-haired, disheveled-looking Southern boy with the recent tatoo on his upper right arm any more than she wanted to hear his voice raised in anger. She was tired of watching him slide.

Daniel hated to see her cry. He tossed the blankets off and, wearing nothing but his briefs, went over and held his spouse. She continued to sob in his arms.

"I'm sorry, Ayse."

"What's going on, Daniel? Why's everything changing? Remember our honeymoon in the mountains? Isn't that how it's supposed to be for us? Ever since I've returned from Istanbul, you've been distant. Do you want a divorce? If that's what you want, I won't contest it. I love you Daniel, but our marriage isn't going well. It isn't going well at all."

Daniel didn't answer. She was right. Their marriage wasn't going well. He was drinking more than he should have and he had started to venture farther and farther into the cave of the early morning bar scene. A seedy, ill-kept cave. It was an unhealthy crowd to hang with, and Ayse sensed it months ago when he first started coming home late.

It was a derelict and pleasure-seeking entourage — waitresses with enough emotional baggage to fill a freight train, bartenders, bar backs, trance club DJs high on Ecstasy, dealers, druggies, gamblers and a thousand variations on a theme, all descending after hours to Jimmy Boy's pad or Bubba's cheap apartment. Anyone who made the offer to host the traveling circus after the three o'clock closing bells sounded in Buckhead.

By four, at whatever place they were, there would be a poker game going in the kitchen, three couples having at it in the bedrooms, basements or closets, and a dozen people lying around the living room too screwed up to move. Daniel was becoming one of them.

Ayse's rhythmic sobs only served to remind him of his shortcomings. But it wasn't their marriage, or Ayse that was the engine of his slow demise. It was his anger. He could not let go of what his father had done to him.

Daniel took the eight thousand dollars from Ayse when she arrived in Atlanta and, using the money carefully, purchased an old Toyota, leased their apartment, and shopped the local Salvation Army and Goodwill stores to furnish their first home.

But Daniel took Ayse's money reluctantly. He had wanted to provide for her, and he was bitter toward his father for keeping him from his inheritance. Had that money been there for them, as well as Ayse's, they would be well on their way to making their game plan work. They wouldn't be living in a tiny apartment, or driving a twelve-year-old Toyota with the front passenger door banged up.

Now, it all seemed like an impossible dream. Even on a good week, with Daniel pulling near sixty hours at the saloon, it was hard to cover the bills and find any money left to put away. It was like the myth of Sisyphus, forever pushing a giant rock up a steep hill that ends by having the rock roll down again the next month when the rent was due, or the Toyota needed new brakes. Daniel's back grew weary from shouldering the responsibility of such a burden. He found a camaraderie with the after-hours crowd, commiserating together until the approaching dawn chased them back to their respective lairs.

The bar crowd appealed to Daniel, each member with his or her tale to tell. Sordid stories to bemoan in a sea of tequila or a line of cocaine. Tales of abusive ex-husbands, drug addictions, sex addictions and a desperate litany of their own stones to push uphill. A lonely, disenfranchised crowd.

Daniel and his anger were being swallowed whole by these midnights. Slowly digested in the stomach of the endless after-the-bars-close party and the victims that were invited. Ayse could sense it, and it was why she had come to the apartment to check on her husband. It was why she had skipped lunch and driven miles through Atlanta's horrid traffic. Driven just to see Daniel and reassure him everything was going to be fine so long as they held fast to the love they had for each other.

"I'll come home early tonight," Daniel whispered in Ayse's ear while he held her. "I'll tell Steve that I can't do the late shift. It's slow on Thursdays anyway.

Jimmy Boy can handle it. I'll be home before midnight."

"Thank you, Daniel."

"I'm sorry for yelling at you, Ayse. It's just a lot harder than I thought it would be."

"It is harder, Daniel. We should have thought of that when we were standing on that cloud in Gatlinburg. We should have known."

Ayse's voice trailed off into a world familiar to all young lovers who have known this crucible. A world spawned of late payments, unexpected car repairs and families that have walked away from their children. A brave old world.

Book of Midnights

Wednesday, Nov. 4, 2:35 a.m.

I can't sleep. What use was it for me to come home at midnight anyway? Ayse's asleep and I'm still wide awake. I should be pushing drinks down at the club. Having a ball.

I had to go out and pick up a six-pack at the convenience store an hour ago. Ayse doesn't like us to keep alcohol in the house. It's a Muslim thing that reminds me too damn much of a Baptist thing. God-damned rules and regs. That's what the world's religions all wind up being, a bunch of screwed up rules and regs.

Muslims and Jews won't eat pork, Hindus won't eat cows and Catholics eat only fish on Fridays, provided it's Lent. Baptists won't drink any alcohol but Catholics serve wine for Communion. Who knows if the particular bus you're on is going to end up in Heaven?

I'll have to drink the entire six-pack before going to bed. Not a big problem. It tastes good and I've already finished three cans. Three to go.

I'm thinking about suing my Dad. That son of a bitch has no right tying up my money. I'm thinking about hiring the meanest kick-ass attorney in Atlanta and taking that preacher to court. That'll teach him to mess up my life.

What gives him the right to tell me who I can and can't marry? I can't stand him. He thinks he's got the keys to the pearly gates in his front pocket and that no one is going to get into Heaven unless they ask his permission.

Screw him. I don't need his permission. It's my life and it's always been my life and I can do as I please.

Ruth, my sister, can go to hell with him. She called me last week at the bar to ask how it's going. I don't know how the hell she found out where I was working, or where they got the telephone number, but it doesn't surprise me. Ruth knows everything. She knew about my partying and she had heard Ayse was back in Oglethorpe.

Baptists are like that. It's a cult. A Jesus-freak cult with spies everywhere. You can't wipe your ass without a dozen Baptists knowing about it. It has to be someone who came into the bar. Yeah, that's funny in a way.

It was probably some alcoholic Baptist who came in for a few bumps at the saloon and squealed on me. Noticed I was a sinner, working at a bar and serving a drunken Baptist. That's the pot calling the kettle black. A drunk turning in a bartender.

Daniel stopped writing in his journal long enough to finish off his fourth can of Ice House. He was drunk. He had grabbed a hot dog on his way into work at seven and had not eaten since then. The beers were his dinner.

He opened another can and took up his pen and notebook to continue.

So Ruth gives me the whole spiel. That I had better start repenting, start thinking about divorcing Ayse and come to my senses. I told her to buzz off. It felt great to tell my sister to get lost and I'd do it again tomorrow given the opportunity. I asked her how she got my number but she wouldn't say. It was the private line and not the phone number we've got listed in the yellow pages. That's usually tied up because we let our customers use it.

She hung up on me. I suppose I should have been more polite. But why? She and Mom sit back and let Dad take a wrecking ball to my life and wonder why I'm angry. Damn straight I'm angry.

I'm angry at all of them — Dad, Mom, Ruth, the whole congregation. I'm angry at God. Oh, the hell with it, why bother using caps. I'm angry at god. Who is god? What has he ever done for me? As far as I'm concerned, we just made him up a couple thousand years ago because we were afraid of dying.

I'm not afraid of dying. Dying is just like being thrown into a dark, black hole where somebody shovels dirt over you to keep the stench down.

Daniel took another hard pull from his can of beer. He finished it in one long, calculated drink, crushing the thin aluminum container in his hand after finishing it. He set the crushed can beside the other empties in the plastic bag beside him.

He picked up the fifth can of Ice House and popped the lid. He was going to continue writing but didn't. He decided to drink instead. Knowing Ayse would be upset with him if she found the plastic bag full of empty beer cans come morning, Daniel knew from the start that he would have to ditch them before morning.

He had planned to go for a late-night stroll and toss the empty six-pack into the Dumpster behind the 7-11 store where he'd purchased it. It was his way of getting rid of the evidence. If he were to leave the cans in the apartment complex's

Dumpster, Ayse might see them before the next pick-up. She knew Ice House was his favorite, and there may be questions asked. Questions Daniel didn't want to answer.

No, thought a drunken Daniel, I'm better off getting rid of any trace of this shit. I've got to be careful. I've got to watch my backside with these religious types, like Ruth and Ayse. They're like spies, snooping through the trash, listening in on your phone conversations. Who knows what they've got going?

By three a.m., Daniel Harris was stumbling toward the Dumpster behind the 7-11. It was a beautiful, early autumn night in Atlanta. The wind was calm and the sky clear and the starlight endless.

But Daniel never looked at the pantheon of stars above him. He kept his eyes on the ground, watching for an unexpected curb to trip him while on his quest to hide the evidence. He opened the heavy plastic cover to the Dumpster, threw in his empty six-pack and stumbled home.

By four in the morning, Daniel was passed out on the Salvation Army sofa in the living room of a one-bedroom apartment in the two hundred and eighty-seven-unit Monterey Apartment complex in northeast Atlanta. He didn't feel like crawling into bed with Ayse for fear she would smell the beer on his breath.

He had come home early to spend some time with her. It didn't matter. He was on his way now and there would be no stopping him.

Thanksgiving Dinner

"Please pass the gravy," said Randy, already working on his second serving.

"Here it is." Hatice passed the gravy bowl to Randy. She was careful not to spill it on Ayse's linen tablecloth. The tablecloth, which had been in her family for years, served well to cover their scratched dining room table.

"Everything's so delicious," remarked Kasha.

"Not only is she beautiful, she can cook," added Daniel, winking at his lovely wife.

"Oh, you are all too kind," said Ayse, blushing a trifle from the flurry of compliments that had been given to her by everyone since dinner had started. "It's just a turkey. They're not that hard to cook."

"It's the best turkey dinner I've ever had," said Randy.

"It's the first home-cooked turkey I've ever had. Now I know why Americans love Thanksgiving. What a feast!" exclaimed Hatice.

"A toast to the chef," said Randy, raising his glass of chablis.

"To Ayse, my sweetheart!" Daniel clinked his glass of wine with Randy. Eventually, with their arms stretching over the mashed potatoes, the yams and the green beans prepared with a Turkish flair, all of them managed to gently kiss each other's wine glasses in celebration of this dinner together.

Small conversations followed. Laughter and remembrances of years past filled the air and mingled with the aroma of a fourteen-pound turkey. Ayse smiled and listened. Dinner had been good all day long — everything she'd wished for.

She looked around the table and felt comforted by the improvised family Daniel and she had discovered. They needed these friends, especially during the holidays. They needed the sense of belonging that had been taken from them. Ayse's family, both geographically and emotionally, were still too distant. She had not spoken a word to, or received a single e-mail, from her mother since her departure from Istanbul.

Daniel's family, though within reach, would have no part of them. He had not heard from anyone since his telephone conversation with Ruth.

As he ate, Daniel couldn't help but think of Thanksgiving dinners past. Rebecca in the kitchen, coming out with dish after dish of okra, homemade biscuits, mashed potatoes, and a huge turkey. His nephew Jason underfoot, the Christmas albums playing and the bowl games to follow. The three of them, Dad, Chet and himself telling the coach what play to run next, somehow amazed that he never heeded their advice.

Daniel missed it. He never thought he would, but as he sat around their makeshift dinner table, it dawned on him that he missed seeing his family. It made him sad to think he would never again have a Thanksgiving at home. He knew his father wouldn't rescind his decision to sever Daniel from the family. It wasn't how Clay worked. When a decision was made, especially one of this magnitude, it was made for good. It was carved into stone as deeply as were the Ten Commandments.

It started to make him angry again, so he forced himself to stop thinking about it. To stop dwelling on the fact that he would never be able to go home again. And why? he reflected. Because I fell in love.

"Dessert anyone?" Ayse's announcement broke Daniel's preoccupation.

"Not now, Ayse, I can hardly move," said Randy, still seated at the table. "Maybe in a while."

"In a bit, Ayse, I'm stuffed," echoed Kasha.

"Well, when you are ready you can all have a piece of my very first pumpkin pie. I hope you don't mind being part of my test group."

"You're taking too many biology courses, Ayse," said Randy.

"Let's catch a game," suggested Daniel, needing to stretch after devouring a huge dinner.

Everyone got up. Daniel and Randy took a half-dozen steps and plopped back down on the sofa, fighting for the remote. Hatice and Kasha helped Ayse clean up. Within minutes a bowl game was blaring, dishes were being clanged and clattered, and the afternoon was wearing on as it was across a million homes in the Peach State.

Things, for the moment, were good again, thought Ayse as she washed the dinner dishes and made small talk with her two college friends. Daniel had taken the last week off, and he had enjoyed his break from the long nights at the saloon. They had made love every night and the past five days had served to remind her how wonderful it was to be with him.

It was his anger that worried her. She saw it flare up time and time again and wondered if he would ever be able to let it go. To put his father's actions behind him and let himself be free of his resentment. He still talked of a lawsuit but, thus far, Ayse had kept him from proceeding.

Daniel wanted to get even. To punish his father in retribution for the pain Clay had caused him. But Ayse knew it would not end if Daniel decided to file a lawsuit in an attempt to gain access to his grandmother's money. All it would serve to do would be to further inflame his father. A legal battle would not resolve the war that had developed between them, but engage it.

She knew intuitively that Clay would react with more anger, more retribution if Daniel were to raise his hand against him. There was much, much more damage Clay could do. He knew enough people in the state to make Daniel's life a living hell if he chose. He knew sheriffs and police commissioners, people who could dedicate their resources to making things difficult for both of them.

Powerful people who could pull Daniel over some night after the saloon closed and serve him a DUI or worse still, racially profile me, bringing me down for questioning every time a bomb exploded somewhere in the world, or a plane was hijacked. No, Ayse reflected as she cleaned the roaster in which the turkey had been cooked, it was far better to leave Clay and his armies of the faithful alone. They could get Grandmother's money when he and Rebecca left this earth. They could wait. Waiting was safer.

"What about that pumpkin pie?" yelled Randy from the sofa.

"I thought you said in an hour?" yelled Kasha in response, drowning the roar of the Nebraska fans on TV.

"I was wrong. Pretty, pretty please..." Randy had turned around to give the three girls his best puppy dog look. They laughed. They were all feeling a bit tipsy from the chablis. None of the girls drank alcohol to speak of. They rarely drank a beer, and had never so much as tasted hard liquor. So the two glasses of chablis had gone straight to their heads and with Ramadan a month away, Hatice and Kasha were determined to have one more glass before returning to their dorm.

Dessert was served just as daylight succumbed to darkness. Around eight o'clock everyone excused themselves and the party dissolved. Jackets were put on, kisses exchanged and small packages of leftovers given to each of the guests.

It had been a wonderful holiday, felt Ayse as she bid her friends farewell and closed the door behind them. Daniel and she would finish the last bottle of wine and within the hour, find themselves beneath the blankets of their bed. The intoxication of wine would meld with the intoxication of making love.

But Ayse couldn't help but worry about tomorrow, when Daniel would have to return to his job at the bar. She worried he might start in again, coming home late and drunk, shouting at her, falling into bouts of depression. She didn't dwell on it, instead she lost herself in the love they were sharing and let it go at that. Tomorrow may never come.

Macon, Georgia

Clayton Aaron Harris relaxed in his easy chair. An ancient Bing Crosby album spun in the old console record player. His entire music collection was embedded on long-playing vinyl and he saw no reason to change. He knew where every scratch on every worn record was and, unless they started skipping, he didn't mind. The old records added to the character of the song, as though Bing would have wanted to sound scratchy and used.

Clay had his Bible in his hand — the Authorized Bible. The King James version of the holy word whose roots sprang from Henry VIII's desire for a new wife in 1533. It was then when England broke with the Holy Roman Church to form the Church of England and start down the long road that eventually brought Baptists to America. Clay's Bible, a new translation made by a committee of 54 Protestants and completed in 1611 in Reformation England, had gone unchanged for nearly four hundred years, not unlike his record collection.

There were some members of his congregation who might have insisted that Jesus spoke in Middle English, although the historical proof of such a thing would be impossible to verify. Jesus, it is believed, was bilingual. He spoke in Greek and an ancient form of Aramaic. The old testament was written in Hebrew. But Clayton Harris cared little about the actual history of his Bible. He knew nothing about the fact that dozens of books originally a part of the collection of books that make up the Bible had been removed and destroyed by members of the early church under the guise of heresy.

Gone was the Gospel of Peter, The Gospel of the Twelve and the Gospel of

Philip. Only papyrus fragments of these lost books exist. Fragments of Epistles, Gospels, Acts and the Psalms of Solomon that were edited out by members of the Holy Roman Church in St. Jerome's sanctified, canonized version of the Bible. A Bible that, as modern archeology has proven, was as much the work of men seeking religious and political authority as it was the word of God. Men seeking power amidst the decline of the Romans and consolidating that power by claiming to have the only authorized edition of the holy book in their court. All else was heresy, a crime punishable by death.

The Gnostics of Egypt, the Coptics of Ethiopia, the Eastern Orthodoxy, and dozens of other early Christian sects feared for their lives. They fled the Holy Land shortly after the destruction of the Temple in Jerusalem, finding safe harbor in distant monasteries deep in the sands of Egypt or the mountains of western Turkey. Believers soon to be hunted out not by the Romans, but by the very Christians who professed to be following God's word. Followers who confessed to Jesus as they burned the heretics alive on pyres made from codices of these false Bibles.

Centuries of inquisitions, witch hunts, and infallible proclamations wherein heretical denominations were found guilty, condemned and methodically destroyed by fellow Christians. A Bible with two thousand years of translations and re-translations. The word of God going from Greek to Latin, then returning to Greek, then to French or German or English or Hebrew. With each and every edition was copied by tireless scribes who labored under the thumbs of omnipotent popes and medieval tyrants. Despots whose thirst for earthly power and wealth far outstripped their concern for the teachings of some Jewish mystic named Jesus.

That was the Bible Clayton Harris read, the King James Bible. It was, according to millions of unquestioning believers, the final, irrevocable word of God. It was a Bible designed by a committee of clerics. A Bible whose roots stemmed from King Henry the VIII's need for a divorce from Catherine of Aragon. The word of God.

Clay could smell dinner wafting from Rebecca's kitchen. She had called him at work earlier in the afternoon to ask what he might like for dinner. He told her he felt like having pork chops. So Rebecca had gone to Winn-Dixie to pick up four fat, fresh pork chops. She was smothering them in onions and green peppers and cooking them slowly in a cast-iron frying pan.

She had picked up fresh corn and grits and the smell of her cooking drenched the downstairs. Clay was getting hungry. He had put down his Bible a while ago, carefully pulling the thin nylon ribbon across a page to mark a section of II Corinthians that he would resume reading after dinner. Now he sat back to listen to Bing Crosby's static-laden voice echo through the downstairs. It all fit together perfectly; the smell of pork chops, the voice of a dead singer on a scratchy phonograph and a Bible reworked to fit the needs for an ancient king. It was modern Christianity.

"Dinner's nearly ready, Clay!" shouted Rebecca from the kitchen. "Go ahead and take a seat at the table."

Clay pulled the wooden lever of his La-Z-Boy recliner back and brought it to an upright position. He summoned every ounce of his energy to overcome the inertia that had gathered during his hour-long rest. Putting the Bible down on the small, dark mahogany end table beside the plaid recliner, he walked over to the dining room.

There were two places set. One for him at the head of the table and one for Rebecca beside him. The table was large enough to seat six. It was a finely polished mahogany table with three leaves that were seldom inserted anymore. There were fine linens placed below the plates to prevent scratching the finish. The surface of the table smelled like Lemon Pledge.

As Clay waited, Rebecca made several trips back and forth to the kitchen. She did so without comment or reservation. She had been serving him dinners for nearly forty years and she did so faithfully. It was her role — her dutiful obligation as his wife and mother of their children. Clay had never made a dinner or cleaned up afterward. No one had ever questioned this arrangement, not even their daughter Ruth, whose familial arrangement with her husband tended to be less traditional.

After the dishes were neatly arranged on their dining room table, Clay said grace. "For what we are about to receive, let us be truly thankful. Amen."

"Amen," echoed Rebecca, slightly out of sync with her husband.

Clay had been saying the same grace for decades. Neither the tone of his voice nor the cadence of his prayer had varied over the years. Only the sound of his aging voice differed from the very first time he had said his short invocation. At that, the difference was imperceptible.

"Please pass me the pork chops," said Clay to his wife.

Rebecca picked up the covered dish that held the four steaming pork chops and passed it to her husband. She said nothing.

"These were always Daniel's favorites, your pan-fried chops. You can rest assured he hasn't tasted one of these since marrying that Muslim girl," commented Clay as he forked the largest of the four and placed it on his empty plate.

Rebecca was stunned. This was the first mention Clay had made of his son since the end of summer, three months ago. Then it was a brief comment on how poor the lawn looked since Daniel had gone off and gotten married. Even during their Thanksgiving feast two weeks ago, neither Ruth, nor Chet, nor anyone had made mention of Daniel. It was as if he were dead. Rebecca felt inclined to respond to her husband's snide comment.

"I don't think it's appropriate for you to be speaking like that about Daniel and his wife. I see absolutely nothing wrong with abstaining from eating pork if a person's religion forbids it."

Clay, who was in the process of buttering his corn, put down his butter knife in disbelief. Rebecca Jean Harris had actually engaged him. It was a rare and startling event in the Harris household.

"It's a stupid, barbarian commandment. Everyone knows the only reason it's forbidden is because pigs once carried trichinosis. The Jews, who you would think might know better, forbid their people to eat pork as well. There hasn't been a case of trichinosis in the United States in a hundred years."

"Well, we don't drink alcohol, Clay, and even Jesus drank wine. His first miracle was turning water into wine, *"Jesus said to the servants, "Fill the jars with water": so they filled them to the brim.*

Then he told them, "Now draw some out and take it to the master of the banquet."

They did so, and the master of the banquet tasted the water that had been turned into wine. He did not realize where it had come from, though the servants who had drawn the water knew. Then he called the bridegroom aside and said, "Everyone brings out the choice wine first and then the cheaper wine after the guests have had too much to drink; but you have saved the best till now."

This, the first of his miraculous signs, Jesus performed at Cana in Galilee. John, Chapter 2, Verses 7 through 11."

Clay's pale complexion flushed with anger. This was so unlike his wife, quoting Scripture and challenging him. What could have possibly come over her?

"I know my Scripture, Rebecca!" he said in a loud, flustered tone. "You are quoting from the New International Version again, and you know I dislike that translation."

"Well, my point is, as Baptists, we choose not to drink wine. There is nothing in the Bible that forbids us from drinking. Jesus drank wine. It says again in Matthew, Chapter 26, Verse 27, *"Then he took the cup, gave thanks and offered it to them, saying, 'Drink from it, all of you. This is my blood of the covenant, which is poured out for the forgiveness of sins.'*

"That's not how the King James Bible reads. It says, and I quote, *And he took the cup, and gave thanks, and gave it to them, saying, 'Drink ye all of it: For this is my blood of the new testament, which is shed for many for the remission of sins.'*

"But I say unto you, I will not drink henceforth of this fruit of the vine, until that day when I drink it new with you in my Father's kingdom.

"You are misquoting and misinterpreting the Holy Scripture, Rebecca, and woe to any woman who does so."

Rebecca found herself frustrated and cornered. She had not wanted their conversation to end up in another of Clay's unwinnable Bible studies, knowing he could run circles around her when it came to Scripture. So she conceded.

"Well, maybe Christ didn't drink any wine, but he certainly didn't mind his friends and followers enjoying a glass or two.

"That's not my point anyway, Clay. My point is that you shouldn't stand in judgment of Daniel's wife or her religious beliefs. We've never even met her. She might be a wonderful young woman, but for your stubbornness, we'll probably never find out."

Clay saw the root of the problem. This wasn't about pork chops or wine, this was about a mother missing her son.

"I've a right to be stubborn, and I've a right to sever that boy and his unbeliever wife from our lives. We had forbidden Daniel to see that woman again, and the next thing we find out is that he has run off and married her.

"You might miss him, Rebecca. And I can't lie to you, I miss him too. But what he did was unforgivable. He disobeyed us and he embarrassed our family before the entire congregation. For doing such a thing, he shall never set foot in this house again. Not so long as I am amongst the living!"

Clay pushed back his chair, stood up, and threw his linen napkin on the dining room table. He walked toward the front door and took his sweater off the hall tree.

"I'm not hungry. I'm going for a walk."

"Oh, Clay. I didn't mean to upset you..."

The door slammed behind him before Rebecca could complete her sentence. She knew at this point it didn't matter. Nothing she could have said would have prevented him from heading out that front door. He was furious, and the walk, reasoned Rebecca, would be good for him. The walk would cool him down.

She had needed to say something, and he needed to know that his wife was not at all sure they were doing the right thing. Rebecca missed her boy over Thanksgiving and with Christmas a few weeks off, she knew her longing for him was only going to worsen.

She loved her son. She knew what he had done was wrong but, without Clay's unbendable resolve keeping her from doing so, she would have forgiven him. She wanted to meet Ayse. She wanted to find out what this woman was like, what she saw in her son. Rebecca wanted to know what their plans might be.

Where were they going to live? Were they going to remain in Atlanta or move across the ocean, returning to Turkey? Was she pretty? Was she gentle and sweet like her son?

These were the questions Rebecca asked of herself while Clay's heavy footsteps walked an empty suburban road as a wintry evening settled over Georgia. Footsteps that landed hard and determined against the dark asphalt. Eyes that watched the darkness approaching, dimming the first hints of autumnal color in the forest surrounding their neighborhood.

Clay kept walking. He was hungry and tired but he took note of neither. He focused solely on his boy and what trouble Daniel had brought into his life. The comments Clay overhead at church — the gossip and the rumors surrounding their elopement. The talk of the Muslim girl being pregnant.

Now it had come to divide his family. Why had God done such a thing to one of his true believers? Clay wondered as the sun fell beneath the tree line. What had he done to deserve such a punishment?

He walked steadily down the winding road that meandered through their subdivision. Darkness fell and, as it did, a cold wind picked up, rustling the dying leaves. Ten minutes along, a light rain began to fall. Clay, absorbed in his anger and frustration, continued walking, taking little note of the weather.

The rain intensified. It fell in icy sheets, soaking the countryside and making the darkness cold and damp. Clay began to shiver, and as he did, he realized that he'd walked much farther than he had planned. His agitation had distracted him, and now, almost a mile from home, he discovered his cotton sweater was soaked through. He became chilled.

I'll just turn around and head back home, he decided. It's less than a mile. Maybe one of my neighbors will be coming down the road in a few minutes. I'll flag him down and catch a ride.

Rebecca stood in front of her bay window, watching the rain come down. It was pitch black outside and the raindrops blew against the window pane as though someone were throwing gravel at the glass. She was worried.

Where on earth could Clay have gone to? It had been half an hour since he stormed out the door, and with the rain starting, she had expected him to be back momentarily. But he hadn't come back. She decided to get into the Explorer and try to find him.

Rebecca went to the garage and started the SUV. When she opened the garage door, a gust of wind blew in, cold and bitter. She backed out and turned around, heading down her long driveway to the main road.

Which way? she asked herself. Which way did Clay walk? To her right, the road led toward the entrance, past a dozen estate-sized properties, and then to the highway that led to North Baptist Church, or farther along that same road into downtown Macon. To her left, the road continued to the north. There were only three homes in that direction, some conservation easements and a score of vacant lots. It ended in a cul de sac a mile and a half away.

He wouldn't have gone left, reasoned Rebecca. It was getting dark when he went storming out of the house and he wouldn't have gone left. He would have gone right, where there are lights from the surrounding houses. Clay's not that foolish.

With the windshield wipers pounding, Rebecca pulled out and drove south. She flipped her headlights on bright, hoping to find her husband in the pouring rain. She drove slowly, meticulously, not wanting to miss him in the darkness.

But Clay had been foolish. He had turned to the left at the end of his driveway, wanting to be alone and undisturbed as he walked. Rebecca's headlights would not find him.

By this time, the rain had soaked through to his shirt and T-shirt. His shoes and socks were drenched. Only the upper section of his pants remained dry, though they were fast becoming saturated in the ceaseless rain. Clay found himself getting cold. Too cold.

Rebecca crawled along the road looking for her husband. She knew he must be chilled to the bone by now, recalling that he hadn't grabbed his umbrella before leaving the house. He wasn't thinking. He was so upset.

Clay walked fast, trying to keep his body temperature up by moving quickly. The rain continued falling, and by now he was totally soaked. He thought about running, but realized he might stumble and fall in the darkness. Falling down, possibly hurting himself, would only make matters worse.

No, I'll be fine. I'll walk up to the Webbs' place and knock on their door. They'll call Rebecca for me and she can run over and pick me up. I should have grabbed an umbrella. What in the world was I thinking?

Rebecca had already gone a mile up the road in the wrong direction. Clay was nowhere to be found. She knew that by this time he would be half freezing, and still the rain kept on. He must have gone into one of the neighbor's houses, she speculated. There's probably a message for me at the house.

She turned around at the last driveway before the highway and started heading back home. She reached down and turned the heat on in the car. She looked at the digital thermometer on the dash. It read 46 degrees. She was getting worried. A person could catch his death out here tonight.

Clay's teeth were chattering uncontrollably as he walked briskly up to the front door of Dr. and Mrs. Webb's house. He pushed the doorbell and heard it chime. Their golden retriever started barking and Clay smiled to himself. They'd be letting me inside in just a minute. He waited.

A minute passed and the dog stopped barking. He pressed the doorbell a second time. The dog started barking again. At that moment Clay knew there was no one in her house to tell him to hush up. The doctor and his wife were in town, attending a Christmas party. Clay reached down to open the door to let himself in. It was locked.

Though the front porch overhang offered Clay shelter from the rain, his clothes were so soaked that it mattered little. A gust of wind kicked up, and as it swirled around him, Clay became colder. He had to keep moving. Standing there, his teeth chattering, his thoughts racing in fear, Clay realized he was in trouble. Serious trouble.

He was beginning to succumb to hypothermia, and he knew it. His house was still a half-mile away and he wondered if he would be able to make it home safely. His legs were cramping from the cold. He couldn't stop shivering.

As he stood on that porch, alone and frightened, he looked up to the heavens. Why are you doing this to me, God? What have I done to deserve this? Is it my time, Lord?

But the Lord did not answer him. A cold wind blew across the porch and served to remind Clay that he could not stay under it any longer. He was too wet and chilled. He had to try to make it home.

Rebecca pulled up her driveway and pushed the electric garage door opener as she approached the house. She would head inside to see if Clay was already back home and, if not, check her phone messages before going down the road in the other direction. Surely someone's called by now, and I'll need to go pick up my impetuous husband.

She left the Explorer running and went inside to check their answering machine. No messages.

Oh my goodness, he must have headed north. Why on earth would he have gone that direction? Aside from the Webbs' place, and two other homes, there's nothing but woods that way. What was he thinking?

Clay wasn't thinking. He was praying. He was walking as quickly as he could manage toward the warmth of his home and he was scared. As he became colder his thoughts became disoriented and confused.

What began as a fit of anger had now placed him in harm's way. He prayed a car would come along and save him. But no car appeared. He wondered, for the first time in his life, if he had done something wrong. If God was punishing him for his decision to disconnect Daniel from his life.

Why won't it stop raining? he asked God. But God didn't answer him. For the first time in his life Clay reflected on his own mortality. Is it my time? Am I going to standing before the Almighty this very night? His thoughts becoming delirious, and he questioned his unbending resolve to eliminate Daniel from his life. What if I'm wrong, God forbid. What if I'm wrong?

Rebecca hurried into the Explorer, backed out, turned around, and drove down the driveway. She headed left this time, praying she would find he husband before having to call the police. She knew this wasn't good, and became mad at herself for upsetting her husband earlier. It's all my fault, she thought.

A half-mile down the road, she found him. He was stumbling along the edge of the asphalt, crying. He was freezing.

"Oh my goodness!" exclaimed Rebecca as she helped her shivering husband into the car. "You're chilled through and through."

Clay didn't respond. His face was pale and his teeth rattled incessantly. He looked at her with such a sense of fear in his eyes that it spoke volumes.

Rebecca turned the heat up as high as it would go and continued north to the next driveway to turn around. The rain did not stop.

Ayse waited. Her roasted lamb shanks lingered in the oven on the lowest possible setting. Her eggplant casserole and rice pudding withered in their respective sauté pans. The small dining room table was set as two tall candles flickered in the dimly lit apartment. Daniel was late, probably caught up in Atlanta's perpetual snarl of traffic.

It was a year ago, thought a young, Turkish princess to herself as she sat on the sofa, a year ago today we were married. It was a heavenly afternoon in Gatlinburg, the day we became husband and wife. The day we entered the Cloud Nine Weddings' Chapel as lovers and walked out a married couple. The next few days, at our campground in the Great Smoky Mountain National Park, were the happiest days of my life.

Ayse was reminiscing. Camping, making their simple dinners on the Coleman stove, hiking all day long and returning to their tiny tent each night to make passionate love beneath a cloudless sky — all made for memories that would not fade. They had only one photograph of their five days in the mountains, and that was the black-and-white of them in the wedding chapel.

Ayse looked toward it, sitting framed on a used sideboard, to remind herself it was true. That she was living in America, deeply in love with a Christian and still attending Oglethorpe. These were the thoughts that comforted her as she sat and watched the digital clock in the kitchen change its red numbers from 7:10 to 7:11 to 7:20 to 7:40.

At 8:00 p.m., Ayse could no longer hold on to the belief it was traffic that kept Daniel from coming home. She let go of the good memories and as she did, the reality of their current relationship crept in. It was like a surge of black, dirty tidal water inundating her dreams.

Daniel was an alcoholic. Ayse didn't want to acknowledge, nor deal with it. It was just too hard for her to accept. But in her heart she knew it. She had found half-filled bottles of vodka hidden around their apartment and had left them undisturbed. She knew it was a sign he was addicted to alcohol. Daniel had hid the bottles well, knowing he might need a shot in the middle of the night. Anything to quench his unquenchable thirst.

He had been sliding since the day his father had called to disown him, embarrassing Daniel before his new bride. Making her husband feel powerless and unwanted. Ayse had watched Daniel descend. Step by step she witnessed her spouse lowering himself into the underbelly of the Buckhead after-hours crowd. At first he had just stayed an hour or two after the bars closed. Over time, it gradually worsened.

After the infamous Buckhead Bar's New Year's Eve party, Daniel didn't come home at all. He stumbled in to shower at four in the afternoon, made love to Ayse, and headed back to the bar for his six to midnight shift. She didn't ask where he had been. She didn't want to know.

As 8:30 lit up the liquid crystal display on the digital clock in the kitchen, Ayse blew out the candles. Once slender and tall, the wicks now stood an inch above their silver-plated holders, the candle holders covered in the drippings of melted wax. He wasn't coming home.

Daniel, Ayse presumed, was drunk.

She was right. Daniel had finished his shift at seven and right afterward, done little more than move from one side of the bar, where he was pouring drinks, to the other side, where he was drinking them. It had become his standard routine. Most of his two-week paychecks were converted into a horrendous bar tab at twenty percent off retail. He was drinking away his earnings, their rent money and the groceries. He was drinking away their future.

The manager was keeping a very close eye on the kid from Macon. He had seen plenty of young, novice bartenders drown themselves in vodka sevens and screwdrivers. To him, the pattern was a familiar one. After the booze came the drugs — then the all-night parties and the infidelities that followed.

Soon thereafter, if Daniel remained on his present course, the tills would start ringing up short. The night manager would start marking the bottles with an invisible magic marker, checking those same bottles the following morning with a black light. He would be looking for a missing inch here, a half-inch there. Shrinkage that had nothing to do with evaporation.

Once he could be singled out for stealing, either booze or cash, Daniel would be fired. Tossed out on his ass like a dozen country boys before him. Sometimes getting fired would serve to snap them out of it. The smart ones would heed the message, would start sobering up and turning their lives around.

Others wouldn't. They'd continue to slide, to tumble downhill until there was no vertical left in their dull, flat universe. The fools would fall, and fall hard.

Over the course of a few years, they would age a decade. They would work odd jobs, going out with casual labor pools or taking dishwashing positions until they had enough money to go on a binge, then do it all over again. They would lose their girlfriends, wives, their families, friends and their self-esteem. Jail or mental-health facilities would keep an empty cot waiting for them, knowing it would only be a matter of time before they stumbled in, too beaten down to endure another cycle.

Daniel was slowly, methodically joining their ranks. He was no longer an apprentice bartender. A year into the business he could whip up a 'gin fizz' or a 'strip and go naked' with the best of them. He knew his drinks, his customers and his job. He was now an apprentice drunk. He could put away a half liter of Smirnoff in an hour, finishing the remainder in a dim-witted fog.

Once he had three or four shots in him, all bets were off. Appointments languished into skipped appointments, meetings never happened, anniversary dinners disappeared into the corner section of a twenty-five-foot bar amid a crowd of fellow lonely drunks. Daniel wasn't coming home.

He had forgotten about their anniversary dinner. He'd stepped outside after his shift to smoke a joint with a regular and decided to go back in, stoned beyond reason, to have a couple of quick bumps before driving home. By eight-forty, as Ayse sat alone and ate her lamb dish beside the unlit, melted candles, Daniel was passed out at the end of the bar.

Jimmy Boy let him sleep, knowing that if he tried to wake him he'd just get angry. As angry as a rattlesnake.

Ayse blamed Daniel's father. But she curtailed her blame because she understood how difficult it must be for Clay. Elif, her own mother, had yet to speak with her, even though a year had gone by.

At least she had her father. He had stopped by to meet Daniel four months ago while passing through Atlanta on business. That was back in January, and Daniel was on his best behavior. It had gone well, and they were thrilled that of the four parents, at least one had honored them with a visit.

But in the end, Mustapha's visit only served to make Daniel more disappointed in his own father's actions. A week after Mustapha left, Daniel was drinking even harder. No matter what the news was, Daniel turned it into a reason to step up his liquor intake and smother the noise that he was hearing deep within himself. A noise that couldn't be silenced.

At 11:14 on the red digital clock, Ayse, while putting away the dishes, heard someone fumbling with a set of keys at the front door. She walked over and unbolted the door from the inside. She opened it to find her prince standing before her in the pouring rain.

He looked lost. His eyes were puffy and bloodshot, his posture slouched and his clothes looked as if they had been slept in. They had been slept in.

"Honey, I'm home," he said in a bad Jack Nicholson imitation.

"Go shower, please."

"Go screw yourself, Ayse."

Daniel walked in, and fell onto the couch with such a tumble that it might have cracked the tired sofa in two. He let his keys fall from his hands as he succumbed to the spinning.

This was their anniversary celebration.

Book of Midnights

Friday morning, 4:30 a.m.

I'm really stoned. Jimmy Boy and I did a couple of lines after the bar closed and now it's five in the morning and I'm totally zoned. Melissa was going to have a party but she got sick from something she ate and had to call the party off at the last minute so that's why I'm home. Ayse's asleep. It's the only time I see her anymore, when she's asleep.

That's fine with me. All we do is fight. She's just like my god-damned dad. She's always nagging me, "Stop drinking so much, those cigarettes are going to kill you." "Drive careful, try to make it home early tonight." Bitch, bitch, bitch. She might as well call my father and discuss my "problems" with him. The two of them would have a ball dissecting their little case study in substance abuse. Well, screw 'em all.

What the hell was I thinking when I asked her to marry me? Was I nuts? We're too different. We're worlds apart.

I read a story in the Atlanta Journal *yesterday about a young couple in India who were stoned to death by their families. She was a member of the Brahmin caste and he was a member of the laborers' caste. Like Ayse and I, they married without anyone's permission. It was in a small village near Delhi, but I can't remember its name.*

When the two families found out about the marriage, they hunted the couple down and stoned them to death. Wow. Imagine killing your own kid because they fell in love with someone outside of their caste. That's what they're doing to us, they're killing us. Mustapha's been the only one who's supported us in any way, the only one who hasn't lifted a boulder to hurl at us.

It's all because of religion. Religion sucks. People get on their high horse and the next thing you know someone's holding someone else's feet to the coals. You've got Sunni Muslims hating Shiites, Catholic pedophiles, Hindu stone throwers, Jewish Nazis and every combination thereof.

A world filled with religions and cultures, classes and castes. A world filled with powerful old men and stubborn old women who ruin it for everyone. Who take it all away and leave nothing but a basket full of throwing stones. Ayse deserves better than this. Better than me showing up at four in the morning, messed up and angry.

Ayse should go back to Istanbul where she can find someone who will give her what she deserves. Some kind Islamic man whose family will welcome her into his life and treat them with kindness. She hasn't done anything to deserve this shit storm we're living in.

I won't make it back to Oglethorpe. Ever. Not at this rate. So far, we've managed to save four hundred dollars. I've pissed away the rest. So much for my college education. She's still got another year left before graduation but I don't want us to go on like this.

We've got to divorce. She's got to go home and I've got to keep working at the Buckhead Saloon. Make that Suckhead Saloon. Working and drinking. That's my plan. It's a great plan. I wonder what's on TV?

At the Crypt of Civilization

The stainless steel door felt cold on her back. Ayse leaned against it, her tears falling on the terrazzo floor beneath her. All was lost.

As she huddled there, crying, Ayse remembered the days when the two of them would meet here — laughing, and joking about all the odd things Dr. Jacobs and his colleagues had decided to place in the crypt: the set of Lincoln Logs, a Schick electric razor set, an image of the Buddha. An eclectic sampling of the human race chosen by an eccentric professor just before the start of the Second World War. Just before the first atomic bomb was built.

It was over. Ayse was going home. She was going back to Turkey. Daniel had insisted they break up. He had come home drunk and high from the bar two nights ago and said he wanted a divorce.

Why? she asked. Because he was tired of the bullshit. He was tired of the stoning both of them were having to endure. He knew it would never end. His father would never change, and Ayse's mother would probably never speak to her again and it just wasn't worth it. They had hardly any money, the Toyota needed work again and that would wipe out Daniel's meager college fund. It wasn't working.

Love wasn't enough. Love was just more bullshit, said Daniel to a woman who loved him more than life itself. A woman who had sacrificed so much only to be willing to sacrifice a thousand times more if he should dare to ask it of her.

But he didn't ask it. So Ayse sat there, her back against the cold, heartless steel, and bawled. She cried a river of tears. A river that flowed through her veins and swept her downstream into an ocean of despair.

We'll not make it, thought the lonely girl in the empty hallway. Not if we go on like this. There won't be anyone here to open this vault six thousand years from now. Not with all the hate and misunderstanding there is in the world. Not with all the standing armies — the chemical, biological and nuclear weapons. Not with all the Saddam Husseins in the world.

The vault will remain sealed, laying buried beneath the rubble of Hearst Hall after some catastrophic war brought on by an assassination, or a surprise strike by some religious zealots hellbent on their personal vendetta. Government-sanctioned madness.

The world will be a nuclear wasteland, imagined the saddened young woman, curled up on a hard stone floor with her backpack full of textbooks lying beside her. There won't be anything left of the forests, the cities, or all the creatures that grace this paradise we call earth.

They will all have perished in a final apocalypse of fire when the thousands of nuclear weapons are unleashed. Those that survive the first strike will die from the radiation poisoning, wishing early on that the initial blast had taken them.

These thoughts did not befit her, but she could not shake them from her troubled heart. She had called her father last night to ask if he could pay for her flight to Istanbul. He wondered what was the matter. She said they would talk later, when she was in Bebek. She told her Dad not to bother to make it a round trip ticket. She didn't know when, or if, she would ever be coming back to America.

Mustapha didn't press the issue, hearing the anguish in his daughter's voice. He knew things were going badly, but he didn't want to interfere. Daniel and Ayse already had the weight of the world on them, and he felt his own weight would only add to their burden. Theirs was, from the day they eloped, a near impossible path to walk, and he could tell from the quivering in his daughter's voice they were stumbling. He would make arrangements for her flight home the following day.

So Ayse huddled in the hallway, her body wrapped in a ball, crying in search of God. A god who had let her down, though she didn't understand why. Still she prayed for her husband and for their marriage. She had told Daniel two nights ago that she would not divorce him. Not now, not with him so mixed up with the booze and the drugs he was taking.

He answered her in anger. Near the end of their conversation, in a fit of rage, he struck her across the side of her face. If he wanted a divorce, she would agree to it, he screamed. But she would not grant him one. Not yet.

She told him she was willing to go back to Istanbul. That they both needed some time alone. That she needed to be away from the madness that had become an everyday part of their relationship. The swearing, the hidden bottles of liquor, the all-night parties. She agreed to go home, but not to end their relationship. She knew she needed some time alone, and that Daniel needed to turn his life around.

After he struck her, she began yelling back at him. They fell into a rage. Her unexpected anger filled the void of their small apartment. She told him he needed to snap out of it, to stop feeling sorry for himself and move beyond his father's misguided behavior. He needed to get out of Buckhead. To find himself a job where he could have some self-respect. She screamed at her husband, telling him to stay away from the trash he was hanging with.

Things were said that night that should not have been said. Dishes were thrown, voices raised beyond reason. A half-hour into their full-blown fight, one of the neighbors called the police, fearing someone was going to get hurt.

When the two officers knocked on the door, Ayse became fearful. She knew they might take her in for questioning. She was dark-skinned — Islamic. She might be one of them. She had heard the stories about racial profiling. Arabs and Middle Eastern people being kept without charges. A knee-jerk reaction to the terrorist incidents.

But the policemen didn't take her in. They told them both to keep it down. They saw the bruise on Ayse's face and the broken dishes and knew what had transpired.

A lovers' quarrel, like a thousand domestic disputes before. They all end. Some horribly.

But a rare few end in murder, or in a murder/suicide. Couples who let the rage overwhelm them. Scenes where the dishes turn to knives and the kitchen floor becomes covered in blood and the stench of death.

The police remained in their apartment until Daniel and Ayse calmed down. They told them that if the neighbors called the police again they would have to arrest someone. They would have to take them both downtown and book them for disturbing the peace. The thought of such a thing happening, and the sight of the two Atlanta policeman standing in their apartment, frightened them into submission.

Daniel and Ayse realized they were losing it. They knew they were succumbing to the stones being hurled at them. Worse than that, they were now picking those stones up and throwing them at each other.

Ten minutes later, the police left. Daniel and Ayse had both taken a long, deep breath. After the squad car drove away, the repentant couple cleaned up the broken dishes. They sat beside each other on the sofa and began apologizing to each other for their behavior. They were tired, remorseful and afraid. Within an hour, the apologies turned to zippers. They soon found themselves stretched out on the used sofa, making love.

For a brief moment, awhirl in the sexuality of their youthful bodies, they returned to themselves. They were no longer in a low-rent apartment on the north end of Atlanta, but in their tent again. They were up in the mountains of southern Tennessee, at a remote campsite under a starlit night, making love.

The sex had taken them to a place their minds could only imagine. They threw themselves into the act of intercourse with reckless abandon. Where two angry, screaming spouses had been an hour ago, two impassioned lovers lay. The duplicity made sense as their senses overtook them. Love was everything and nothing. Love was the last shelter left in this terrible storm.

After they were becalmed, still lying on the sofa, Daniel reluctantly agreed with Ayse that they should give it some time. They should separate first and, if nothing improved, divorce within the year. He told her he would start looking for a better job after she left and that they could stay in touch via e-mail. He conceded.

But he was lying to her, and to himself. Within his heart he had no intention of leaving the underworld of Buckhead. He couldn't wait to have Ayse gone, knowing that when she was finally out of his life there would be no one left for him to answer to. Then he could cut the last cord and finally be free. Free to sleep with whom he wanted to, to screw himself up as much as he desired. Free to vanish into the subterranean world of cocaine and vodka, ecstasy and marijuana. Free to fly.

Ayse had sensed it. That was why her back was against the crypt as she sat there weeping on this beautiful spring morning. She wept because the world was ending. Her world. Our world. This world where no one would be around to celebrate that day on May 28, 8113 A.D. when the Crypt of Civilization would go unopened. Unopened and unknown. She cried because of it. She cried for us all.

A Return to Istanbul

The drone of the jet engines lulled Ayse to sleep. They had left the coastline of America behind them an hour ago and as the last few remnants of daylight vanished in their wake, Ayse fell asleep.

She cried off and on for the first hour of the flight. Had there been anyone sitting beside her, she would have withheld her tears. The seat beside her was empty, as were most of the seats on this flight. Ayse was glad for it.

She could stretch out and try to get comfortable while the darkness swallowed the plane. In that darkness, the sound of the three engines at cruising speed became the only reality there was. The reality of these long, transoceanic flights — soothing and tenuous at once.

Ayse wasn't feeling well. She had turned down the dinner offered to her earlier. She hadn't felt well during the past week, with cramps and an overall malaise that was impossible to pin down. Ayse thought it must be her nerves, her worries overwhelming her as her flight back to Istanbul grew closer. This flight away from Daniel and back to the familiar, if not bitter, terrain of Bebek.

She knew what her mother was going to say. She knew Elif would be there to meet her, and the first words out of her mouth would be something to the effect of, "I told you so."

"I warned you early on this relationship wouldn't work. They never do. There's too much bad blood between us. Look how they have treated us over the centuries, Ayse. Remember the Inquisition, where we were burned alive as heretics and made to flee all but the southernmost tip of Spain. The unprovoked attacks of the Crusades, the way they always side with the Israelis over the Palestinian issues. No, the contempt the Christians have for us runs too deep for you, or your love for one of them, to change it.

"You were young and you let your heart steer your course. You were blinded by your heart. Now you must leave him, you must let go of your youth and stay here in the city of your birth. You will find a good Turkish boy who will be thrilled to have such a beautiful bride. You must let go of Daniel, Ayse. You must come back to your family and your home."

She knew it was coming, just as she hoped her father, who had actually met Daniel, would serve to temper her mother's harsh words. She prayed Mustapha would convince Elif to go easy on her, give her the time and space to make up her own mind, decide her own future.

Ayse had played out a thousand scenarios as her stomach turned and the whir of the big engines held steady, though she knew it did little good to fret about it. She was tired. Finals, her nerves, these last few days with Daniel, had exhausted the young princess.

She took the flimsy airline pillow and propped it against the bulkhead of the airplane cabin. Then she unfolded the thin, blue blanket with the Delta logo stitched on the corner, and curled up into a tiny, lovely ball. She covered herself. Within a few minutes, safe and warm seven miles above the Atlantic, she fell fast asleep.

❂

A gentle tap on her shoulder woke her. When Ayse first opened her eyes, she didn't know where she was, or who was wakening her. She took the longest time to focus, to remember she was still on an airplane. She felt the tap again and looked over to see a woman sitting beside her.

It was the flight attendant. The same woman Ayse had encountered years ago when returning home to announce her love for Daniel to her family. The flight attendant, Ayse observed, looked much the same. She was wearing a dark-blue Delta blazer, matching slacks and a clean white blouse. Her light brown hair hung straight and long, neatly trimmed just below her shoulders.

Ayse could see her eyes still held a sparkle, a warmth that emanated from this lady's glance — comforting and becalming. It was as though they held some kind of fire behind them, a fire that could warm the coldest of nights.

The flight attendant smiled and spoke to Ayse, "I have come to be with you."

Ayse remembered looking for her that morning as the jumbo jet descended into Heathrow. She was not on the plane. This time she looked at the elegant flight attendant and realized she hadn't noticed her while boarding, or while dinner was being served.

"Who are you?"

"I am who I am," answered the kind lady seated beside Ayse. "It is not important to know what you cannot know. What is important is that we talk."

"But how do you come and go on these planes like this?"

"I am where I am," she replied, surprising Ayse by saying it in flawless Turkish.

Ayse was amazed. Her intuition told her not to question anything else. She looked into the woman's eyes and found solace there, as they were portals into a large, open room with a grand stone fireplace standing opposite the entrance.

Ayse took the flight attendant's soft hand and walked with her toward the two overstuffed chairs sitting before the fireplace. A fire was burning and the glow from the embers served to soothe the unsettled Turkish girl.

She looked around the room. There were long, medieval tapestries hanging on castle walls. They depicted knights in armor, bishops blessing them and maidens approving of their valor. The floor's dark, wooden planks were covered with a floral-patterned Hereke carpet from Eastern Turkey. The woolen carpet was enormous, the pattern familiar to a girl raised in Istanbul.

Ayse took a seat in one of the overstuffed chairs and smiled at the flight attendant as she descended into the other chair. The flight attendant saw Ayse smiling and asked, "Are you comfortable here? Can I get you anything?"

"No, I'm fine. This is a wonderful room. The fire's very comforting. There are so many embers. Has it been burning a long time?"

"Yes it has. This fire's been burning a very, very long time."

The two women sat there, staring into the burning logs without saying another word. The warmth of the fire soaked into each of them, until it had warmed not just their bodies, but their souls. They looked at each other and, after smiling warmly at one another, they began to talk.

"You told me everything was going to work out, but you were wrong," said Ayse.

"Time, my child, everything in time."

"But surely you know what has happened. Daniel is falling apart. He drinks, he stays out all night, he even struck me in anger.

"See, look, the bruise is still here on my cheek."

The flight attendant could clearly see the bruise in the firelight. She did not comment on it. She continued, "I told you never to falter in your love for Daniel. Do you doubt your love for him now, after he has done these things to you?"

"No, because he is so mad at his father for disowning him. I know it's not because of me, but I don't know if I will ever see him, or be with him again. He wants a divorce. He wants to end it."

"Ayse, from this day forward you will always be with Daniel, and he with you."

"But that's not possible. Daniel has asked me for a divorce, my mother would welcome it, and I doubt my father would fight to save our marriage. I doubt that

I will ever see Daniel again."

Ayse began to weep, her tears glistening in the light from the fireplace. The flight attendant rose from her chair and came to comfort her.

"Daniel's within you, Ayse. Time is a river into which you cannot see. All that matters is your love for him. Love him even as he destroys himself. Love him beyond the boundaries. For it is as He has spoken, *'Through God all things are possible.'*

"'It may be that God will ordain love between you and those whom you hold as enemies. For God has power over all things — God is oft forgiving, most merciful.'

"You must trust me completely when I tell you these things."

Ayse recognized the passage the woman was quoting. It was from the Qur'an. She was speaking in Arabic, and though Ayse knew little of the language, she understood the words perfectly.

The flight attendant held out her hand to Ayse. Still whimpering, Ayse reached and took hold of it. When she touched it, a charge of energy unlike anything she had ever known ran through her body like a massive electrical shock.

But there was no pain to this electricity, only a warm, inexplicable vibrance that blanketed her misgivings, soothing her restless heart. Ayse fell back to sleep, holding this woman's hand.

The change in pitch of the jet engines woke her. The flight attendant, who had come to sit beside her in the night was gone. Ayse did not ask the other flight attendants where she might find this woman with the long, straight brown hair and inviting smile. She knew she could not be found.

She wondered for the longest time if it was just a dream. The castle-like setting, the large room, the warmth of the massive hearth, and the shock of the woman's touch — it must have been a dream. A wondrous dream.

Dreaming or not, it didn't matter. For Ayse knew that neither waking nor sleeping meant anything to the graceful lady in the blue Delta uniform. All that mattered was her being there, her visitation.

Ayse's ears began to ache as the plane descended into England. Her stomach churned and the worries she had forgotten earlier began resurfacing from the depths of her heart. It would not be easy, these next few days.

She thought of her lover and remembered the day she kissed him long and sweet atop Kennesaw Mountain. Long and sweet. She did not regret loving him, not for an instant. These thoughts would give her the strength she needed in the days to come. With love, all things are possible.

Buckhead

*D*aniel woke up in the back seat of his Toyota. The smell of his vomit staining the edge of the seat and the pool of half-dried puke on the floor reminded him of the night before. He was in the parking lot behind the Buckhead Saloon. In the fog of his hangover, he couldn't remember throwing up, or passing out afterward.

As he lay still, smelling the stench of his own retch, his memory began coming back, albeit fragmented and without clear definition. He remembered dropping Ayse off at the airport. He was sober then. She was crying. He had carried her bags for her to the curbside check-in. They kissed one last time, then he drove off.

He came back to the bar to celebrate. Yes, that's what he did. He was glad it was over — the relationship, the marriage, the mess he had made of his life. It was finally over. He came back to the Buckhead Saloon to get drunk and rejoice in his new found freedom. It must have been around seven when he pounded down his first shot of tequila. The first of many.

What happened afterward was fuzzy and disjointed. There were girls involved, and they were all dancing in a nearby club. Maybe some pills of some kind. As he tried to put the pieces of his debauchery together, he realized he was hungry.

He remembered he had forgotten to eat. Or maybe he had eaten something. Three or four hot dogs from a convenience store. Did I have ice cream? He couldn't remember. He raised his head to look down at the vomit beneath him and saw pieces of hot dog in it. He had eaten at some point during the night, but he was hungry again, and with good cause.

I'll clean the car today, it stinks. But I've got to get some food in me. Food, aspirin. Shit, I've got to work this afternoon at four. What time is it?

He looked at his watch and saw it was already eleven-thirty. It was cloudy out, and it looked like rain. He got up from the back seat, glad he had decided to sleep in the car and not attempt to drive home. He was barely able to walk, let alone drive when the bars shut down at three.

He got out of the car and stretched. It felt good to stretch after sleeping in such a cramped position. A young guy on a bicycle glanced over at Daniel just as he raised both of his arms up, stretching them over his head. The cyclist didn't see the clean, suburban preacher's kid from north Macon.

He saw a burnout. The bicyclist noted the stain of vomit on Daniel's dirty T-shirt. The fact that he was barefoot, unshaven and standing beside a faded Toyota with bald tires and a dozen rust spots spoke of another lost soul in a city filled with them. The biker saw a drug dealer, a young alcoholic, a loser, a dropout and little else. Wanting to distance himself from this young man, the biker picked up the pace of his pedaling and continued down the alleyway.

Daniel put on his tennis shoes and climbed into the driver's seat. When he reached for his keys in his right pocket, he pulled out a napkin with some writing on it. *Melissa, 770-483-0981.*

It wasn't his handwriting. She must have been one of the girls he met while playing pool. He couldn't remember what she looked like. It didn't matter. He threw the note over his shoulder and it fell into the vomit. There would be plenty of Melissas in the months to come. Too many.

Daniel started up his car and pulled into the alleyway, following the direction the cyclist had traveled a few minutes earlier. He was heading home to shower. His head hurt, his clothes stank and his neck was stiff from sleeping on his shoes. Life was good. He was free.

In Ayse's Room

*S*he placed her cell phone beside her bed. It was one-thirty in the afternoon, and the call she was expecting could come at any moment. Although she suspected the news, Ayse was filled to overflowing with anticipation. For her, it would be the greatest news in all the world.

In the meanwhile, to keep herself distracted, Ayse was reading a novel. It was an American novel and she was reading it in English. She had been told about the book by Hatice, her girlfriend from Egypt. It had been part of the required reading for one of Hatice's Narratives of the Self prerequisites at Oglethorpe. It was called *All the Pretty Horses*. Hatice had given it to Ayse just before her flight to Turkey.

Upon reading it, Ayse knew why her girlfriend had given it to her. It told the story of a love between an American cowboy and a Mexican girl, a tale that mirrored the story of the love between her and Daniel. But Ayse was disappointed with the book. She was upset with both of them for letting their love perish, especially the girl. As she neared the end of the novel, it only served to make Ayse more determined than ever to overcome the hardships of staying with Daniel. It made her want to endure.

As Ayse thought of her lover, her cellular phone rang a refrain from Beethoven's *Ode to Joy*. Ayse picked it up and pushed the call button. She put the phone to her ear, her hand trembling, and in Turkish, said "Hello."

"This is Dr. Nevzat Aksaray's office. Is this Ayse...Harris?" The woman on the other end of the line had a difficult time pronouncing Ayse's last name. English, thought the nurse, is an impossible language.

"This is she."

"The test results have come back and I am glad to tell you...well, congratulations, you are expecting a child."

Ayse paused. To the nurse on the other end of the line, she paused for only a second, but within her heart she paused eternal. She flew on wings of a thousand doves, thrilled to her core with the knowledge that she was no longer just herself, but that she now shared her youthful body with another — the child in her womb.

"Thank you. Thank you for calling."

"Dr. Aksaray has asked me to send you some informational material on the early stages of pregnancy, the first trimester. Do you want us to send it to your U.S. address, or to your home in Bebek?"

"To the Bebek address, please."

"We'll also need to set up another appointment for you next month, are you available on July seventeenth, three p.m.?"

"That will be fine. Could you include a reminder card in your information package? I've been having some morning sickness and I don't want to forget the appointment."

"Yes, that would be the right thing to do."

"Thank you so much, and goodbye."

"Goodbye."

Ayse hit the end button and disconnected the call. She didn't turn her cell phone off, knowing she would want to call Fatimah in a few minutes with the news. But Fatima could wait. For the moment, the only person Ayse wanted to share the news with was herself.

She set the novel on her nightstand and laughed as she did. "You see how different our stories are," she said to the Mexican girl in the novel. "I'm pregnant with Daniel's child and I will not let go of him. I will do as the flight attendant asked, I will love him without reservation."

The Mexican girl in the novel did not respond. Perhaps she wished she had been as strong as this Turkish woman. Perhaps she envied Ayse.

Ayse sat on her bed, drawing her legs up to her chest and wrapping both of her arms around them. It was one of her favorite positions and this afternoon, because of the news, she realized she wasn't alone any longer. A child lived within her.

The lady on the airplane had spoken the truth. Daniel would, from this day forward, forever be a part of her. He was inside of her now, growing, thriving, becoming an infant to be brought into this world. Half-American, half-Turkish, half-Christian, half-Muslim, the child of a world in the throes of becoming smaller.

A world filled with wonder and infinite possibilities, thought an expectant mother, dreaming of her unborn child's future. A future undivided by religions and politics. A world at peace.

Ayse decided to tell her parents in the next few days. Elif had already suspected Ayse's pregnancy, seeing how ill she had felt these last few weeks. It would not come as a surprise to either of them, although Elif would have something cruel to say — something about the reality that Ayse was a continent away from her husband.

Elif, although resigned to the fact that her daughter was not going to give up on Daniel, was still being difficult. Upon Ayse's arrival in Bebek, Elif had hoped she could talk her daughter out of their ill-fated marriage, but to no avail. Ayse maintained that the only reason she was in Turkey was to give Daniel some time to put his life back together. She would not leave him. They would survive this crucible.

For Ayse, curled up on her bed, the child inside of her was proof. Proof they had a future. Proof that love can survive.

She wondered when it might be time to call Daniel. It's still too soon, she thought. I might lose the baby, Allâh forbid, in the first trimester. That news would only serve to darken Daniel's world.

No, I must wait. I must wait until I'm certain the child I am having will be fine before I tell him. Four, maybe five months from now I can tell him, then he will welcome me back to America and stop all this talk of divorcing. I will wait.

On the Empty Apartment

Six weeks had passed since Daniel had last kissed his wife, bidding her farewell at the airport. They had communicated twice since then — a single phone call a few weeks ago, and an e-mail Daniel had yet to reply to. He missed her immensely but wouldn't dare admit it.

As he sat up in bed, watching reruns of television programs that should never have been produced in the first place, he felt lonely. He had the night off, and, after last night's fiasco, had decided not to head out to party again.

Last night he hadn't slept. He and a friend had dropped acid at midnight. It was the first time he had ever taken acid and the trip he took convinced him he would never do LSD again. It was, he'd concluded, too weird and too intense.

He ended up on a tattered couch somewhere in the bowels of Atlanta, reminding himself to keep breathing. Breathe in, breathe out, he repeated to himself as the sun rose over the eastern suburbs of the South's first city. A sun that rose to freeways clogged with commuters and summer smog. Breathe in, breathe out.

At one point, he was tempted to ask his friend to take him to the hospital. But his friend was in the bedroom of this girl's apartment where Daniel was crashing and he didn't want to disturb them. So he waited out the high and eventually came down far enough to handle it.

He had slept most of the afternoon in a futile attempt to regain his sense of reality. Now he was wide awake and alone. Alone in an apartment that looked like hell. Dirty laundry, unwashed dishes and empty containers of take-out

Chinese littered his one-bedroom apartment in a collage of decadence. Daniel didn't care.

He hit the remote and turned off the TV. It was all so stupid, the mock reality of sit-coms and cop shows. Who really gives a shit? he thought.

Daniel reached over and found his current notebook, his lifelong *Book of Midnights*. He would be asleep by midnight and he felt compelled to write the poem he felt brewing inside of him, before it slipped away. Without thinking about it, in his empty apartment that grew emptier by the day, he took up his pen and paper and wrote.

August 3, 10:45 p.m.

Love is Gone.
All is an empty field in winter,
The brown clods of earth turned over,
Fallow.
Without her, spring shall not return.
The earth will never again taste life.

All is a graying sky that never changes.
A light rain falls in an atmosphere charged with sorrow.
Hollow.
Without her, the rain is ceaseless,
The cold wind drives this dampness to my soul.

All is a playground without children.
Swings lie motionless, metal slides go empty.
Voiceless.
Without her there is no laughter.
Children no longer grace the world.

All is a place where things lie rusting.
A junkyard of cars that will not run.
Broken.
Without her no one will repair them.
Highways sit empty, journeys never start.

All is a landscape of aloneness.
Leafless forests of blackened, naked trees.
Desolate.
Places cold and forsaken, windswept and barren.
Birds no longer sing, death freshens in the breeze.

All this since she has left.
For the coward in me, only these ruins remain.
Temples of fluted columns standing on rocky hillsides.
Religions sans saviors, worship without gods.
Joy has vanished.
Love is gone.

Daniel Mark Harris

He reread the poem to himself several times before tearing it out of his notebook and throwing it on the floor among the trash. For a brief instant, he had considered sending it to Ayse via e-mail but now, after rereading it, he knew he couldn't. She would never see this poem.

Daniel was the coward in his own bad play, performed upon a stage no one was watching. This poem would serve no purpose other than to make her come back, and as much as he missed her, he had no intention of having her return. Stubborn and firm in his decision — Daniel was Clayton's son.

Kicking the rubbish at his feet aside, he got up and walked to his refrigerator. He felt hungry. Inside, he found three cans of beer, some moldy bread and a jar of strawberry jam. Pinching off the mold, he cleaned up two pieces of bread and smothered them with what was left of the jam. Dinner.

He walked back and flipped on the TV. He cracked a beer and ate his sandwich while watching *Dateline*. It was a special about some small-town murder that had yet to be solved. He didn't care who had killed and who had been killed. It was only white noise in a vacuum for him.

Mother and Daughter

Elif stood at her daughter's bedroom door for the longest time. She didn't know whether to knock and hand-deliver the package to her daughter, or leave it on the hallway floor, where Ayse would discover it the next time she left her room. She looked down at the label for a second time, knowing what it must contain.

The package was from Dr. Aksaray's office. It had arrived in the mornings mail. Elif had surmised that Ayse was with child, and the delivery of this package confirmed her suspicions. She had known of Dr. Aksaray's practice and had heard good things about him. Elif was glad her daughter had chosen such a reputable physician to bring her child into this world.

After standing in the hallway for longer than planned, Elif decided to knock and hand the package to her daughter. It is time, she thought as her weathered knuckles made three light taps on the bedroom door.

Ayse heard the gentle knock and looked up from her novel, "Who is it?"

"It's your mother."

Ayse hadn't expected this, thinking it was probably Halil wanting to check her hamper for laundry. The sound of her mother's voice through the door caught her off guard. What would her mother want with her this time of day?

Elif added, "May I come in?"

"Yes, Mother, please do."

Elif opened the door to her daughter's bedroom. She looked around, noting the daughter's room looked as it always did — tidy and clean. So different from her two sons' rooms.

"This package came in the mail for you today. You were expecting it, weren't you?"

Ayse could see the large Manilla envelope in her mother's right hand. She couldn't read the label from across the room, but knew it must be her pre-natal instruction kit from Dr. Aksaray's office. It would include a sample of vitamins, dietary information, warnings on what to avoid, such as cigarettes and alcohol, and an assortment of related materials.

"Yes, I was expecting it."

Elif walked towards Ayse's bed slowly. As she did, Elif lifted her right arm up and extended the envelope to her daughter.

Ayse accepted the package from her mother, then took a long, studied gaze at the woman standing before her. For the first time in years she noticed that her mother looked old. Her dark gray scarf served to cover most of her hair, but what few strands protruded from beneath it were equally gray. The lines around her eyes were gathering, as were those around the corner of her tightly drawn mouth. Even her hands looked older than Ayse remembered. She saw a slight tremor in her mother's hand as she handed her the package.

Elif was changing. She was making the transition from mother to grandmother. Her daughter, carrying a grandchild within her, took notice of that change.

"You're pregnant, aren't you," said Elif unexpectedly.

"Yes. But how did you know?"

"I know my daughter. I know she doesn't wake up every other morning feeling nauseated. I know what it's like to be pregnant for the first time, Ayse. These are signs a woman would have to be a fool to miss.

"When I saw this package in the mail today, it confirmed my suspicion."

"Are you happy for me, Mother?"

"Yes and no. I am happy you are with child, because I know you will be a wonderful mother. There is nothing in the world more fulfilling than bringing a child into this world. There is nothing more important. For this, I am happy.

"But as for Daniel and your marriage, it is still hard for me, Ayse. You know how I have felt about him from the start. Mustapha has met him and he tells me that he is a good man, but this was a relationship I was against from the day you first met. That's what makes this pregnancy of yours difficult for me – not knowing what will become of the two of you."

"Oh, Mother, I love you so."

The words sprang from Ayse's lips without her thinking. As Ayse spoke them, she slid her legs down off the side of the bed and she reached out to hug her mother. Elif, seeing that her daughter needed her, collapsed into Ayse's arms. There, with them sitting on the edge of Ayse's bed, they held each other in an embrace that lasted a century.

Without words, tears sprang from their eyes and fell upon the chenille bedspread. Tears of joy and regret — tears of disappointment and love. They cried with abandon, wrapped in each other's arms like Madonna and child.

After a while, Elif spoke, "I love you too, Ayse. All I want for my daughter is happiness. If you love Daniel as you say you do, then I will stop objecting to your marriage."

"Do you really mean that, Mother? Because it means so much to me, and so much to Daniel. He's lost without the love of his own family. His knowing that Father and you are supportive of us would help him to hold on, to help him get through this."

"Yes, Ayse, I mean it. I see the love in your eyes and I know it does not fade with time or the distance you have between you. Whoever this man is, he must be someone special to deserve the love you bestow upon him."

"He is wonderful, Mother."

"Have you told him about the child?"

"No. I don't want to tell him yet. I want to be certain I will have the baby before I call. I will wait for a while, when the chances of losing the baby become very slight. The news of him finding out that I miscarried would only make matters worse. I think it's best if I wait. What do you think, Mother?"

"Yes, you're wise to wait. Wait until you are sure the baby within you is strong and healthy before you tell him.

"Ayse, is there anything I can do to help the two of you get back together?"

"Yes, you can hold me."

Elif smiled at her young, lovely princess and wrapped her arms around her. Ayse was right. All she needed was the knowledge that Elif would accept and bless their marriage. That meant everything to Ayse, and the thought of it filled her heart with joy.

The two of them remained on the edge of the bed for the longest time. Elif took Ayse into her arms and gently rocked both her daughter and the child within. The afternoon passed.

Mother and daughter sat in a princess's bedroom in a suburb of Istanbul in a world filled with discord and held each other. Tears fell like rain. Heartbeats synchronized and the gulls circled high above the minarets of the Blue Mosque. Allâh, the all-forgiving, was showing his mercy to the world.

The Call to North Macon Baptist

The Georgia sun had long since burned away the night. The morning's mist had retreated into white, summer clouds which, in turn, would build into Atlanta's afternoon thunderstorms. A ritual of weather unchanged by the twelve lanes of I-75 and the young, disenfranchised preacher's kid sleeping past noon.

Daniel didn't care about the world beyond his trashed one-bedroom apartment any more than he did about himself. Both were expendable.

He pulled the dirty sheet over his eyes as the light of day poured through his bedroom window. The dark green sheet kept enough light out to allow him to continue sleeping through his hangover. Daniel no longer belonged to the lucid world of daylight. He had become a creature of the night.

Last night was spent in a variation on the same descending theme. He had closed up the bar with Jimmy Boy at three, then the two of them went to the dance club after smoking hashish. There, they picked up two girls and ended up in a high-rise apartment building somewhere smoking crack and having sex until the sun began stealing the stars away.

He drove home and passed out in his bed after inhaling two greasy burgers from an all-night truck stop. He was hungry after having sex with a perfect stranger. Hungry and tired.

As one o'clock rolled around, Daniel found himself waking up. He knew he had to get to work by four, so he forced himself out of his stupor and got out of bed. He needed a shower.

After relieving himself he stumbled into the kitchen to make himself an oversized cup of instant coffee. He opened up the hot water tap until it poured scalding and shoved a coffee cup beneath it. Two heaping tablespoons of Folger's dissolved in the hot water. His coffee tasted bitter and lukewarm by the time he drank it. He didn't care. He needed the caffeine, and would have chewed raw coffee beans to get it.

He put down his coffee cup and headed into the bathroom to shower. He caught a glimpse of himself in the mirror above the sink and the sight of his own unshaven face startled him. It was bad and he knew it would only get worse. Ayse was gone. He no longer had a mother, or a father — so the twisted entourage of the bar crowd became his adopted family.

They kept each other company amid the ever-encroaching darkness. Theirs was a world of shots, chasers, powder, pills, sex, dust, needles and noise. The noise of stereos screaming punk music and young girls giving themselves away in a search of heroes who had long since vanished from this world. This brave new world.

Daniel climbed into the shower and stayed in it until he used up all the hot water. He shaved using cold water and it felt strangely inviting. He only wished he could have made it colder. He wished he could have turned up the cold like you turn up the hot. Turned it up to the point where ice formed on the shower head and the water pierced his skin like frozen daggers.

After shaving, he dried himself with a towel that had soured a week ago. He hated the smell of the soured towel on his clean body but not enough to take the time to launder it. He covered up the odor of the towel with deodorant and aftershave. Then he went over to the fridge to see if there was anything safe to eat.

There wasn't. The quart of whole milk he considered drinking last night had turned into some foul smelling cottage cheese and the jelly was riddled with mold. He would have to go to the nearby convenience store for some hot dogs or something, anything as long as it didn't cost much.

He looked in his wallet to see how much cash he had. Seven bucks. He wouldn't get paid again until Friday.

"Shit," he said to himself as he closed his wallet and slipped it into his back pocket. "Where does all my money go?"

He knew the answer. He knew where it went because his weekly bar tab was deducted from his pay. He knew it went for gas, cigarettes and reefer. He knew it went for ten dollar hits of Ecstasy and grams of coke and whatever else was available.

The phone company had just sent him a second disconnection notice and the rent on the apartment was two weeks' late. Daniel had arrived. He had arrived at a place that was as bleak and forlorn as the Gobi Desert. An urban desert.

He put on his shirt and started for the front door when the idea struck him. He had been thinking about doing it for months, but had always found an excuse not to follow through. Maybe it was the hangover, or the fact that he was broke and would remain broke for the next three days. He wanted to speak to his father.

Daniel wanted to tell his Dad it was over, that Ayse had moved back to Istanbul and their divorce was imminent. He wanted to tell his father he was sorry. That's what he wanted to say, he wanted to tell his father he was sorry. Sorry for screwing everything up — sorry for the marriage, for messing up his schooling, for getting drunk every night, for getting laid last night by a girl whose name and face were already forgotten.

He wanted to stop falling. He would ask forgiveness from Clay and return to Macon, glad to mow the expansive lawn again. That it was all just a crazy, screwed-up mistake.

As he reached for the telephone, his stomach started churning. He wasn't sure if he could remember the church's number, knowing his father would be in his office by now. His hand shook as he punched in the area code and phone number to North Macon Baptist Church. The number came back to him automatically.

"Hello," answered Rose, the church's long standing receptionist.

"Is Clayton Harris in?"

"May I ask who's calling?"

"It's me, Daniel, his son."

"Daniel, is it really you?"

"Yes, Rose. It's been a while," said Daniel, recognizing her voice from the start.

"Hold on while I put you through to your father. It's nice to hear your voice again."

"Thanks, Rose."

Rose pushed the intercom into Clay's office. She knew he was in, and for the moment, not busy with one of the church council members, or on another call.

"Mr. Harris, I have your son on line three."

"Daniel?"

"Yes, it's your boy."

"I'll take the call."

Clay put down the budget report he was reviewing and pushed line three on his handset.

"Hello, is this Daniel?"

"Yes, Dad. How are you?"

"I'm fine, son. But I told you a year ago never to call me again."

Daniel's stomach locked up when he heard his father's bitter tone. I should have known he'd behave this way, he said to himself.

"But Dad, Ayse and I are split up."

"That's not my problem, Son. You should have thought about this before you ran off and married her. It's too late for you to be coming around asking for my help at this stage.

"You've shamed me in front of my congregation and I've no intention of ever wanting to see you, or hear from you again. *And if thy right eye offend thee, pluck it out, and cast it from thee: for it is profitable for thee that one of thy members should perish, and not that thy whole body should be cast into hell.'* Matthew 5, Verse 29. You were my right eye, Daniel. Have I made myself perfectly clear?"

"Yes."

Daniel heard his father's phone hit the receiver. He was disconnected.

The Red Carpet Motel

Megan studied the interior of the room. She couldn't remember the name of the motel any more than she could remember the name of the naked young man beside her. Neither mattered.

Nothing mattered. The brown Formica desk, mounted firmly to the wall, holding the nineteen-inch color television with the broken remote didn't matter. The two cheaply framed prints of some obscure garden scene done in dime store Impressionism didn't matter. The stained bedspread, the worn carpeting and the rusted steel hangers permanently attached to the rusted bar, the moldy shower curtain and the toilet that ran all night didn't matter.

The only thing that did matter to Megan was that this guy sleeping beside her in the sex-stained sheets didn't have any diseases, and that she needed to pick up her two kids from her ex-husband in forty-five minutes or he'd be pissed at her for a third time this week. Those were the only things that occupied Megan's clouded thoughts.

I'll shower at home, she decided while slipping as quietly as she could manage out of the bed. I don't want to wake him, not now.

She put on her panties, her bra, slipped into tight-fitting jeans and put on her off-white, low-cut blouse in a cat-like silence. She looked around for her sandals and found them kicked under the bed. She kept thinking she was forgetting something but in the fog of her hangover she couldn't think of what it might be.

Whatever it was, it too didn't matter. She put on her sandals and walked stealthily toward the motel room's front door. She took note of the rate card posted on the inside of the cheap metal door and remembered the motel room was her idea and not his. She liked motel rooms, especially cheap ones. They seemed to make illicit sex that much more illicit.

For a second Megan thought about pulling a twenty-dollar bill out of her wallet and leaving it on the bed stand beside Daniel to cover her half of the room charge. He was worth twenty dollars, she thought, recalling how this young man had performed. Hell, she thought, this boy's worth five hundred dollars.

But she didn't pull out a twenty. She opened the door, trying to block as much sunlight as possible as she slid out and closed the door behind her. Thirty minutes remaining before her ex would start fuming. She would have to skip showering until after she dropped the boys off at school. Divorce sucks, she thought as she climbed into her rusting Dodge minivan. Sucks big time.

❂

Daniel woke an hour later. He reached over to touch the girl beside him only to find her gone. Nothing new. She had slipped away like a score of other urban courtesans before her. Techno girls wearing too much makeup and easily seduced into spending the night with a good-looking boy from Macon. Club girls and club boys finding each other amidst shots of Jägermeister or Cuervo, a line of nose candy, Ecstasy or the latest, most fashionable street drugs available.

Party people who never ask last names and know that, if they behave, they can look forward to an end game of flesh, sweat and orgasms. Urban creatures who crawl back to their chosen, strobe-soaked lairs every night to repeat the same self-satisfying ritual again and again in some vain attempt to make the noise go away. The noise that keeps getting louder.

Daniel looked around the motel room in a studied fashion not dissimilar from Megan's observations earlier. Maroon drapes covered the window next to the door, blocking the sunlight. Nondescript prints of nondescript scenes painted by nondescript artists hung on the walls. A room made attractive only by its low cost and ready availability.

Daniel got up and went into the tiny bathroom to urinate. He noted that none of the towels had been touched. She must have slipped out without so much as showering, he thought while relieving himself. She was a great lay, he recalled, remembering the series of events that lead them to the Red Carpet Inn just north of Buckhead's nightlife. A great screw even without a name.

He finished pissing and thought about taking a shower. He decided to wait. He threw his naked body down on the bed and grabbed the remote for the TV. It didn't work. He got up and turned on the TV manually. It was still tuned to MTV, which the two of them had turned on last night for background music to a chorus of groaning, headboard banging and muffled screams. It was loud, and with his head still throbbing from the virtual drugstore of chemicals pumping inside of him, Daniel hit the mute button before the band Disturbed had finished an ear-crushing measure. The mute worked.

In silence, the crazed gesturing and wild cinematography of the music video was surreal. Without the music, the band seemed angry without any reason. Their faces contorted, their eyes wide open as their arms lashed out at their guitars as though they were beating them to death. Looking at them on mute, their message was clear — the world wasn't worth saving.

As Daniel watched the silenced video, he remembered he didn't have enough money to cover the cost of the room. He had thirty bucks on him and some loose change. The girl was supposed to leave him a twenty.

He looked to the night stand on her side of the bed and saw nothing. Maybe she left it in the drawer. He rolled over and opened the small, single drawer in the night stand and found two items in it. One was a copy of Gideon's Bible. The other was a Zip-Lock Baggie containing a dozen hits of OxyContin.

✪

The Bible, he thought to himself, while taking the book in his hand. It might as well have been the Qur'an, or the Torah, the Upanishads, the Tao Te Ching, the I Ching, Dhammapada, or the Book of Certitude for all it's done for me, reflected an embittered boy. They're all useless. They do nothing but divide us into angry mobs, each and every mob standing ready to defend their holy words to the death if called upon. Ready to cross the river and lay siege to the heathens on the other side.

The history of the world's great religions stands as grim testimony to the dysfunctional family of man. Daniel became increasingly angry as he sat there, holding the holiest of books.

"God," said Daniel aloud...."God can go to Hell."

He put the Bible back. Then he took the Baggie in his hand. He knew by their color and shape they were OxyContin, or Oxys as they're called on the street. The chick without a name must have left them by accident. Take one pill when you're drinking and the alcohol buzz is magnified tenfold. Take two and you had to be careful. Take twelve and careful didn't matter.

Daniel opened the Baggie and looked at the half-finished beer beside him. He poured all twelve of the pills into his clammy hand and, while yet another punk band screamed its desperate song in silence, threw his head back and ate all twelve. He took a long, hard pull of the flat, lukewarm beer and washed down his breakfast.

It was time. It was time to put the noise inside of him on mute. Time to go. To say farewell to his alienated bride, his zealous, self-righteous father and this strange, nihilistic lifestyle.

He took the TV off mute and left it playing loud as the effects of the pills took hold. He felt relaxed. His head propped up against a cheap motel room pillow. His body naked but not uncomfortable.

Daniel finished his can of the warm beer and waited for the next video. The VJ announced a song by one of Daniel's favorite groups, System of a Down. The choice of songs seemed uncanny to him, but fitting. Within a few seconds the song *Chop Suey* was blaring, filling the room with its rhythmic malaise.

"Father, into your hands, commend my spirit. Father, into your hands. Why

have you forsaken me? In your eyes forsaken me. In your thoughts forsaken me. In your heart forsaken me. Oh, trust in my self righteous suicide. I cry when angels deserve to die."

It was perfect, he thought as he started fading into a narcosis that would soon overwhelm him. I like this band, he thought as he dissolved, dissolved until there was nothing left conscious enough for him to think. Nothing but an eerie numbness he welcomed.

Within a few minutes everything went away. The noise, the room he couldn't pay for, the bullshit and the world it thrived in. The angel of death was coming for him. The angel was Daniel's choice.

Housekeeping

There wasn't any DO NOT DISTURB sign hanging on the door of room 228. Checkout was still thirty minutes away, but lacking any other indication, aside from a blaring television, that the guest was still in the room, Juanita Solerno gave three loud knocks on the metal door and stood waiting. No response. She reached for her master key and slipped it into the lock. Juanita opened the door slowly, learning from her years of motel housekeeping that if they are still in bed or getting dressed, they'll notice the door opening and shout at her to come back later.

No shout came. Only the loud, booming sound of a music video. Hearing the television set blasting away didn't stop her. Half the tenants checking out of The Red Carpet Motel left their TVs on. People are lazy, she thought to herself as she walked into the room and turned the TV off manually.

As she turned around to head outside and pull in her housekeeping cart, she saw him. He was perfectly still, as pale as the stained sheets. Juanita screamed, dropping her set of room keys as she did.

She had never found a dead person before. She had found blood, needles, sex toys of every shape and description imaginable, but never a body. One of the other girls on staff had once found a body. It was a businessman. He was dressed in a three-piece suit, sitting in an empty bathtub with a hole blown through the back of his head and a .45 Smith and Wesson lying on the tiled floor beside him. The bathroom was a mess.

This wasn't a businessman, but a young man, observed the maid as she studied the ashen-gray body before her. Too young, she thought, too young to die. She couldn't help noticing Daniel's fine physique, even in its morbid stillness. This is a beautiful boy, she thought. Such a shame! Such a shame!

Still shaking, Juanita went to the telephone that rested on the bed stand beside the naked body. She picked up the phone and punched zero for the front desk.

Mr. Smithson, the day manager, picked up the call.

"Front desk...how may we help you?"

"It's me, Juanita. There is a dead boy in 228. You must come up here at once."

"Oh my God! Stay there, Juanita, I'm on my way."

Mr. Smithson dropped everything, bounded out the front door of the lobby and up the single flight of stairs. He saw Juanita's cart outside the door and went in. Juanita was still standing next to the bed stand, receiver in hand, staring at the boy.

"Are you sure he's dead?"

"He's so white, Señor Smithson. Surely he must be dead."

Mr. Smithson walked over to Daniel's side of the bed and bent down beside him. He put his ear right up to Daniel's half parted lips and listened. He listened and he prayed. He prayed to the same God Daniel had just told to go to hell.

A few minutes passed in macabre suspension. The room was frozen. Daniel's body, naked and pallid in the morning light, formed the centerpiece of the tableau. The expression on the face of the Mexican maid, the motel manager leaning over the dead boy, all added to the horror. Mr. Smithson, as he listened for any sign of life, looked down and saw the empty Baggie. A drug overdose, he thought. The third one this year.

He discerned a breath. Faint, nearly undetectable, but a breath.

"Call 911, Juanita."

"He's still alive?"

"Yes, I think he is, but barely."

The manager started slapping Daniel's ghostlike face. If the boy had taken depressants, it was important to keep him stimulated until the paramedics could arrive. It was important to try to wake him, get him to come back from the darkness that had swallowed him.

Juanita was on the phone, talking nervously to an operator about the emergency. She was giving her the motel's address, the room number, all the details needed to dispatch an ambulance to the scene. Juanita's hands were shaking as she held the phone next to her face, tears were welling in her dark Hispanic eyes.

Time started moving again. But it moved slowly — reluctantly. Mr. Smithson tried to prop up the naked body but found it heavy and difficult to move.

Juanita completed the call and stood there, sobbing uncontrollably, watching her boss trying to revive this fine-looking boy. It was all so horribly sad, she thought to herself. Horribly sad.

Within five minutes they could hear the sirens. The front door of the room had remained open, and they heard the two doors slam from the EMS vehicle that had just pulled up outside. As the two paramedics rushed through the door, the manager let go of Daniel's limp body and it fell sideways on the bed. He and Juanita stepped back and watched as the team began working on the boy. The manager put his arm around the shaking maid, trying to console her.

The paramedics had been in this motel room before, if not Room 228, then Room 119, or 334. A thousand motel rooms identical to this one. Some with needles lying in the corner and ashen gray whores staring at the ceiling. Some with pipes still filled with crack and the patient in full cardiac arrest from an overtaxed heart that couldn't sustain the rush. Most were young. Young and foolish. Some survived. Some didn't.

One of the paramedics stuck an endotracheal tube down Daniel's throat while the other took his pulse. One forced his eyes open to shine a bright light into his pupils while the other man hooked up wires to run an EKG. They pulled him down and rolled him into a position that made it easier for the boy to breath.

"Do you know what he took?" asked one of the medics while inserting a nasogastric tube in Daniel's nose.

"Drugs of some kind. There's an empty Baggie on the floor and a lot of empty beer cans. I think he was trying to commit suicide."

One of the paramedics picked up the Baggie and gave it a smell.

"Downers of some kind. Maybe Xanax, possibly Oxys."

"Let's pump him here."

They slipped a nose tube into Daniel's stomach and hooked the other end of it to a machine. Within minutes fluids and acids flowed from Daniel's stomach into a large plastic vial. Daniel remained unconscious.

"Is there an elevator?" asked one of the emergency workers.

"Yes, on the far end of the building," answered the manager.

"I'll get the gurney, are you okay for now?" asked the paramedic of his fellow worker.

"I'm fine. He seems to be stabilizing. They'll probably give him the cocktail when we get him to Piedmont."

"Yeah, but we'll let them make the call. I'll be right back."

The paramedic exited the door and took the stairway to the emergency vehicle in the parking lot. It was still running, with its red and blue lights flashing in the noonday sun. Outside, a small crowd had gathered. Anonymous passerbys and a few late checkouts looked up toward Room 228 to try to catch a glimpse of what was happening. They commented to each other as they gaped.

"I heard someone's having a heart attack," one of them said.

"Yes, that's what I heard too," seconded an onlooker.

Misinformation flowed through the small crowd as it always does at scenes like this. Heart attacks, strokes, accidents, all became topics of speculation as the medic wheeled the gurney to the elevator. No one had thought of suicide. No one but Daniel and the motel manager.

Within minutes the stretcher was returning to the ambulance. When the onlookers saw Daniel laid out upon it their story changed. He was too young for a heart attack. The story changed to a drug overdose of some kind. Maybe a knife wound covered discreetly by the clean white sheet. Was it a gunshot wound?

"See the tube in his nose," remarked one of them who had some working knowledge in matters like this, "they use those to pump stomachs."

"Such a shame, he's too young to be messed up with drugs like that," commented another bystander.

One of the paramedics hopped into the driver's seat while the other stayed in back with Daniel. The sound of the siren startled the crowd as the ambulance pulled into traffic, heading directly toward the emergency room at Piedmont Hospital.

The crowd dispersed. Mr. Smithson walked out of the motel room in a daze. He sent Juanita home for the day. She had seen enough.

"Go home, Juanita. You'll be paid your regular wag today. By going into his room like you did, you probably saved his life. But you're in no condition to work."

"Muchas gracias, Señor Smithson."

Juanita went to the housekeeping room, took off her apron and walked to the bus stop where she would normally catch the three-forty-five. Today she would be home early and she was glad. She was still sobbing quietly to herself as she stood alone at the bus stop. I hope he makes it, she prayed.

Mr. Smithson went back to the front desk and sat down. He breathed a long sigh of relief and told the clerk at the desk to cover him for a while. Hold all calls. It was all just a part of his job as a low-rent motel manager. The awful part.

✪

Large white rectangles danced in and out of focus. A plastic bag hung beside him, though he couldn't see the tube coming out of the bottom. The tube that led directly into his right arm. Everything was blurry — his vision, the sound of people speaking, his sense of self.

After a spell the rectangles above him became ceiling tiles. The plastic bag was an intravenous drip and he knew without looking that it fed into his arm. The noises were patients crying out in pain as doctors and nurses tended to their wounds and ailments. The clatter of surgical tools, the sound of someone coughing, the loud screams of a baby who had fallen, all became decipherable. Daniel was alive.

He realized he was in an emergency room. That someone must have found him before the dark angel did. Someone rescued him. He was angry with that person, whoever it was. No one had the right to rescue him. He wanted no part of his own redemption. He wanted to be dead.

A nurse appeared out of the fog and stood beside him. He had been unconscious for seven hours.

"You're lucky to be alive," said the nurse, seeing his eyes were open and he was awake.

"No, I'm not."

The nurse picked up his chart and wrote something on it. She smiled, pretending to ignore his sarcastic comment, turned and left the curtained enclosure where he was lying. Daniel went back to staring at the bone-white acoustic tiles.

Why am I here? he reflected. I don't want to be in this god-damned hospital with this tube in my arm and this air in my lungs and these thoughts in my head. I want to die. To end it. Perish, cease, stop, quit, expire, end, end, end this shit-storm called life.

A half-hour later a man came into the room. He didn't look like a nurse or a doctor. He had on a plain, long-sleeve white shirt and brown pants that didn't fit. He approached the bed, picked up Daniel's chart and studied it.

"OxyContin, huh?"

Daniel looked at him with the eyes of a cornered panther. The cold, calculated stare from a pair of steel-blue eyes that spoke volumes. Daniel didn't say a thing. He deduced the man standing at the foot of the bed was a shrink of some kind. He was not about to engage him in conversation.

"Your toxicology report says you took a handful of Oxys. A big handful. You washed them down with beer. There are traces of cocaine, marijuana and alcohol in your blood. You were legally drunk when you took the pills. You didn't take them to get high, did you?"

The panther inside the boy hissed at the psychologist. The hiss was loud and threatening, even in its silence. Daniel remained quiet.

"What's going on, son?"

No reply from the cornered beast. Just a hollow gaze that told the psychologist this patient was suicidal. A stare that compelled the doctor to make a few notes on Daniel's chart, then coolly place it back on the hook on the end of the bed.

"Get comfortable, boy. You're going to be here for a while."

With that, the man left, closing the curtains behind him. Five minutes later two orderlies came in and strapped Daniel's arms and legs down. His journey to nowhere was just beginning. The panther let go a scream that sent shivers down the backs of a dozen hardened veterans of the emergency room at Piedmont Hospital. This, they knew instantly, was a cat who wanted to die. The scream eventually soaked into the acoustic tiles covering the ceiling. Death did not want Daniel Mark Harris. Neither did life.

A Phone Call to Atlanta

*T*he number you have called has been disconnected and is no longer in service; please check the number and try again," spoke the computerized voice on the other end of the line. It was her third attempt, and Ayse knew with certainty that she was dialing the correct number. Daniel was not there.

She had waited six weeks to make this call. Six weeks of doctors' visits, blood tests, vitamins, supplements, and morning sickness, all to ensure herself that she would not lose his child. The waiting was over. As she entered her second trimester of pregnancy, her morning sickness fell away and a feeling of confidence overcame her. She knew her baby would be born. She knew as only an expectant mother can know.

She had waited until six p.m. to call their apartment in America, knowing it would still be ten in the morning when Daniel's phone rang in Atlanta. He might have worked late and she didn't want to wake him too early. But there was no one to answer her call at the one-bedroom apartment where their first child had been conceived — the apartment was empty. The walls had been repainted and the carpet cleaned. All of their furniture and personal belongings had been moved into a storage facility along North Peachtree. The landlord had taken their deposit monies to move their belongings, clean up Daniel's mess and make the apartment presentable to the next young couple trying to make a life of it in Atlanta.

The utilities had been shut off for lack of payment. The telephone line was disconnected three weeks ago. There remained no trace of either Daniel or Ayse on the bare, freshly painted walls of their first apartment.

Same old shit, thought the landlord as he watched the moving van pull away to the storage unit two weeks ago. In sixty days' time, after posting two notices, he would sell off the contents of the storage unit to a used furniture dealer to cover the balance due on the rent. The perennial disappearing act of young couples. Same old shit.

There were only two phone calls left to make, calculated Ayse. Her first call would be to Randy, who was still living in the dorm he and Daniel had once shared. The second call, if Randy wasn't able to help, would be to Daniel's home in Macon. Ayse dreaded making the second call. Dreaded it terribly. She had never spoken to either of his parents and prayed Randy could tell her where her husband was.

Ayse decided to wait an hour before trying Randy's number. She knew he'd often head back to his dorm at noon for a peanut butter and jelly sandwich and if she were lucky, her call would find him there today. She buried herself in another novel to pass the time.

When eight p.m. arrived, she dialed the sixteen digits needed to make the long-distance phone call to the United States. It took forever to complete. After a long, anxious pause, Ayse heard the phone ringing six thousand miles to the west.

On its third ring, Randy picked up the phone.

"Hello."

"Randy, it's me, Ayse." There was a curious echo in the line.

"Ayse, what a surprise. How are you? Where are you?"

"I'm fine. I'm calling from Bebek, from Turkey. It's long-distance. Randy, I need your help."

"Anything, Ayse. I'll do anything to help."

"Do you know where Daniel is?"

"No. Nobody does. I was at the bar last week and they were asking me the same thing. He has a paycheck waiting for him there but nobody's seen him. I thought he might have gone to Turkey, to be with you."

"No, he's not in Turkey. I haven't spoken with him or had an e-mail from him in two months.

"Do you think he's okay?"

"I don't know. Maybe he patched things up with his mom and dad and he's back in Macon. Have you tried calling his parents?"

"No, I'm afraid to."

"Don't be. You're still his wife and you've got a right to know where your husband is."

Ayse sighed. Yes, she was still his wife. His pregnant wife, though she hesitated telling Randy about her condition before telling Daniel.

"Did he tell them at work he was going back home to Macon?"

"No. They told me he just up and vanished. He was supposed to come in at four o'clock one afternoon about six weeks ago and he never showed. No phone call, no letter, nothing. No one on campus has seen him and I heard your old apartment is up for rent.

"You might want to give them a call to find out where all your things are."

"Yes, that's a good idea. Maybe the landlord knows where he is."

"If there's anything I can do, Ayse, you know I'll do it for you. Are you coming back to Oglethorpe?"

"No, not anytime soon."

"We miss you."

"I miss you too, Randy. Say hello to Hatice and Kasha for me, please."

"I will."

"Goodbye."

"Goodbye and good luck."

"Thanks, Randy. I'll need it."

Ayse hung up the phone and started worrying. This wasn't a good sign.

She looked at her clock and realized she would have to wait another hour before calling the supervisor at the Monterey Apartment complex. She remembered he broke for lunch and it was presently twelve-fourteen in Atlanta. Unless he was out showing someone an apartment, he'd be back in the office by one.

Ayse dived back into her novel. It was a welcome refuge from her worries.

✦

At nine-fifteen Istanbul time, Ayse looked up the number of her former landlord and again called America. The phone rang four times before the answering machine kicked in.

"Thank you for calling Monterey Apartments, located in the heart of north Atlanta. We are currently leasing one- and two-bedroom..."

The tape shut off and a man's voice came on the line. "Monterey Apartments, how may we help you?"

"Hello. Is anyone there?" inquired Ayse.

"Yes, it's a real person. Sorry about the tape, I was out in the parking lot with some customers when I heard the phone ring. The tape always kicks in like that. I turned it off."

"This is Ayse, Ayse Harris, do you remember me?"

"Yeah. The Muslim girl, right?"

"Yes. I'm calling from Turkey. I'm looking for Daniel, my husband. I tried calling the apartment but our phone's been disconnected. Do you know where he has moved to?"

"No. But I'm glad you called. In fact I was just showing your apartment to another couple a half an hour ago."

"Where's our furniture, my computer?"

"They're in storage. When Daniel disappeared the rent was already a month late. We posted an eviction notice on the door but as far as I know, he never saw it. After the legal requirements were satisfied, I hired a moving company to take all your stuff and put it in a mini-storage facility up on Peachtree.

"That's where it is now. If you hadn't called, I'd have sold them to a used furniture dealer in a few months to pay for the back rent and the cost of keeping the storage unit."

Ayse took a deep breath, imagining the worst, and continued speaking with the apartment manager on the other side of the world.

"You have no idea what happened to Daniel? Where he moved to? Where I might find him?"

"No. But I did keep an eye on the obituaries for a month or so after he disappeared. He was hanging out with a pretty crazy crowd and it wouldn't have surprised me had he turned up in the obits. They have plenty of young folks making that section of the paper: drug overdoses, car accidents, drug deals gone bad, you know the sort of stuff.

"But his name never showed. I had his car towed out of here too, but in the condition that car was in, I don't think it'd be worth your time trying to buy it out of the salvage yard. You probably owe more in towing and storage fees than the car's worth."

"Thanks," said Ayse sullenly.

"What do you want me to do with y'all's stuff?"

"Sell it to pay for the rent we owe you. It's not important."

"If there's any money left, I'm obligated to send the excess to you."

"Give it to charity. Or ship it to Daniel if you ever find out where he's living."

"I doubt that," said the manager.

"So do I," added Ayse.

"Well, sorry I can't be of more help."

"Thanks anyway."

"Bye now."

"Bye."

Ayse hung up the phone and burst into tears. Her stomach tightened and for an instant, she wondered what was going to happen to the child within her. Would that child ever have a father? Would Daniel and his baby ever play together, or know the joy of sharing each other's company?

Where was he?

As she cried, Ayse prayed to Allâh that Daniel had gone home. That he and his father had reconciled and he was back in suburban Macon, working for that painter friend of his father's or mowing lawns. She prayed he was safe. Prayed her next phone call would find him with his family again, like the parable of the prodigal son.

But Ayse knew she could not make another call today. Her tears fell upon the bedspread and her heart raced across the open field of a thousand unspoken fears. Her call to Macon would have to wait. A day, a week, perhaps longer.

It was a call she did not relish making, but she knew she had to find her husband, and to do so she would have called Satan.

Central State Hospital

A sprawling tropical storm covered south Georgia the day they transported Daniel. Grayness and rain overwhelmed the landscape, filling the rivers and streams to overflowing. Just west of Macon — Crawford, Taylor and Marion counties — were declared disaster areas.

Tornadoes tore through mobile home parks and strip malls and the Flint River rose overnight to levels unseen in forty years. The storm, named Gabriel, had moved across the Florida Panhandle a day earlier, just west of Panama City. Winds had topped fifty miles an hour when Gabriel's poorly defined center had pushed into the Emerald Coast. But after the ill-defined eye made it up and over the hill country west of Tallahassee, the winds abated.

All that was left was the rain. A ceaseless, untiring rain that made the noonday sun of the Peach State feel useless and unwanted. It was a cement gray sky that shadowed the long, rolling hills along Interstate 20 that morning. A gray whose color mirrored the pavement upon which the customized medical van traversed, as though the freeway itself was poured from hardened cloud.

Daniel peered out the tiny, wired reinforced window in the back of the van. He kept silent. He had not spoken to anyone — except saying three words to the nurse and letting go one harrowing scream — since his failed suicide. Nobody could get through to him. Not the doctors, the staff psychologists, or the nurses trying to pry him open during the three days he'd remained at Piedmont.

The staff decided not to release him. Not yet. It was clear by his silence and the anger in his eyes that he would present a clear and present danger to himself if they put him back on the street. They knew from experience that the next time an ambulance came in with Daniel Mark Harris, there would be no rescue. The back of the skull would be gone, the neck broken or the wrists slashed in a final act of self-immolation. The next time he tried suicide, chances were that Daniel would succeed.

The hospital had contacted his father, the Rev. Clayton Harris, and informed him in great detail of his son's condition. Like Pontius Pilate before him, Clayton Harris washed his hands of the boy, telling the psychologist he no longer had a son. He told them in no uncertain terms they should treat him the same as they would any mentally ill patient. He had no interest in the outcome. In fact, he added, it was too bad Daniel had failed.

The doctors made note of the minister's comments and shook their head in disbelief. They had seen it all before, but seeing it again didn't make it any easier. Fathers despising sons, mothers loathing daughters, families screaming at each other across hallways while surgeons did what they could to save the victim. The emergency room at Piedmont Hospital bore out grim testimony to the reality that most people aren't murdered by strangers. They're murdered by their own families.

Domestic violence thrived in this great Southern city, just as it did in all the Midwestern, Eastern and Western cities across America. Families falling apart, dragged into hell holes of hatred and malfeasance. Bruises, indifference, bullet holes and knife wounds all carved by the disgruntled wife, the embittered husband. The statistics proved that it wasn't a terrorist organization from the other side of the world you needed to be afraid of — it was your brother.

With no alternatives available, the decision was made to commit Daniel Harris to Central State Hospital for further observation and until such time as the staff at that facility deemed it safe for him to be released into the world. There were facilities closer than Central State Hospital, but Daniel's driver's licence indicated he was still a resident of Macon County, and state law dictated he must be cared for at the facility that serviced his region.

After three days of being strapped to his bed, Daniel was placed in a straight jacket, walked out of his room and taken to a remote section of the hospital. It was the loading area where the hearses picked up the corpses and the ambulances the crazies. Once to the loading dock, Daniel was unceremoniously placed into an unmarked white van. Two drivers sat in front, protected from their passenger by a thick iron grate with a small, secure doorway leading to the rear. They could see Daniel sitting on the bench along the driver's side of the van. If he screamed, they could hear him. Just like the lunatic they'd ferried to Milledgeville two weeks ago. Screaming and banging his head against the heavy metal grate between them. Banging it so hard that his face was bloodied and bruised by the time they finally strapped him down to the bed on the other side of the van.

But Daniel didn't scream or make a sound. He stared out the back window and watched the highway disappear. Watched the four lanes of I-20 vanish beyond a hill or fade into the misty, incessant rain. In the distance Daniel could hear the gothic rumble of thunderstorms spawned by Gabriel. The rumbling neither frightened nor concerned him. His internal storms were worse.

❂

The two men driving the van were glad this boy wasn't like the last delivery. In the rear-view mirror the driver kept a steady eye on Daniel but he knew early on this one would be no trouble. This one had pulled inside himself like a tortoise in a maelstrom. They wouldn't have to pull over and muscle him into the bed like the last one. This was a good one — depression was easier than rage.

They pulled into Milledgeville around three p.m., nearly an hour behind schedule. The rain and the road conditions had caused the delay and, as they turned off 441 south toward the hospital, they knew no one would call them into question about the unexpected delay.

They took the back road in, winding through the poor, black section of town and along the street that took them past the Chapel of all Faiths and a half-dozen deserted buildings. In the dismal, relentless drizzle, the abandoned buildings of Central State Hospital appeared more forlorn and abandoned than ever. The driver, who had been doing these runs for thirty years, knew the story of Central State Hospital well.

He had watched the slow retreat of this infamous facility through the years. He watched as building after building had been shut down and deserted. He knew about the asbestos, the fact the state couldn't afford to have these empty shells torn down because of the costs involved. So the empty shells remained — windows broken, roofs leaking and basements filling with mold and stagnant water.

Central State Hospital had become a ghost town of madness. A single building, with a large white dome and a stately, governmental look to it, held all that was left of the more than twelve thousand patients who were once confined to Milledgeville. That was during the height of the hospital's fame — or infamy as many would see it. From the twenties through the sixties, when the now empty buildings were filled to overflowing with the insane, the forgotten. When the massive campus had a staff of twenty-thousand and every hallway was laden with the catatonic, the manic, the retarded and the lost.

Estranged, unwanted people dropped off at the doorstep in the middle of the night or brought in by ambulance not unlike the van Daniel was riding in. Crazy people, or people made crazy by those who surrounded them.

The driver remembered the days of electroshock therapy and the thin, stainless steel knives of frontal lobotomies. Knives that sat in plain display at the small museum beside the Powell Building like a pair of thin letter openers. But no letters were ever opened with these long, slender surgical tools. No, they were carefully slipped up under the eyes and used to disconnect the frontal lobes from the rest of the brain. Used to silence the screamers, the dangerous and the criminally insane.

Those days were gone, thought the driver as he got out of the van and went around to unlock the back where Daniel sat in silence. Now the tools were Xanax and Prozac, antidepressants and antipsychotics. The volts of electricity were replaced by blue pills or yellow pills containing neurochemical compounds that methodically brought the patient back into the real world. Whatever real was.

As he and his partner took Daniel's hand, he knew Daniel wouldn't be staying here very long. No one stayed at Central State Hospital long. Hardly no one that is. There were always the exceptions. The ones whom the drugs couldn't reach. Those and the nightmarish patients in the plain red brick building to the west. That was the building that housed the criminally insane. It housed the inmates who had killed and eaten their parents, drowned their own children, or raped their neighbor's daughter. Patients who were serving life sentences drooling on themselves, swearing to take revenge on enemies who'd died years ago. Inmates whose cells had no keys that would fit their release — lifers.

Everyone in Georgia knew about Milledgeville. It was what it was and no amount of political correctness would ever change it. It was the nut house, the loony bin, the last place in the world anyone would want to be. A cornerstone laid over a century ago in the oldest building on the campus said it best — "GEORGIA LUNATIC ASYLUM — 1883."

That was where they were taking this blue-eyed boy from Macon. The rain kept falling as the driver pressed the admittance button on the back side of the building and looked up at the security camera above the door frame. The electric lock sounded a loud, disturbing buzz as they pulled the heavy glass door open.

Daniel walked into the building without speaking. He was home. He was in Milledgeville.

Ayse's Last Call

*T*wo days had passed since Ayse had last tried to phone her husband. Two days of agonizing over the next call she had to make — the call to Macon.

As much as she dreaded having a conversation with two people who had never once shown any inclination to meet or get to know her, the thought of not knowing where her husband had disappeared to was worse. As she picked up the phone, her hand was perspiring, her mouth dry.

She had waited until one in the morning to call, not wanting to bother Reverend Harris at work. Calling Daniel's parents at home meant she wouldn't have to call the church. There was something about calling the North Macon Baptist Church that would have made it impossible for Ayse, something ancient.

With her heart pounding, she held steadfast and dialed the volley of numbers needed to place the call. She had never known such trepidation.

On the other side of the world, a phone in the kitchen rang. Rebecca was standing near it, making a pie crust for the peach cobbler they planned to have for dessert later. She reached over, half expecting it to be another phone solicitor, and answered it.

"Hello."

"Hello," said Ayse.

Rebecca heard the foreign accent of the young woman on the other end of the line. It couldn't be, she thought. Ayse continued.

"Is Mr. or Mrs. Harris home?"

Ayse thought the woman answering the phone was probably a servant, like Halil.

"This is she, I'm Rebecca Harris. May I ask who's calling?"

"It's Ayse, your daughter-in-law. I'm calling from Turkey."

Rebecca didn't know what to say. She stood frozen, debating her next move. She knew Clay would be furious with her if she continued speaking with Ayse, but she wanted to know why she was calling. Her curiosity won out, and Rebecca proceeded. "You know how we feel about the marriage. Why are you calling us?"

"It's Daniel. Is he back home? Is he staying with you?"

"Of course not. He has his own apartment in Atlanta, at least that's the last we heard. His father would never allow him back into our household, not after all he's put us through."

"But he's not in Atlanta. They evicted him from our apartment a month ago. All of our things are in storage. Randy, Daniel's old roommate, hasn't heard from him in weeks."

"Did you call the bar he works at, that saloon in Buckhead?"

"Yes, Mrs. Harris. He left without notice. They're holding a paycheck for him and they have nowhere to send it. He's disappeared, Mrs. Harris, and I'm worried about him."

Rebecca grew concerned. It wasn't like her son to behave like this. Surely someone must know where her boy was.

"But you two are split up, aren't you? Why should you care what's happened to him?"

"I care because I love him. It was your son's idea to separate, Mrs. Harris. I wanted to try to make our marriage work but he had become so angry, and it was hard for us. I may not be in America, but that doesn't mean I don't love Daniel. I do. I will always love him."

The quivering in the young girl's voice bore out the sincerity of her testimony. Indeed, this girl, this Muslim girl, noted Rebecca, does love her son Daniel.

"Well he's not staying with us. I'll discuss this call with my husband when he gets home from the church. Perhaps he's heard something. If he has, how can I reach you?"

Ayse gave Rebecca her home phone number in Bebek and told Rebecca that it's eight hours later in Istanbul.

"I will call you if Clay has heard of Daniel's whereabouts. But if he doesn't know anything, I won't bother you again."

"No, you must let me know one way or the other. If you don't call, I will sit and wonder what, if anything, you have found out. Please Mrs. Harris, let me know either way. It's important to me. Even though we are separated, he's still my husband. Wouldn't you want to know everything if your husband had vanished?"

Ayse was right. Rebecca was reminded of that night she nearly lost Clay in the freezing rain. Left hanging there, without knowing one way or the other, would be an awful thing to do to this young lady. If Clay knew anything about Daniel's whereabouts or if he knew nothing at all, Ayse had a right to know.

"Yes. You're right. I'll discuss this with Clay and call you tomorrow with the details of our conversation. Daniel's always been a good boy, and I'm sure he's just fine. He probably needed a change of scenery. I'm sure he's relocated somewhere and just doesn't want to be bothered.

"By marrying you, he's made such a mess of his life."

Rebecca's comment cut like a blade into Ayse's heart. It was a mean-spirited thing to say. Ayse remembered again their glorious afternoon in Gatlinburg at the Cloud Nine Wedding Chapel and could not understand how Mrs. Harris could say such a thing.

For an instant, Ayse wanted to respond. She wanted to engage Mrs. Harris over the fiber optics that would have transported her own frustrations and anger back across the Atlantic. She wanted to say it wasn't their marriage that had made a mess out of Daniel's life, but his parents' unwillingness to support their marriage.

The disownment, the protection order, all of Clay's legal maneuvering, did more to bring down their marriage than anything else. How could Mrs. Harris say such a thing?

But Ayse bit her tongue and refrained from quarreling with Daniel's mother. This was not the time, nor the place for such an altercation. Ayse responded as though Rebecca's comment was never made.

"I'll wait for your call tomorrow. Thank you, Mrs. Harris."

"Goodbye," said Rebecca as she hung up the phone.

"Bye," replied Ayse, a second after the call had been disconnected.

For a spell, Rebecca reflected on the woman on the other end of the line. She wondered what this girl was like. What her son must have seen in her. Was she pretty? Did she wear a scarf over her head like so many of those Muslim women? What did she believe in if not in Jesus?

These thoughts occupied Rebecca's time as she laid out her pie crust and rolled it flat with an old wooden rolling pin she had inherited from her mother. Clay would be home shortly. Sometime during dinner, carefully, skillfully, Rebecca would steer their conversation around to Daniel and his whereabouts.

She would need to be careful, as Clay became very agitated by any mention of his boy. Any discussion of Daniel could send him off in a tirade of anger, an avalanche of Bible quotations. Their separation was an open wound, and talking about it was like pouring salt into it. Rebecca knew this and laid out her plans accordingly.

If he was withholding information from her, she had a right to know. Tonight, she thought quietly to herself while pouring the peach cobbler filling into the pie pan, tonight will be interesting.

Clay Harris arrived home just after six. It had been a long day at the church and he was looking forward to a relaxing evening. Following a ritual from which he rarely deviated, he pulled the car into the garage, bringing the windshield up to where the tennis ball hanging from the rafters touched it, turned the car off, and went inside.

There, in the hallway, Rebecca had neatly placed his copy of the *Macon Telegraph*. He picked up his newspaper and proceeded into the kitchen. Rebecca had already poured him an extra-tall glass of homemade iced tea. He would kiss his wife on the cheek without saying a word and proceed to his favorite recliner, newspaper and tea in hand.

Once comfortably seated, he would pore through the news of the world with a calculated aloofness, as though it were his obligation not only to catch up on the various murders, wars, scandals and mayhem offered, but to pass judgment on each and every incident. He didn't read the news, he ruled on it, and there was no room for debate once his ruling had been issued. Rebecca kept out of it.

After covering the world news and deciding how best each and every situation should be handled, Clay moved into the local section, paying particular attention to the obituaries. He read each and every obituary as if he were reading over a legal contract. Skipping only the notices posted of the deaths of Macon's blacks, Clay would sometimes spend fifteen minutes reading the obits. There was a morbid curiosity that drew him to this section night after night. Perhaps it tied in with his love for the Book of Revelation, perhaps the root of his fascination with death and funerals could never be understood.

As he studied who had survived the deceased, where and when the service was to be held and whose funeral home was handling the arrangements, Rebecca set the table. Sometimes Clay would shout over to her with a comment like, "Did you know Mrs. Beckworth passed on?" or, "I had heard Mr. Cowley had taken ill, but I didn't think his condition was all that serious."

If Rebecca were in the dining room, she would answer him with an acknowledgment, saying something like, "Isn't it a shame," or "I'll keep them in my prayers." But if she were in the kitchen, she would only hear an incomprehensible holler from the living room. She would know that someone he knew, or had met at some point in his life, had passed on. It was a morbid habit, one to which Rebecca had become accustomed. Sometimes Clay would know of the funeral long before the obituary announcement hit the *Telegraph*. He knew because he would be presiding over it.

Macon was a small town, and its deaths fascinated Clayton. Someday, he knew, one of these notices would be his.

"Dinner's ready," Rebecca called across the empty house to her husband.

"I'm on my way," he replied in a loud, preacher-like voice.

They sat down, directly across from each other overlooking the high-gloss finish on the dining room table. The three leaves had been removed, so the distance between them was less than it was during the holidays.

Clay said grace, thanking the Lord for all their blessings and for the food placed upon the table. It was the same grace he said at every meal.

Rebecca said, "Amen," and remained quiet. She passed the country-fried ham, the mashed potatoes, the red-eye gravy and homemade biscuits without comment. She knew if she were going to bring up Daniel, it had best be over the cobbler and not before. A hungry Southern preacher is not a person you want to take chances with, and bringing up the topic of their son was always a risk.

"This is plum deeelicious," remarked Clay while cutting up more of the fried ham steak on his plate.

"Just wait until I serve you dessert," said Rebecca.

"I know what it is, I couldn't help but smell it when I came in."

"It's your favorite — peach cobbler."

"There ain't nothin' in the world better tasting than cobbler made from fresh Georgia peaches. Nothin' at all."

They finished eating and Rebecca rose to clear the table. Clay stayed seated, sipping a cup of decaffeinated coffee. He liked his coffee with so much cream and sugar in it that it tasted more like a mocha milkshake than it did coffee — a decaffeinated milkshake.

Rebecca brought out the cobbler, hot from the oven, and set it on a trivet between them. She went back into the kitchen and returned with a carton of vanilla ice cream. Looking at her husband lovingly, she said, "Help yourself."

Clay did just that. Halfway through his second serving Rebecca knew it was time to bring up Daniel. Stuffed on her home cooking, his mouth still savoring the taste of cobbler, Clay was satiated and distracted enough for her to broach such a sensitive topic.

"I was wondering..." said Rebecca calmly.

"Wondering what?"

"Well, I was wondering if you've heard anything about our boy lately? You know, through the grapevine."

Clayton Harris stopped eating his second slice of cobbler and looked long and hard at his wife. Did she hear something? Why was she asking me about Daniel?

"Why are you asking me this?"

"Well, Ruth and I were just curious. We were talking about her brother the other day and she asked me if I had heard anything since she found out about their splitting up. I said I hadn't. She wondered if you had heard anything, seeing that you know more people than both of us combined in Atlanta."

Rebecca's tactic worked. Clay found it natural enough for Ruth to be asking about her brother, and, even as much as he disliked talking about Daniel, he was willing to share what information he had. They had a right to know.

"Yes, I got a call a few weeks ago."

"Who called?"

"It was a doctor from Piedmont Hospital in Atlanta, a shrink of some kind."

"Is Daniel okay?"

"He's had some kind of nervous breakdown. The woman asked if we were willing to take him in, or get some kind of help for him and I told her we're not interested. Not after what he's put us through."

Outwardly, Rebecca remained calm. Inside, she went into a raging fit over her husband's decision to abandon their boy once again. *He should have consulted me. I have a right to know,* thought an infuriated mother to herself.

"What else did they say?"

"They said he's depressed. That they couldn't keep him at Piedmont any longer and they were moving him to Milledgeville."

"Oh no!" Rebecca's hands went to her face, and she couldn't hold her tears back. The anger, like some electric switch in purgatory, flipped to anguish.

Clay remained seated, not wanting to appear anything other than stalwart and steadfast in his decision to abandon their child. He sat there, cold and unmoved, and watched as his wife buried her weeping eyes in her aging hands.

"He'll be fine," he said. "They'll fix him up with some of those new drugs they use over there and he'll be back up in Sodom and Gomorrah, I mean Atlanta, in no time."

"But our son's in Milledgeville, Clay. That's Daniel, our little boy."

"And if any mischief follow, then thou shalt give life for life, eye for eye, tooth for tooth, hand for hand, foot for foot, burning for burning, wound for wound, stripe for stripe. Exodus, 21, Verses 23 through 25," quoted Clay sternly.

Rebecca looked at her husband and knew what he was saying. Daniel had wronged him and caused him great suffering and embarrassment before his congregation. Milledgeville, in Clay's mind, was Daniel's just punishment. Clay would not intercede, or come to his son's rescue. He was too proud for that. Daniel was on his own.

Rebecca wiped her tears with her napkin and rose from the table. It wouldn't be any use for her to continue crying. She knew where her son was and she knew Clay would see her tears as a sign of weakness. She collected herself and went over to pick the dish of cobbler up off the trivet. It was still warm. Warmer than her husband's heart, she thought as she carried the dish back into her kitchen. Warmer by far.

Rebecca's Call

Two days slipped away before Rebecca could garner the courage to telephone Ayse. She was so troubled by the knowledge that her boy was in a mental institution that she had hardly slept the past few nights. She tossed and turned though the endless hours wondering what it must be like for him at Central State Hospital. Wondering if he was safe from the others — the schizophrenics, catatonics and victims of this modern age.

Only after she decided it would be better to lie to Ayse, could Rebecca make the call to Turkey. It was a white lie. A small, harmless lie to tell Daniel's distant bride. Half the truth was enough, Rebecca had decided.

Clay was busy with a church council meeting the morning Rebecca sat down in her kitchen and began punching in the long string of numbers it would take to connect her to Turkey. Rebecca had never made an international call, and as the telephone rang a quarter of the way around the world, she marveled that such a thing was possible.

Ayse was home alone that afternoon. Her mother was out with Abdul to buy saffron and nutmeg at the spice market in the old city. Mustapha was in Italy on business. Only one of the housekeepers was home when the telephone rang, and she was busy with the laundry. The phone rang twice before Ayse got to it.

"Merhaba," said Ayse in Turkish as she picked up the phone.

"Hello," replied Rebecca, wondering for an instant if she had dialed the right number.

"Hello, is this Rebecca?" asked Ayse, breaking into English.

"Yes it is."

For two restless days Ayse had awaited this call. She too had gone sleepless while the nights crawled by. She was anxious to hear news of Daniel.

"Did you find out anything?"

Rebecca hesitated for a split second, wondering if it might not be better to tell Ayse the truth.

"Yes, Clay knew where Daniel was."

"Can you tell me where he is?"

"No, not exactly."

"What do you mean, not exactly?"

It was at this juncture Rebecca decided lie to Ayse. Clay was right. Daniel would be released from Milledgeville soon, so why should I subject Ayse to the fact that her husband had been confined to an asylum?

"He's taken a job in Athens, Georgia."

"Where's Athens?"

"It's just east of Atlanta."

"Why would he go there?"

Rebecca continued filling in the details of her lie. She had walked herself through this conversation a hundred times before making the call, but the reality of telling it to Ayse made her feel extremely uncomfortable.

"He told an old friend from high school that he needed to get out of Atlanta. He said the crowd he was seeing in Buckhead was getting to him, and he's taken a job working in a lumberyard in Athens. It was offered to him by an acquaintance of someone he'd met at the bar. He told his old high school friend that he liked his new job."

Ayse was relieved and disheartened. Why hadn't he called her, or at least contacted his friend Randy with the news of his relocation? Maybe Daniel just needed a break from his past. Maybe it was better this way.

"Is he okay?"

"His friend told Clay that Daniel sounded fine. He just needs some time is all."

"Do you have a number, or an address where I might be able to reach him? I have some news I need to tell him."

Rebecca wondered what the news might be. Perhaps Ayse was finally giving up on their relationship and asking for a divorce? No, her voice did not convey that message. It was something else.

"Clay said Daniel's friend didn't have any way of contacting him up in Athens. He was staying at some small motel until he could find an apartment and he didn't have a phone in the room. He was calling from a pay phone."

"But you could give me your message and I could pass it along."

"No, Mrs. Harris, I have to tell this to Daniel myself. Thank you for offering though, and thank you for finding out that he is all right. It's such a relief to me knowing he's not in any real trouble. It's been hard for me to sleep, wondering where he might be."

"I understand. You can put your mind at ease. Daniel's perfectly safe."

"Thank you, Mrs. Harris. Thank you so much."

"It was no trouble, Ayse," said Rebecca. Then, almost as an afterthought, she continued, "Sometimes I wish my husband wasn't so stubborn. I want you to know that I never wanted Clay to do what he did to Daniel. It's not that I thought your marriage was a good idea, because it wasn't. It was foolish. But I didn't approve of the protection order Clay put on Daniel, nor the way he tied up my mother's money. I want you to know this."

"Thank you for telling me that," said Ayse. "If you hear anything more, would you please call me again?"

"Yes, I'll call you if Clay or I hear anything. But what are you going to do, Ayse? You can't keep a marriage together like this. Not with both of you thousands of miles apart."

"All I can do is pray that it works out, Mrs. Harris. Only God knows what will happen."

"Yes, only God."

There was a brief silence. The two women realized, as if by accident, the God they spoke of was the same — the God of Abraham, the God of Jesus and the God of Mohammed. For a passing minute they were not all that different from each other. They were the same.

"Goodbye, Mrs. Harris," said Ayse in closing.

"You can call me Rebecca from now on, Ayse."

"Goodbye, Rebecca."

"Goodbye, Ayse."

Ayse placed the telephone back on the receiver and smiled. Daniel was fine, she now knew. He was working in some lumberyard in a small town in north central Georgia. Her mother-in-law had actually warmed to her enough to allow her to call her by her first name, Rebecca. Ayse took her hand and rubbed it gently over her abdomen, already swelling with his child. God had answered her prayers. God was merciful and good. Merciful and good.

His Empty Room

Heavy gauge wire formed a checkerboard pattern behind the thin gauze-like curtains of the window. As the morning light poured in from the east, the metal squares divided the daylight into cubes, as though the sunlight were being methodically platted into section and range, lot and block. The sheer curtains did their best to disguise the fact that this room was a cage, but the two small square slots on the bottom of the window, allowing a pair of hands just enough room to slip through the grating and open the single-hung window beyond, verified that it was. It was a cage. There would be no escaping through this second story-window. It provided no entrance into the world beyond.

Daniel saw none of this. He sat on the edge of his single bed and stared at the blank wall six feet in front of him. The second bed was empty, awaiting another sad arrival from the world beyond the mullioned frames. Another delivery of these twilight people.

In his empty room, in Daniel's innermost thoughts, there was no sunlight pouring in through the tall, seven-foot window beside him. There was no daylight, or joy, or the chorus of songbirds resonating from the expansive campus beyond. There was only the smell of burning rubber, and a thick, acrid smoke that choked his every waking thought. Tires were burning inside Daniel Mark Harris. Truck tires and car tires and tractor tires all thrown on a raging bonfire that burned without sense. Daniel sat motionless, staring at the wall, watching the black, polluted smoke curl and engulf the world. Glad that it did.

He knew where he was but he didn't care. He knew about Milledgeville. Everyone in Georgia knew about Milledgeville. Its reputation was legendary.

Daniel stopped tossing tires onto his personal pyre and studied the room. They would be coming to get him soon, and he knew it. He had only a few minutes to scrutinize the cage he was kept in. There were two beds in the room, one beside the window and the other against the opposite wall. A cheap night stand with three drawers stood between the beds. There was a single, framed print on the wall between the beds. There was no glass covering the print. The print portrayed a single blue vase holding a dozen pink roses. It was nondescript. It was there to add an element of warmth to the room. It failed.

There was a highboy dresser at the foot of the second bed and wall-to-wall carpeting on the floor. Industrial carpeting — beige, thin, and durable. The ceilings were very high. Daniel looked upward and guessed they must be at least twelve feet high, possibly fourteen. These rooms were designed before the advent of air conditioning, when the hot, summer air would collect near the ceiling, allowing the cooler air to remain below. There was an aluminum air-conditioning vent near the ceiling. Daniel knew that even standing on the highboy dresser, he would not be able to reach it.

He studied the metal grate covering the window. Was it strong enough? Was it high enough?

A loud knock disrupted Daniel's survey. There would be time to find a way out, he thought to himself as he looked toward the orderly unlocking his door. There would be time.

"Breakfast's being served," announced the orderly to the young man sitting on the edge of his bed.

Daniel made no reply. He got up and walked toward the attendant, unwilling to change out of his light- blue hospital scrubs before going to the small dining area located on the just off the commons area.

"You're new here, aren't ya?" asked the attendant as he walked beside him down the wide, institutional hallway. "You come in yesterday, I'll bet. I was off yesterday."

Daniel didn't respond.

"No one told me you was even in there, 'til five minutes ago. Y'all gonna be late for breakfast. Not that the oatmeal they're servin' will be cold or anythin'. They keep it nice and hot all mornin' case patients wants seconds."

The orderly kept talking at Daniel as they walked down the terrazzo floored hallway. Daniel looked straight down at his slippered feet. He heard the man speaking but paid no attention to what he was saying. Instead, Daniel focused on the sound of his slippers shuffling across the floor, making a skidding sound like someone sanding a piece of hardwood.

"Cat got your tongue?" asked the orderly as they arrived at the small dining area.

Daniel looked at the orderly with a cold, calculated stare. His eyes, once so alive and filled with wonder, were distilled to a cold, arctic blue. The color of a glacier hanging on the side of a frozen mountain — chilling and primal. His stare told the orderly that it wasn't the cat who got Daniel's tongue, it was insanity.

The orderly stopped talking. He knew from experience this was a bad one. He had studied the chart before going to Daniel's room to wake him for breakfast. He knew this one meant trouble. Although this boy had failed once in his attempt to leave this place called life, the orderly sensed he would try again. Soon, he thought as he walked back to the nurses station for his next assignment. Real soon.

The dining area served its meals cafeteria-style. The patients first picked up their trays and plastic silverware and then proceeded past two cafeteria workers who took their order, spooned it on to plastic plates and awaited the next patient. There were seldom many choices and they made little difference. The food was as institutional as the bricks, mortar and roofing tar that kept the rain out of the Powell Building.

The cafeteria workers handed Daniel a bowl of oatmeal, some biscuits and a glass of watered-down orange juice. Daniel looked at them with his glacial stare and said nothing.

He ate by himself. He didn't enjoy the food. It was like eating ashes. The orange juice tasted like water. Everything had taken on an element of surrealism since the overdose, and Daniel found a twisted pleasure in it. He hated it all. Disdain became the norm. The entire world was carved out of some dull black mud. He couldn't wait to get away from it.

After eating, Daniel stood up and left his tray where it sat. He walked away, listening to the sound of his slippers sanding the surface of the stone floors. In the common area, he found an old, overstuffed chair in the corner of the room and sat down. He watched the others, his fellow inmates, as they interacted and occupied the room before him. He found no pleasure in any of it.

Twenty minutes passed and it seemed like a week. A thin, smiling black man came up to him and knelt alongside of his chair. It was another orderly. He was dressed in the same white pants and white shirt as the other man. But this man was taller and thinner. He had short, curly black hair and a distinctive gait about him. He had a small, thin mustache and a warm smile that preceded him like the beam of headlights on a rainy night. Headlights on bright.

"Good morning, son. My name's Joshua J. Taylor and I'm here to take your vitals. You still got vitals, doncha, son?"

Daniel stared straight ahead, ignoring the man squeezing his right wrist, feeling for his pulse. Joshua kept speaking to him, ignoring the fact that Daniel wanted no part of his monologue.

"What's y'all doin' in a place like this? A fine, healthy young man like you is. Your heartbeat is as strong and steady as any I've ever taken, and look at you, sitten' there starin' at nothin like it was sumtin'.

"This ain't no place for a good-looking young man like you is. You gotta get yourself all fixed up here and get on with your liven'. That's what I'm thinkin'."

Joshua took out his blood pressure equipment and completed the task of monitoring Daniel's health. He knew there would be evaluations done on the boy today. He knew the staff psychologist would be coming around after lunch, taking Daniel into his small office, and trying to get a read on what was going on inside. Joshua had seen a thousand young men and women come and go in the years he'd worked at Milledgeville. Some left cured. Some returned. Some left in a box, finally able to complete their own death wish despite the best attempts by the staff to prevent it. Some, only a few, never left at all.

"Y'all get y'self better, ya hear. An' you can call me JJ if ya like," said Joshua as he walked away, heading toward the next patient on his rounds.

Daniel sat there, throwing another massive rubber tire on the fire. The stinking, dark smoke soon filled the common area. Its stench crept into every corner of the room and saturated the dining area, making the food taste of burnt rubber. Burnt rubber and ashes.

Joshua looked back at the blond-haired, blue-eyed boy sitting by himself. This was a bad one, thought Joshua. The devil's got a hold of this boy, and he's gonna need all the prayin' I can give him.

Knowing that, Joshua started praying.

Joshua's Farm

The faded silver roof of the old Dodge revealed a half-dozen spots of rust as it pulled out from the parking lot behind the Powell Building. Joshua noted the rust as he walked up to the car and reminded himself for the hundredth time that he needed to stop at Preston's Hardware and pick himself up a can of matching spray paint.

I've just gotta take care of those spots before they eat clean through my hardtop. Can't have me no leakin' K-car, Joshua said to himself as he sat in the broken-down front seat and turned the key, hoping she'd do him the honor of starting. She did start that afternoon, and they were now on their way home, taking a left at the stop sign atop the hill, eventually finding their way to State Highway 22, driving toward Haddock.

The old, nineteen eighty-seven Dodge had been good to Joshua and his family. He bought it used in 1993 with only sixty-two thousand miles on it. The odometer had broken at one hundred and forty-three thousand miles in 1998. The Lord only knew how many miles she had on her now.

She was finally starting to pour through the oil, and the reality of needing a newer used car weighed heavy on Joshua's mind. Maybe that's why he never bothered stopping by Preston's store. What good was fixin' a bunch of ordinary rust spots when you knew darn well the engine was about to blow? It was just a matter of a thousand more highway miles and a few months' time, decided Joshua. Miles and time, just like all of us.

Joshua kept a keen eye out for deer as he drove along Highway 22. There were so many deer in Baldwin County there was talk of increasing the legal limit this fall to nine per license. That was up from eight last fall. Joshua and his family had mixed feelings about the herds of deer that had come to overrun the county in recent years. He liked the fact his freezer was filled to the brim with deer meat, but they wreaked havoc on his gardens. Worse still, the thought of hitting a big buck scared him to death. People hit deer constantly in Baldwin County, sometimes with disastrous consequences.

Because of the deer, he couldn't concentrate on his prayin' like he used to. He could easily sing his favorite hymns, but praying kept him too distracted, and he couldn't afford to be distracted traveling along this stretch of road at dusk. Such a distraction could wind up putting a two-hundred-pound buck through his windshield like it did to Lloyd Smith's pick-up three weeks ago — darn near killed him.

So Joshua sang quietly to himself as he drove the seven miles toward the town of Haddock. When he came to a small, local road that entered from the north, he took a right and proceeded down the clay-colored gravel for another three miles. It was called Mill Road, although Joshua didn't know if it was named after a wood mill or an old grain mill. For all he knew, there may never have been a mill down Mill Road. It was just a name someone had picked for an old wagon trail a hundred years ago. An easy name.

His odds of hitting a deer increased dramatically after leaving the highway. Second- and third-generation scrub forest abutted Mill Road, broken only by deserted fields and pasture land. It was ideal whitetail deer habitat. The only good news was that Mill Road was in horrible condition — wash-boarded to death, twisting, turning and potholed to the point of possibly being the worst stretch of dirt road in Georgia. That kept everyone's speed under thirty miles an hour. It's a world of difference between slamming into an animal at sixty as compared with twenty-five, reflected a cautious driver.

But the appalling condition of Mill Road created its own set of headaches for Joshua J. Taylor. It had wiped out his car's electrical system. The radio had been shaken into silence, and the rest of the electrical system had been reduced to random connections. If you flipped on the headlights, chances were that the windshield wipers would kick in. If you turned right, the emergency flashers would go on. If you signaled a left turn, the automatic transmission would sometimes downshift into second. Mill Road was hard on his Dodge Reliant, but it kept Joshua moving slow enough to avoid hitting all but the swiftest doe.

Three miles of kicking up a cloud of red Georgia dust ended when Joshua turned right into his driveway. He was home. He was back on the farm. He slowed the car up to a lumbering crawl, ever watchful for his two older boys playing kickball with an old basketball or his girls picking a bouquet of wildflowers. Flowers that bloomed profusely along the edge of his driveway. He didn't want to risk an accident with one of his four children, so he took the Dodge down to walking speed as he climbed the driveway to the knoll where his double-wide stood.

Joshua and his wife, Mariah, had purchased the farm from her Uncle Everett twelve years ago, just a few years after Joshua began working at the hospital. It wasn't really a farm, per se. It was a three-and-a-half-acre patch of red Georgia clay sitting atop a knoll, cleared and planted with gardens, peach trees, and strawberry patches. It was surrounded by the same scrub forest that pressed the flanks of Mill Road — lowly jack pines, undernourished Southern pines and a mixture of hardwoods, poplar and brush. The lush, flourishing pines, black oak, and walnuts had been logged off eons ago, leaving behind only this low, endless scrub.

Joshua parked the Dodge in the same ruts it had wiggled out of at seven-thirty that morning. As he got out of the car, his four-year-old, Melissa, ran to him, threw her arms around him, and gave her father a hug worth returning. He lifted her little body into the air and twirled her around several times in response.

"Me next, Daddy," said his six-year-old. "Me next."

"Just wait yer' turn, little darlin'," replied Joshua.

He finished playing with his girls and proceeded into the mobile home with his empty lunch box in hand. His wife was in the kitchen, preparing a fine stew of venison, sweet potatoes and carrots. They would have fresh collard greens on the side and when all the aromas came together, the entire inside of the long, narrow mobile home smelled glorious.

"How's yer day, honey?" asked his wife.

"Just fine, and yer's?"

"Fine, provided them boys of yours return before it gets dark. They's out explorin' again."

"It's a good thing, explorin'. Keeps em' out of trouble. They made it all the way down to the river last week, an that's gotta be four, maybe five miles west of here. They're learnin' these woods better than I'd ever knowed 'em. Maybe they can give me some good spots to put up a deer stand this fall."

"You can shoot all the deer you want right off the front porch, JJ. They've always got their darn noses in our corn patch."

"Yeah, but it don't hurt any to have me a backup plan."

Mariah carried on with peeling the potatoes with her paring knife. She smiled and hummed as she did, happy to be watching her two girls skip rope in the yard outside the kitchen window. They'd tied one end to the clothesline pole and took turns twirling the long rope for each other. Oh so sweet they is, thought Mariah.

Joshua looked over to his wife lovingly, seeing her standing there peeling potatoes, smiling, watching her children grow up. With each successive child she bore him, Mariah had gained a few pounds, but Joshua never said anything about it. By now, Mariah was a big woman, with legs bigger around than most of the poplar in Baldwin County.

Mariah was much darker than her husband, with skin so black that it was as if she'd just stepped off an equatorial slave ship. Joshua, by comparison, was brown-skinned, and it was clear to everyone who saw him there was white blood flowing in his veins. The same white blood who owned the ships that had carried the great, great-grandparents of his wife to Savannah.

Mariah was a good woman and a dedicated mother. She kept at the gardens, the chores, the laundry, and rode shotgun over the kid's schoolwork like a junkyard dog looks after his spare parts. The Taylor kids came home from school with As and Bs, period. That was the way it was in the Taylor household. When one of them came home with a C, he had to explain it to Mariah, and even though she'd hear him out, no explanation on earth could convince her he couldn't do better next quarter.

Joshua continued his conversation with his wife. She was used to listening to her husband when he came home from work, knowing that his job at the hospital weighed heavily on him.

"We got a new patient in yesterday. A boy named Harris from 'round Macon, I guess."

"Yeah," Mariah responded, letting her man know she was hearing him.

"It's a shame. It's a real shame. He's about the best-lookin' boy I'd ever seen admitted to Milledgeville. He's got the looks of a movie star about him — nice white teeth, blond hair, blue eyes. Big old square jaw, solid cheekbones. It's a cryin' shame.

"He's got it bad, Mariah. He's got that look. I don't know how they get their lives mixed up to the point to where they get that look, but this boy's got it. He looks at you like you was trying to cut his heart out of em', then stand there and show it to him while he died. He's gonna be in fer a spell, I suspect."

"What'd he do to get himself admitted?"

"He tried to kill himself up in Atlanta. Took a handful of pills and some liquor. They found him just in time but I don't think he's none too happy about livin', not by the look a him."

"Yeah."

"He's not talkin'. He's locked up solid and wound so tight he might bust right out of his skin if he lets go. I can see it in his eyes.

"He's gonna need us, Mariah. He's gonna need us and he's gonna need the help of Jesus to make it out of that dark place the devil's taken him to."

"Amen, JJ."

"Keep him in your prayers, Mariah. This boy'll be needin' all the prayers we can give 'em. Just keep thinkin — **WWJD** — Mariah. What Would Jesus Do? He'd be there for that boy. That's the only question worth asking, what would Jesus do?"

Joshua stopped talking to his wife. His point had been made and it was clear to Mariah that his new mission had been found. Mariah had seen him come home over the years with much the same story again and again. There was always someone at the hospital who needed extra attention. To many of the lonely patients at Central State Hospital, Joshua wasn't an orderly, he was a godsend.

Once he found someone like Daniel, while still taking care of his regular duties, he would set aside all of his extra time to focus on that patient. Sometimes it was a young woman with an eating disorder that had gotten out of control, sometimes it was a patient who had become so paranoid he couldn't find his way out of bed every morning, and sometimes it was a withdrawn white boy from Macon who was carrying a load too heavy for his shoulders to bear.

To Joshua Taylor, it didn't matter. His mission was clear, laid out before him by the power of his faith. He had to save these folks from the devils that had taken them. Taken them from their children, their families and the world.

Mariah looked at her husband and she could see his lips moving and his eyes closed. He was praying for this lost child already. This was good. What would Jesus do? asked Mariah. He'd be sending in Joshua J. Taylor.

The Night Shift

After eight p.m. the staff on every floor in the Powell Building was reduced to a skeleton crew of three — two orderlies and a nurse's aide. Dinner was over by then and most of the patients were safely locked in their rooms by nine. Most nights slipped by without incident, lost in the solitude of empty hallways, unfilled chairs and silent television sets. Most but not all.

Moses McCarty heard the crash at eleven thirty-five. He woke the new kid who was dozing off on the couch beside him and together they rushed down the dimly lit hallway toward the area where the noise had come from.

They split up as they neared the end of the hall, Moses taking all the rooms on the right and Stan Thomas inspecting the rooms on the left. There were no more noises to be heard, so the only hope of finding out where the crash had come from was by looking into each and every room at this end of the ward. It could be a while.

The first four rooms they inspected were fine. Several of the patients in them had been awakened by the din and, as the orderlies unlocked their doors, they were standing there, looking perplexed by whatever had happened. They appeared confused, unaccustomed to midnight disruptions.

The fifth door Stan looked into was Daniel's, and it was apparent that his room was the source of the disturbance. Stan hollered over to his co-worker, who was halfway down the other side of the hallway, "Moses, it's over here."

Stan unlocked the door. As he opened it, a plume of fine white dust, like a puff of smoke, poured into the hallway. Moses arrived and went in ahead of Stan, flipping the overhead light on as he did. The scene before them explained the cause of the noise as well as the source of the dust. It was a disaster.

Daniel was lying on the floor, just beside the foot of his bed. Large chunks of plaster, pieces of broken glass and the entire seven-foot tall section of metal grate lay on top of the boy, pinning him to the floor.

"Is he alive?" asked Stan, watching as Moses hurriedly lifted the heavy grate off the boy, holding it with both hands. As he did, he noted the rope attached to the grating and traced it back to where it was wrapped snugly around Daniel's neck.

"I doubt he is. Come here and hold this grating for me. I've got to get the noose off this boy before I check his pulse."

Stan rushed over and lifted up the metal grating. The rope, carefully fashioned out of torn bed sheet strips, was too short to allow them to move the grating all the way onto the bed without dragging the boy along.

By this time, the nurse's aide had arrived. As she looked into the room, she let out a restrained but harrowing scream. Daniel looked dead. He was pale, and pieces of the shattered window had fallen on his face, causing any number of lacerations. As they watched, Moses reached over and worked the noose loose. It had cinched up so tightly against Daniel's throat that Moses was certain the boy had broken his neck in the fall.

Deep red bruises traced every twist in the handmade rope as Moses carefully worked it free. After loosening the rope enough to slip it over Daniel's bloodied face, Moses took hold of the grating with Stan and together, they pushed it on top of the bed. It was so large that it covered the entire mattress, like a steel blanket woven from coarse metal twine.

"It don't look good, Ma'am," Moses said to the young nurse as he knelt down beside the crumpled body. He took his right hand and slipped two fingers just under Daniel's right jaw, pressing them firmly against his carotid artery, searching for a pulse. As he did, he looked up toward the heavens and prayed.

There was a long, silent pause. After what felt like an eternity, Moses looked over and smiled at the frightened aide.

"You best go back and call in a doctor, Cindy, this boy's still with us. We best not try to move him or anything 'cause his neck might be broken."

The nurse gave a sigh of relief, turned, and scurried back down the hall toward her small, glassed-in office. Cindy dialed the emergency number she had been instructed to dial seven months ago when she was first hired at Central State Hospital. She had never needed to dial that number before, but she knew exactly where it was. She was glad the boy was alive, not wanting to have had a suicide occur on her shift.

Moses and Stan brushed off the dust and pieces of shattered glass and sat on the bed opposite Daniel's. Stan was still standing, visibly shaking.

"Damn, I's sure could use a cigarette," said Moses loudly.

"I thought you quit."

"I just started again."

"What'd ya think happened?" asked Stan.

"Oh, he tried to kill himself, sure 'nuf. Looks to me like he didn't pay any attention to the nine o'clock lights-out rule. He must have spent the last few hours tearing his bed sheets into long, thin strips. Then he must have taken three or four of them and wound them up tight, fashinin' a rope out of 'em."

"How'd he get the rope up that high?"

"Well, looks to me like he moved the highboy over beside the window and tied one end of the rope to the top of the metal grating. He made a noose on the other end and slipped it over his neck. He was smart. He didn't jump off the highboy, figurin' he'd get up too much speed from such a height, possibly breaking his rope."

"You think he used the bed? You think he just stepped off 'a it?"

"Yeah, that's what he did. He must of got it set just right and when he had the rope nice and tight, he just walked off the edge of the bed, thinkin' his feet wouldn't make it to the floor. Trouble being, the age of this old Powell Building didn't help him out any."

Moses pointed toward the top section of the window. "Look up there, do ya see what happened?"

"Half the wall's gone."

"Yup, the weight of this here boy was just too much for these old walls to handle. Thirty years ago that grating would have held and we would have come in here at six-fifteen in the morning to find a corpse on our hands. But too many winters and too many summers have gone by, and when he walked off the edge of the bed and started kicking like the hanging kind always do, the grating just pulled right out from the wall and crashed down on top of him. Made for one hell of a mess.

"The grating must have kicked back into the window as it fell, causing the glass to shatter, and the plaster to cover the room in dust. I'm sure he never figured on the gratin' to give way."

"No, it looks to me like he wanted to die pretty bad."

"Yup, he sure did. But he didn't make it."

A few minutes later the staff doctor arrived followed by two emergency workers. They crowded into the room with a gurney and Daniel was whisked away into an elevator and down two floors to the ward where they treat patients for injuries, fevers and diseases.

Moses and Stan were left to sweep the room and haul the grate away. The nurse went from room to room, calming the patients down, telling them there had been an accident but no one had been hurt.

By two in the morning, the second floor, south wing of Central State Hospital was back to normal. Two floors below, a handsome white boy was strapped to a clean white bed, unconscious but breathing. Daniel had severely strained his neck, but it was not broken. He had tried again to meet the angel of death. The angel did not want him.

Suicide Watch

"Y'all remind me of Jonah, son. You've heard the story of Jonah and the great fish, haven't ya?"

Daniel gave Joshua a spiteful look. He didn't like the attention this black man was giving him. He hadn't asked for it, nor was he interested in listening to him. But in this circumstance, Daniel's oath of silence worked against him. He could not tell him to leave, to go to hell, so Joshua continued.

"Well, even if ya've heard it before, I think it's good to hear it again. A good story like this can't hardly be told too often."

Joshua got comfortable on the bed across from Daniel's. The patient who was sharing the room had already gone out into the common area for the day, and Daniel, still bandaged and recovering from his injuries, remained. Under a suicide watch, Joshua, a nurse, or one of the other orderlies, would check on Daniel every fifteen minutes. There would be no time to fashion a second rope with which to hang himself. Daniel was condemned to live.

Joshua went on, "Well, a long while ago, there was this fellow named Jonah. He lived in Jerusalem during the Bible times and one day the Lord says to him that he's gotta go up to Assyria, which is somewhere in Iraq, to save this town full of sinners.

"But Jonah didn't much like the idea of saving the people who was liven' in Nineveh. He would rather have God destroy 'em than save 'em. So, instead of doing what God wants him to do, Jonah gets on this ship and heads west instead of east. Bad move. What's Jonah thinkin' anyway? Was he thinkin' he can slip out a town without God knowin'?

"Well, they get out to sea a ways and a great big storm comes up. Jonah's already told everyone on board that he's trying to avoid havin' to go preach to the Assyrians and, the crew figures he's bringin' them a heap a bad luck. After some heated discussion, the crew decides to pitch old Jonah in the sea, hopin' and prayin' that after they do, God will calm the storm.

"Sure 'nuf, that's just what happens. They toss Jonah overboard and the sea settles down. But instead of drownin', Jonah gets swallowed up whole by a big fish. Most people think it was a whale, but it don't rightly matter what kind of fish it was, only that it didn't eat Jonah, it just kept him there in his belly.

"And that's where you are, Daniel. You're in some kind of belly of some kind of huge fish right now. It's dark and it's foul smelling and you'd rather be dead than alive, ain't that right?"

Daniel stared straight ahead. He was listening, but he wouldn't give Joshua the pleasure of knowing it. No sign of acknowledgment of any kind came forth from the young man staring at the ceiling. Still Joshua continued. "Yeah, I can tell yer listenin'."

"Well, once Jonah's all eaten up by this whale, he says this prayer to God. This is a good prayer for you to hear, cause it seems to me that yer inside the same darkness as Jonah was. But I can't remember it clearly enough, so I'll just thumb through this lil' ol' Bible of mine 'til I comes across it."

Joshua opened his diminutive Bible and began leafing through it, quickly thumbing past Isaiah, Ezekiel and Obadiah, until coming to the book of Jonah. Finding the chapter and verse he was searching for, Joshua read the passage aloud to the muted soul beside him.

"In my distress I called to the Lord,
and he answered me.
From the depths of the grave I called for help,
and you listened to my cry.
You hurled me into the deep,
into the very heart of the seas,
and the currents swirled about me;

all your waves and breakers
swept over me.
I said, 'I have been banished
from your sight;
yet I will look again
toward your holy temple.'
The engulfing waters threatened me,
the deep surrounded me;
seaweed was wrapped around my head.
To the roots of the mountains I sank down;
the earth beneath barred me in forever.
But you brought my life up from the pit,
O Lord, my God."

"See what I'm sayin'? Those bandages around your head are like the seaweed wrapped around Jonah's head. And you're drownin' in some kind of ocean I can only guess at. But you need to know the Lord is merciful, boy. The Lord was merciful to the evil Assyrians, to Jonah, and the Lord is gonna be merciful to you.

"He let you live, and there's a reason for that. We don't know what the reason is, because that's the Lord's business. But as sure as I'm sittin' here, the Lord had a hand in that big heavy grate pulling free. As sure as I'm sittin' here today, I'll be sittin' here tomorrow. Because it just ain't right that you're in this place. Ain't right t'all.

"And no matter how long I gotta sit here, I'm gonna help you get out of that whale's belly and help you get on with livin'. Just like old Jonah, you've gotta turn yourself around and come back to Jesus. That's my plan, son, and I just want ya to get comfortable with it."

Daniel didn't flinch. Joshua had no way of knowing what was going on behind the eyes of Daniel. No one was allowed in — not the staff psychologist, not the nurses, and certainly not this skinny black man wearing glasses and quoting the same Bible that had helped to put him here. The mouth of the whale was sealed shut and the darkness comforting to the Jonah inside.

"Call me if ya need anything," said Joshua as he picked up his blood pressure cuff, his stethoscope and walked from the room. He would be back in fifteen minutes to check on him. Hour after hour, day after day, week after week, month after month, year after year, it didn't matter to Joshua. Daniel, Joshua believed, would eventually come back from the grave he had buried himself in. That was the level of faith Joshua had in God — a faith beyond challenge.

Ozel Meltem Dogum Hastanesi, Istanbul

*T*he contractions were increasing in frequency and strength. Ayse had never known such pain. She had been in labor for eight hours, and as her muscles tightened once again and the beads of sweat gathered on her forehead, she kept her thoughts focused on the child she was birthing. In doing so, her pain became bearable, became her price tag to motherhood.

Elif stood beside the bed and comforted her daughter, just as Elif's mother had comforted her twenty-two years ago at Ozel Meltem Dogum. Elif would wipe the sweat from her daughter's neck and forehead with a towel and hold her trembling hand when the contractions came. As they increased in intensity, Ayse's fingers tightened around her mother's aging hand, nearly crushing it. Elif said nothing. Her daughter's pain became her pain, as it was meant to be.

At two-thirty-seven in the morning, on a cold February night in Istanbul, Ayse delivered Daniel's son, Ibraham Yalçin Harris. He was a healthy, seven pound, four-ounce-child with dark hair and Daniel's steel blue eyes.

Within minutes, Elif held him. Ibraham was wrapped in a small cotton blanket and still damp from the passage of birth, she pressed the infant to her bosom, remembering the wonders of motherhood.

After Ayse regained her strength, and with the attending nurse's nod of approval, Elif passed the swaddled Ibraham into her daughter's extended arms. She watched as the circle completed itself. How another generation was born into this world filled with joy and tragedy. Elif looked at Ayse's dark eyes and saw them radiate with a warmth only a mother fathoms.

Elif knew of the journey to come. The long, sleepless nights, the diapers, the coughs and fevers, the falls, the worries, the disappointments and the duties. As difficult as raising this boy would be, especially without a father, Elif knew it would be offset by the euphoria of motherhood. The smile on her daughter's face told Elif what she already knew: Ayse would be a good mother and little Ibraham would have all the love he would ever need.

Ayse looked up and, although exhausted, spoke softly to her mother in Turkish, "I wish he were here."

"Yes, I know you do, Ayse. But he is here. Somehow, he is here."

Ayse smiled warmly at her mother, seeing Elif's eyes filled with tears, her head covered in a cotton cloth in the fashion of the older women of Turkey. But Elif had changed since Ayse's return from Atlanta. She no longer fought against her daughter's love for this young man from Georgia. Elif knew Ayse's love was genuine and unfaltering. No matter the outcome, thought Elif, Ayse had found the man she was meant to find. The birth of this grandchild, Ibraham, was God's blessing upon all of them.

For beautiful Ayse, it had been a difficult nine months. No word of Daniel from Athens, no letters, no e-mails, nothing since the conversation with his mother five months ago. Ayse could only assume he was safe and well. But as she became heavy with his child, she longed to hear from him.

Ayse would wait for the mail every day, praying to Allâh that it would bring news of her husband. Even the arrival of divorce papers from her husband would be a welcome sight. At least then she could let him know about the child she was carrying. But no divorce papers arrived.

Many times over the past five months, Ayse had held the telephone, staring at Rebecca's phone number. But she never called Daniel's home in Macon, nor would she when she returned to Bebek with Ibraham in two days' time. This new grandchild would remain unknown to Clayton and Rebecca Harris, just as it was to their son, Daniel.

Ayse had faith that time would unveil its mysteries to her. Time would allow Ibraham to grow and flourish, to run through the hallways of the big house in Bebek and learn about the wonders of his own existence. Time would solve the secret of when and how Daniel would learn of his son. This she knew in her heart, as Ayse had a great faith. Faith that all things would come to pass under the will of Allâh. In this, she differed little from a humble black orderly named Joshua J. Taylor. She could not see him during that same hour of her child's birth, reading his tattered Bible, comfortable in his worn recliner in the living room of his mobile home, praying to God — the same God.

Praying to Him who knows all in Joshua's quiet, patient inner voice. Asking that God make it safe for Daniel to leave the belly of the whale, to be released from that place of infinite darkness. That God grant safe passage for Daniel to return to the daylight of living.

For both Ayse and Joshua, time and faith were their steadfast allies. It would all come to pass, Ayse felt as she listened to her newborn's delicate breathing, all in time and faith. Joshua prayed as well, knowing God would be merciful to the young man from Macon. Time and faith, felt each of them, at the same minute, six thousand miles apart. Belief in a kingdom larger than life.

Sunday Morning

A brisk March wind kicked up the red dust in the lot, dirtying the assorted cars parked there. The wind was from the north, but it no longer spoke of winter. It was gusty and warm, speaking the language of spring. Green shoots of summer grasses were pushing through the washed-out straw of winter, buds were forming on the dogwoods in the forest beyond. Life was stirring again, reborn by the quickening sun and the lengthening daylight.

Inside the rural church Joshua, Mariah and their four children all stood singing *Amazing Grace* with a conviction that shook the old church windows more than did the blustery wind. It was Sunday morning, and, like every Sunday morning without fail, the Taylor family was worshiping — worshiping Jesus.

Amazing Grace, how sweet the sound,
That saved a wretch like me...
I once was lost but now am found,
Was blind, but now, I see.

T'was Grace that taught my heart to fear...
And Grace, my fears relieved.
How precious did that Grace appear...
the hour I first believed...

When the song was over, and the congregation settled back into their pews, a heavy-set black minister walked in front of the robed choir and started speaking, "Who's here to be touched by Jesus, this fine mornin'?" Rev. Brown asked in his deep, impassioned voice.

A series of responses came forth. They came in no particular order, often overlapping each other, or shouted simultaneously. Words like "I'm ready for you, Lord," and "Praise God," "I've been touched by the Lord," "Amen," and "Hallelujah," sprang forth from the mouths of the faithful as the preacher surveyed his gathering of sinners.

He took note of each and every one of them. The preacher knew their individual stories, along with the sins that accompanied them, by heart. He looked across the sixty-odd people sitting in rows before him and he saw more than their shiny shoes and Sunday best. He saw Miss Eliza Garvin, whose father had died of prostate cancer last fall. He saw Byron Lewis and Alyssa Cook, now back with their respective spouses after a torrid love affair two years ago. He knew Cyrus Johnson still had a gambling problem and Monique Tillman had acquired a taste for moonshine.

There were a few out there, amidst this crowd of sinners, who had been blessed. There were Mr. and Mrs. Samuel Sykes, who gave more to the church than they could afford. And the Taylor family, whom he admired because they worked hard to keep their lives simple and near to God. The minister knew Joshua was a man who read his Bible and put what he read to use. That's what he admired about Joshua and his family — they were the doers.

That's what it was all about for Earl Brown, the battle between the doers and the talkers. Half his sermons were dedicated to that topic and if he felt he could have gotten by with it, the other half would have been about the same thing. Because, according to Reverend Brown, that was the problem. Everyone talked about being Christian, but few and far between were those who behaved like one.

The situation reminded the reverend of an old saying he'd heard years ago in the seminary. The saying was attributed to St. Francis of Assisi. St. Francis used to say a Christian should always preach the gospel of Jesus at all times, and if necessary, use words. To Revered Brown, doing Christ's work was the only true measure of the faithful. As the wind whipped through the tattered steeple, the good Reverend began preachin'.

Throughout the service, Joshua's mind kept wandering back to Daniel. Seven months had passed and he was still unable to crack through the shell Daniel had encased himself in. He worried it would soon harden to the point where no one could get in. He'd seen it before. There was George Asher on the fourth floor. He had arrived at the hospital twenty-three years ago. No one had been able to reopen his self-sealed tomb. The doctors, the staff, everyone knew that George would never walk out of Central State Hospital. He'd be wheeled out on a gurney.

Something had to get through to that boy before long, or he might join the desolate ranks of the forgotten. The permanently withdrawn. The quiet ones whose suffering remains internal. Whose silence is their private prescription to the grave. Joshua prayed throughout the service that God would give him a sign, a signal of some kind that the time was drawing near when Daniel would want to leave his dark sanctum. Joshua needed a sign, like the olive branch in the dove's beak for Noah. Joshua prayed deeply and forthright, like a monk cloistered in a monastery on the edge of the world.

Worship continued, with several more hymns sung in earnest, and a sermon delivered with unimpeachable conviction. It was another of Brown's messages about the doers and the talkers. Joshua paid little attention to it, so immersed were his thoughts in prayer. Soon, Joshua prayed, help us soon.

Words

"What is it with you? Why is you so wrapped up in yourself like this? Was it a woman who broke your heart? Is that why you're here? Was it your family? Did they seal you up like some mummy in this mausoleum y'all are livin' in?

Daniel stared straight ahead, ignoring Joshua's string of questions with a studied detachment. He heard him clearly, Johsua's words coming into Daniel's mind like an unwelcome, cold rain. He'd heard everything over the past year. The quotations from the Gospels, the paraphrased Bible stories, the prayers and the pleas, but Joshua had no way of knowing this. For JJ, there was only a blank stare, a steady, healthy heartbeat and a young man growing older in a mental institution.

The doctors had no more luck with Daniel than did Joshua. He had battened himself down so tight that no one could enter. They had been prescribing antipsychotics and antidepressants, among an array of other pharmaceuticals, but nothing seemed to dislodge him from his determined course — a course into a flat, endless ocean.

To the nurses, the staff and all the others save Joshua, Daniel Mark Harris had become a piece of furniture on Wing 2-B of the Powell Building. He woke up every morning, ate a generic breakfast and wandered into the common area where he would find a comfortable chair, safely removed from the other patients, and sit. He did not watch television, or read, or participate in any of the group activities. He sat.

At lunch he would shuffle back into the dining area, take his place amid the other patients, eat overcooked Southern food, and return to the common area or retreat to his room. Dinners would come and go, come and go, come and go and the lights would be flipped off at nine. His catatonic ritual would be repeated the following day, and the day after that.

By now, everyone but Joshua felt Daniel was going to be a lifer. Unless something broke, he would remain in his internal wasteland until they found him wrinkled and breathless one morning fifty years hence. Found him dead in his room. Dead and at peace with the demons that haunted him.

Joshua finished taking Daniel's pulse and blood pressure and recording them on his small clipboard. He was about to get up from the wooden chair he had placed beside Daniel when an incident broke out across the common area. Four patients who had been enjoying a friendly game of gin rummy suddenly began screaming and shouting at each other. Shouted accusations of cheating could be heard in every corner of the ward, and Joshua knew from experience a fight was imminent. Placing his clipboard and pencil on the chair he was sitting in, he ran across the room to the scene of the ensuing mayhem.

That's when it happened.

Daniel reached down, picked up the clipboard with his chart attached and studied it. He read Joshua's notes and reviewed his vitals. His heart beat was sixty-three beats per minute. A heartbeat a second, he thought. His blood pressure was one hundred and thirty-one over eighty-four.

He took the pencil out of its holder between the metal clamp and began writing. He wrote, *Could I have a pencil and paper, please?*

Daniel calmly, methodically set the clipboard back on the chair and went back into his trance. He had not used his voice in so long that he'd become afraid to break his oath of silence. But he longed to write. He wanted to continue his *Book of Midnights*, and he knew Joshua would supply him with the materials needed if he asked him to.

Soon after the cheating incident had been resolved and the fight between the inmates narrowly averted, Joshua returned to pick up his chart. He didn't notice Daniel's note. He grabbed his clipboard and went down the hall to his next patient.

"See you this afternoon, son," he said while walking away from Daniel.

Once comfortably seated beside Mrs. Sloan, Joshua picked up his clipboard and was about to bury Daniel's chart at the bottom of the pile when he noticed the request. At first he didn't put it together, wondering how these words had ended up on his chart. He couldn't imagine this message was from Daniel's hand.

But as he studied it more carefully and retraced the events of the past twenty minutes, Joshua could draw no other conclusion. It was possible. In fact, it was the only plausible explanation.

Joshua resisted the urge to run back to ask Daniel if he had written this on his chart. No, that wouldn't work, he reasoned. He was scheduled to take his vitals this afternoon, and he had decided that rather than asking Daniel if he was responsible for this message, he would simply provide him with the paper and pencil he had asked for and leave it at that.

Maybe he doesn't want to talk, Joshua asked himself. Maybe he wants to write.

If it was Daniel who wrote the note, thought Joshua, this is the answer to my prayers. It has been nearly a year, and it's time. It's just not the answer I'd expected, he thought. But then again, it never is.

Joshua smiled to himself when he thought about it, recalling one of his favorite jokes. It was told to him by Reverend Brown some years ago on a glorious Sunday morning at Hillside Baptist Church. The Reverend had walked over to Joshua during the brief social they held after the worship service and asked him a question. "Joshua, I've got a question for y'all."

"What is it, Reverend?"

"How do you make God laugh?"

Joshua thought about it, knowing Earl Brown had something up his sleeve, and responded, "I don't know, how do you make God laugh?"

Reverend Brown smiled a huge Southern smile and said without flinching, "You tell him your plans."

Joshua laughed. The preacher was right. He knew that all the plans we make matter little to the One who knows.

That's what's happened. All along, my plan was to get Daniel to speak, recalled Joshua. God's plan was to have him write.

Over lunch break, Joshua drove into town and purchased an inexpensive notebook and a half-dozen pencils with his own money. As he approached the cash register, he looked up toward the heavens and mumbled something about God having a sense of humor.

He returned to the hospital, punched in, and waited. He had a score of tasks to attend to before he'd be able to get back to Daniel. He would not rush, or show any sign he'd received the message. It was better this way, he felt.

When three o'clock rolled around Daniel was still sitting in the overstuffed chair he had been in all morning. His face was expressionless and distant as Joshua pulled a small wooden chair up beside him. For a moment, Joshua was convinced someone else must have written the note. Surely it could not have been the frozen, motionless boy beside him.

But Joshua put his doubts away. There is no room for doubt when it comes to miracles, he thought. As he recalled the story of Thomas after the resurrection of Christ, Joshua sat down beside Daniel and smiled. He had sharpened one of the pencils in the nurse's station and had the pencil, along with a notebook, in a paper bag beneath his clipboard.

Without saying a thing, he slipped them out of the bag and placed them, one at a time on Daniel's lap. The empty notebook first, followed by the pencil. Daniel looked down and saw them. The notebook was gray, Daniel noted. That was the same color as my last notebook — gray. It's not even a color, just a shade of black.

Daniel didn't look at Joshua, or acknowledge the gift. He took the pencil in his hand, opened the notebook and started writing. Joshua didn't lean over to read whatever Daniel was scratching down. It didn't matter. He jotted down Daniel's heart rate and blood pressure without so much as taking them. They had not changed in months. He did make a note of Daniel's change of behavior and the fact he was writing.

Then, without a word, Joshua got up and walked away from the young man from Macon. He had to continue his rounds. As Joshua headed across the common area, tears fell from his eyes. He wanted, more than anything, to drop right then and there to his knees and thank the Lord for his kindness.

Joshua knew his prayers had been answered. That the Lord works in mysterious ways and this was the moment he'd been waiting for. It was not what he had expected, but it seldom is. Daniel wouldn't speak, but he would write. Years of working at the hospital had taught Joshua that it mattered little how each patient climbed out of the fish's belly. All that mattered was that somehow, someday they began their labored ascent.

Joshua made note of the date, May 17, nearly a year since Daniel's arrival. God is good, thought the thin, black man with glasses as he approached his next patient, infinitely good.

His First Pencil

Words exploded out of Daniel. They came in waves, like breakers smashing against a jagged coastline from some unnamed storm at sea. They crashed, they hurled back against themselves in a wash of fury and foam. The words came from all directions, leaving behind the rules of syntax and meaning, surging in disarray on the empty pages of his notebook.

Emotions collided with reason, definition slammed against passion, and as he crouched there in his bed, writing frantically beneath the dim candlepower of a waxing moon, his pencil melted away. Dissolving one word at time into a manuscript of madness. As the first lead gave way, Daniel used his fingernails, or his teeth to keep a point on the pencil. If he was too immersed in a thought, and the pencil was losing its ability to write, he would press down so hard on the surface of his notebook that the words were more etched than written.

He had not uttered a word in a year. His new *Book of Midnights* became a voice in the harrowing darkness that held him. More than a voice — a scream.

Anger formed the core of his manic soliloquy. Anger at God, at his father, at his family, at a world that had once promised everything only to abandon him at the doorstep of this asylum. His words burned into the pages, as if he were writing with a blowtorch. A year of silence spilled out of him in three days. The entire notebook was nearing completion when his first pencil gave out in a rage of unconnected phrases.

God doesn't give a damn my father is so much like god and goddamn my father too where is Ayse now is she still in school I wonder who created this whole thing doesn't anyone know? and why are there so many different gods when there is only one world?

why gods at all? Why Baptist or Buddhist or Islam or Moses or Jesus or Krishna or Zeus or Lao Tzu or Shiva or Catholic or Zoroaster or Ra or Gabriel or Satan or St. Francis or Episcopalian or devils or angels or ghost dances or Judaism or Ahura Mazda or Adam or Eve or Mother Teresa or David Koresh or Shinto or Jainism or stigmata or miracles or Stonehenge or mosques or temples or inquisitions or Muhammad or prophets or martyrs or saints and sinners or dharma or reincarnation or death or Krishna or Hinduism or Bibles or sacraments or creeds or crucifixions or catacomb or hell why is there a hell when life itself is hell enough

why is this man doing this for me finding this pencil which is now gone like my Ayse is gone and my father is gone that son of a bitch has taken everything because i hate him i hate him i hate him i hate him and if there is a hell he should be delivered to it tomorrow why is JJ here?

why?

Daniel tried to bite off the last bit of stubble on the pencil he had been writing with but it was no use. Although the lead ran right to the edge of the metal wrapping encasing the unused eraser, he could not work the last half-inch of the pencil. It was too small to hold and without the supporting pine wood, the lead crumbled. Daniel knew he needed a new pencil from Joshua, and soon thereafter a second notebook.

He would have to ask Joshua for them. With the last remaining shard of lead he tore out a sheet of paper and at the very top, in letters nearly impossible to read, he wrote the single word he had finished his notebook with. The word — *why?*

Then he wrapped the tiny, half-inch remnant of his first pencil in the page and clutched it in his hand. He would give it to Joshua after breakfast.

✪

After breakfast Daniel went to his usual chair, his note gripped firmly in his palm. There, he waited. Joshua made his way to Daniel at ten that morning. Joshua had observed Daniel with his notebook and pencil in hand since giving them to him three days ago. He noted their absence this morning as he approached to check his vitals during his normal rounds.

As Joshua approached Daniel, he was amazed to discover Daniel was not staring straight ahead, but focusing on him. Joshua went over, pulled up a wooden folding chair and brought it beside Daniel's. When he sat down, his stethoscope hanging around his neck and his clipboard in hand, Daniel, still staring at him, reached out and handed him his note.

The sweat from Daniel's palms had saturated the paper. Joshua carefully unwrapped the damp paper and found the tiny fragment of a pencil within. Not noticing Daniel's question, Joshua looked at the young man before him and said, "I take it y'all be needin' another pencil."

Daniel smiled. Not a big, heartwarming smile, or anything that someone who lived in the world beyond the Powell Building would consider a smile. Just a crack in the white marble facade that had become this boy's face. Joshua smiled back. The ice was melting.

When Joshua went to set the paper down to take Daniel's blood pressure, he saw the sole, diminutive word half written, half etched at the top of the page. Joshua picked up the piece of paper, and looking from the bottom of his bifocals, read the word aloud. "Why?"

"That's a right good question, Son — Why?"

Joshua sat beside Daniel a while in quiet reflection. He knew his answer was important to the lonely soul beside him. But Joshua knew he couldn't answer the question. Not for Daniel Mark Harris. He could only answer the question for himself, and hoped that his answer might make sense to Daniel.

With that in mind, he looked at Daniel and said, "Come on, get up and follow me for a minute."

Daniel looked at him quizzically. He climbed out of his chair and stood beside the black man. Taking Joshua's lead, they walked toward the eastern side of the common area where a half-dozen mullioned windows captured the rising sunlight. They walked to a window near the center of the room and stopped. Joshua pulled the curtains back, allowing them, through the metal grating, a clear view of the world beyond.

The window had been cracked open earlier by someone working the night shift. As the two of them stood there, the cool morning air sifted through the window, tempering the warmth of the ascending sun. Beyond the window the view continued down beyond the parking lot and across the courtyard. To the south, they could see a handful of abandoned buildings. Further off, only the steeple of the Chapel of All Faiths was visible, protruding above the trees in its silent reverence to God.

The trees were spectacular. Black oaks and maples, magnolias, sycamores and black cherries, all arranged in careful rows descending the hill.

The sky was clear, its majestic blue set off dramatically by the rich, summer green of the leaves. The wind was light, and the leaves shimmered as delicate breezes rushed down the hill, carrying the morning dampness away. Songbirds could be heard — Southern cardinals, mockingbirds, catbirds calling in the canopy.

To the north, a group of patients was being escorted to the gymnasium by a nurse and three orderlies. Through the cracked window they could hear the members of the group speaking, but their words were blurred and muffled by the distance. There was laughter, and you could see two of the orderlies jokingly pushing each other, as though teasing one another about a new girlfriend.

Joshua didn't say anything. He stood beside Daniel inhaling the scene before him without comment. The earth was so alive that it was impossible not to admire the energy beyond the mullioned window. After a while, Joshua spoke.

"That's why, Daniel. Because I got up this mornin' and the dew was heavy on the grass and the gardens and my little girl, Melissa, ran into our bedroom and threw her arms around me and I knowed right then and there that it's all just a dream. But it's God's dream and you and I can only see the smallest, quickest piece of that dream.

"Them birds's are singin' because God's dreamin' them singin'. The sun's shinin' because God's dreamin' stars and universes and infinities that stretch far, far beyond all a what we can know. You're a part of His dream and I'm a part of His dream and that's why we're here right now, lookin' out this window.

"Do you think it's all just a big coincidence? It ain't, Daniel. Every breath you take is because God gives you that breath. That day you come in here a year ago, I took one look at you and I said to myself that you don't belong here. I don't know how you got here, and seein' that you ain't talkin' much, I don't know if I'll ever know how you got yerself to Milledgeville. In a way, it ain't important. What's important is that you get on out a here.

"God's got His plans for you 'cause he loves you, Daniel. He loves all of us, and if we just say to Him, 'Go ahead, God, show me the way', then He will. He'll take you by the hand and walk you through the darkest valley without harm. Because it's a powerful dream He's dreamin' and He can make happen whatever He chooses to happen.

"All we is, is stardust, Daniel. We ain't but a speck of dust in this whole vision of somethin' much bigger than ourselves. Much, much bigger. It ain't about us, it's about love. God's love. That's why he sent us Jesus, just to show us how much He cares. That's why I'm standin' here talking to someone who ain't never spoken a word since he came to this place, because God told me it's the right thing to do.

"I ain't no fool. I ain't gonna spend one minute of my time arguin' with God. I'm just doin' his work, and happy to be asked to do so. That's why, Daniel. That's the only reason I can think of."

Daniel stood motionless. His view of the world outside blurred as tears welled in his eyes. He knew this man beside him had gone to extraordinary lengths to spend time with him. Whoever this Joshua was, he must have been sent to him by God. There could be no other explanation.

For a moment, Daniel wanted to speak, but he stopped himself from doing so.

It wasn't time yet, but that time was drawing near. Daniel was changing. He could see himself walking in the courtyard beyond. He could see Ayse's face again, her dark eyes, her smile. Joshua's love had pried open the mouth of the great fish and had allowed the daylight to enter. Daniel was awakening.

✪

The months flew by. Sometimes, on the weekends, Joshua would come back to the hospital to visit and the two of them would spend hours together. Joshua would answer Daniel's lengthy written questions with even longer monologues. Daniel had yet to speak and Joshua had not asked him to. He would talk when he was ready, and Joshua rejoiced in what dialogue they had, never complaining once to the boy about his silence.

They discussed everything. Joshua told him about himself. His early years, hanging with the wrong crowd in Milledgeville. He told him about his friend, Tyler Jones, whose face had been blown off with a shotgun at seventeen. How Tyler and he had gotten into dealing crack and marijuana in high school and how Tyler had smoked up the money he owed his supplier.

"That was my wake-up call, Daniel. The day I heard they'd shot Tyler in the face, that was the day I woke up from my own nightmare. We had the funeral right down the street at the Chapel of All Faiths. There wasn't a dry eye in that church the day we laid Tyler to rest.

"He was a strong, good-lookin' seventeen-year-old child and he was killed for nothin'. I sat there, lookin' across the aisle at his mother and father grievin' so and cryin', and I know'd that I had to turn things around or next time it'd be me in that coffin. It'd be my family sitting in the front row.

"It wasn't easy to stop bein' who I was. I was somebody back then. I had me a gun, a nice car, girls, money, everything was mine for the havin'. But you know what I really had, Daniel? I had nothin'. I had nothin' because that's what all that stuff is — it ain't but nothin'. If you ain't got a connection to sumthin' bigger'n you is; you is so small that you could own the whole world and not have nothin'.

"As I followed that hearse, takin' my friend Tyler to his grave, I looked down in the glove box where I had a roll of hundreds stashed and I realized my friend was dead forever. That's right when it happened. I broke down and cried to where I couldn't drive my fancy car no more. My sister took over driven' and we made it out to the cemetery and as they lowered my best friend into the ground, I promised Tyler I'd make good to him. Not by going out and killin' the kids who had killed him, what good would that do? No, I'd make good by quittin'.

"So the next day I quit. I quit sellin' and usin' and even thinkin' about any of it. I paid Tyler's money to his dealers and sold everything — my car, my stereo, and I throw'd my gun in the river. I joined the AA in Milledgeville and they took me through the twelve steps. After that I found me a church and that church took me to Jesus.

"I got me this job at the hospital almost twenty years ago and now I've got the real deal. I've got a rusty old Dodge that barely runs, a wife that can cook up a mean meal and four of the best children in the world. I ain't rich and I don't care that I ain't. Every night I pray to God that Tyler's doin' fine, and I thank the Lord for the path he's let me walk. The path that put me here, talkin' directly to you."

Daniel understood. He knew he was Tyler, or another version of him — a self-destructing young man on the road to nowhere. The Buckhead crowd was the same as Joshua's old crowd. Parties, girls, XTC, pot, tequila, Oxys, Xanax, whatever you could get your hands on to make it though the night. No wonder Joshua had taken it upon himself to spend time with me, thought Daniel, he couldn't bear witnessing another shotgun blast to the face. Life had been hard for Joshua and knowing that helped Daniel lower his defenses. They grew closer.

"I want to talk," Daniel said four months after he had handed his first note to Joshua.

"That's good, Son. Talkin's good," replied Joshua, as if hearing Daniel's voice came as no great surprise.

Daniel tried to clear his throat, realizing how difficult it was for him to speak after a year and a half of silence. He didn't recognize his own voice at first. His voice sounded raspy and uncertain, like his thoughts.

"Thank you, JJ," he said.

"Don't thank me, thank God. He was the one who put us together here on Ward 2-B. He's the one to thank."

Daniel didn't know where to start. Where would he begin his own arduous tale? Does he start with Ayse, and the trouble they had, or does he go further back, to his father?

"I've had some trouble with God, JJ, and I'm still having trouble with Him."

"No, Daniel, there you're wrong. You're havin' trouble with people, that's a far cry different from havin' trouble with God. We all got our share a trouble with people. Some peoples are good, some ain't. Trust me, Daniel, God got his share a trouble with people. Heck, he's had his share a trouble with angels. It's hard to imagine, but Lucifer himself is an angel."

"It's my father."

"Yeah?" Said Joshua inquisitively. He knew it was time for this boy to begin unloading whatever freight he was burdened with. It was no longer time for Joshua to be talking to Daniel. It was a time for him to be listening.

"My father's a minister. He's a powerful person in Macon and he's made my life miserable. He runs the North Macon Baptist Church, the largest church in the county, and he's the reason I'm here," confessed Daniel.

"Why blame him?"

"Because he hated her."

"Hated who?"

"Ayse."

Joshua was patient. The dislocated nature of Daniel's conversation was typical. He had spoken with dozens of patients like Daniel through the years, and from that experience, he knew that when they first started talking about their path to Milledgeville, it was often in a broken, disordered fashion. It was the hardest part, coming out of the darkness. Joshua knew he had to give them plenty of room or risk watching them retreat back into the belly of the whale.

"I ain't never heard of this Ayse before."

"Ayse's my wife. At least she was. I haven't seen her in a long time. Not since she went back to Turkey."

"She's from Turkey? Ain't that near Russia?"

Daniel looked up at Joshua and laughed. Yes, Turkey was near Russia, in a way.

"Part of Turkey's in Asia, part of it's in Europe. Ayse lives in Istanbul, a city that bridges the two continents."

"Oh yeah, I heard about Istanbul. They've got some right big churches there."

"Churches and mosques. Ayse's Islamic. She's not a Christian, JJ. What do you think about that? My father hates her because of her beliefs."

"Is she good people?"

"She's wonderful."

"Then I think it's fine she's Islamic. Ain't my place to be passin' judgment, Daniel. That's one of the few quotes I've made an effort to learn, *'Do not judge, or you too will be judged. For in the same way you judge others, you will be judged, and with the measure you use, it will be measured to you.'*" Joshua, almost as an afterthought, added, "Jesus said that, and his friend Matthew wrote it down for him."

"Don't you want to convert people to Christianity, JJ? Don't you want to save her soul?"

"Ain't mine to save, Daniel. And if she's a good person, who am I to tell her what to believe? I know lots of people in these parts who've become Muslims. Some are good people, some ain't. Just like Christians, or Jewish folk, or anybody, some's good people, some ain't. Just 'cause I'm a believer in the words of Jesus doesn't mean I have to go around forcin' the rest of the world to see things my way. That ain't bein' a Christian, it's bein' a bully."

Joshua continued. "I see it this way, Daniel. My preacher, Reverend Brown, likes to separate us into doers and talkers. I think he's right. But I've got another explanation. Ya see, there's two kinds of Christians in this world. There's the so called Christians, with a capital C. They's all those people who'll be the first to tell you how good and holy they is, and then there's the other kind of Christians, those with a lowercase c. I like to think of those christians, the ones usin' the lowercase, as the little people. They're the kind that don't spend a lot of time preachin' and carryin' on, because it's all just the sound and the fury as far as they're concerned. It ain't the real deal.

"Reverend Brown's got a right fine way of puttin' it. He says that it ain't about quotin' the Bible up and down or going to church every Sunday that makes us Christians. Heck no, he says — going and sittin' in church every Sunday don't make you turn into a Christian anymore than sittin' in your garage every day's gonna make you turn into a Cadillac. It'd be a whole lot easier if it worked that way, but it don't.

"Christians, the capital C, churchgoing, Bible-thumping kind, make sure you know that they's right, an you's wrong. The other ones, the lowercase christians, know that all God's children's are right. That's what people forget. Jesus was a christian, a lowercase christian his whole life. That's why he hung round with the tax collectors and the whores, the lepers and all the lonely people. He forgave sinners and worked miracles on the sick and even died for us with a humbleness no one can approach. That's what a christian oughta be."

"It sounds to me like you daddy's a Pharisee. Just like those old Pharisees Jesus used to get all riled about. All those rich, uppity folk that hung out in the temple passin' judgment on everyone and making rule after rule. All the while exchangin' money and exploitin' the poor in the house of God. Only these modern day Pharisees are buildin' fancy churches full of game rooms and movie theaters and whatnot. What's all that got to do with Jesus?

"Your Daddy sounds like one of them — a modern-day Pharisee. Big church, fancy car, big congregation where he can do his preachin'— his hootin' and a-hollarin' about all those sinners below him every Sunday. Ha, it's time for the rest of that Scripture, *'Why do you look at the speck of sawdust in your brother's eye and pay not attention to the plank in your own eye? How can you say to your brother, 'Let me take the speck out of your eye when all the time there is a plank in your own eye? You hypocrite, first take the plank out of your own eye, and then you will see clearly to remove the speck from your brother's eye.'"*

"That sounds like your father, Daniel. Going around with a big old plank in his eye telling everyone else how bad they're behavin.' Ain't nothin' new. I hear them all the time on TV and on the radio and all they're a-wantin' is for us fools to send them money so they can keep their ministry. Their ministry ain't nothin' but a church made o' glass. Ya can see right through it, Daniel.

"They's just what Jesus warned us about. Those's the same people who got Jesus crucified. It don't surprise me you're mad at your Daddy. But that's the problem. You've got to get past your anger, Daniel. That anger is your own plank."

Joshua was right. Daniel had come to hate his father for what he had done. He wanted Clay dead, just as Jonah wanted the people of Assyria dead. But Joshua wanted something else, he wanted Daniel to embrace forgiveness. Joshua saw the trouble brewing in Daniel's eyes and continued.

"You've got to forgive your father. You've got to do the hardest thing there is to do, Daniel. You've got to love your enemy. You've got to find a way to love your father. That's what it's gonna take for you to walk out of here, ya understand?"

Daniel didn't respond. He turned reflective again, and, for the moment, retreated to the edge of the darkness. He knew Joshua was right, but that didn't change his feelings.

Joshua got up from his chair and said, "I'd best leave you alone for a spell. You've got some thinkin' to do."

With that, Joshua got up and walked over to his next patient. He said a prayer as he did, praying Daniel wouldn't retreat into himself.

"God," prayed Joshua, "please keep this boy in your light."

Ibraham's First Steps

*H*e's determined, isn't he?"

"Yes, he's like his father."

"He falls so many times, but he always gets back up and tries again," said Elif as they watched Ibraham attempting his first few steps.

"That's how Daniel is and, I suspect, his father before him. They are a proud and strong-willed people, these Americans. Daniel has told me stories of his forefathers. They came to America hundreds of years ago and moved westward as pioneers. Ibraham is a little pioneer, Mother. He's like the American pioneer, Davy Crockett, a Turkish Davy Crockett."

They laughed together. Ibraham was only eleven months old, but he had been crawling and walking along the edge of the furniture for months. Ayse felt certain he would try to walk soon, and she was right. With his mother and grandmother watching him, Ibraham made a wobbly dash from the edge of the sofa to a nearby coffee table. His legs swayed and his body teetered but he kept his balance and made the passage without incident. Ibraham looked toward his mother, beaming with pride.

"See, he's walking!" exclaimed Elif.

"Yes, he is. Now we've got our hands full. We've got to keep an eye on him, Mother. Who knows what kind of mischief he'll be getting into."

"Just like your older brother, Yücel. Ibraham will be our new little trouble."

The women watched Ibraham. Upon making it safely back to the chair he looked to both of them for approval. He had Daniel's deep blue eyes and Ayse's thick black hair complete with dimples and a smile that could melt the heart of any woman.

"I wish he could see his boy," said Ayse reflectively.

"He will; someday he will."

"But it worries me, Mother. So much time has gone by and no word from him. Nothing — not a card, nor a letter, not a phone call, nor an e-mail. Just this long silence."

"All in time, Ayse. He is fine, working in some lumberyard in Georgia. He will call you when it's time, and I think that time is drawing near. I pray to Allâh every day he will return to you, and return to be a father to this beautiful boy. We must be patient, Ayse, because the will of Allâh cannot be hurried. You must always remember that the word Islam means surrender. We must surrender to God's will."

"Yes, your words are well spoken, Mother," said Ayse in sad agreement.

They went back to watching Ibraham. Ayse got on the floor, six feet from the edge of the chair to which he clung. She held out her arms and encouraged the toddler to walk into her awaiting embrace. Ibraham looked at his mother with the look of a boy completely in love with his parent, smiled bravely, and let go of the chair. He fell almost immediately, being turned around from the moment he'd let go.

Ibraham, ever persistent, crawled back to the chair, steadied himself, and made a second attempt. This time, although it appeared as though he might have fallen twice in his short walk, he made it. He reached into his mother's outstretched arms, then fell forward into her lap, giggling and proud.

As Ayse wrapped her arms around him, she remembered the flight attendant. Ayse recalled their conversation, and how she was puzzled by her comments. Now she knew. Daniel, or a part of Daniel, would be with her from that day forward. She kissed the forehead of her boy and smiled.

Elif looked on in delight, seeing what a wonderful daughter she had. On the other side of the world, Daniel slept quietly in his locked bedroom at Central State Hospital. He too was learning to walk again, learning to keep himself from falling. There was a symmetry of purpose between the father and his son at that moment that Ayse could not have known. All in time and faith would this be revealed to her. All in faith in time.

Autumn

I don't like talking to the doctors. I like talking to you," said Daniel angrily.

"I know that, Daniel, but I can't get you outta here. Only the doctors can release you from this place and you've gotta know that."

"The hell with them. I don't want to get out!"

Daniel paused for a minute, then asked Joshua, "Does my father know I'm here?"

"Yes, your records say they called him when you were first admitted."

"Then you can be damn certain Ayse knows. I doubt my father would miss an opportunity like that — telling her that our marriage has driven me here, to the loony bin.

"But if she knows I'm here, where is she? If she really loves me, why hasn't she written, or called, or tried to reach me? Answer me that JJ? If Ayse doesn't love me any longer, then I don't want out."

"Maybe she doesn't know. Maybe your father didn't never call her. Don'cha think it's only fair for you to try to reach her?"

"Why should I? She doesn't care about me. She doesn't give a damn."

Joshua shook his head in dismay. Daniel, he knew, was choosing the path of least resistance. He had become addicted to the lifestyle of the asylum. He knew when breakfast, lunch and dinner were served. He knew he was safe and secure inside the concrete walls of the Powell Building. He could just remain there, with Joshua, and everything else would eventually go away. He wanted it to go away.

Joshua had seen this behavior before, a hundred times. Patients who found their comfort zone within the confines of the hospital. Long-term inmates who refuse to show any signs of improvement to their psychologists. They become lifers, staying just sick enough to ensure their permanent incarceration. Asylum junkies, hooked on the Spartan but stable comforts of a mental institution. Afraid to leave, to go back into the difficult world that delivered them to Milledgeville.

Daniel was speaking, but only to Joshua. The doctors could manage but a few words out of him now and again, but nowhere near the depth of conversations Joshua could achieve. As was his duty, Joshua had relayed many of their conversations to the staff, but until they could verify Daniel's improvements, there was little they could do. He would remain in the hospital until they deemed him sane enough to leave. That meant he would have to speak to them as lucidly as he spoke to Joshua. Daniel refused to do that.

"What'd ya plan on doin', spendin' the rest of yer life in this place? Is that what you want? Don't ya want to be with your wife again? To make love to her again? This ain't no place for you, Daniel. There's a whole world waitin' for you out there and you can't keep hidin' in here 'til you're old and gray."

"Why not, JJ? What's so great about the world? There's more madness out there than there is in here. There are lunatics everywhere out there, just like my father. Crazy Christians, crazy terrorists, crazy kids who kill their parents and parents who kill their kids. It's just one big madhouse, JJ. I'm better off in here, where the metal grates keep the real crackpots and kooks out."

"Oh, Daniel, y'all never leave here thinkin' like that."

"I don't want to leave here. I like it here."

"What about your wife?"

"She can stay in Istanbul. She's probably already filed for a divorce. She can marry a Turkish Muslim and they can take over her father's carpet business and live happily ever after. I don't care about Ayse anymore. I don't care about anything. To hell with it! To hell with all of it!"

Joshua didn't respond. He was on to something, something more important.

"You ain't never told me her father's in the carpet business."

"Sure he is. It's expensive to put a foreign student through Oglethorpe. He had some contacts, some retail outlets in Atlanta. That's why they chose Oglethorpe. Her father's business, Yalçin Imports, brings in carpets from Afghanistan, eastern Turkey and Turkmenistan, and sells them in Europe and the United States. That's how they managed to put Ayse through college.

"Don't think for one second the people in Turkey are poor and illiterate, JJ, because Ayse's family's far from it. They have a maid, housekeepers, a gardener and all the trappings. They even have a chauffeur, Abdul."

Joshua listened attentively. Without being aware of it, Daniel had finally given Joshua what he had been searching months for — Ayse's last name. With it, he could finally contact her. He would now be able to call her, but to find her number, he would need her father's first name as well.

"Abdul's a fine Muslim name, don't ya think? Is that her father's name too, Abdul?"

Daniel looked at Joshua suspiciously. He suddenly realized he had said more than he should have. But the other side of him came forward, the brave child who, like the son he knew nothing of, was willing to let go and try to walk. Torn between the two, he decided to provide Joshua with Ayse's father's first name, knowing there was an unspoken risk in doing so.

"Mustapha. His name's not Abdul, JJ, it's Mustapha. I met him once when he came to Atlanta on business. He is not a bad person. He's not like my father."

Joshua smiled and corrected Daniel, "Your Father's not a bad person either, Daniel. He's just a little lost. Hate the sin, not the sinner."

Joshua had to get going. He had been talking for half an hour and there were other patients who needed his attention. Joshua would report that Daniel was improving daily, talking freely and coherently. The psychologist who was scheduled to see Daniel tomorrow would observe none of this. Daniel would appear sullen and withdrawn, unable to cope with the pressures of reality. Nothing would change.

Long Distance

Joshua squirmed nervously in the kitchen chair. Mariah saw the situation as comical, and tried to keep herself from laughing. For Joshua, it wasn't a laughing matter. To him, there was something intimidating about doing such a thing, as if the act violated an unspoken principle he felt compelled to uphold. Mariah looked at him straight away, giving him one of her 'you best be payin' attention' glares. Joshua knew she meant business.

"How long y'all gonna hold that phone in yer hand?" she asked, her voice cutting through the cool morning air of the kitchen.

"I ain't never made a call like this before, and I need some time to think it over," replied Joshua. "What if I make a mistake, or misdial?"

"If you misdial, you just call up the operator and get a credit for makin' a mistake. Yer sittin' there actin' like you gonna do a stretch of hard time if you dial the wrong number. People call overseas all day long, doin' business and stuff, and there ain't nobody ever been arrested for doin' it."

He knew Mariah was right. Still, it didn't seem right. Joshua stared down at the fifteen numbers he needed to dial and froze. How can it be that easy, he kept thinking to himself? It's confusing to think that it's only seven-thirty in the morning here and already three-thirty in the afternoon in Istanbul. Why ain't it the same time everywhere?

Mariah, washing last night's dishes, put down her dishrag, looked at poor

Joshua and started laughing.

"It ain't funny," he said.

"Do you want me to dial the number for you?" asked Mariah.

Joshua's dark eyes lit up and a big smile, bigger than any smile he had managed to muster in the past twenty-four hours, spread across his thin black face like a smudge of white clouds.

"Would you?" he asked.

"If it'll keep that big ol'' grin on your face, I will."

Mariah dried her hands on her apron and walked over to her anxious husband. She reached out for the phone and Joshua willingly relinquished it to her. It was a portable phone, with the keypad on the inside of the handset. She turned it over and held it in her left hand, her right hand poised to dial the numbers.

"Read me the numbers, JJ. All of 'em, nice and slow. It'll be easier not to make a mistake that way."

Joshua started reading her the fifteen-digit telephone number, starting with the international dialing code, the country code, the city code, then the final seven numbers that would direct the call to the Yalçin residence a quarter of the way around the world. Joshua breathed a sigh of relief as Mariah punched in the string of numbers. She was used to calling long distance. She had family in Mississippi and a sister living in South Carolina whom she called regularly. Joshua dreaded calling long distance. There was something disconcerting to him about speaking with someone who was that far away, as if it should be illegal.

"D'ya think this call'll be expensive?" asked Joshua as Mariah put the receiver up to her ear.

"Give a little less at church this Sunday if you're worried about the cost, JJ. This call's about doin' God's work, JJ. Ain't nothin' too expensive when you're doin' God's work." Mariah paused for a minute, waiting for the international connections to be made. She lowered her head and looked at her skinny husband sitting beside her. She thought it funny, the fact that he could go out tomorrow and shoot a ten-point buck, or take down a fifty-year-old live oak with his axe, but the act of making a long-distance phone call reduced him to a helpless pile of jitters. Men are ridiculous.

"Here, it's ringing," said Mariah as she handed the phone back to her husband.

Joshua reached up and took the phone from her, glad to have avoided the task of dialing. He put the receiver to his ear and listened.

"It's a funny-sounding ring, ain't it?" he remarked to Mariah as she walked back toward the kitchen sink.

"It's a Turkish telephone, JJ. That's prob'ly how they all ring over there."

"Ola," answered the housemaid in Bebek.

"Hello," said Joshua timidly. "Is Ayse there?"

The maid knew the caller was speaking in English. Mustapha received calls from England and America all the time. She found it unusual that this caller was asking to speak with Ayse, but thought it must have something to do with her schooling in America.

"Ayse, telefon. Ayse!" she shouted.

Ayse was in the living room with Elif. They were watching Ibraham drag pots and pans from the kitchen cupboards into the dining room. He had been at this task since lunch, when he first discovered the cupboard that held the metal cookware. It was a noisy endeavor, but Ibraham loved every crash, rattle and bang the stainless steel pots made when they hit the tiled floor. It was a little boy thing, and Elif and Ayse had been enjoying the last hour immensely.

"I'm coming," responded Ayse in Turkish.

As she walked up the central hallway toward the phone, the Yugoslavian housemaid handed it to her and said, "Englis."

Ayse took the telephone in her hand and paused. She was caught off guard by discovering the caller was speaking in English. Her instincts told her immediately it was about Daniel, and the thought of hearing something from him, or hearing his voice again, made her heart race.

"Hello," she said with a tremor in her voice.

There was a delay in the line, common to calls that traverse such great distances.

"Hello, Ma'am. Is this Ayse, Ayse Harris?"

"Yes, it is. May I ask who's calling?"

"You don' know me, Ma'am. My name's Joshua, Joshua J. Taylor, but most folks just call me JJ. I work with your husband, Daniel."

Ayse made note of Joshua's strong Southern accent. She imagined this must be the way they speak in Athens.

"You work with him at the lumberyard? Has anything happened to him?"

Joshua was confused. What lumberyard was she talking about?

"No, I don't work at no lumberyard with him. Daniel ain't workin' in no lumberyard, Ma'am. He's in a hospital, Central State Hospital, in Milledgeville, Georgia."

Ayse's heart fell from her chest and spilled across the marble floor of the hallway. Daniel was in a hospital. Was he hurt?

"Is he okay? What's happened to him?"

Joshua knew there was something wrong with this conversation. He was confused about her reference to a lumberyard, and he could tell that Ayse thought Central State Hospital was a regular hospital. It dawned on Joshua that Daniel's wife had no idea where her husband had been these last twenty months.

"Ma'am, Daniel's just fine. He had some trouble last year but he's been doin' fine. He's been at the hospital for quite a spell. But this ain't no regular hospital, Ma'am; this is a mental-health facility. Your husband's a patient here."

Ayse's heart kept falling. It had found a way to pierce the marble and fall to the cold, concrete basement below. Daniel was in a mental hospital. The sound of Ibraham crashing a large pot cover down on the floor in the dining room did nothing to distract her. It clanged loudly, but Ayse didn't hear it. She was collapsing.

Joshua could sense Ayse's implosion through the static-filled silence of the phone line. He realized he had to say something.

"Are you still there?"

"Yes."

"Daniel's just fine. He came here over a year ago and for the longest time he was havin' trouble. But I did some prayin' for him and the Lord reached out and pulled him out of trouble. He's doin' fine. That's why I'm callin' y'all. He needs you. He needs to know you still love him. Do ya, Ma'am? Do ya still love him?"

Ayse burst into tears. No longer able to stand, she put her back against the hallway wall and slid to the cold floor beneath her, wailing as she descended. From the living room, Elif could hear her daughter's desperate sobs, and knew it must be news of Daniel — bad news.

Joshua heard Ayse crying and felt helpless. He waited. Mariah saw the look on her husband's face and knew the situation was solemn. She kept washing the dishes, praying to God Almighty as she did.

A long, tear-filled minute passed. It seemed even longer, like time stretched itself into a highway that no one ever traveled. Ayse was on that highway.

"Yes, I still love him," she whispered to Joshua between her sobs.

"Praise God!" said Joshua in response.

"Praise God!" Mariah echoed her husband's expletive while she scoured a cast-iron frying pan. She knew Joshua had heard some good news. He always said, "Praise God!" when he heard good news.

Joshua continued. "What Daniel needs now is a reason to live. Without you, he's got no reason to go back to the world. He's fine with me, but he keeps stonewallin' them doctors. It's because he doesn't want to leave the hospital. It happens more often then you'd think.

"But if you could come to America, pay a visit here and tell him what you just told me — tell him that you love him — he have a reason to get on out of here. He's a good-lookin' boy and a fine person, but he needs your help, Ayse, and that's why I'm callin' you. He don't belong in this here hospital no more."

Ayse listened. She wondered who this Joshua was — a man that would go out of his way to help her husband. She could hear the honesty in his voice, the sincerity.

"We have a son now, JJ. A boy named Ibraham."

"Daniel never said nothin' to me 'bout havin' no son."

"He doesn't know. He couldn't have found out. I've not told anyone in the states."

"Please bring your boy with you. It'll make him want to bust right on outta here."

"Yes, I will."

"When can you come?" asked Joshua, wanting to make sure he was going to get a commitment from Ayse before hanging up.

Ayse had regained her composure, envisioning their family reunion. "Soon. Two weeks, maybe sooner. It will take me some time to get things in order. I will have to book the flight, rent a car, there is so much to do before I can leave."

"I understand. Let me give you my phone numbers. My work number's 478-455-5690 and my home number is 478-495-8891. My wife Mariah is home most a the time so's it's best to call and leave me a message here.

"But please don't call the hospital. If you talk to him now, he might try to convince you not to come, an' that would be a terrible mistake. It'll be much better if you just show up and surprise him. That way he'll have no way of preparing for it."

"What if he doesn't want to leave the hospital after seeing us?" asked Ayse, wanting some assurance that her long journey would not be in vain.

"Oh, when he sees you and that boy of his, he'll want to get out of this place faster then a chicken chased by a bobcat. You gotta trust me, Ma'am, I've been doin' this too long not to know that your trip'll be worth it. He's still crazy 'bout you. It's just that he doesn't know how you feel 'bout him.

"If you love him like you says, then you come over here right quick and get him."

"I will," said Ayse. "I'll come and get him."

"Then call me and let me know when y'all be arrivin' in Atlanta."

"I'll call you in a week, JJ. Thanks so much for calling."

"You're welcome. Goodbye then."

"Goodbye."

Ayse hung up the phone. She stood up, still leaning against the wall. She was overflowing with emotions. What if Daniel rejected them? How had he ended up in a mental institution? Will he love Ibraham? Will he be all right?

She walked into the living room and looked at her mother, sitting on the sofa, covered in her Muslim head scarf . Elif was watching Ibraham play with the metal pots and pans beneath the dining room table. Elif saw her daughter and knew there was news of her estranged husband. Elif held out her arms, and without a word being said, Ayse came over and fell into them. She was a little girl again, safe and warm in her mother's arms. There would be time enough to tell her mother what she had learned, but for now, it was better to be held. Far, far better.

Book of Midnights

Four spiral notebooks lay collecting dust under Daniel's bed. The first notebook had been completed in less than three days, filled to overflowing with the ravings of a young man who had been kept silent too long. The second notebook, that Joshua gladly provided, took over a week to complete, and as his words raced across the blue-lined pages, they started to regain their sense of syntax. As Daniel's writings rediscovered the rules of usage and structure, the manic pace of his pencil slowed.

Every notebook thereafter lessened its pace. Daniel's hungry pencil returned to a place where meanings became comprehensible. He wrote with a steady, studied hand. He became a scribe of midnight, using a small, pen-sized flashlight Joshua had purchased for him.

Daniel could not have known of Joshua's conversation with his wife, Ayse, three days ago. The coincidence was one of karmic symmetry. He picked up his pen after awakening in the middle of the night. Awakening from a dream that left him frightened and afraid.

In his dream he was walking inside of North Macon Baptist Church. He was crying out for Ayse but she was not there. His voice echoed eerily in the empty church, making him acutely aware of his loneliness. It became cold in his father's church, colder than a winter's night atop Kennesaw Mountain.

He walked to the alter and stood behind the pulpit where his father's Bible lay open before him. Daniel looked down at the Bible and the scripture read, *Though I speak with the tongues of men and of angels, and have not love, I am become as sounding brass, or a tinkling cymbal. And though I have the gift of prophecy, and understand all mysteries, and all knowledge; and though I have all faith, so that I could remove mountains, and have not love, I am nothing.*

Upon reading this passage from 1 Corinthians, in a translation unfamiliar to him, Daniel woke. He had thrown off his blankets and sheets, and found himself shivering. His roommate slept without interruption as Daniel got up to close the open window. Autumn had arrived, and the winds outside were blowing hard from the north.

Daniel grabbed his notebook, his pencil and flashlight and climbed back into bed, wrapping the blankets around him. He lay on his side, placing the light next to the notebook, giving him just enough light to write. With his back to the other bed, his roommate wouldn't be disturbed by Daniel's writing.

Tuesday morning, sometime around 3:00 a.m. Milledgeville

Gone

Gone is the sound of her voice.
The chants of her prayers on a hand-woven rug.
Her sense of God, and of purposes beyond the touch
Of her devoted hands. Purposes divine.

Gone is the mystery of her eyes.
A sweet, lyrical darkness into which I fell.
Set free in some vertigo of emotions,
Falling, falling, falling into her Asian eyes.

Gone is the scent of her skin.
The sensuality of her mouth, her tongue
Like sex itself, moist and aqueous.
Lips that pleaded to be kissed.

Gone is her tumbling hair, auburn and black
Cascading down her shoulders, framing
Her imploring smile, her sense of woman
That drew me toward her like a willing moth to the perfect flame.

There is nothing left.

My heart walks alone on this windswept
Hillside, walks in patient circles above a
Valley filled with the huge encampment of human madness.
There, I still feel her in the wind.
Like the sound of rain falling on a forest of orchids,
Like a post card from a paradise I cannot find,
Like a year without air,
I long for her.
My Ayse.

A Mother's Farewell

yse stood in the doorway of her room. It had changed. Her dresser had been moved to one of her brother's empty bedrooms to make room for Ibraham's crib. A mobile hung above the wooden crib, with six paper angels suspended from the ceiling. They were his guardian angels, looking down on Ibraham as he slept each night. A large box of disposable diapers stood beside the crib, with only a dozen diapers taken out of it, enough to last them the next few days.

Everything had changed. Ayse was a mother now. A mother about to be reunited with the man she could only pray would still want her. A man who was living in a mental institution six thousand miles to the west.

Halil was watching Ibraham in the kitchen, and Abdul was scheduled to show up momentarily to take Ayse's bags to the car, then drive her and her mother to the airport. Elif was in the living room, reading her Qur'an. Elif was going to send them off. She was saddened by the news of her daughter's departure but supportive of Ayse's decision to return to America. Saddened by the knowledge that she would no longer hear her grandson's tiny footsteps running down the tile. She was going to miss his laughter, his adorable smile.

"A boy must have a father," Elif had said to her daughter on more than one occasion over the last week.

Elif sought refuge in the words of her scripture. As Ayse took one last studied look at her room, wondering when, if ever, she might sleep in her room again, Elif, sitting in her favorite chair downstairs, read the following passage from her bible, the Qur'an:

It may be that God will ordain love between you and those whom you hold as enemies. For God has power over all things; and God is Oft-forgiving, Most Merciful. Qur'an 60.7

This passage spoke to Elif. Like many Muslims throughout the world, she felt Christians were her enemies. She had just cause for her feelings. The Christians had been persecuting the Muslims for over a thousand years. Ever since Pope Urban called for a crusade against the Turks in 1095 at the Council of Clermont in southern France, the Muslims had felt victimized by the Christian world. That First Crusade was a success. The Christians, at a great cost of human lives, had recaptured the Holy Land. But their victory was short lived.

The Turks retook the County of Edessa soon thereafter and the Second Crusade, or Holy War, began in 1147. The fighting continued for centuries, resulting in this heritage of hate. The Third Crusade, the Fourth Crusade, the Children's Crusade, and those that followed left little more than death and destruction in their wake. From that time forward, the West, the Christians, could not be trusted.

Elif Yalçin knew the division between them continued today, as modern day Turkey made every attempt to gain admission to the European Union. Despite their efforts in becoming a democratic, secular state, Turkey was denied entry. The crusades weren't over, and the radical elements of Islam held that they would never be over until America and their co-conspirators, the Jews, were annihilated. The extremists', the terrorists' hatred for the Western world ran deeper and far more bitter than Elif could conceive of, but the roots of their disdain of the United States and Europe sprang from the same seeds.

All Elif asked of Christians was to follow the teachings of Christ. Many spoke of doing so. Few did. They seek revenge, they conspire against Muslims. Who among them turns the other cheek? Perhaps that's why Ibraham had been born to her daughter, to show me that a bridge between us is possible, she reflected. Maybe that's why Allâh ordained this love between my daughter and a Southern boy from Macon. If it is so written, she thought, then it is meant to be.

❂

"Ibraham, it's time to go!" Ayse stood at the bottom the stairs, her carry-on in hand, calling for her son in the direction of the kitchen.

"One minute, he's having a snack," responded Halil in Turkish.

Ayse looked over to her mother and said, "He's always having a snack."

"He's a growing boy, Ayse. I know from raising your two older brothers, these boys have no bottom to their appetite."

Ayse put her bag beside the front door and walked toward her mother. Elif pulled the satin ribbon across the page she was reading and closed her Qur'an.

There would be plenty of time to read her holy book once they were gone.

"I'm frightened, Mother."

"Yes, I know."

"What's going to happen?"

"Only God knows the answer to that question. But it is important that you listen to your heart in this matter. Whoever this Daniel is, God has arranged to call you back to him. The phone call you received from Mr. Taylor last week was no coincidence, Ayse. It was a sign, a sign you cannot ignore.

"Allâh ordains your reunion, and though it will break my heart to have you absent from this household, I will not stand in your way."

"Oh, Mother."

Ayse fell into her mother's arms, and they both wept without shame. Ayse felt so terrible in taking her grandson away from her mother, but knew there was no other way. As she knelt beside her mother, tears flowing down her cheeks, she recalled what the flight attendant had told her years ago. "When your mother knows your feelings run deep, she will come back to you, and she will hold you in her arms like she did when you were a child. She will bless you and set you free to discover the beauty of your feelings."

So it all came to pass, just as the flight attendant said it would.

❂

The sound of Abdul coming in the back door interrupted their embrace. Ayse could overhear Halil and Abdul speaking, and a second thereafter, the sound of her son's laughter. No doubt Abdul was tossing her little boy up in the air, catching him when he was halfway to the floor in a game Ibraham never tired of. Abdul had become like a father to the boy, and Ayse appreciated all the time he spent playing with Ibraham. With children of his own, he knew what boys were all about.

Mustapha, who had planned to go along to the airport with them, had been called out on pressing business in Italy the day before. As much as he hated to go, missing his daughter's departure, he knew he must.

Ayse was disappointed, but she realized that without his financial support, her return to America would be impossible. Mustapha's business was her business, so they had said their sad goodbyes yesterday before his flight to Rome. He promised her that as soon as all was settled he would visit them in Atlanta. She knew he would keep his promise.

"Your little Turk wants to know if you've packed all his toys. Have you?" Abdul asked as he walked into the living room with Ibraham in his arms.

"Most of them," replied Ayse. She looked at her boy and added, "But not the rocking horse Grandpa bought for you, it's a little too big."

It was time to go. Abdul could see that the women had been crying, but said nothing. He, too, was saddened by the thought of not being able to throw aloft this charming toddler any longer. Abdul fought back his own tears.

Abdul set the boy down and told Ibraham to stay downstairs. "I'll go up and get the bags," he said.

"Thank you, Abdul. I'll put in the car seat."

Soon the four of them were on the highway to Ataturk Airport. The quiet inside the Lexus was interrupted only by Ibraham making noises with the toy fire engine he held in his hand.

Elif prayed their reunion would go well. Ayse hung in suspension, unsure of what tomorrow would bring. Abdul drove, his tears finally overtaking him as he pulled onto the departure ramp. It was time to go.

A Family Reunion

oshua checked the large clock on the far wall of the reception room. It read 2:12 p.m. Ayse was running late.

It had been a long time since Joshua had been in the reception room downstairs, and it seemed larger than he remembered. A heavy oak desk sat in the center, encasing the girl working behind it in a thick glass enclosure, as though it were a ticket office. He used to know the woman working behind that desk, Marilyn, but she had retired years ago. The new girl was a stranger to Joshua, though she seemed friendly enough.

Four wingback chairs sat in the room, two on either end. Between each set of chairs sat a small dark-cherry coffee table. Atop each table lay an assortment of outdated magazines. For an area this size, there wasn't enough furniture. The room felt empty and cold.

Some old photographs of the hospital filled the showcases on either side, just behind the chairs. The color shots were badly faded, looking not unlike the much older black-and-white shots framed beneath them. Those grainy photographs were taken in the twenties when the Powell Building was new and the deserted buildings down the street were filled with patients, nurses and therapists.

But the room felt strange to Joshua — abandoned. He did not want Ayse to wait here with her child. It would give them the wrong impression, an impression of loneliness and isolation.

As the large, institutional clock ticked past 2:15, Joshua carefully thought through his plan again. As soon as Ayse and her son arrived, he would introduce himself politely, then whisk them through the inner set of front doors to the elevator. He would push the button for the second-floor and they would go up one flight. Then he would escort them through the two sets of secure doors between the central section of the building and the south wing. Once inside Ward 2-B, he planned to hurry them into the small waiting room just beyond the last pair of locked doors on the right. There, he would ask Ayse and her child to wait. Then he would go back to the common area and get her husband.

Daniel didn't know anything about these plans. Over the past two weeks, Ayse and Joshua had made all the arrangements. The flight from Istanbul, the room at the Magnolia Motel three miles from the hospital, the rental car with the child's seat, all were planned in complete confidence. Daniel could not be told anything because his knowing might make him run from the encounter, retreating back into the abyss from which he was steadily emerging. It had to be unexpected — unannounced.

Joshua had just taken a seat in one of the wing-back chairs when he saw the front door open. There, coming through the doorway, walked a young, lovely woman carrying a child in her arms. She was striking. Her dark eyes looked over and caught Joshua's gaze. They were vibrant, so alive. Her black hair hung past her shoulders, reflecting deep, reddish hues in the afternoon light.

As Joshua approached her, he noticed how much her broad facial bones resembled those of an American Indian. Her skin was dark, but more sand-colored than that of a Native American. Joshua could not have known that it was her Mongolian ancestry that gave Ayse these resemblances — a bloodline that lent itself to both races through the millennium.

The boy in her arms was sleepy. They had spent last night in a motel near Atlanta, and Ayse and her boy were still recovering from the time change. Ibraham, only partially awake, had been cranky all morning. The toddler didn't understand what was going on, only that he was going to meet someone Ayse called his Daddy.

"You must be JJ."

"And you must be Ayse."

They shook hands and smiled at one another as they greeted each other.

"Thank you so much for all you've done for my husband."

"No, thank you for flyin' half way 'round the world to be here today. This must be Ibraham. What a fine-lookin' boy."

Ibraham wiped his sleepy eyes with his small hands and looked at the black man. He smiled at Joshua, but shyly.

"He's tired. It's been a long journey."

"Come then, let's give Daniel his surprise."

Joshua nodded at the receptionist and when he did, she buzzed open the inside foyer doors. They went around the corner and found the two large elevators that serviced the building. Joshua pushed the up button and one of the doors opened, allowing the three of them to step in. Within a minute, they were on the second floor, heading toward Ward 2-B.

After sliding Joshua's ID card through two separate sets of secure doors, all three of them were soon inside Ward 2-B. The hallway was empty save for a single patient hobbling away from them. She was an older, gray-haired woman who looked lost and forsaken in the wide hallway. Ayse, upon seeing her, knew where they were.

Joshua unlocked the visiting room and they went inside. Ayse was amazed at how small it was. She had expected something larger. The room felt crowded, as if there was more furniture in it than the room could hold. There was a wooden rocking chair, a single wingback chair of the same style as the four downstairs in the lobby, and a small love seat sitting in front of the only window. An oval coffee table rested upon an imitation needlepoint rug that covered most of the terrazzo flooring. Two nondescript paintings hung on the walls and heavy mauve drapery covered the window behind the love seat.

There were two doors on the far wall, one leading to an attached bathroom, the other going into a second small foyer that led back to the hallway. With Ibraham still held in her arms, Ayse walked over and sat on the love seat. The room felt crowded to her, uncomfortable. Maybe it's just me, she thought, recalling how stressful the last few weeks have been.

"Y'all just wait right here, an I'll go fetch Daniel. I'm gonna tell him he's got some visitors. He'll be right surprised, 'cause he ain't had no visitors since he come in here. So y'all just sit tight, okay?"

"Are you sure this is the right thing to do?" asked Ayse.

"Oh, I'm sure, Ma'am. I'm right sure."

Joshua went out through the door they had entered. Ayse waited. Her thoughts raced wildly as she did. Would he look the same? Would he be the same Daniel she had left two years ago? Does he still love me? Will he recognize his son? There was no answer to her questions, just the racing worries of a woman's apprehensions.

✪

Joshua found Daniel sitting in his favorite chair, writing in the new notebook Joshua had purchased for him a week ago. Daniel smiled as Joshua approached, thinking it was a bit early for his afternoon vitals, but glad to see him regardless.

"Big surprise today, Daniel. Big surprise for you."

"What's that, JJ?"

"Y'all got visitors."

Daniel didn't respond. A bone-chilling rush of fear ran through him as if his blood had been replaced with crushed ice. This isn't good, I'm not expecting visitors, he thought.

Daniel was terrified as to who these visitors might be. Was it his mother and sister? Randy, his old friend? Who was it?

"I don't want to see any visitors!" he stated emphatically.

"Yes you do."

"No. I won't see them. I don't have to."

"She's come a long, long way to see you, Daniel. You must meet with her."

It was Ayse. The ice thawed. It melted so quickly that it left him flushed and disoriented. How could this happen? Why's she here? Is she here to divorce me? Why did she wait so long before coming to the hospital? But Joshua had said visitors. Who's with her? Was it her father, Mustapha?

"It's Ayse, isn't it?"

"Yes, she's in the visitin' room at the end of the hallway."

"Who's with her?"

"I can't tell you, it's a surprise."

Daniel didn't question Joshua any further. His heart ran ahead of him, flying toward the small room at the end of the hallway. He had never been in the visitors room, never having had guests before, but he knew exactly where it was.

He rose, nervously, and followed Joshua. He was still dressed in his light-blue robe, his pajamas and his slippers. His hair was uncombed and his eyes had the glassy look of his self-imposed imbalance, but he didn't care. The thought of seeing her filled him with a curious mixture of dread and joy. The joy of seeing her face again and the dread that she might be here only to make certain he would never see her again. His stomach was churning, and for a minute, he felt as though he might become sick.

Joshua saw him pale as they approached the doorway leading to the room. Before letting him in, he turned to Daniel and asked, "Y'all gonna' be okay?"

"Just give me a second, JJ," he answered, the color drained from his face.

"Don't be gettin' sick on me, Daniel. This girl's gone through a lot of trouble to make it here today, and she a waitin' on ya. She needs ya."

Joshua's comment comforted him. Daniel took several long, deep breaths. Everything flashed before him — his decadent parties after the bars closed in Buckhead, the last time he saw her, catching the plane at Hartsfield, the metal grating pulling free from the strain of the handmade rope around his neck, his notebooks filled with longing for her, the day they were married in Gatlinburg, their meeting place by the Crypt, the first day he spoke to her, everything fell from the shelves of his thoughts at once, leaving his heart buried beneath the rubble. He knew he would never be ready to see her.

"I'm okay," he said as Joshua opened the door to the room.

✦

He saw them sitting on the love seat. Ayse appeared more wondrous and beautiful than he remembered. Her long hair shone, her eyes sparkled as they filled with tears. But it was the boy in her arms that made his heart stop beating. A young child — his child — and he it knew immediately. The blue eyes, the dark, auburn tint in his hair. A child of two cultures.

Ibraham knew it as well. He clung tightly to his mother, afraid and excited. This, thought the child, is a daddy. For a moment in time, everything ceased to matter in the world but the rush of three hearts. A father finding his son, a son his father, and a wife with tears of joy pouring down her cheeks. A family reunion.

Joshua interrupted the silence. "I best be leavin' ya here alone for a spell. Y'all got some catchin' up to do."

Joshua left the room and smiled a smile wider than the Blue Ridge Parkway is long. He looked up at the ceiling and, speaking loud and clear to no one but the Creator, he shouted out, "THANK YOU LORD!"

Somewhere far, far above, in a whisper known only to the space between the stars, the Lord replied, "You're welcome."

The First Weekend

"O'course it ain't gonna be easy. Ain't nothin' easy 'bout changin'. Never has been, never will be. But sometimes we all gotta change. You've been in this hospital all this time wrapped up in yerself like some kinda bug in a concrete cocoon. Now it's time to fly again, to spread your wings and see what it's like to be alive.

"And o'course you're afraid. Wouldn't be natural if you weren't afraid. It's darn comfortable for you here in this hospital. Ya got your three squares a day, nice clean bed to tuck into, everybody watchin' after ya. It's easy to get comfortable in here, too easy. Heck, I've got folks been in here over forty years runnin' gettin' comfortable like you is. They ain't never gonna walk out that front door again, they're gonna be brought out the back door on a stretcher, cold and stiff.

"But they ain't got what you got. They ain't blessed with a wife who loves you more'n you can appreciate and a little boy who needs his daddy. No, these are blessings the Lord has given you that you need to appreciate and respect, Daniel. These are what I call godsends, things God gives to us to make us know how much he loves us. And if there's one thing I know for certain, it's that God loves you a bunch."

Joshua had been talking to Daniel all morning. Ayse was expected after lunch and Joshua had decided earlier in the week to dedicate Friday morning exclusively to his good friend. It was Daniel's first time out in almost two years. Plans were for the three of them to drive back to the two-bedroom apartment Ayse had leased in suburban Atlanta and spend their first weekend as a family together. Maybe take in a museum, like the old days as freshmen at Oglethorpe.

Order take-out Chinese or pizza Saturday night. Rent a video.

Two nights were all the doctors would allow Daniel for now. A brief, trial run into the world of freeways, apartments and, most importantly, choices. Choices most of us take for granted. Choices that petrified Daniel, that stole him from the sheltered, repetitive ritual of life in a mental-health facility and placed him back into a world of chaos. The chaos called sanity.

"Can I call you?" asked Daniel.

Joshua had anticipated his request, and from his shirt pocket he pulled out a small note. He handed it to Daniel and winked.

"I know'd you was gonna' ask me that. On this piece of paper is every number you might need this weekend if you find y'all need to do some talkin.' I've got my home phone and the hospital number — 'cause I'm puttin' in some overtime tomorrah, and I've even got the church's number if you need to reach me Sunday mornin'. You can call me in the middle of the night if you think y'all be needin' someone to talk to.

"But all those numbers I just give ya ain't important. The important number's in your heart. There's only one number we need, Daniel, and that's His number. You remember what we talked about yesterday, don't you?"

"Yes, but you can tell me again," replied an anxious Daniel.

"People go round forgettin' what His number is and that's when they get into trouble. They think they're more important, all puffed up with themselves, and they forget that the next breath they're inhalin' is given to them by God.

"We're all just a heartbeat away from eternity, just a single heartbeat. And we got ta learn to appreciate it's God's love that lets us wake up every mornin' to the joy of livin'. It's God's love catches us when we fall. His big ol'' hands are like a catch net, like the kind they use in the circus. He's up in Heaven watchin' us do our crazy somersaults and flips, each of us with slippery hands and each of us never been up on that trapeze before. And He knows that sooner or later we're all gonna fall. We're all sinners. It's important to know that, Daniel.

"I fell, and I fell hard. You fell too, we all gonna take that tumble someday and when you find yourself at a place where you can't hang on anymore, you just let go. You just release your grip and stop frettin'. You don't worry none 'bout money, or where your next meal is comin' from or nuttin' of the kind. The minute you let go, the minute you have faith, the Lord, well, He catches you. It's like He's pulled His net up so close you don't fall but for an instant before He's catched ya in His net."

Joshua smiled at Daniel, confident he was listening.

"Does He ever miss us, JJ? Does He ever fail to catch us?"

"No, He never misses. People miss, though. They just start falling and they don't want no part of His love. That's when the devil catches them. That's when they start thinkin' they don't need no faith, no Jesus, no world beyond this world. They's thinkin' this world is world enough.

"They start hoardin' their money, their boats, their cars, their big houses and fancy ways a liven' and then they start thinkin' this here stuff is better than the Lord's blessing.

"Oh, I pray for them kind'a folks every day, Daniel. I pray they come to find out that all that stuff don't do nothin' for them. All that stuff is just a big pile of junk and trouble. They got to worry 'bout how they gonna pay for it all. How they gonna insure it, how they gonna get even more and more of it. What the heck are they thinkin'? You can't hang onto nuttin' if God wants to take it from you — not money, not power, not your health, nuttin's out of His reach. It's all just junk and trouble.

"God looks down at the richest man in this world, flyin' his big ol'' Lear jet 'cross the sky thinkin' he owns 'bout half the earth below him and, the next thing you know, that jet's havin' all kind a engine trouble and a minute after, that jet's plowin' head first into the dirt. You think all his power and money's gonna help him now? No way, Daniel. He's standin' a'fore the Lord, just as naked and poor as the guy in front of him, explainin' how he lived his life here on earth.

"Naked and poor, Daniel, that's how we'all look when He's lookin' at us, naked and poor.

"If that man lived good, and there's plenty a rich man that's lived good, then he's gonna' be fine. But here's the catch, Daniel. If he spent too much time worshipin' all those things he owned, and not enough time helpin' others with his wealth — sharin' and givin' away the things the Lord blessed him with — he'll have a heap of explainin' to do. And ain't no tellin' if the Lord will let him stay in the Kingdom, or send him to that other place we'all been warned about — the one where the heat's turned up real high."

Daniel sat on the edge of his bed mesmerized, listening to the words of this unimposing black man sitting on the bed across from him. He loved to hear Joshua talk, explaining to him a perception of God's grace that ran so simple and deep that it never failed to capture his attention. Daniel had come to admire Joshua's sense of Scripture, and delighted when Joshua pulled out his thumb-worn, pocket-size Bible to, as Joshua would say, "shine some 'lumination on the subject."

He studied Joshua's face. His glasses reflected the bedroom's window as he spoke, and Daniel couldn't help but observe the pattern of the metal grate in the glare. He remembered tying one end of his bed sheet to a similar grate. He thought of his father as he studied the face of Joshua. How different they were. Poor and unassuming – powerful and pompous. Humble and willing to help — arrogant and quick to condemn. Joshua had befriended Daniel without expectations.

This person, thought Daniel, Joshua J. Taylor, his black skin contrasting sharply with his white teeth as he sat there, grinning like a slice of moon, had saved my life. It was more than that, reflected Daniel — Joshua had saved my soul.

Ayse and Ibraham arrived at the hospital at one-thirty. They waited in the downstairs lobby while Joshua escorted Daniel downstairs. Ibraham, running wildly, rejoiced in the fact that the spacious lobby was empty. For a toddler of sixteen months, it was like discovering an indoor soccer field. Ayse allowed him to run, knowing he would spend another two hours strapped in his car seat while they drove back to the city.

Daniel came through the lobby doors looking apprehensive. Ayse ran up to him, wrapping her arms around him in a hug that stole away his fears. Joshua stood back and admired her instincts. That's a good woman, he thought, that's a woman who'll do that boy good.

Ibraham was on the other side of the room when Ayse rushed to embrace her husband. He stopped his running and studied the two of them. He had never seen his mother holding another person like she held him. Ibraham knew it meant something, but he was too young to understand. All he could tell, in his childlike heart, was that it was good.

"Y'all drive safely now. I've got to be goin' upstairs, tendin' to my patients," said Joshua.

They broke away from their lengthy embrace. Daniel turned to his friend and said, "Thanks for everything, JJ. I'll see you Sunday night."

"Yeah, I reckon we'll have some talkin' to do 'bout then."

Ayse didn't say a word. She let go of Daniel's hand, walked over and hugged Joshua. Joshua, feeling a little embarrassed, hesitated, then wrapped his long, thin arms around this beautiful Islamic woman. This was her way of thanking him. There was no cause to speak.

Ibraham dashed across the room and started tugging on Ayse's coat, interrupting their friendly embrace. Joshua saw him out of the corner of his eye and said, "I think it's time y'all better get goin', 'cause yer boy's gettin' jealous. Y'all have a good weekend now."

"We will, JJ, we will," said Daniel as the three of them walked toward the front door.

"Mama, Mama," cried Ibraham as he reached his arms upward, indicating his desire to be carried.

Ayse acquiesced to her son's wishes. She bent down and picked up Ibraham, supporting him with her right arm as they went out through the front doors of the Powell Building. Daniel started playing peek-a-boo with his son, who was using Ayse's dark hair as a hiding place. The boy laughed every time Daniel would surprise him, saying, "peek-a-boo," as he did. This, thought a little boy who was beginning to like this stranger, is what a daddy is.

As they walked to the car, Ayse thanked Allâh for his mercy in allowing them to be reunited as a family. It wasn't going to be an easy road from this point forward, but that never bothered her. Nothing worth fighting for is easy, thought Ayse as she buckled her son back into his car seat.

She looked over the top of the car at Daniel just before the two of them got in. Ayse on the driver's side, Daniel across from her. Daniel winked, beaming with a joy he hadn't known in years. Her lips moved the words but did not speak them. Silently, like a mime in a world filled with empty noise, Ayse's lips spoke to her husband. They said the words that were forever in her heart. "I love you, Daniel."

Three Weeks Later

"It's time for me to leave soon, isn't it?"

"Yup."

"It's time for me to go back out there, find a job, and start over, isn't it?"

"Yup, but don't be forgettin' that we start over every day we're down here."

"I'm going to miss you, JJ."

"Why you sayin' somethin' like that. I ain't goin' anywhere. I'll be right here, anytime you need me."

"I know, JJ. But I'm going to miss our talks."

"Remember what I told ya. You can always talk to God. He's always willin' to listen. That ain't sayin' He'll be agreeing with you all the time, 'cause he won't. Reverend Brown says God always answers our prayers, it's just sometimes he answers them with a big ol'' 'NO.'

"And don't be gettin' fooled by what happens on this day or that day in particular. There's things that happen in life that don't make a much sense when they happen. But later on, maybe a year later, maybe ten years later, you start to seein', understandin' why it happened. That's God's will, Daniel, and don't be fightin' it by tryin' to swim upstream against the current. All you end up doin' then is drownin'."

Daniel respected Joshua's words of wisdom. He had fought against the current for two years after leaving Oglethorpe, and he hadn't accomplished anything more than filling his lungs with water. Once he started listening to Joshua, once he started to let go, to trust the flow of the river, he began to heal. Now it was coming time to leave the hospital, to return home to his wife and child. It was another eddy in the great river of life.

His first weekend out had been a success. They had taken in an OmniMax show on dinosaurs at the Fernwood Museum and spent Sunday morning on top of Bald Mountain, placing Ibraham in a child-carrier backpack as they hiked to the top. They were at the hospital by five that same evening with plans for another outing the following weekend. This time Ayse would pick Daniel up on

Thursday, extending his journey into the world a day at a time.

The doctors and the staff approved. It would only be a matter of weeks before they authorized Daniel's release. He had come a long, long way from his vow of silence. His anger toward his father was fading, but there were still issues he needed to deal with. These, reasoned the psychologists, would take years to work through, but were no longer of a nature that required his remaining in Central State Hospital. Daniel was soon to be set free.

"There's one last thing we have to talk about afore you leave, Daniel."

"What that, JJ?"

"It's sumthin' ya gotta do when ya get out of here. Ya don't gotta do it right away, cause it ain't gonna be easy for you, 'specially during these next few months. But at some point in your life, if you really want to get better, it'd be the right thing to do."

Daniel didn't know where Joshua's conversation was going. He had heard so many of his sermons before that he had come to anticipate where most of Joshua's conversations were headed before he finished them. But this one was new to him, and as they sat there, Daniel in his bed beside the window, and Joshua sitting on his roommate's bed like he loved to do, he wondered what Joshua was getting at.

Joshua reached down and got out his Bible. With a careful hand as studied as the man who wrote it, he soon found the Scripture he was searching for. He didn't read from the Bible in his hand as he quoted the scripture from it. He didn't need to. He just wanted Daniel to know where these words came from.

"It says here in the Gospel of Mark, somethin' y'all need to do, *'And when you stand praying, if you hold anything against anyone, forgive him, so that your Father in Heaven may forgive you your sins.'*

"You know who Mark's talkin' 'bout, don'cha, Daniel."

Daniel's heart recoiled. He knew at once. He knew and his heart hissed at the thought of it. It was too much to ask.

"I can see in yer eyes that you know who I'm thinkin' of, who needs yer forgivin'. I'm thinkin' 'bout your father, Reverend Harris."

Daniel looked within himself at the darkness he had emerged from and, for an instant, wanted nothing more than to go back into it. Here was an issue he had yet to deal with.

Why should I forgive him? asked Daniel to himself as he glared at Joshua. Clay nearly destroyed my family. He had never came to visit, wrote me a letter, or gave a damn. To hell with him, spoke the cobra still slithering within this angry young man. To hell with him.

"I know you ain't ready for this conversation. But I can't wait until you're ready because I ain't gonna be with ya when ya are. Y'all be up in Atlanta, probably workin' a good job, gettin' along fine with your boy and your wife. Maybe y'all even have another kid or two, who's to say. But sooner or later, your gonna have to deal with your feelins' 'bout your father.

"Your gonna need to do the hardest thing in the world there is to do. Your gonna have to pick up that phone, or sit down with a pencil and paper, and write him a letter forgivin' him. And he ain't gonna be none too happy 'bout it when you do. Mor'n likely he'll be screamin' and a hollarin' at ya. He'll say you ain't got no right to forgive him and that he's the one that should be doin' the forgivin'. He'll be thowin' more Scripture at you than a truckload of Gideon Bibles.

"But don't you let him cross you up none. It's not 'bout him. It's 'bout you. You're carryin' one heck of a load of anger on your shoulders Daniel, and I can see that it's still weighin' ya down. You muster up the courage to forgive your father, truly forgive him, and I promise you that weight will become a thousand times lighter.

"And remember, it don't matter what he does. He can shout and scream all his days 'bout you marryin' that Muslim woman. He can carry on 'til his last breath if he wants to, but all you gotta' know is this: once you forgive him, you're free.

"And I ain't talkin' no lip service forgivin' here, Daniel. I'm talkin' the real thing — keepin' your father in yer prayers, carin' 'bout him, givin' him the love you can't even think 'bout right now.

"This is the last thing, cause after you forgive your daddy, as sure as I'm sittin' here this mornin', you're gonna be free. Like it says in the last part of that passage, *That your Father in Heaven may forgive you your sins.*

"That's why Jesus died for us, Daniel. He died to teach us how to forgive. It ain't no eye for eye, tooth for tooth no more. Them's da old rules. The new rules are to turn the other cheek. The new rules are to forgive your father, Reverend Harris, just as our Father in Heaven forgives us."

Daniel squirmed beneath the heatlamp of Joshua's words. It was the one conversation he didn't want to hear. Somewhere, deep within his soul, he knew it was true, but his heart ran from that knowledge. Time would have to pass, perhaps a lifetime, before Daniel would be willing to deal with it.

Joshua, seeing how Daniel was recoiling from him, said no more. He got up, said goodbye and left the room. Daniel almost laid back down on his bed, wanting to pull the covers up and over his face, finding solace in the whale's belly once again. But he stayed sitting on the edge of his bed, across from a mentor who had vanished. That last dragon, the most wicked, the one that breathes the hottest of flames, is always the hardest to slay.

Life in Atlanta

The drone of endless traffic filtered through the bedroom window. From a distance, it sounded like the wind — urban wind. It was the sound produced by a hundred-million tires slowly wearing themselves into dust as commuters and truckers, snowbirds and travelers traversed the six lanes of I-75 a half mile to the east of their apartment.

Daniel was still in bed, although the winter sun had already climbed above the bare trees of Kennesaw Mountain and the huge commerce of Atlanta had long since begun its midweek grind. He had an appointment for a job interview at three, so there was no impetus for him to rise and shine with the rest of the world. He was awake, but quiet. He listened to the hum of the traffic with a reflective, studied indifference.

Where was everyone going? he wondered, though he knew the answer before asking. Why is everyone in such a hurry?

Ayse was in the bathtub with Ibraham. On occasion, above the ceaseless drone, Daniel could hear them, the sound of splashes followed by an echo of laughter. They loved taking baths together — bubble baths. Mother and child connected. Ayse would carefully scrub her son while he played with an armada of floating rubber ducks, battleships and, like children everywhere, the bubbles. The sound of their happiness mixed oddly with the sound of the semi-trucks and sirens in the distance. Everything in the world changes, reflected Daniel, while everything remains the same.

Life in Atlanta had not been easy. Six weeks had passed and Daniel had yet to find a job. Ayse's family had been supporting them. Her father had spoken with Daniel several times explaining that it was not welfare, but a loan to help them get back on their feet. Being Islamic, it was interest-free.

Daniel didn't like the fact that he was still unable to support his family. He was growing frustrated by his predicament. Tired of being called back for the second interview only to be dismissed when he attempted to explain the two-year gap in his resumé. Dismissed at the mere mention of his stay at Milledgeville — no phone calls returned, no job. At one point Daniel thought it might be easier to say he was in prison. Armed robbery would have been less offensive to the interviewer than the three words that kept him unemployed — Central State Hospital.

As Daniel lay thinking about his dilemma, through the thin plywood door of the bathroom, he heard Ayse and his boy getting out of the tub. She was speaking to Ibraham in Turkish, and the foreign sound of the language appealed to Daniel. Ibraham was being taught both languages, and Daniel agreed with Ayse that it was the right thing to do. What few words Ibraham spoke, he drifted easily from English to Turkish. He soon learned that Daddy understood only one of the languages, while Mama understood both.

The bedroom door opened and the two of them came out of the bathroom together. Both naked, both of them as innocent as the tub full of bubbles they had emerged from. Ibraham ran across the room and jumped on the bed with his father. It was time to wrestle. Time to do battle with the little, blue-eyed Turkish Ottoman. Daniel defended himself by lifting his son high above him, arms and legs flailing wildly, then tossing him down beside him, landing him playfully on the mattress.

Ibraham would get back up, laughing that joyous laughter only a child can make, and dive, head first, into his father's arms. Ayse, letting them entertain her, got dressed as they played. There was laundry to do, then shopping for groceries before Daniel took the car into Atlanta, and, after he left, dishes to wash. Ayse had spent more time than she had planned with Ibraham taking an extended bubble bath and now she needed to get going.

"What time's your interview?"

"It's at three-thirty, downtown."

"What kind of job is it?"

"It's an advertising firm. I can't even remember the name of the company, not that it matters," said Daniel while throwing his son on the bed for the fourth time.

"Don't be so negative, Daniel. It doesn't help."

Daniel gave Ayse a cold, angry glance. She knew why he wasn't able to find a job, and having a negative attitude had nothing to do with it.

"When I spoke with my father yesterday, he gave me an idea. He said he doesn't want you to mention Milledgeville or the hospital at your interviews anymore. He told me to tell you that from now on you just tell them you were with me in Istanbul for the last two years.

"Tell them you were working with my father, Mustapha Yalçin and Yalçin Carpets. My father said he will send you a letter on his stationery verifying that you were working for his firm. You can tell the interviewer you had decided it wasn't right for you. Tell them you didn't like the carpet business."

"Ayse, that's an outright lie."

"Daniel, you're never going to get a job if you keep bringing up Milledgeville. I know Joshua told you to be honest about what's happened, but the people who are trying to hire an employee don't know you. They hear one mention of your stay in a mental hospital and the interview is over.

"JJ would understand. He has to know what kind of reaction people have to those who've been to Milledgeville. So don't bring it up today. It's the only way they're going to consider hiring you, Daniel. Just tell them you've been in Turkey with your wife, working for her father in his export business, please."

Daniel went back to wrestling with his little Turk. He had heard his wife but didn't want to acknowledge her. Since coming home from the hospital he could be like that, withdrawing into a silence that was comforting to him. Becoming, if only momentarily, like Jonah again.

Ayse went to her purse and took out her leather billfold, the one she had purchased in the Grand Bazaar a year ago. She opened it and took out one of her father's business cards. Without saying anything, she walked over and handed it to her husband. He took it from her reluctantly, reading it aloud to her as she went back to dressing.

"I worked for *Yalçin Carpets, the Finest Quality in Imported Carpets,* right? What did I do when I was there, weave?"

Daniel's sarcasm didn't set well with Ayse. She gave him a cold grimace and continued putting on her worn bluejeans and a light cotton sweater. Perfect clothes for a cool, late autumnal day.

After she finished dressing, Ayse went to the hamper, reached in and pulled out an armful of dirty laundry. Her day had begun. She would need to get to the grocery store before Daniel took the car, so it was time to get the wash started. With the boy, she was glad she'd leased an apartment with its own washer and dryer. Between the three of them it seemed as if the laundry never ceased. She pried open the bedroom door with her knee and went down the hallway toward the small laundry room just off the kitchen.

Daniel and his boy kept battling. Ibraham had the heart of a warrior, descended from the same bloodline that had produced men like Mahmet the Conqueror and the powerful Turkish sultans. He was spirited and seldom cried, even when he was hurt. Daniel admired his tenacity. He realized Ibraham had also descended from hearty, stalwart Scots and Brits who had blazed a rugged trail westward through the primal forests of America.

It was a good mix, thought Daniel as he fought off another attack from Ibraham the Fearless. A world mutt, reflected Daniel, my boy's a world mutt. A new generation of children whose heritage stems from an earth where international travel takes hours instead of months. Where computers, televisions and phone lines make distances irrelevant. This brave new century where Vietnamese marry Italians, Chinese wed Norwegians and children become the offspring of melding cultures and creeds. The Global Village, recalled Daniel as he held his boy high up on the soles of his feet — Marshall McCluhan's prophetic vision of the future.

Daniel spread his feet apart, catching Ibraham midair in his fall. The boy laughed loudly, having a great time of it wrestling with his father. This is our tomorrow, thought Daniel as he set his son on the floor and got out of bed. My son is a world mutt and Ayse's right — I was in Istanbul learning the rug business from her father. As it turns out, I'll tell them, I'm allergic to wool. The perfect cover for madness.

"No more today," Daniel said to Ibraham, who was standing beside him, arms outstretched, waiting to be roughed up again. "No more."

Daniel looked at his toddler lovingly. He saw his own blue eyes reflected in his boy's and conceded defeat. "Okay, one more toss and that's it. I mean it."

He picked up Ibraham, holding him within inches of the ceiling, turned around and threw him unto the very middle of the bed. Ibraham bounced a foot upon landing, looking as if he were about to break in two. Then, he fell back to the bed for a second time and started giggling. This is what a daddy is, thought the child. I like daddy.

Mosby & Simms wasn't a large advertising firm. Compared to the three giants — Fitzgerald & Company, BBDO Atlanta and WestWayne, Inc. — they were hardly a player. They had a handful of solid accounts, and the fourteen employees, including the founders of the firm, Chuck Mosby and Dwight Simms, worked hard for their clients. Their offices were located near downtown, and from the apartment where Daniel and Ayse were living in Marietta, it was a forty-five minute drive. Much longer during rush hour.

They were located on the seventh floor of the Piedmont Building, leasing a little over two thousand square feet for their enterprise. The receptionist, Mary Beth Russell, was the first to greet Daniel as he stepped into the office complex. Being twenty-six and single, there was an immediate inclination for her to push Chuck Mosby into hiring this applicant. Daniel was the best-looking young man to come through the doors at Mosby & Simms in recent history, and Mary Beth made quick note of it. She didn't care if Daniel was right for the job, he was right for the office.

"May I help you?" she asked as Daniel approached the reception desk.

"I'm here for an interview with Mr. Mosby. My name is Daniel Harris, and," he looked down at his watch, noting he was a few minutes late, added, "I believe my appointment was at three-thirty."

"Please take a seat Mr. Harris, while I let Mr. Mosby know you're here."

Mary Beth got on the inter-office phone and rang her boss's office. She couldn't take her eyes off Daniel, and she was glad he eventually buried his handsome face in a copy of a trade magazine. It was when he lifted the magazine up to peruse through it that she noticed his wedding ring. Figures, she thought, men are just like parking spots, all the good ones are taken. Still, he'd make a nice addition to our staff, if nothing else just to look at — office eye candy.

"Chuck, this is Mary Beth. There's a gentleman out here to see you. A Mr. Harris."

"Give me five minutes, then send him in."

"Will do, Chuck." Mary Beth lowered her voice to a whisper and added, "If I get a vote on who to hire, this one gets mine."

"I'll assume he's good-looking?"

"If you only knew."

"You're too much. You can personally escort him to my office if you'd like, Mary Beth."

"I'd like. Thanks, Chuck."

She hung up the phone and turned to Daniel. "Chuck will be about five minutes, if you don't mind."

"That'll be fine. Thanks."

Mary Beth went back to her paperwork between sneaking glances at this fine-looking young man sitting in her reception area. If Chuck doesn't hire this guy, I'll kill him, she decided.

The five minutes flew by quickly. Mary Beth found a good stopping place in her never-ending avalanche of invoices, memos, and messages. She buzzed her boss again on the intercom.

"Chuck, this is Mary Beth, can I bring him in?"

"Sure, I'm all set," replied her boss.

She looked up and spoke to Daniel, "Time's up. Let's head back to Chuck's office."

"Okay."

The two of them proceeded down a hallway toward the back of the office suites. There were any number of standard-issue, light gray cubicles on either side of the hallway. Daniel could barely see over the tops of them, but when he did, he noted a half-dozen people on the phone, or working on their computers, their desks covered in proofs, slicks, and the stuff of advertising.

"Here you go." Mary Beth made three small taps on her boss's office door.

"Come on in!" said Mr. Mosby loudly.

Betsy opened the door and introduced the applicant to Mr. Mosby, slyly winking at him as she did.

"Please take a seat, Mr. Harris."

"You can call me Daniel," he said while sitting down in one of the two chairs placed before Mr. Mosby's unimposing desk.

"And you can call me Chuck."

"Thanks."

"If that's all, I'll be back to my desk," said Mary Beth, lingering in Chuck's office longer than needed.

"That's all for now. I'll give you a buzz to escort Mr. Harris out when we're through."

She closed the door behind her and returned to her desk. God, is he cute or what, she thought as she went back to her desk. Too bad he's married.

✿

"Thanks for coming in today. I've got a couple of questions about your resumé I wanted to review with you, as well as get a feeling as to why you think the advertising business might have a future for you. Do you mind?"

"No, that's why I'm here," said Daniel nervously.

"There's a gap in your resumé that doesn't add up. It says here you were bartending in Buckhead after two years at Oglethorpe, but then you seem to disappear. The rest of the application looks good, and I like what you wrote with regard to your interest in creative writing, but I need to know where you were during that time, if you don't mind."

Daniel hesitated for a minute before answering. He had been telling everyone the truth, in part because he felt that it was what Joshua would have wanted him to do. Daniel would freely volunteer information about his protracted stay at Central State Hospital, but by now he realized that in doing so, every job opening closed the instant he mentioned it. He remembered Ayse's suggestion, and, somewhat timidly, he answered Mr. Mosby.

"I was in Istanbul."

"Istanbul, Turkey? What were you doing way over there?"

"My wife's from Istanbul. Her father owns a carpet export business and she wanted me to give it a try."

"Well, what happened?"

"Turns out I'm allergic to wool."

"You're kidding." Chuck started laughing. The thought of this young apprentice sneezing his way through his workday struck him as humorous. "So I take it you didn't stay on long?"

"No, the job lasted less than a year, then my wife had a child and we stayed in Istanbul at her parents' place. It was like an extended vacation. Her parents have quite a bit of money.

"I looked around at a few opportunities in Turkey, but we decided to return to Atlanta. Istanbul is nice, but the pay's not what it is in America."

"No, I suppose not. Well, that fills in the time gap. Let me ask you a few more questions. Why do you think the advertising industry would work for you?"

Daniel answered Mr. Mosby's question, along with a half dozen more. The interview lasted thirty minutes. It went well. Daniel talked about his lifelong journal, *The Book of Midnights,* and his desire to write. Chuck Mosby liked what he heard. They were looking for someone to work on ad copy and small features for two in-house newsletters they produced for several clients. Once the two-year absence was explained, the two men found themselves enjoying each other's company. For the first time in months, Daniel felt he had a chance of getting the position.

As the interview wound down, Chuck Mosby got his receptionist on the intercom.

"Mary Beth, we're pretty much wrapped up in here, do you want to come down and see Daniel out?"

"You bet," she replied on her phone, knowing Chuck would make note of her enthusiasm.

"See you in a bit. Well, Daniel, I can tell you Mary Beth wants you to get the job. But I'll have to remind you that you're married and you've got a child, if you know what I mean."

"I was a bartender for a year in Buckhead, Mr. Mosby. I know what you mean."

Mary Beth showed up a minute later. She knocked, chatted briefly with her boss, then escorted Daniel to the reception area.

"How did it go?"

"Well, I hope."

"Me too. Chuck will probably get back to you in a few days with his decision. I hope you get the job."

"Yeah, that'd be great."

Daniel Harris went down to the parking ramp to find his car. He knew it had gone better than any of his recent interviews. For once, he felt he had a shot at it. As he started the car, he was anxious to tell Ayse. Tell her, and thank her for her suggestion about living in Istanbul.

Istanbul, he reflected as he started driving north to Marietta, that would be a nice place to visit someday.

✦

Two days later the phone rang at their apartment in Marietta. It was Mary Beth calling. Daniel was to show up at Mosby & Simms the following Monday at eight-thirty sharp. Mustapha and Ayse were right. Life was good.

The Birth of Sarah, Several Years Later

Nothing could have prepared Daniel for that morning. Not the birthing classes they had attended, or the videos they had taken home to watch. Nothing could approach the actual experience. Being there, for the birth of his daughter, Sarah, was one of the most powerful moments in his life.

The pregnancy had not gone well. Unlike Ibraham's pregnancy, Ayse had a difficult time carrying Sarah. Her morning sickness was much worse, and she had trouble near the end — spotting and any number of false labors. There was even talk of a Caesarean if the fetus didn't change position in the final weeks of her pregnancy.

But with the help of her doctor, they rotated the child and the birth went better than had the pregnancy. Sarah Yalçin Harris was born a healthy seven-pound, three-ounce baby girl on a beautiful summer morning in Atlanta. A morning full of cries, contractions and the first breath of their second child.

Coming home from the hospital, Daniel felt an overwhelming sensation of being a part of something larger than himself. Even more than the love Ayse and he shared, to him it was the feeling of being part of a family. As though the birth of Sarah completed the circle. He could not define, or put his feelings into words, because these emotions were new to him. He was leaving behind the things of youth and becoming an adult, a parent of two children — proud yet apprehensive.

Later that night, after tending to Ayse, and spending extra time playing with an envious Ibraham, Daniel, though exhausted, decided to make an entry in the *Book of Midnights.*

The entries to his journals had become infrequent. With all the copy writing he was doing at Mosby & Simms, Daniel seldom had the energy left to keep up with his journal. There were times when two months would pass between entries, and a single notebook could take over a year to fill. It was so different from the first notebook Joshua had handed him in Milledgeville, a notebook he completed in three days' time with a pencil he sharpened with his teeth.

Life, since leaving the hospital, had been good to Daniel. Every day, every chance he had, he thanked God for that. He and Ayse had not taken it upon themselves to join a church yet, but they both felt that, in time, they would. Ayse had remained a faithful Muslim, and it never bothered her husband. He felt it was her devotion, both to her God and to himself, that had saved their marriage. Devotion, thought Daniel as he picked up his notebook, is a good thing.

They were still living in the apartment in Marietta. Daniel had paid back a considerable portion of the monies they had borrowed from Mustapha only to find out that, as soon as Ayse and he found a house, he and Elif were willing to loan them the down payment. They would need a bigger place soon, and Daniel was glad for the support Ayse's parents were giving them.

The relationship with his own father remained unchanged. There would be no crack in Clay's steadfast opposition to the marriage. There was no belated blessing, no contact whatsoever. The only change was from Rebecca, who had called twice in the past year. Once to apologize to Ayse for telling her Daniel was working at a lumberyard in Athens, and a second time to tell them she was trying to get her husband to agree to see the grandchildren, once the newborn had arrived. Rebecca argued to Clay that it wasn't fair to hold the grandchildren responsible for the sins of their parents. Thus far Clay said, no, the grandchildren were not his.

With the newborn safe beside her mother, and Ibraham asleep in his room, Daniel took up his journal and a sharpened pencil and sat down at the kitchen table. This is what he wrote.

As She Lay Still and Sleeping

I awoke early this morning.
The alarm went off, you stirred momentarily
Then fell back to sleep.
I showered, got dressed and as I walked to the bedroom door
I looked once more at you — my Ayse.

Your hair spilling across the white linen pillowcase
Like a dark, mysterious river winding through a field of snow.
You had pulled the blankets down during the night
And your bare shoulders rose and fell with every breath.
Shoulders the color and curve of sand dunes — sensual and warm.

I realized how much you've meant to me.
When I was hard upon that storm of life God laid before me,
Your prayers and faith, your devotion to our marriage.
All to save me from myself.
Save me from the waves, the wind, the abyss.

With every breath you took I loved you more.
Then, as you lie still and sleeping beside Sarah,
I kissed my boy, and quietly left our home.
I drove on crowded highways, listening to the clamor of the world.
I merged and stopped and accelerated as the radio blared.

Oh, Ayse, what world is this we have?
Where nations talk of war while old men sleep in streets?
Where the fields are planted fallow as our children die of hunger?
Where money persecutes justice,
And the prayers that most need praying remain unsaid.

I turned the radio off as I pulled up to the office.
It was more bad news, of killers running loose,
Of rage and pain and desperate men alone.
My thoughts turned back to you as I sat behind my desk,
Buried in memos, faxes, voice mail — Imperatives all.

I can't resolve the conflicts that unend, nor can you.
Men will go on killing, hating, just
As we will go on loving one another.
The world wobbles on its crooked path through time
As she lay still and sleeping.

Daniel Mark Harris

"It's my understanding that Daniel Harris, my son, is currently in your employment. Is that correct?"

"Yes, Daniel's been with us over five years now. He's a good man, a hard worker and a real asset to our firm," answered Chuck Mosby.

"Well, then you need to know he's a liar."

"Excuse me, Mr. Harris?" Chuck was blind sided by Daniel's father's comment.

"My boy, Daniel, he's misrepresented himself to you from day one."

"I don't understand."

"He was never in Istanbul. If you want proof, ask to see his passport. He doesn't have a passport. You can't travel overseas without a passport, Mr. Mosby, and that's a natural fact."

Charles Mosby was perplexed. He had never heard Daniel talk about his family, and wondered from the moment Mary Beth patched Mr. Harris through, why Daniel's father was calling him.

"Where are you going with this, Mr. Harris?"

"He was in Milledgeville, Mr. Mosby. My boy was institutionalized for two years at Central State Hospital. He lied to you, just like he lied to me about seeing that Muslim girl he married.

"My boy's got issues, Mr. Mosby, serious issues. He's tried to kill himself and he's of an unsound mind. They had to keep him in restraints down there, and he could pose a potential threat to you, your clients and your employees. I know that if I were the owner of a big advertising firm like yours, I'd want to know if one of my employees had falsified information on their job application. I'd be right concerned about the fact that he had spent a considerable amount of his life in an insane asylum. Wouldn't you? Don't you want to know the truth about my son, Daniel?"

Mr. Mosby didn't respond. He knew the answer was yes, that as Daniel's employer he had a right to know, but there was a deeper, more troubling aspect to this conversation, something more sinister than the truth.

"Yes, I suppose it's something I should be made aware of," said Mr. Mosby.

"If it were my company, I wouldn't hesitate a minute in showing him the way out the door. He's a liar and a lunatic, Mr. Mosby. If it were my company, I wouldn't have any of it. I thought it my Christian duty to set the record straight for you. I disowned Daniel years ago and I have a standing protection order against him should he ever dare show up in Macon."

Chuck Mosby was astounded. He couldn't believe what he was hearing. He needed more information. "How did you find out Daniel works here?"

"I've got a lot of Baptist friends in Atlanta, Mr. Mosby. Some of them are clients of yours, although I've promised not to disclose my sources. Let's just say I found out through the grapevine."

"Well, this is all news to me. I want to thank you for calling me and setting the record straight, Mr. Harris."

"It's Reverend Harris, but you can call me Clay, Mr. Mosby."

"Then thank you, Clay. Mr. Simms and I will look into the situation immediately."

"I figured you would. You don't want to start losing any business, do you Mr. Mosby? It's easy to lose business when you're employing nut cases like my ex-son."

"Certainly, Clay."

"Well, goodbye then. I left my number with your receptionist if you need to get back to me for any further information."

"Thanks, we'll be in touch. Goodbye."

Chuck Mosby hung up the phone and shook his head in disbelief. In his twenty-seven years of being in business he had never received such a bizarre phone call. It was, in effect, a father attempting to get his son fired from a job he was excelling at. He picked up the phone and called his partner on the intercom system.

"Dwight, can you come over and see me. I've got some disturbing news about Daniel."

"Daniel Harris? What's the problem?"

"I'll tell you when we meet. Say half an hour?"

"Yeah, that works. I'll see you then."

❂

Mid afternoon Mary Beth informed Daniel he now had a previously unscheduled meeting with Chuck Mosby and Dwight Simms tomorrow morning in Chuck's office. In the years Daniel had been with the firm, he had met with both partners at once only half a dozen times. He knew it must be something important, so he pressed Mary Beth for more information.

Mary Beth didn't have any idea as to why they were asking to meet with him, and she told Daniel as much. She said it sounded serious, because of the tone in Chuck's voice.

"It might have to do with the huge Delta Airlines account you recently landed, but I'm not sure," she added. Daniel let it go at that, knowing that whatever the reason, he would find out the following morning.

Then, just as Daniel was leaving for home that same afternoon, Mary Beth said something that sent shivers down his spine.

"Oh, Daniel, I forgot to tell you something — your father called."

"Are you certain?"

"Yes, he's from Macon, right? I've got his number right here, I'm sure it's a Macon area code."

Mary Beth handed Daniel her message pad and showed him his father's telephone number. The message was for Mr. Mosby. Daniel studied the message and checked the number twice, hoping it was all a mistake, a mixup of some kind. It wasn't.

Daniel suspected the worst. Now he knew the reason for tomorrow's meeting. He handed the message back to Mary Beth and asked, "Did he actually get through to Chuck?"

"Yes, I think so, they were on the line for five, maybe ten minutes. I know because I had two other calls holding. It's been a busy day. And congrats on landing that Delta account, Daniel. We've been trying to get a piece of their business for years. I know Chuck and Dwight are absolutely thrilled about it."

Daniel didn't react to Mary Beth's accolades. A look of panic overtook him. His color vanished. The smile he normally sported at the end of his workday was replaced by a grimace. Mary Beth couldn't help but notice the sudden change in his demeanor.

"Are you okay, Daniel?"

"No, I'm not. I've got to go home," Daniel answered in a quivering voice.

"You look as white as a sheet. Are you sure you can drive?"

"I'll be fine. I'll see you tomorrow."

"Drive carefully. I'll see you at eight-thirty."

Daniel didn't say goodbye. He opened the door to the office and went down the hallway to the elevator. When the elevator arrived, it was curiously empty. As he pushed the button for the lobby, the elevator made a sudden, jerky motion as though a cable had snapped. The car caught itself, and the descent to the ground floor went fine. In Daniel's heart, the cable had snapped.

The cable snapped and Daniel was falling again, back into the belly of the whale. Darkness, even in the bright daylight on the long drive back to Marietta, was engulfing him. He thought of Joshua, and how Joshua told him there were going to be days when he would have to be brave. This was one of those days. He hurried home to Ayse, his heart still tumbling into hell as he did.

❁

A night of troubled sleep heralded in the sunrise. Daniel and Ayse talked late into the night. They had discussed a thousand different scenarios without resolve. Why had his father called Chuck Mosby? How did he find out where Daniel was working? What did his father and Chuck discuss? Why was he being called into a meeting with both partners tomorrow morning?

Daniel had deduced that Clay had told them about his stay at Milledgeville. That and the fact he had lied on his application. Both would be grounds for his dismissal. If he were fired, what would they do? They talked about moving to Istanbul. Anywhere in the world so long as it would be far, far away from the twisted reach of his father. They talked about what they would say to Ibraham, if he was let go. How would they explain his dismissal to her parents? They talked, like two adults in a crisis, just to have the comfort of hearing each other's voices late, late into the darkness. The darkness of impending disaster.

✪

"Take a seat, Daniel," said Dwight Simms.

Daniel walked in and sat in the chair beside Dwight. Chuck Mosby sat behind his desk, with a look on his face that foreshadowed the conversation to come. Daniel was perspiring, his throat dry and his stomach tied in knots. In a somber, business like tone, Mr. Mosby began. "Do you know why we've called this meeting?"

"No."

"Two reasons, Daniel. One, to thank you for all your hard work in landing the Delta account. And secondly, to talk to you about your father."

Daniel froze. He was right. It was about his father — that son of a bitch — that asshole. Why can't he leave me alone? A sense of powerlessness flooded over Daniel as he braced himself for the news. Mr. Mosby continued.

"Your father, the Rev. Harris, called me yesterday and informed me about your stint in Milledgeville. He also made it clear that you had lied on your job application. I want to ask you something right now, and it's important to both Dwight and me that you answer us honestly. Have you ever been to Turkey?"

"No."

"Were you, in fact, a patient at Central State Hospital during those two missing years?"

"Yes, but..."

"Are you still crazy, Daniel?" Chuck interrupted.

"No, it's just my father..."

"To hell with your father!" blurted Dwight Simms.

"Yes, I second that, Dwight. And, I would like to make a motion, as one of the two voting partners of Mosby & Simms, that Daniel Mark Harris, because of his outstanding work on landing one of the largest account we've seen in years, presently and posthaste be made the new, junior partner of Mosby, Simms...and Harris."

"I second the motion."

"Congratulations! We'll discuss your bonus and the terms of the new partnership this afternoon."

Daniel didn't understand. Everything was upside down. He was there, ready to defend himself against his father's accusations, but it was over. Instead of being fired, he was made a partner. He had to say something, to try to make sense of what had just occurred.

"But what about my stay in Milledgeville?" he asked.

"Christ, Daniel, you've got to be nuts to be in the advertising business anyway. Whatever happened down there was just your field training. And as far as your father goes, I can't stand those self-righteous religious zealots anyway. If he makes a few calls and we lose some accounts, well, good riddance. The days when the old saying, *there are more Baptists in Atlanta than there are people,* no longer applies. We'll get by without them.

"But why a father would place a call to have his son fired is beyond me. He must really have some kind of axe to grind."

"It's because of my wife, Ayse," said Daniel. "It's because she's a Muslim."

"Well, GLORY BE and PRAISE THE LORD," exclaimed Dwight sarcastically. "I thought the Crusades were over, but I guess they're not. Ayse's a fine woman, Daniel, and she's raising your two kids better than half the mothers in this city. In my opinion, your father's just another narrow-minded, Bible-thumping asshole. He's no business meddling in our business. Isn't that right, Chuck?"

"That's right, Dwight. I can't wait until his contacts tell him we made you a partner, the youngest partner in town. He's going to shit."

"Now, Daniel, let's have lunch this afternoon to celebrate. We've got a lot of details to sort through and we might as well get started ASAP. What do you say, can you break for lunch with your new partners?"

"Yes, of course."

❂

Daniel left Mr. Mosby's office in a state of shock. After calming down, he phoned Ayse a half-hour later to tell her the news. She could not believe what he was telling her, but knew it was true. When she hung up she thanked Allâh for showing them His great mercy.

In Milledgeville, Joshua looked out the window in what used to be Daniel's room and wondered how life was treating his dear friend. As the Georgia sun climbed the staircase of the day, Joshua sensed that life was good for Daniel. It was as if he knew.

Soon, thought Joshua to himself as he prayed for Daniel, I'll hear from him soon, and then I'll know for certain. I miss him, but that's the price you pay for setting them free, reflected the reverent orderly as he left Daniel's room and walked down the hallway toward Elizabeth Bragg, his newest endeavor. Love them enough to set them free, that's all Jesus asks of us — to set them free.

Clay's Concession

"It isn't fair, Clay, and it never has been. They're growing up without us."

"I've cast Daniel out of my life, and I have no intention of allowing his children, the children of that marriage, to come into our lives," stated Clayton Harris over a dinner that was growing cold.

"Well, so be it, and you're welcome to your opinion. But I'm not asking you this time, I'm telling you. I spoke with Daniel a week ago and the arrangements have all been made. The two children are going to spend the afternoon here tomorrow and that's final.

"I've gone along with all of it up to this point. I didn't think it was right, but I allowed you to have your way with our son. I don't agree with his decision to marry her any more than you do, but this time you've gone too far. Now you want to hold the children responsible for the sins of their father, and that, I won't allow."

Rebecca was furious with her husband, a behavior foreign to Clayton Aaron Harris. She had always been a good wife, submissive and subordinate to his every whim. She had objected several times to his actions, especially the phone call he'd made some years ago to Daniel's employers. She thought it a loathsome act, and begged him not to do it.

He ignored her, telling her he felt it was his Christian duty to expose the sins of his son — the lies and manipulations. But Rebecca was no longer convinced of the purity of her husband's motives. To her, his actions stemmed from a bitterness toward his boy's success. Success he found despite Clay's every attempt at ruining his life. His phone call was an act of revenge. Just another attempt at getting even for embarrassing Clay before his family and his congregation.

When his plan backfired, Rebecca was elated. It proved there were forces at play that were more powerful and benevolent than her husband's version of Christianity. She had never forgiven Clay for making that call, and now, with her son climbing the ladder of success as a full partner at Mosby, Simms & Harris, she felt it was time to try to bridge the gap between them.

Knowing Clay would never concede to seeing Daniel or Ayse, Rebecca had focused her efforts at trying to convince him to see their grandchildren, Ibraham and Sarah. Ruth's boy, Jason, was in junior high school at this point and Rebecca longed for the sound of children's voices in her empty house in Macon. She wanted to hear their laughter, bake them pecan cookies and see their smiling faces. Rebecca was determined to get this concession from her husband. She continued.

"Are you going to drive to Locust Grove with me tomorrow or not?" asked Rebecca, letting Clay know her decision to pick up Ibraham and Sarah was final.

The only remaining question was whether or not he was coming along.

Clay didn't answer. He sat at the kitchen table, recalling the cold rain he had suffered through nearly a decade ago. He remembered stumbling along the road, shivering uncontrollably. He remembered being afraid. He recalled seeing the headlights of the Explorer come around the bend, and how his wife had to help him get inside the car. How he soaked in the tub for an hour just to get warm again. Then, without looking up, he answered his wife. "Yes, I'll ride with you."

"Good. We'll have to leave here by nine to meet Daniel at the truck stop just off I-75. He said you can't miss it. Do you know the one I'm talking about?"

"Yes, it's a big 76 station. I've stopped there on my way to Atlanta before. You can't miss it.

"But let me warn you in advance, Rebecca. I'll not get out of the car when you go in to pick the Grandkids up from Daniel. I've sworn on my Bible that I'll never — and I repeat, NEVER — set my eyes on that boy again. He's out of my life and I'm glad for it."

Rebecca didn't respond to Clay's mean-spirited comment. She thought Clay had carried his malice too far. It was over for her. It had been nearly ten years since the wedding in Gatlinburg, and it was time to put it all behind them. That was how she felt, and that was why she had written to Daniel at his office three months ago, politely asking if he would allow them to meet the children.

When Daniel opened the letter, noting the return address and his mother's handwriting, he read it and reacted much like his father. No, was his first response. Why should I allow her the privilege of seeing my children after all they've put us through? To hell with Clay.

That evening, after the kids were in bed, he shared the letter with Ayse. She cried when she read it, knowing her mother, Elif, missed Ibraham and had never met Sarah. Mustapha had visited them twice since the birth of their daughter, and he was planning to be back in Atlanta before the end of the year on another business trip.

Ayse felt Rebecca was extending an olive branch to Daniel and his family, and she wanted to allow the visit.

"Daniel, surely no harm can come of this. Why are you against it? Rebecca is doing everything she can to bridge the gap between us. I doubt it was easy for her to convince your father to allow this. Why should you be the one to deny your children the right to know who their grandparents are?"

Daniel answered her in an acrid tone. "But I don't think it wise to allow my children to be anywhere near that bitter, heartless old man."

"Maybe the children will lessen his bitterness. Maybe that's why this change of heart has come to pass. Maybe this too, has been written.

"Thus far, all Ibraham and Sarah have really known of our families is my father, Mustapha. Ibraham was too young to remember his short time with my mother, and Sarah wasn't even born. It's clear to me in reading her letter that your mother has taken the first step in trying to mend this rift between us. It would be so unfair of you to say no. You would be behaving just like Clay."

Ayse was right. Daniel hated to admit it, but he knew it was true. He hated to think he was his father's child, but he was.

Daniel wanted, more than anything, to remain steadfast in his decision not to allow it, but he could not. His thoughts turned to Joshua. He recalled their last conversation together, wherein Joshua told him he would never be free until he had forgiven Clay.

Maybe, just maybe, this would be the first step toward that forgiveness. His anger ran deep, and he wanted to deny his mother's request, but Joshua had taught him to bend. It was time to bend.

"I am behaving like my father, aren't I. But it's not fair, Ayse."

"No one said life would be fair, Daniel."

Without saying so, Ayse knew she had convinced her husband to allow the visit. She could see it in his eyes as she looked at him across the polished surface of their dining room table. He had surrendered, and she was proud of him for doing so.

Later that same evening, they made passionate love as the children slept in their bedrooms down the hallway. In the morning, she asked if she could call Rebecca in the next few days to make the arrangements. Daniel told Ayse he would make the call.

❂

His mother's voice sounded familiar, but tired. Halfway through their telephone conversation Daniel realized he had not seen his mother in a decade. He imagined that she had aged, just as he had grown up to be a young, successful ad executive in the bustling metropolis of Atlanta.

She told her son she was proud of him for becoming so successful and that she missed him dearly. She was anxious to see her grandkids but, before the visit could be finalized, she would need to get her husband to allow it. She wouldn't ask for his permission, she told Daniel in a decisive manner, she would tell him. The visit was on.

They'd decided to meet on Saturday, halfway between the two cities, at a truck stop just off the freeway near Locust Grove. Daniel would drive them down on Saturday morning, explaining to his nine-year-old son and five-year-old daughter that they were going to spend the day with their grandparents. Ibraham thought it sounded cool, different. Sarah was a little intimidated, but willing to go along so long as her brother was there. Because it was their first visit, Rebecca and Daniel decided to keep it short and sweet. If all went well, overnights would be discussed, but not for a while. Daniel would drive down to pick up the children at the same location just after dinner, spending the entire afternoon at his office catching up on paperwork

✵

That's how it unfolded. As the sun rose without fanfare that morning in October, two cars left their respective driveways just after nine in the morning. One held a young father and his two children, the other two aging grandparents. Soon, both were driving on I-75 — one heading south, the other north.

Just past ten-thirty, Daniel arrived at the designated meeting place on the west side of the freeway. They went in the restaurant at the truck stop and took a booth. Daniel had promised them each a glass of milk and a donut for behaving well on the ride down. Daniel ordered a cup of coffee.

Ten minutes later, Rebecca walked through the front door. She looked down the booths and tables and spotted her son with his two children. Daniel looked good, thought his mother. His eyes still shone their endearing blue and his face was still as well-sculpted and handsome as ever. But he was no longer the college kid she had driven back and forth from Oglethorpe. He was a young man, dressed in an upscale polo shirt and well-pressed khaki Dockers. She walked toward him, uncertain of how he would greet her after all these years.

"Hi, Mom," he said when his mother was still twenty feet away.

"Hi, Daniel."

He stood up and embraced her. It was not what he had planned to do. He had planned to remain aloof, but upon seeing his mother again, he couldn't maintain the distance he had wanted to. It had been too long.

"You look fantastic, Mom. Did you drive up here alone?"

"No. Clay's still in the car. He doesn't want to see you. You know how stubborn he is. I tried to convince him to come in, but it's no use. He'll go to his grave with his bitterness, and there's very little you or I can do to change that. I'm sorry about your father, Daniel."

"Me too."

They turned around to see the children staring at them. Sarah had traces of chocolate donut smeared at random across her pretty face and Ibraham had donned an impressive milk mustache. Rebecca smiled, helping to put them at ease. She went over and sat across from them, slipping into the booth beside her son.

"My, my, my, what adorable little children!" she exclaimed.

"Are you our grandmother?"

"Yes, but you can call me Rebecca if you'd like."

Sarah looked at Rebecca and smiled. "Want some of my donut?" Sarah asked, extending her half-eaten chocolate donut toward her grandmother.

"No, no thank you, Sarah. But I've got cookies waiting for you at my house."

"What kind?" asked Ibraham.

"Pecan cookies. Do you like pecans?"

"I like all kinds of cookies," replied the boy.

Rebecca studied her grandchildren. Ibraham was wearing a short-sleeve baseball jersey with an Atlanta Braves logo on it. Sarah was wearing a simple floral dress, with white lace around the collar. Her skin was darker, more Mediterranean than was her brother's. It must have come from Ayse, thought Rebecca. Ibraham had Daniel's eyes, but Sarah had her mother's dark eyes. Rebecca was pleased with what she saw.

"We should be going, I don't want your father to wait in the car too long. It was hard enough to get him to agree to this visit in the first place."

"Well, you're going to need a booster seat and some things for Sarah. How should we handle it?"

"Could you run out and bring them in for me? When you leave I can go out and get Clay and he can help carry them to our car."

"It seems so crazy at this point, doesn't it, Mom?"

"Not to him."

"No, it wouldn't seem crazy to Clay."

Daniel got up and went out to his car, leaving the three of them to visit while he retrieved their bag of toys and the booster seat. When he got out to the parking area, he looked around for a Ford Explorer. He didn't even know if they still owned an Explorer, and, when he remembered how long it had been, doubted if they did.

There were forty cars, trucks and SUVs in the parking lot. Any one of them might be his parents' car. In a way, a curious way, Daniel wanted to catch a glimpse of his father. He took one more glance at the parked cars and between the tinted windows and the cars parked along the fringe of the expansive lot, he could not find the one his father was hiding in.

But Clay, with his seat reclined listening to an FM preacher on the radio, immediately spotted Daniel. His eyes, the same blue as his son's, watched his every move. Somewhere in his heart, he too, wanted to greet his boy, but he held himself back. There would be no meeting between them that morning.

Daniel walked to his car and unbuckled the booster seat. He found the bag of toys in the trunk and carried them into the restaurant. As he approached the booth, he noticed the three of them were having fun. Ibraham was laughing while Sarah tried to feed her grandma a portion of her messy chocolate donut. Rebecca was smiling, delighted to be playing with her grandchildren. Ayse was right, thought Daniel, it was good for them to know his mother. He placed the booster seat and Sarah's bag of toys beside the booth. He didn't sit down.

"Here they are, Mom. I've got to run." Daniel reached for his wallet and took out a five-dollar bill.

"Put your money away, Daniel. I'll get the bill. Thanks for letting us visit with the kids today. You don't know how much this means to me."

"They're good kids, Ma. Enjoy your afternoon. I'll meet you here between seven and seven-thirty tonight, okay?"

"I'll be here."

"Call me if you need anything. Use my cell phone number though, as the office lines will be switched over to the answering service. Here, take one of my cards. They have all my numbers on them."

Daniel slipped his money back into his wallet and removed one of his business cards. He handed it to his mother.

"Mosby, Simms & Harris," she read aloud. "It has a nice ring to it, don't you think?"

"Yes it does."

"Goodbye, Daniel, and thanks again."

"Bye, Mom."

Daniel went to his car and pulled away. He slipped onto the ramp heading north toward his office and thought about the past ten years. He would like to have caught a glimpse of his father, but hadn't. His mother looked much as she always had, but older. Older than he had imagined she would look. She must be sixty by now, he thought. Clay must be sixty-four, if I remember correctly.

Daniel pulled up to his office at eleven-thirty. He phoned Ayse and said it had gone well. She was glad. He buried himself in his work as time slipped away. There was always work to do at the office. Always. The hours passed without notice.

Hillside Baptist Church

As Daniel drove east on I-20, he recalled taking that same route over a decade earlier. He didn't drive that day, on his lonely ride to Central State Hospital. He sat in back of an ambulance as remnants of tropical storm Gabriel soaked the summer greenery. He watched a windy landscape sketched in halftones of gray. He didn't look forward. He stared backward, out the rear window of the van. He watched everything disappearing behind him — his wife, his dreams, his world.

Daniel still thought of that nihilistic journey, and suffered for it. He had waited years to return to Milledgeville, and even with that much time between him and Ward 2-B, his blood ran cold as he exited the Interstate to catch Highway 441 south.

They weren't going to go to the hospital today, though Ibraham had asked several times if they could drive by it. Drive by the place where Daddy was once sick. The place where he stayed until he was better.

Daniel was better. His marriage was strong, his children content, and his financial situation better than he could ever have imagined. The Delta account was followed by some of CNN's business, followed by a half-dozen additional major accounts over the years. Mosby, Simms & Harris was now a factor in the Atlanta advertising scene. It was nominated for seventeen Addy Awards, and renowned throughout Cobb County for its creative approach to marketing. Business was better than good, it was excellent.

It was Ayse's idea to make this sojourn. For years, Daniel had talked about seeing Joshua again and Ayse wanted the children to meet him. But Ayse could sense Daniel's reluctance to go near the hospital. There, in his memory, too many ghosts still roamed. Only time would make the ghosts vanish, and that time was now.

They were originally planning to come the night before, and spend Saturday evening at a motel, meeting Joshua and his family for Sunday morning services the next day. That plan fell apart when Daniel learned he had to be in the office until six the night before. Sometimes, business was too excellent.

So their plans were modified. They decided to rise and shine early and make the two-hour drive from their home in the Vinings the following morning. They would have to be under way before eight to make the ten a.m. service at Hillside Baptist Church. Thus far, the trip was on schedule and, unless Joshua's directions were incorrect, they would arrive a few minutes early.

At nine-thirty they drove past the entrance to Central State Hospital. From the road, they could only see the white dome of the Powell Building. Ayse pointed out the hospital to the children.

"Ibraham, Sarah!" she called, turning around to gain their attention. "See, there's the hospital where your father stayed when he was sick."

"Can we see the inside?" asked Ibraham.

"No, not today, Ibraham. We don't want to be late for church."

Ayse didn't mind attending a Christian church with her family. She had become well adapted to the American concept of worship, even if she found it odd. To her, every moment of life was connected to God. To Christians, it was as though one hour a week was sufficient. It made little sense to her, but she never made mention of any of this to Daniel.

They had decided to expose their children to both Christianity and Islam, and because of that decision, had joined an Episcopal church in the Vinings two years ago. They attended service every Sunday without fail, and Ayse had become quite an asset to the church's women's group, the E.C.W. Ayse, with Daniel's approval, would read the children passages from the Qu'ran, and during the summer months, all four of them would go to mosque on Fridays.

This morning would be a dramatic change from the studied hymns of Episcopalians and the sanctity of Friday's mosque. This morning's worship would take place in a small, rural black Baptist church in south central Georgia.

There would be hands waving, voices raised in enthusiastic praise, and hymns sung loudly and raucously. The preacher wouldn't present the word of God like a dissertation on abstract theological concept, he'd preach the Gospels full of enthusiasm and verve, knowing souls were being lost to the devil's hand every day.

Daniel knew what kind of service they would soon participate in. Ayse, whose mosques preserved a piety more serene than the Episcopalians, would be in for quite an experience. The children would watch in awe. Daniel knew this because, as a young man, he had attended several black Baptist services in Macon. He had a number of black friends who had, over the years, invited him to worship with them. It was worship that meant business.

By this time Daniel had passed through town and, per Joshua's instructions, was heading west on Highway 22 toward Haddock. From there he took a right on Mill Road. But he would continue past Joshua's driveway to the north. He would eventually take a left, along Douglas Road, until he came up to the top of a long, steady climb.

Once at the top of the knoll, he would double back south, following a winding driveway to the very top of the hill. The parking lot was at the top of that hill. A short pathway down the western slope took you to the church itself — Hillside Baptist Church.

As soon as Daniel turned off Highway 22, the landscape changed and the signs of the local poverty became obvious. Shotgun shacks and double-wide mobile homes propped up on cinder blocks became the norm. It was hard to find a house that resembled anything like the four-bedroom ranch they owned in the Vinings. The yards were filled with abandoned vehicles of every make, model and year. One house, from all appearances, was a rusty, converted school bus. But there were gardens, plenty of gardens. Some were carefully tended, some looked abandoned.

In most of the yards, there was a proliferation of junk. Nothing worth anything more than the space it occupied — old hot water heaters, washing machines, refrigerators, what have you. Daniel laughed to himself as they drove past the clutter — they were indeed a long, long way from Atlanta.

Daniel found Joshua's directions to be faultless and, in a few minutes' time, they pulled off Douglas Road, ascending the dusty driveway to the church's parking lot. The lot was filled with cars, trucks and mini-vans. His car, new and clean, stood out from the aging, rusted collection.

The four of them got out and walked down the pathway toward the church. The condition of the church mirrored the condition of the automobiles. It needed paint, a few of the stained-glass window panels had been replaced by inexpensive clear glass, and there was some obvious storm damage to the steeple.

Joshua, who had been keeping an eye out for Daniel and his family since arriving at the church, approached them as they neared the chapel.

"Well, Lordy be, look who's comin' to praise God this fine mornin'!"

"JJ," said Daniel as he walked up and embraced his old friend. "It's so good to see you again."

"It's good to see you, Daniel."

They finished their long, genuine hug and took a step back, inspecting each other as they did.

"Why, you're even skinnier than I remember," said Daniel in jest.

"Yeah, and you're lookin' fit as a fiddle."

"You remember Ayse?"

"Of course I do. It's nice to see you again, Ayse. Thanks so much for coming down and visitin' us this fine Sunday mornin'. And who are those little critters?" asked Joshua, pointing to Daniel's children.

"This is Ibraham, whom you met when he was just a toddler and this little darling is our daughter, Sarah. Can you two say 'Hello' to my friend JJ?"

"Hi, JJ," said Ibraham sheepishly.

"Hello, JJ," said Sarah, falling behind her mother's skirt as she did.

"It's good to see you again," said Ayse. She stepped forward and gave Joshua a big hug. She knew how much he had meant to Daniel in the hospital, and she knew that without Joshua's intervention, Daniel might still be there. Joshua returned her embrace, smiling at Ayse as they pulled apart.

"We'd best be gettin' inside. My wife Mariah and the kids be savin' a spot for y'all. The preacher will be gettin' started here in a few minutes, so there's no time to be wastin'."

The five of them went in and found the pew Mariah had reserved for them. Within a minute, the electric organ started playing the opening hymn and the ten o'clock service began. The church, except for a few empty seats near the rear, was filled. All totaled, there were sixty-four parishioners attending worship service that morning. Unlike the Episcopal church they worshiped at in the Vinings, where three separate services were held each Sunday, this was the only service held that morning.

There was a small service held Sunday evening, with fewer than twenty-five members in attendance, and the Wednesday night service sometimes held fewer than a dozen of the faithful.

Still, Reverend Brown held his head high and his faith higher. He worked part-time at Preston's Hardware store to help augment his preacher's income, and there never seemed to be enough money to get the things, as the good reverend put it, "that needed fixin' fixed," but, overall, he felt the Lord was good to them. It wasn't about money at Hillside Baptist Church, because nobody who belonged to the church had any.

Joshua felt their poverty a blessing. When it came to being naked and poor in front of the Lord on the day of judgment, the members of Hillside Baptist Church would have a clear advantage over a lot of other folks. They were already poor, figured Joshua. It's just the naked part that would take some getting used to.

The worship service that followed was an explosion of faith. Voices were raised in a chorus of devotion that could have drowned the roar of a jet engine. The congregation threw themselves into the service just as Reverend Brown threw himself into his sermon. This week, he talked about the talkers again. Those Christians who make themselves all too visible and hold themselves as all too holy. Daniel thought the good Reverend Brown might have known his father personally, so well was he describing him.

After the service Joshua invited them to his home for a good old-fashioned country breakfast. Daniel and Ayse readily accepted. After attending a brief social after service, they followed Joshua back to his place. As they eased up the hill where Joshua's trailer was parked, Daniel noted that it looked like most of the other mobile homes they'd driven by along the way, only a bit tidier.

Once out of the cars, Joshua's youngest, Melissa, came over to visit with Sarah. Melissa was now fourteen years old and an honor student at Milledgeville High. She asked Sarah if she had ever skipped rope before. Sarah said no, but she'd like to. Within minutes, with Ibraham on one end of an old clothesline, and Melissa on the other, Sarah was giving it a try.

✪

Breakfast was ready within the hour, a country breakfast, with grits, cornbread, sausage and eggs. It was enjoyed by all. Afterward, Ayse and Mariah went about the business of cleaning the kitchen, while Daniel and Joshua took a stroll. It was warm under the midday sun, but a cool spring wind kept it pleasant. As they walked, the two of them talked. There was much to talk about.

"I've brought something for the church, JJ."

"You gonna run us some free ads up in Atlanta? I don't think that'll bring in too many more worshipers down here next Sunday, do you?"

"No, it's not a free ad, JJ. It's just a little something to help you get by. Maybe by the time we come back next year you can put on a new coat of paint and fix those damaged boards near the top of the steeple."

Daniel paused and pulled his billfold out of his back pocket. In it, neatly folded in half, was a personal check. He handed it to Joshua without unfolding it.

"That's mighty kind of you, Daniel. Our congregation is a mite on the poor side. Paintin' and fixin's right expensive. I'll be sure to get this check to Reverend Brown."

As he spoke, Joshua unfolded the check. He was shocked to see it was for five thousand dollars. As much as he wanted to, Joshua didn't say anything. He grinned at Daniel, as if understanding this was Daniel's way of thanking God for saving him from the belly of the whale, then he slipped the check into his pant's pocket. The two of them went back to their walk.

"Are those tomato plants?" asked Daniel.

"Yeah, we got them in just 'bout a month back. Every one of those yellow flowers should end up bein' a fine-tastin' tomato in six, maybe eight weeks' time."

"You've got nice looking gardens, JJ."

"Me and the wife work on 'em pretty regular. It was easier when all the kids were still at home, but the four of us still do okay with 'em. I think after the last two fledge on outta here, Mariah and I are going to cut back some. There's too much garden here for two people to handle without the children."

They eventually returned to the small, covered porch Joshua had added to his mobile home. Beneath it, in the comfort of the shade, sat two old rocking chairs and a number of weathered pressed-back chairs. Daniel and Joshua took up residence in the two rockers and relaxed, watching the Georgia sun bake the red clay as if it were in some immense kiln that never quite made it harden.

Joshua continued. "Tell me 'bout your father, Daniel. Have you forgiven him yet?"

Daniel became defensive. "I can't do it, JJ, I just can't. He tried to get me fired from Mosby & Simms some years back. He tried, but fortunately, he failed. Clay won't let go of it, and I don't think he deserves to be forgiven."

Joshua didn't respond. He sat there watching as his two girls brought Ibraham and Sarah back from a hike through the surrounding woods. Joshua was thinking, choosing his next words carefully.

"You know the story of Daniel, don'cha?"

"Yes, of course."

"Then you remember that Nebuchadnezzar, angry with Daniel, cast him into the lions' den to be eaten. Do you remember what happened next?"

"The lions couldn't eat him, because an angel of God had shut the mouths of the lions. The king rejoiced when he found Daniel alive and well the next morning."

"You're in that den to this very day, Daniel. The Lord has surrounded you with His angels but He grows weary at your own self-righteousness. Until you forgive your father, these beasts stand at the ready to consume you.

"You must take it upon yourself, and soon. Leave your father's malice behind you once and for all. Forgiveness isn't what you think it is, Daniel. Forgiveness is a tool. It's the crowbar by which we are freed from the enslavement of our ill-tempered feelin's. Freed from the endless cycle of revenge. So long as you hold on to your anger and bitterness, you shall never be free of those lions.

"That check you just handed to me for the church. It means an awful lot to us. It'll fix all the broken windows, repaint the outside and put a fresh shine on the sanctuary, but it's worthless when compared to the value of forgiveness. Ten thousand checks mean nothing when measured against the value of saying 'I forgive you, Father.'

"Remember when they asked Jesus how many times we must forgive? *'Seven times seventy'*, that's what Jesus answered them. *'Seven times seventy.'*"

Daniel sat in the rocking chair beside his friend and remained silent. He recalled the last conversation he had had with Joshua before leaving the hospital. A conversation not unlike the one they were having today. Daniel didn't want to discuss it back then any more than he did now. But in his heart, he knew there was truth in Joshua's advice.

They didn't speak again about his father. They spoke about life in Atlanta, about where the kids were going to school, about Joshua's plan to retire in ten more years, after he'd put his thirty-five years in. They passed the time like inherited money, spending it freely and without concern. Two friends enjoying an afternoon together on the front porch of life.

Inside, the ladies poured some iced tea and took it to their husbands, still sitting on the veranda. Mariah and Ayse joined the men and the four of them whiled away the remainder of the afternoon in small talk and laughter. Moments together as sweet as the tea. The children kept busy in the yard, playing tag, chasing the chickens.

Around four, Daniel announced that it was time they head back to Atlanta. He had a big day tomorrow and the children had to go to school. He said they would try to make it down next spring, if not sooner, and invited the Taylor family to visit them in the Vinings. Farewells were said, and hugs were exchanged. The afternoon came to a close with the shutting of car doors and a trail of red dust down the long, winding driveway.

One Year Later

Daniel couldn't let go of his conversation with Joshua about forgiveness. Hardly a day passed without Daniel contemplating that call to his father. It had been over a decade since he had heard Clay's voice, and the thought of hearing it again, for any reason, filled him with dread.

But Daniel wasn't a young man any longer. He was a partner in a successful advertising firm, the father of two beautiful children and the husband to one of the kindest, most tolerant Muslim women in the world. He had a large, four-bedroom home in one of the best subdivisions in Atlanta. There were two cars in the garage and he earned a salary well into six figures, not including bonuses. He was a man now, and he knew the time was drawing near for him to confront the lions.

He made the call on a Tuesday morning. It was in the spring, a year since Joshua had advised him to do it. Daniel was in his office, his door closed. Mary Beth was instructed to hold all calls. This was a conversation that could not be interrupted.

As he picked up his telephone, Daniel noticed his hand was trembling. He reached down and dialed his father's office number, a number that had not changed or been forgotten by his only son. Daniel knew the best time to reach his father was in the morning, before meetings and appointments took him into the workings of the North Macon Baptist Church. It was nine-fifteen.

The phone rang twice before his father's secretary picked it up. He didn't recognize the woman's voice, unaware Rose had retired two years ago. He was a stranger to the woman who answered the phone, as she was to him.

"Good morning, North Macon Baptist Church. How may I help you?"

"Pastor Harris, please."

"May I ask who's calling?"

"Daniel Harris, his son."

The receptionist paused for a minute. She didn't know Clay had a son. He'd never said anything to her about Daniel, though she'd seen Ruth on numerous occasions.

"I'll put you right through."

Daniel was put on hold while the receptionist made the connection. The background music consisted of an overly orchestrated rendition of *Wayfaring Stranger*. Ironic that this particular song is playing, thought Daniel as he listened and waited.

His father's voice, sounding older but just as forbidding, interrupted the song, "This is Clayton Harris. Who's calling?"

Daniel froze. He wanted to hang up. He wanted to run away, just like he had been running all these years. But he didn't. He thought of Joshua, said a prayer, and answered his father's question.

"It's Daniel, your son."

"I told you never to call, or speak to me again. I can have you prosecuted for making this call. You're aware of that, aren't you?"

"Go ahead, Dad, report me to the authorities if it helps. But could you please hear me out before sending the sheriff up here to Atlanta."

Clay didn't respond. Daniel continued with his dialogue before his father could hang up.

"I called to say I forgive you. To tell you that I no longer hold any of it against you, and that..."

Clay interrupted his boy, mid-sentence. "Forgive me! You've got a lot of nerve calling me here at the church to pontificate on forgiving me. I'm the one who's got the forgiving to do, and I'm not about to forgive you. Not for what you've done, Daniel. Not now and not ever.

"You disobeyed your father the day you wed that woman. I had warned you, Daniel Mark Harris, that there would be repercussions, but you wouldn't listen. You've no right to be calling me today, telling me you've forgiven me. I haven't done anything wrong. All I've done is kept my word. I'm the one who should be doing the forgiving here, and I'm not inclined to do so. Not so long as I walk God's earth."

Daniel took a deep, studied breath and responded, "That's not important, Dad. It's not about you, it's about me. Joshua was right. I just want you to know I'm praying for you. I forgive you and, in time, maybe I can even find a way to love you again. That's why I called."

Clayton Aaron Harris was furious. For once in his life he couldn't find the words, or the scripture, to define his anger. His wrath was so overpowering it wanted to crawl outside himself and rise up like some monster. Crawl out and lash at his son like a poisonous snake filled with venom. He screamed back at his boy.

"Don't you ever, ever call me again, Daniel! Do you understand me, Son? AM I MAKING MYSELF CLEAR?"

"I won't call again. I don't have to. Goodbye, Father."

Clay Harris slammed the receiver down forcefully enough to have cracked the phone in half. He could not believe his son's nerve.

Daniel put the receiver down gently. He felt it fly away from him — the bitterness, the anger, the resentment. He knew immediately that Joshua was right. The angel took his hand and led him safely out of the lion's den. The beasts looked longingly at Daniel as he left their lair. They would never be able to devour him.

God's grace poured into him. He smiled to himself and said a long, silent prayer for Clay. Daniel was free.

Istanbul

It was dark. It was as if the night had swallowed the world as the 767 soared above the waters of the Atlantic. But those waters, wind-driven by gales unseen, had also disappeared into the void. All that existed in the world were the flashing lights at the end of each wing, and the dimmed cabin of the airplane. Everything else had vanished.

Sarah's head lay on Ayse's lap. As Sarah slept, Ayse ran her slender fingers through her daughter's fine, black hair. The motion soothed her, and put Ayse in a reflective, thoughtful mood. She had wanted to make this trip years earlier, but there was always a reason to delay her journey home. Now, with Sarah turning nine, and Ibraham thirteen, it was time to show her family the fabled city of her youth — the city of Istanbul.

The kids were excited. From the day Ayse had taken them to the local photo shop for their passport photos three months ago, Ibraham and Sarah had talked of little else than their upcoming voyage to Turkey. They read books about the Byzantine Empire, the Crusades and the Ottoman sultans. They practiced their Turkish with their mother for hours on end, ecstatic at the thought that they could soon speak with other Turkish children, hear other voices talking in their private language.

Daniel as well had been swept up in the anticipation of their forthcoming journey. He had never been overseas before and he was ready. Business was brisk, and he knew that leaving for three weeks might cost Mosby, Simms & Harris some billings, but it didn't matter. It was time to pay homage to his wife's world, and that was all Daniel focused on. It was time to meet Ayse's family, to explore the city of her youth. He could dive back into his work and make up for lost business upon his return.

As his son, Ibraham, buried himself in a hand-held computer game, and the world outside vanished into a starlit abyss at thirty-five-thousand feet, Daniel tried to imagine what Istanbul would be like. It was so old, so steeped in human history, that it was difficult to compare to the youthful, vibrant Atlanta. Still, there remained a kinship between these two cities that Ayse had spoken of many times over the years. They were good cities, filled with a tolerance and energy that could not be denied.

Ayse had grown to love Atlanta. It was the new South. She seldom felt awkward or out of place wearing her head scarf or her conservative fashions. Elsewhere in Georgia, dressed like a Muslim, she would garner looks and comments due to the small-town nature of the rural South. But in Atlanta, no one took note. Amidst the saris, the perforated punks, the GQ businessmen, and the threadbare clothes of the street people, Ayse was just a part of the matrix. No one singled her out, nor would they have cause to. She belonged to the sense of urbanity Atlanta had embraced.

Istanbul too, had its own sense of self. But the blood in its veins ran deeper and richer than did the young, almost teenage energy of Atlanta. Istanbul was drenched in history. Emperors, dynasties, wars and palaces collided in this montage of a city. Cultures rich with their own sense of pride found niches in the narrow streets amid the taxis and Turks. Coptic and Greek Orthodox churches mingled with multi-domed mosques, Jewish synagogues stood beside Roman ruins. Pagan and sacred, pious and profane melted together in Istanbul, standing like a lone sentinel between the mysteries of Asia and the reason of Europe.

Ayse loved Istanbul. This was her town, stretched like a long, bejewelled necklace around the rich blue currents of the Bosporus. She longed to see it once again.

As night wore on, Daniel and Ayse followed their children into sleep. Daylight would come soon enough. Before falling asleep, Ayse knew she would not see her flight attendant on this voyage. There was no need for her at this juncture in her life. Everything was settled now. Even their families, save Clay, had come to accept the marriage. Rebecca would come to take the children for a long weekend three, sometimes four times a year. Mustapha would visit every other year, and once Daniel's sister Ruth had actually stopped by for a visit. She arrived with Chet and their only son, Jason. God had been good to them, and for this Ayse was grateful. She fell asleep thinking this, knowing that God is indeed merciful.

❂

It was late afternoon when the plane landed at Ataturk Airport. Abdul had come alone to greet them at the airport. Ayse and Abdul hugged warmly, then she introduced her children to him in Turkish. The children responded in Turkish and Abdul replied with kind words of encouragement and a beaming smile. He took their carry-on bags and whisked them off to the Lexus, while they went to the carousel to collect their suitcases.

Mustapha and Elif were awaiting their arrival at their home in Bebek. A large, Turkish feast was planned for dinner and Elif wanted to make certain it was prepared to perfection.

Once in the car, and heading down the highway to Bebek, Daniel realized he was actually there, in Istanbul. After the long flight, and a virtually sleepless night, Daniel had to pinch himself to make certain it wasn't a dream. As Abdul wound his way through the heavy traffic on Kennedy Caddesi toward Beyoglu, Daniel's eyes feasted on the views of the Sea of Marmar and the sights and sounds of the city.

They passed the fish market, with turbot hanging above bins brimming with shrimp and langostino, smelt and fresh lobster. A fish market unlike any Daniel had seen before, attesting to the bounty of the surrounding seas. He caught glimpses of Russian freighters, pouring in and out of the Black Sea laden with grain, coal, and cargo bound for distant ports. Old, rusty ships — weathered and pounding against the seas long beyond their years.

As they approached the edge of the Old City, Daniel saw street vendors and roadside vegetable hucksters. Their wooden carts filled to overflowing with cherries, oranges and strange fruits and vegetables Daniel didn't recognize. He saw old men selling souvenirs and young men selling prayer rugs and hand-woven carpets. They drove past the ancient, crumbling walls of the city, built by Theodosius II during the Byzantine era. He saw Yudikule Castle, with its seven limestone towers overlooking the Bosphorus, standing as a stalwart reminder of Istanbul's war-torn past.

High on the hill, above the oldest section of the city, stood the resplendent Blue Mosque. Its six minarets soaring skyward as the late afternoon sun drenched them in a golden wash. Daniel remembered reading about its controversial history. Built by Sultan Ahmet I, it caused a great uproar during its construction, when the Islamic world feared it would rival, if not usurp, the great mosque of Mecca. As Daniel studied it from the rear seat, he found its beauty beyond words.

They crossed the Golden Horn on the Galata Bridge, lined with bearded old men holding fishing rods and smoking Turkish tobacco. Daniel and the children saw a few of them reel in small, silvery sardines. Once across the horn, they followed the flowing Bosporus, passing the sprawling Dolmabahçe Palace, and the high, impenetrable walls that protected it. Shortly thereafter, they left the main road and began to climb the hills bordering the Bosporus, making their way toward Bebek and the house where Ayse was raised.

It is all a dream, even though it's real, decided Daniel. The children, his wife, Abdul, the city itself were all part of this dream. Like Joshua had said, it is the dream of my life, God's dream.

❂

Mustapha had been waiting anxiously. As Abdul pulled in, Mustapha came out the side entrance of the house, with Elif behind him. He hugged his daughter tightly as soon as she got out of the Lexus, following with warm embraces for the children and Daniel. He introduced Elif to Daniel and the two grandchildren. The children joined in the celebration, speaking to their grandmother in their neophyte Turkish.

Dinner was amazing — skewered lamb served with seasoned rice and eggplant dishes whose names Daniel could not pronounce. They shared an after-dinner drink of a licorice flavored liquor named Raki, or lion's milk, as Mustapha called it, and enjoyed honey-sweetened baklava for dessert. Ayse sat across from Daniel and kept a smile on her face that was so bright it rivaled the glow of the rising moon. She was glad to be home again.

❂

The time flew by like doves in search of paradise. They visited all the tourist sites and many special places only a native would know of — small, unpretentious mosques where Ayse's family had worshiped Allâh. Mosques that had only rarely seen an errant tourist. They visited the graveyard where Ayse's grandmother and grandfather were buried. They took in parks, museums and shops uncountable.

With Abdul driving, they took the car to Isnik, to see the famous cobalt blue tiles of that city. They stayed the night, then continued southward to the ruins at Ephesus, where Paul brought the Gospels of Christ to the Greeks. There, the ruins of ancient Greece mingled with Roman and Byzantine remains. They walked amid the empty seats of the Greek amphitheater where the plays of Euripides and Sophocles were once performed.

The children loved every moment of it. They practiced their curious Turkish, curious because it held traces of a Southern accent, and spoke at length to anyone who would lend them an ear. They played tag amidst the facades and fluted columns. They never tired.

Near the end of their vacation, they spent two days shopping at the Grand Bazaar and the many boutiques around the Sultanahmet. Daniel bought gifts for friends and family while Ayse purchased dozens of exotic spices she would be unable find anywhere else except in the massive spice market of the Old City.

As the last day approached, a sadness descended upon all of them. Elif promised to visit America soon, so close had she and the grandchildren become. They had one huge, family farewell together. Both of Ayse's brothers, their wives and families were invited. Even Abdul and his family were asked to join them in this farewell feast that ran late into the evening.

The next day they were at the airport early. It would be a long flight back, chasing the daylight the entire flight home. They arrived in Atlanta in the early evening after making a connection in England. Their journey over, their suitcases stuffed with gifts, they left the intrigue and romance of Istanbul behind them. Weary, jet-lagged and spent, they were all glad to be back home.

On the Answering Machine

*T*he seventh message on Daniel's home answering machine was from Rebecca. As Daniel listened to it for the second time, he could clearly discern the quavering in his mother's voice as she spoke, "Daniel, this is your mother. I know you won't get this until you return, and I hope it's not too late. It's your father. He's had a heart attack. It happened on Wednesday night, after service.

"We had no idea it was coming. He's stable now but the doctors think that the incident may have caused permanent damage to his heart. He still doesn't want to see you, but I thought you'd want to know. Call me right away when you get back from Turkey. Please."

There were thirty-four messages in all. Some for the kids, some for Ayse and any number about business. To Daniel, none really mattered but the seventh. Upon replaying and hearing it for a second time, Daniel sank into the chair sitting beside the phone in the family room. Everything reopened before him, like some wound that would not heal.

His emotions took hold of him, retracing the heartbreaking history of their strained relationship. From the heated debates of high school to their last conversation together, with his father hanging up on him in a fit of rage. Daniel remembered, for the first time in years, the metal grating pulling free from the wall when he stepped off the edge of the bed. He recalled his will to die.

Here, he recognized, was yet another test of his resolve to forgive his father and rise above the mundane. Perhaps the final test, thinking his father might already have died, already left this land of the quick — this place of sticks and bricks.

He picked up the phone and called his mother, his left hand shaking visibly as he dialed.

"Hello," said Rebecca upon answering the phone.

"Hi, Ma, it's me. I got your message. How is he?"

"Oh, Daniel!"

Rebecca burst into tears. Her sobbing stretched across the phone lines and came to rest on Daniel's shoulders as if she were in the room with him. Her pain was laid bare, and her son tried to comfort her as she wept.

"It'll be okay, Mom. I love you. The kids love you. They talked about Dad and you all the while we were in Turkey. They wished you were there with us, but they know the situation. How's he doing?"

"Not well," answered Rebecca, regaining a semblance of composure. "He's very sick, Daniel. He's back home, but it's so hard for me to see him this way."

"What happened?"

"It was after a Wednesday night service, just a few days after you had left for Turkey. He had been in an agitated state all day, and during dinner I told him to calm down, but you know how stubborn he is. Well, his sermon that night was on false gods, and he was on fire, preaching like I've never seen him preach before. He was almost hysterical.

"Maybe it had something to do with your going to visit Turkey, but he lashed out at Islam with a vengeance. He called Mohammed the great Satan. He reminded all of us that the Jihad would not end until every Muslim had been converted to the teachings of Jesus. It was so intense that afterward, several of the parishioners came up to me and said something about it. They felt it was uncalled for, and asked what had gotten into Clay of late.

"I told them he'd been overworked and in need of a vacation. I made up excuses for his sermon while he remained in his office, not in any mood to mingle with his congregation. That's where it happened, around nine. He was busy working on Sunday's sermon when the heart attack struck.

"I found him. I couldn't see him when I walked into the office but I could hear him gasping for air. He had fallen off his chair and was collapsed on the floor behind his desk. It was horrible. We called the ambulance and they rushed him off to Macon Northside Hospital. After two hours in the emergency room, they got him stabilized."

"What's his condition like now?"

"He's not well. The doctors are quite sure his heart's been damaged and there are going to be complications. His prognosis isn't good, Daniel. We're going in tomorrow for some more tests. He tires quickly and he's retaining water. They keep telling me he has a condition called cardiomyopathy."

"Is there anything I can do to help, Mom? Anything at all."

"Pray for him, Daniel. I've asked him if he won't change his mind and see you, knowing how sick he is, but he says he wouldn't think of it. He told me he's going to take this to his grave, Daniel. He told me to tell you he will look down on you in hell someday, and that he doesn't want to see you or your wife."

"What about the Grandkids?"

"I know we were planning to have them over on Labor Day, but I think we should hold off. Clay's bedridden and he looks very ill. I think seeing him like this wouldn't be good for the children.

"The doctors are telling me there are some new drugs that might help, but they need to do some additional testing before administering them. Some diuretics, and some kind of inhibitors that will help him lose some of the water he's retaining. He can't have anything with salt in it, or it could kill him.

"I'll call you in a few weeks after the testing's completed. If they can get him stabilized, I think I can drive to Atlanta and pick up the kids for a long weekend after school starts. You don't mind, do you?"

"No. You know Ayse and I love the fact that you both enjoy the children. At least there's some connection between us. I'll sit down with Ibraham and Sarah tonight and tell them what's happened to Grandpa. I know they'll want to see him as soon as he's well enough.

"Are you taking care of him by yourself?"

"No, the doctor's insisted we have a full-time nurse stay with us until he's prescribed medication and Clay's health improves. She's been fabulous. He's having a hard time sleeping because his lungs keep filling with fluid. He has to sit up most of the time. It's bad, Daniel, and I'm really worried about him."

"Ayse and I will keep him in our prayers."

"I wish he'd let you see him. I know there's still a part of him that wants to let go of it all, but he's so set in his ways. He loves the children though, Daniel, and I'm glad you don't mind letting them visit."

"I'll drive them down personally as soon as you feel he's up to it."

"Thanks, Daniel."

"I love you, Mom. Goodbye."

"I love you too. Goodbye."

✪

Later that evening, with the children still exhausted from their journey, and Ayse by their side, Daniel told them what had happened to Grandpa while they were in Istanbul. Ibraham and Sarah wept in their mother's arms as they heard the news. Sarah, after Daniel had finished, asked, "Is Grandpa going to die?"

Daniel was caught off guard with the directness of his daughter's question. He found himself becoming teary-eyed and afraid. After a minute had passed, he answered his daughter. "Yes," he said. "Unless there's a miracle."

Three Angels

It was winter. The fall had come and gone without notice. The holidays were spent in suspension, as Daniel waited on word of his father, knowing his parting was imminent. The children, Ibraham and Sarah, had visited Macon twice since returning from Turkey. Once at Thanksgiving, and once between Christmas and New Years. They returned to tell Daniel what he and Ayse already knew — Grandpa was very sick.

Rebecca had called a week ago to let Daniel know they were moving Clay, by ambulance, to Emory University Hospital for further testing and, if the tests went well, some new, experimental drug therapy. The prognosis was still very grim, and Rebecca wept openly with her son as she described Clay's condition. His lungs were filling with fluid hourly. Every breath was labored.

She had arranged for Clay to stay at the John W. Rollins Pavilion. She wanted him to have every comfort possible, and spared no expense. He would be staying at one of the six suites on the top floor, with the finest doctors and staff in the South. She sensed he wouldn't leave the hospital alive and felt it was the least she could do for the man she loved.

Daniel listened while his mother confided in him. Rebecca wanted nothing more in the world than for Clay to make amends before his passing, but she had stopped trying to change her husband's intractable decision. Clay was stubborn and proud, and wouldn't even allow Rebecca to broach the topic again. Daniel was already dead as far as Clay was concerned. It made no sense at all to discuss it. Dead and buried.

It made Rebecca's feelings of sadness run deeper. Her son told his mother not to be sad. He had long since forgiven his father and he held no malice in his heart for anything Clay had done, or would do to him. The Lord had delivered Daniel from the lion's den and he would never set foot in it again. He told Rebecca Ayse and he prayed for Clay, and hoped he would find peace in his final days. Ayse prayed to Allâh. Daniel to the Lord. The children prayed to both, knowing in their innocence God and Allâh are one and the same, made separate and disparate only by the semantics of a world filled with men like Clayton Aaron Harris. Christian, Jewish and Muslim men.

Before she said goodbye, Rebecca asked if she could come up to the Vinings the following weekend to take the children over to Emory for what could well be their final visit with their grandfather. They brought great joy to him, and seeing them would lift his spirits. Daniel, knowing this, wouldn't think of withholding his permission for their visit. He held no hatred toward his father — he sought no revenge.

"Of course they can visit him at Emory," he replied. "When do you want to pick them up?"

They made the arrangements. Rebecca would pick them up at nine in the morning and return them by noon. Daniel invited Rebecca to have lunch with them afterward, but she declined, telling her son it would be better if they waited until after. Daniel understood. It was time to wait.

❁

By Saturday the weather had turned cold, not unlike that winter fourteen years ago, when Daniel and Ayse first met. Atlanta had already endured two horrific ice storms and the metro forecast called for a dusting of snow that Saturday morning, followed by gradual clearing and a blow of frigid arctic air. The trees atop Kennesaw Mountain were, in the ebb and flow of the changing seasons, laid bare.

Daniel and Ayse had considered calling Rebecca and telling her she should reschedule the visit, but after realizing there might not be another time to reschedule, they decided to let it be. The roads would be sanded and salted and Rebecca was a good driver. Having the children see their grandfather once more far outweighed the threat of a slippery dusting of snowfall. God would watch over them and keep them safe.

At ten after nine, Rebecca rang the doorbell of the four-bedroom Colonial. It was snowing lightly, and the yard was covered with an inch of pure white powder. Ibraham and Sarah were ready to go, though nervous about going to a large hospital like Emory. Ayse told them not to worry, that it was the best place for their grandfather to be and he was receiving the finest care in Georgia. She helped Sarah put on her red coat while Daniel and his mother talked in the foyer. Ayse could only guess at their conversation, but knew by the somber tones of their voices that it was sadness being discussed. Terrible sadness.

Ibraham put his jacket on and joined everyone in the foyer beside the front door. Soon, the three of them went out into the falling snow and climbed into Rebecca's vehicle. Daniel was glad his mother still drove an SUV. The snow seemed less threatening because of it.

They arrived at the hospital's parking ramp forty-five minutes later. The snow was still falling and the north wind was picking up as the arctic blast pushed southward toward Florida. By Sunday morning the high would be in the teens and, combined with the wind chill, the temperature would feel like it was below zero. It was going to be cold, even for Atlanta.

They parked on the third floor, and Sarah made note of the fact that the floor was called the Gull floor, telling her Grandmother it would help them remember where to find the car afterward. Rebecca smiled at her granddaughter as the three of them climbed into the elevator, glad to have such a thoughtful grandchild.

The elevator stopped on the first floor, one story above the ground level. From there, the three walked down a glass-enclosed overpass that wound from the parking lot, across the street and directly into the hospital. Rebecca had made this walk every day since Clay had arrived a week ago. Today, because of the wind and the blowing snow, she was glad they had built the enclosed overpass. Glad to be out of the elements.

Just before the overpass crossed the street, there was one last stairway that led down to a set of doors opening to the sidewalk below. As they passed the stairway, Sarah unexpectedly let go of her grandmother's hand, ran down the stairs and pried open the clear glass door at the bottom.

"Where on earth are you going?" asked Rebecca as Sarah paused with the door cracked halfway open.

"You'll see, Grandma. Just stay right there and you'll see. It's a present for Grandpa," she said as she went out the door and into the chill of winter.

Just beyond, in a small wooded area across the driveway leading up to a wing of the Children's Hospital, Sarah stopped and looked back at her brother and Rebecca, still standing in the overpass, watching her. She waved, then, with her spirited enthusiasm, she laid down in the light dusting of snow and made a single snow angel. Once completed, Sarah took two steps toward another patch of untouched snowfall, laid back down and made a second. The snow wasn't deep, and the brown grass lay exposed beneath the wings and legs of the two matching angels.

Rebecca watched as Sarah got back up, brushed off the back of her coat the best she could, and return to the entry leading up to the overpass. The snow continued falling. When Sarah reached the two of them in the hallway, Rebecca turned to Sarah and said, "They're beautiful, Sarah. But how do you know Grandpa will be able see your angels from his room?"

"I know," answered Sarah. "Do you think he'll like them?"

"He'll love them," answered Rebecca.

✵

Apart from at their births, Ibraham and Sarah had never been in a hospital. They were blessed with good health, as were their parents, so the sights and sounds of a busy hospital like Emory were unfamiliar to them. They watched in amazement as the hallways bustled with doctors, patients, nurses and aides. Sarah took Rebecca's hand again as they entered the elevator to the fifth floor of the C-wing where Clay was staying. The elevator, like the hallway that led to it, was crowded with visitors and staff, all of them in a hurry.

When the elevator opened on the top floor, they could see the entrance to the John W. Rollins Pavilion. Its set of fine-grained mahogany doors stood in marked contrast to the plain off-white doors throughout the remainder of the hospital. Once through the wide, double doors they entered a carpeted hallway. It looked more like a hotel than a hospital. The brass fixtures, the decorative light sconces, the tray ceiling all added to a sense of Southern elegance.

"Is this where Grandpa's staying?" asked Sarah as they walked down the hallway.

"Yes, it is."

"It sure is fancy," remarked Ibraham.

"Yes, it sure is," confirmed their grandmother.

They checked in at the nurse's station, then proceeded down the hallway to Suite Five. The three of them entered the adjoining sitting room. Rebecca told her grandchildren to be seated while she went in to see if Clay was ready. Ibraham and Sarah obediently sat on the sofa and waited. Rebecca knocked gently on the door to announce her arrival and quietly disappeared into the adjacent bedroom. Sarah picked up an old issue of *Southern Living* and started idly flipping through it, admiring the pretty pictures. Ibraham got up and looked out the window, checking to see if Sarah's angels could be seen.

"I can see them, Sarah!" he exclaimed. "The snow hasn't covered them up yet."

Sarah put down her magazine and went to the window. She looked down from the fifth floor and there, in the small wooded area a hundred yards away, lay her two snow angels, looking lonely amid the rush of traffic and the steady parade of Emory University students and faculty walking by.

"They look lovely, don't they, Ibraham?"

"They look beautiful, Sarah. It was a good idea."

While they peered out the window, Rebecca reentered the sitting area. She came up behind them and said, "What are you two up to?"

"Sarah's angels. Can you see them, Grandma?" asked Ibraham, pointing as he spoke.

"Oh, yes. They're so pretty. Come now, Grandpa says he's ready to see you. You know that he's very sick, children, and don't let his condition frighten you. He has to have those tubes in his nose to breathe. His heart isn't working right anymore, so his feet and legs are swollen. I know you'll understand."

"Don't worry, Grandma. Dad told us all about it. He said Grandpa was probably going to die soon. Is that true?" asked Ibraham.

She looked at her grandson, tears gathering in her eyes and answered, "Yes, I'm afraid it's true, but he wants to see the two of you again and he's glad you've decided to come visit him. Now let's go in and say hello."

The three of them entered a short hallway with a bathroom off to one side. Once in Clay's room, Sarah and Ibraham noted a funny odor but said nothing to their grandmother about it. Grandpa was sitting upright in his bed, and as they entered the room, a huge smile adorned his face. He looks different, thought Sarah.

Clay looked ill. Very ill. His color was pale, nearly gray, and his face had a worn, tired look to it that spoke of his pain. A plastic oxygen tube ran in through his nostrils and an electric monitor was attached to his chest. His breathing was shallow and labored . He could hardly speak.

"Come over to me, my sweethearts," whispered Clay. "You look so pretty in red, Sarah."

Ibraham and Sarah went to the opposite side of Clay's bed. Sarah leaned over, careful not to disturb his heart monitor, and gave her Grandfather a hug. Ibraham stood beside her, tears welling in his eyes. He knew his father was right — Grandpa was dying.

"Do you want to see what I've made for you?" asked Sarah.

"Yes, of course."

"You'll have to come to the window to see them," she added.

"Well, I'll need some help to do that."

Clay pushed a button located on the right side of his bed and a nurse entered the suite within a minute.

"What's the matter, Mr. Harris?"

"These are two of my grandchildren, Sarah and Ibraham. This is my private nurse, Mrs. Wilson."

"Hello, Mrs. Wilson," said Sarah.

"You can call me Nancy."

"Nancy," Clay interrupted, "Sarah has asked me to look at something she's made for me from the window. I have no idea what it is, but could you bring me a wheelchair so I can have a look."

"Certainly. I'll be back in a few minutes with one, Mr. Harris."

The nurse turned and left the room. The three of them made small talk until Nancy returned with a wheelchair. She wheeled it close beside Clay's bed and began the arduous task of getting him moved into it. She detached his oxygen hose and reattached it to a small tank beneath the seat of the wheelchair. The heart monitor was disconnected, as the nurse would remain in attendance so long as Clay was out of his bed. Should anything happen, Nancy would be there for him.

Rebecca helped, folding back the blankets covering her husband's swollen feet. Clay tried to step into the wheelchair himself, but couldn't. The nurse assisted him, and, after a few minutes, Clay, dressed in his flannel pajamas, was seated in the wheelchair. The nurse wheeled him to the window.

Sarah stood beside her grandfather and pulled back the gauze-like curtains that covered the windows. Once the curtains had been pulled away, she pointed down to the small wooded area where her angels were lying. "See them, Grandpa. I made them just for you."

"Snow angels, how beautiful," said Clay. "You know how much I love angels."

"Yes, Grandpa."

He looked back down and turned to ask Sarah, "One must be you, and the other one is Ibraham. Am I right?"

"Yes, one for each of us, but I made them both myself."

Clay turned away from Sarah. Ibraham had taken a seat on the other side of the room and Rebecca was standing next to the nurse beside him. He turned to the three of them, smiled warmly and said, "Aren't they wonderful."

"They're precious, Clay," said Rebecca, who was discreetly asking the nurse for an update on her husband's condition.

When Clay looked back into Sarah's eyes to thank her for making the snow angels, he found himself peering into her dark eyes only to discover they had been replaced by a light so brilliant that by contrast it would made the midday sun appear like a solitary candle on the darkest of nights. Time, as men measure it, ceased. Clay's heart pounded in fear. The world was held in divine suspension. An angel of God had arrived.

It was the angel the shepherds feared the night of His birth, the angel who had slain one hundred and eighty-five thousand Assyrians before the battle, the angel who drove Lucifer from the Kingdom of Heaven. Clay trembled, knowing there was a reason for this fearful apparition.

"Clayton Aaron Harris, minister of the Lord, do you see those two angels below?" asked a voice that spoke within. A voice that sounded deep and resonant, as though the earth itself were speaking.

"Yes," answered Clay in a humbled whisper, his eyes unable to break away from the light.

"Who are they?"

"Ibraham and Sarah."

"No, they are not. They are Daniel, your son, and Ayse, your daughter-in-law. They were not made by Sarah. They were made by the hand of God."

Clay wanted to cry out, but he could not break free from the aura of this being before him. Rebecca and the nurse noticed nothing. Sarah's soul was being held in safekeeping by the spirit possessing her. Ibraham stayed seated beside the bed. Only Clay could see the angel.

The angel pointed to the two-winged figures carved in the snow and continued, "I have been sent by God the most merciful. He forgives you your sins, and asks you to forgive those who have sinned against you. Death awaits you, Clayton Aaron Harris, and I have come to tell you this alone: If you do not forgive your son, his wife and yourself, and ask for their forgiveness in return, those will be the last angels you shall ever see."

Then, in an instant, the light was gone. The voice vanished. It vanished like a gust of wind racing across an empty field. Sarah's brown eyes reappeared, and when she looked at her Grandfather, she saw the look of fear in his face.

"Are you okay, Grandpa?"

The nurse, upon hearing the little girl's remark, rushed over to check on her patient. She took one look at Clay and knew something was wrong. His face was ghostly white, his eyes glossy and distant. He tried, but could not speak.

The nurse took his pulse only to find his ailing heart racing. She told him to calm down, to relax and went beside the bed to push the call button for assistance. Turning to Sarah, she said, "It would be better if you leave, I'm afraid all this excitement has been too much for your grandfather."

Rebecca, seeing the look on Clay's face, and not wanting the children to see what might be happening, ushered the children into the adjoining sitting room. They went without hesitation, sensing the nurse's alarm.

"Is Grandpa going to be all right?" asked Sarah, feeling responsible because of taking him out of his bed to see her snow angels.

"Grandpa's very sick, and I think all we can do for him now is pray," replied Rebecca, holding Sarah close to her as they sat on the sofa.

Ibraham walked over to the window while they waited. He looked down and, because the snow was beginning to drift in the gusting winds, he could barely see Sarah's angels any longer. They were disappearing. Two fragile snow angels fading into a blanket of white, transitory and fleeting, like life itself.

Inside Clay's room, three nurses were busy moving him from his wheelchair to his bed. They were checking his blood pressure, hooking up his oxygen and reattaching his heart monitor. They knew an incident like this could kill him, so fragile was his condition.

Ten minutes passed. When his heart rate returned to normal, Nancy told the other nurses it was safe for them to leave. A minute after they left, Clay spoke to his private nurse, his voice sounding raspy and uncertain as he did.

"Did you see it?"

The nurse didn't understand Clay's remark. "See what?"

"The angel."

The nurse went to the window and looked down. By now the blowing snow had covered every trace of Sarah's angels. Nancy turned to Clay and said, "No, they're gone, I never saw them. I'm sorry."

"No, not the snow angels, the real angel!" said Clay emphatically.

"What angel?"

"The one I saw, the one that spoke to me. Didn't you hear Sarah speak? Didn't you see the angel in her eyes?"

The nurse felt it must be the medication Clay was taking. It might be making him delusional. It was odd, she thought. He had been on the experimental medication a week and this was the first time he had ever shown any kind of reaction to it. She made a mental note to put this on his chart and mention it to his cardiologist.

"It's the medication you're taking, Mr. Harris. Sometimes it has side effects."

"No. It's not. It was real. The angel was inside Sarah, and it spoke to me. That's why I became so afraid. Her eyes, they shone like the sun. And the voice, it was so powerful. It was an angel of God. It appeared to me. Didn't you see it?"

The nurse didn't know what to say. She studied Clay's facial expressions as he spoke to her, hoping to see some sign of his delusional state, but found none. He seemed to think his apparition was real. She decided to bring his wife into the room and go to call his doctors.

"I'm going to get Rebecca; please try to calm yourself," said Nancy as she walked toward the adjoining room. When she entered the small sitting area, she found Ibraham watching the winter storm through the window, and Sarah and Rebecca quietly talking to each other on the sofa. Nancy interrupted them.

"Mrs. Harris, it's all right to come back in now. Your husband's stabilized. It would be best to leave the children here though, okay?"

"Thank you, Nancy. Sarah, Ibraham, you two stay here for a little while and I'll check on Grandpa."

"We'll be fine, Grandma," said Ibraham.

Nancy and Rebecca headed into Clay's room. Once in the short hallway, beside the bathroom, the nurse turned to Rebecca and spoke to her in a solemn tone.

"Your husband's had some kind of hallucination. I've seen this kind of thing before, when patients approach their passing, but he's very upset by it. He's convinced an angel's appeared to him. If you could stay with him for a few minutes, I'm going to make a few phone calls to his cardiologist and internist, to see if this might not be a reaction to the medications he's taking. Please try to calm him down, and use his panic button if you need to reach me."

"You say he saw an angel?"

"Yes, in Sarah."

"Oh my goodness!" said Rebecca in disbelief.

They went into the room and the nurse excused herself. Rebecca pulled up a chair beside her husband and smiled. He looked at her and asked, "Did you see it?"

"See what, my darling?"

"The angel."

"You mean the snow angels?"

"No, the third angel. The one that was in Sarah?"

Rebecca started stroking her husband's fine white hair. She didn't know what to say. She decided, for the moment at least, it was easier to go along with his delusion.

"Yes, I think I saw it. What did the angel say to you?"

"It said it was time to forgive them."

"Forgive who?"

"Daniel and Ayse."

Chills ran down Rebecca's spine. For years Rebecca had prayed for a change of heart from her husband. She had hoped and prayed that someday, before he no longer could, Clay would find it in him to let go of his bitterness. Could it be that God had answered her prayers? No, it wasn't possible. Was it?

"It's just your medication, Clay. The nurse is calling your doctors right now. It was just a dream."

"No, it wasn't a dream, Rebecca. I saw a light in Sarah's eyes. It was so bright it seemed like it would burn you to look at it, but it wasn't hot. And the voice, it was so deep. It sounded like a waterfall was speaking, or like the words were made from thunderclaps. Rebecca, it was Jehovah's angel. I know this to be true."

Rebecca didn't respond. There was no cause to argue with her husband. In a way, she realized it didn't matter. If it was an angel or a delusion, it told her husband something she felt he needed to hear. It was true, God had answered her prayers. The rest was up to Clay.

The Longest Night

"No, it wasn't an angel, Mr. Harris. We've seen these kinds of things before. Drug interactions can cause both auditory and visual hallucinations not unlike those you experienced this morning. We've got calls into our Glaxo and Pfizer representatives to report the incident and we're waiting to hear back from them as to how we should proceed from here.

"The drugs you are taking, at least two of them, are still in the experimental stages and we don't know all the various side effects they might produce. For the moment, we've reduced your dosage until we hear back from the pharmaceutical companies. I can't imagine what they'll say when we inform them one of the side effects they might keep an eye out for are angelic visitations. That will certainly get their attention."

The internist chuckled to himself as he spoke to Clay. The doctor found the incident humorous. Clay didn't. Whatever the cause of the apparition, it seemed all too real to allow Clay to dismiss it as an unanticipated side effect of something called loop diuretics and ACE inhibitors. The angel's ponderous voice still resonated within him, reverberating in his heart like the aftershocks of an earthquake.

"Could I have a reoccurrence?" asked Clay.

"You could, but it's unlikely now that we've reduced your dosage."

"It was so real."

"Yes, it's amazing what these side effects can be like. Over the years I've seen just about everything, although yours ranks right up at the top of my list. Now, if you don't have any more questions, I'll be off to my next patient."

"No, not for the moment. Thanks again, Dr. Clifford."

The doctor made some notations on Clay's chart, let go of one last chuckle, and left the room. Clay was alone for the first time since the incident. Rebecca had come back after taking the children home to the Vinings, and she was followed by the several nurses attending to him, a cardiologist, and lastly, the internist who had just left his room. Rebecca had told him she needed to drive to Macon tonight to get some things for her extended stay at a friend's house in Druid Hills. Aside from the nurses checking on him, the remainder of the night was his alone.

Clay kept thinking about what the angel had said. Fragments of Scripture kept running through his thoughts as he did. He remembered Matthew, Chapter 6, Verse 14, *"For if ye forgive men their trespasses, your heavenly Father will also forgive you."*

There was more; it continued on with Verse 15, *"But if ye forgive not men their trespasses, neither will your Father forgive your trespasses."*

But the angel said God would forgive me regardless of my decision. What did he mean by these will be the last angels I will ever see? Am I not going to Heaven? I've dedicated my life to Jesus, is this my just reward?

No, this is all nonsense. The doctors have assured me that there was no angel. It was nothing more than a drug interaction. A curious, bizarre side effect of my medications. To fret over this is nonsense. I'm not about to change anything. Daniel is a sinner, and he's married to a heathen who follows the ramblings of a false prophet. He and his wife can go to hell. There was no angel.

❂

Night fell. The winter winds slipped southward toward Savannah and the cold kept falling in behind them. Clay fell asleep just after ten. He watched a few minutes of the evening news and dozed off with the television still reporting on the news of the day. Wars in Africa and the Mideast. People murdering people. Political unrest, scandals and the usual melee of the human situation. All told in living color to a dying man asleep in his hospital bed after a day like none before it.

At two in the morning, Clay awoke, choking on the fluid in his lungs. He pushed his panic button and a night nurse was at his side in a minute. The care at the John W. Rollins Pavilion was everything it promised, thought Clay as the nurse helped him sit up straight to breathe. He was glad to be staying at Emory though in his heart he knew he would not leave here alive.

"Is that better?"

"Yes, it helps to sit up," said Clay, laboring to speak.

"You've had quite a day," remarked the nurse.

"Then you've heard?"

"If you're talking about the angel, everyone in the hospital's heard."

"Was it real?"

"I don't know. I've never seen an angel myself, but a friend of mine says she saw an angel once."

"Oh?" said Clay, suddenly not wanting to be left alone. "Could you please tell me about it."

"It was after her young son had died of cancer. She was having a terrible time, not understanding how God could have done such a thing to her and her family. She was very religious. She fell into a deep depression because of his unexpected death, to the point where she even lost her job. Her son was only seven when he died."

"What did the angel say to her?"

"She told me it happened late at night, like she was in a dream. The angel appeared in her bedroom, as she slept beside her husband, and told her the reason Matthew, that was her boy's name, was taken from her was that God needed him more than this world did. The angel told her to start living again, and that her son was in Heaven. Matthew was her only child so, even with the good news, it was very hard for her."

"Did she ever have any more children?"

"That's the strange part of this story, Mr. Harris. After she had Matthew, her doctor told her she could never have children again. There were complications with the pregnancy that made it impossible for her to conceive."

"And?"

"Two years after Matthew died, she had twins. A boy and a girl who are alive and healthy to this day. Whether the angel was a dream or the angel was real doesn't matter to her anymore. The birth of her twins was proof enough. God has a way of speaking to us, provided we're willing to listen."

"Yes, he does."

"Will you be okay?"

"I'll be fine."

"Buzz me if you need anything, Mr. Harris."

"You can call me Clay."

"Buzz me anytime, Clay."

The nurse left the room. Shortly thereafter Clayton Harris found himself afraid, unsure of what he should do. Was the angel real or was it just a chemical imbalance, a freak of nature created by a mixture of two experimental drugs? Then again, did it matter? Dream or not dream, side effect or divine visitation, shouldn't I listen to what the angel said to me?

Time passed slowly, almost imperceptibly. Clay could not see himself forgiving his son, not after all he had put him through. And Ayse? He had never spoken to her, not once, nor ever seen her. Even if he were to forgive them, there was no way his son would come to the hospital. It was too late. He would die and his embittered will would stand. Daniel and his spouse would receive nothing — not one penny.

A civil war raged in the heart of this dying old man. Forgive, punish. Bend, remain firm. Love, seek retribution. Give, keep. Clay could not rid his mind of the angel's voice. His thoughts turned back to an incident that happened long, long ago. To the night he found himself caught in that cold rain, and how he felt, brushing against death. Remembering that judgement was eminent.

Clay sought comfort from Scripture, as he had his entire life. At four in the morning he fell asleep, reciting the Lord's prayer as he did, *"Our Father, which art in Heaven, Hallowed be thy name. Thy kingdom come. Thy will be done, in earth, as it is in Heaven.*

"Give us this day our daily bread, and forgive us our debts, as we forgive our debtors. And lead us not into temptation, but deliver us from evil; For thine is the kingdom, and the power, and the glory, for ever. Amen."

Born Again and Again and Again

By morning, the snow had stopped falling. The clouds had been replaced by a clear sky whose shades of blue belonged more to the Caribbean than the freezing air it held. The snow angels were gone, their outlines vanished beneath the drifting snow. It was calm. Calm and bitter cold, with the temperature outside the hospital hovering at twenty-one degrees.

Clayton Harris was asleep, half upright, half falling over. Exhaustion had overtaken him. Just before succumbing to that weariness, he had decided to dismiss the angel as a delusion and remain steadfast in his estrangement from his son and daughter-in-law. It was the only decision he could make. He had told everyone, from his wife to his entire congregation, that he would never forgive Daniel for marrying that woman, and he felt obligated to himself, and to all the others, to uphold his oath of alienation.

If he conceded, he might be thought of as weak. Clayton Harris, more than anything else in the world, dreaded being thought of as weak. He would rather take his chances with death than admit to being wrong about a decision.

He awoke to the sounds of a nurse in his room, the same nurse who had spoken with him during the dark of the night. She had come in on her final rounds before punching out and going home. It was just before seven when Clay reopened his eyes and came back from a silent, dreamless sleep.

"Good morning, Clay," said the nurse. "Are you feeling better?"

Clay didn't respond. He looked at her with fatigued, weary eyes and shook his head. He was not feeling any better. He was dying of congestive heart failure and saw no reason to pretend anything would change. He shook his head as if to say no, he wasn't feeling well at all.

"I'm sorry. Is there anything I can do?"

"Yes," Clay replied, in a voice that confirmed his infirmity.

"What is it?"

"Tell me your story again. The one you told me last night."

"The one about my girlfriend with the twins?"

"Yes."

The nurse sat beside Clay, first helping to straighten him out and to check his feeble pulse, then to retell her tale. As she told it to Clay, she watched his eyes. They were fixed on her, looking for something he might have missed. Looking for a way out.

When she finished telling him about the birth of the twins, Clay spoke, "I haven't seen my son in fourteen years. I know, and you know, I'm dying. He has hurt me tremendously, but I don't know that I have the courage to call him."

Clay paused. The nurse saw the struggle he was having. It was painful for him to speak at this point, so weak were his fluid-filled lungs and failing heart.

"The angel I saw, the one you heard about, asked me to forgive him before I die. What should I do?"

The nurse, tears in her eyes, realized that as a cold Georgia sun ascended above Atlanta, a dying old man was confiding in her. She didn't have to think about her answer.

"I cannot tell you what to do, Mr. Harris. I know God works his wonders in ways we seldom understand. I don't know if you really saw that angel, nor, in a way, does it really matter. But as I sit here, I can see something lies dark and heavy on your heart. I can see it in your eyes, they're so tired, so filled with sadness.

"Jesus taught us it's not a sign of weakness to forgive. If it was, then God must be weak. We both know, as Christians, He is not. Life is short, for you, Clay, lying upon your deathbed, and for me, whose deathbed is but a few fleeting decades away. Whatever your son has done, however he has trespassed against you, doesn't matter. Were I you, I would call him here today and forgive him. That's what I would do. For in the end, Mr. Harris, love is all we have and all we leave behind."

Tears were streaming down Clay's ashen cheeks. He wept openly and without restraint. With his tired voice trembling like a child who had done something terribly wrong, he asked the nurse to pick up the phone beside his bed and call Rebecca.

She did as he asked, then held the receiver for him. He was too weak to hold a telephone to his ear. Rebecca answered her phone at their suburban home in north Macon.

"Hello."

"Rebecca, it's me."

She could tell Clay had survived another difficult night. She could hear the pain.

"How are you, my love?"

"Please help me, Rebecca. Please."

"Yes, anything, Clay. Anything at all."

"Call Bill Royer and tell him I need to see him this morning."

"Our attorney?"

Rebecca didn't understand why Clay would be asking to see his attorney at this point, the arrangements for her husband's passing having been made months ago when Clay was strong enough to put his affairs in order.

"Yes, I need him here today. And tell him to bring the will."

"Okay, I'll call him right away. But it's Sunday, and he's probably made plans."

"Tell him to change his plans."

Clay started coughing, and soon a thick red phlegm had formed along the edge of his mouth. The nurse, still beside him, wiped it away with a tissue. She smiled at Mr. Harris as she did this, approving of what he was doing.

"Then call Daniel," Clay said after catching his breath.

"Daniel?" Rebecca asked in disbelief.

"Yes. Tell him and Ayse, no, ask him and Ayse if they would be so kind as to come here to the hospital this morning."

"Are you sure, Clay? Do you understand what you are asking me to do? Are you feeling okay?"

Clay looked at the nurse sitting next to him and winked at her. An unexpected smile spread across his face and the nurse saw the darkness fly away from his deep blue eyes. She winked back.

"I haven't felt better in months. Now call my son and tell him that I wish to see him. I've been such a fool, Rebecca."

Rebecca didn't know what to say. All her prayers, her years of trying to make Clay understand what mattered and what didn't matter, were suddenly and unexpectedly answered.

"I'll call them. I'll have Bill in my car within the hour and we should be able to make it to Emory by ten. What do you want me to say to Daniel?"

"Tell him I was wrong. Tell him..." Clay began coughing again, but went on. "Tell him that I love him."

Rebecca burst into tears. Her hand went up to her mouth and she took a deep, short breath of disbelief. This was not happening. This could not be happening. But it was.

She felt as if she might collapse to the floor of the kitchen, her knees no longer able to support her.

She hung up the phone and went to the small kitchen table where they had eaten breakfast together for the past twenty-five years. There, she sat down and wept. It would be some time before she could call anyone. She was so moved by her husband's change of heart that she could not believe what he had told her. She prayed as she cried, and the prayers mixed with her tears like rain falling on a field of flowers.

Daniel, Ayse, Ibraham and Sarah arrived at Emory University Hospital a little after ten that Sunday morning. As they walked across the glass-enclosed walkway, Sarah pointed out where she had made her snow angels the day before. Now, only three inches of wind-sculpted snow remained, covering the dried grass beneath.

Ibraham led, retracing the route he and his sister had taken the day before. As they walked, he told his mother and father how fancy this hospital was, and how big Grandpa's room was.

On the fifth floor, they checked at the nurses' station to be certain they were really being allowed to see Clay, and the nurse said, "Yes, Mr. Harris is expecting you. He's in Suite Five, down the hallway on the left."

Daniel was nervous, unsure of what to expect. He held his wife's hand as they walked down the hallway toward his father's room. They did not speak, but a thousand words were said between them. Ayse had never met Clay, and wondered why they had this sudden, unanticipated request from him to come to Emory.

Ibraham and Sarah were glad Grandpa had asked to see their mother and father. They hadn't understood why he had never wanted to see them before. Daniel had tried to explain, as best he could to his children, that he and his father had had a fight a long time ago, and, in a way, they were still fighting. That's why they never spoke to each other and that was why they never spent any time together.

Just before entering the room, Sarah, in her innocence, looked at her father and said, "Daddy, does this mean your fight is over?"

"I hope so, Sarah. I hope so."

They knocked on the door of Clay's room. Rebecca heard the knock and went to open the door. Bill Royer, their attorney, was sitting beside Clay, holding a clipboard, while Clay was signing his name to the legal forms Bill had brought with him from Macon.

As Daniel walked in, Clay looked directly at him. He then looked at Ayse. In an instant he knew why his son loved her. She was so beautiful, her dark eyes radiating a sense of serenity that calmed the entire room. For an instant, Clay remembered she was a Muslim. Then, just as quickly, he dismissed the thought and returned his gaze to Daniel.

The attorney got up and stepped back, sensing the gravity of the moment. Clay spoke first.

"Can you ever forgive me, Daniel?"

"Yes, Dad."

"Come, sit here."

Daniel let go of his wife's hand and walked around to the other side of the bed, where the lawyer had just been sitting. As he sat down, he leaned over and held his frail, dying father in his arms. No one said a thing. A glorious silence overwhelmed the room. Rebecca went over to Ayse and embraced her, unable to cope with the flood of emotions washing over her.

The children sat down, not able to grasp the meaning of what they were witnessing, but knowing it was important. Intuitively knowing that this was a good thing.

"What have I done?" whispered Clay into his son's ears. "All those years, all that time we could have had together is gone, Daniel. What was I thinking?"

"It's okay, Dad. It's all behind us. We're here, you're alive and nothing else matters. All we ever have is the moment, and this is the best moment of my entire life."

Daniel squeezed his father as hard as he felt it safe to do. With his father's mouth beside his ear, he could plainly hear the strained breathing, the sound of the fluid filling his father's lungs, and the pain he held.

"Ask Ayse to come sit beside me, please."

Daniel looked at his wife, and with his right hand, motioned for her to come join him on his father's deathbed. She walked over and stood beside her husband.

"Ayse, can you ever forgive me?"

"Yes, Mr. Harris. God is most merciful and kind. He has shown us that again today. I forgive you."

As Daniel rose, Ayse sat down where he had been seated. She leaned over and embraced the man she had never seen before. The warmth of their bodies melded into something that reached beyond the differences. She held him as a mother holds an injured child — gravely injured. Tears welled in her eyes. This frail, sick old man had caused them so much agony and suffering through the years. But it was over. It was a time to heal. She let go of her embrace and whispered to Clay,

"God has answered our prayers. The angel on the airplane was right, time is a river into which we cannot see."

Clay could not believe what Ayse had just whispered to him. He looked at her and asked, "You've seen an angel?"

"Yes, I think I have. Twice, on an airplane. But why do you ask?"

Clay paused, realizing it was no longer important. The past was written, there could be no changing or repairing those damaged years behind them. He let go of everything, forgiving himself for being wrong, forgiving his son for disobeying him and forgiving the woman who now held him in her arms. God had filled the room with a joy that sang as loud as all the choirs in the world singing in perfect unison.

"Do you believe in angels, Ayse?"

"Yes. Don't you?"

Clay smiled, and whispered, "Yes, I do now."

Clay grew tired again, his will falling victim to a body that failed him. He thought of death. Not in a bad, or a fearful way, but in the understanding that death was good. We are all born and we all die, he thought. That is how God binds us to one another, through death. In death color doesn't matter — race, creed, philosophy, wealth, power, success, failure all share in the long silence. Only the living debate their differences.

Clay was not afraid. He thought about death as calmly as he thought about living. He was released. The fleeting angels were gone — the two angels vanished beneath the drifting snow and the angel of God standing beside his Creator in Zion. The real angels were in the room with him — two wondrous grandchildren, his wife, his son and a woman from Istanbul who believed in a religion he knew nothing of. Human angels.

That's when it happened. At that very moment, in a room full of family and tears, Clayton Aaron Harris became a christian.

Hast thou no need of your fresh power to find anew thy holy grail — a thing which reckless youth must do because the careful aged fail? Uplifted to that cross Lord God with outstretched hand we wait thy nail.

Thornwell Jacobs

Amen

Also by Charles Sobczak:

Six Mornings on Sanibel *(1999)*
ISBN 0-9676199-5-5 $13.95

Way Under Contract *(2000)*
ISBN 0-9676199-4-7 $15.95

Rhythm of the Tides *(2001)*
ISBN 0-9676199-1-2 $13.95

Questions regarding ordering information and/or comments are encouraged and welcome via:

Toll Free Number:	877-472-8900
Local Number	239-472-0491
Fax Number:	239-472-1426
Email:	indigopress@earthlink.net
Web Address:	www.indigopress.net
Mailing Address:	Indigo Press, LLC
	P.O. Box 977
	Sanibel Island, FL 33957

— VISA or MasterCard Accepted —
Orders may be placed via our website, telephone or US Mail.

A Choice of Angels
Book Club Discussion Questions

#1. Is the relationship between Daniel and his father, Clayton, typical of other teenaged relationships you might be familiar with? Does the fact that Daniel is a PK (a preacher's kid) help to exacerbate Daniel's rebellious nature? Do you personally know of or have stories to share about other troubled preachers' kids, and why they might behave that way?

#2. Do you feel that mixed marriages, whether stemming from religious, cultural or ethnic differences, are appropriate? Would you allow your son or daughter to marry a Muslim if they were in love? Can these marriages work in today's world? As a culture, have we become more, or less tolerant of religious differences since 9/11 and the war in Iraq?

#3. What are the similarities and differences in the marriages between Clayton and Rebecca and Mustapha and Elif? On page 155, Daniel tells Ayse that his mother, Rebecca, wears her own form of veil. Do you think Southern Baptist women are too subservient to their husbands?

#4. Clayton feels betrayed by his son's elopement with Ayse and views it as the ultimate act of disobedience. Is Clayton being fair by disowning his son? Would you disown your child if they did something similar? When Clayton addresses his congregation and publicly denounces his son by asking the entire congregation to disown Daniel does Clayton go too far? Near the end of the novel, when Clayton calls Daniel's employer to have him fired, do you think it was the right thing for Clayton to do?

#5. Are the angels that appear to Ayse and Clayton real or could they be explained by other factors such as dreams or drug interactions? Angels are present in most of the world's great religions: Christianity, Judaism, Islam, Buddhism and Hinduism. Do you believe in angels? Have you ever had an experience or know of anyone who has had an experience with an angel? There are three readily identifiable angels in the novel but unbeknownst to many readers, including the novelist at first, there is a fourth, more obscure angel. Who do you think the fourth angel is and when does she appear?

#6. Joshua J. Taylor describes forgiveness as a tool, a "crowbar by which we are freed from the enslavement of our ill-tempered feelings." Is Joshua's definition of forgiveness the same as yours? In your opinion, who is behaving more like a Christian, JJ Taylor or Clayton Harris? Is it more important to practice our faith in deeds and actions or in Bible quotations and words? Was forgiveness important to Christ? What does the prophet Mohammed say about forgiveness? Is there an inherent, if not irreconcilable difference between the philosophies of the Old and the New Testaments?

#7. When Rebecca discovered that Daniel was incarcerated at Central State Hospital why do you think she didn't insist on getting him out of the facility immediately? Was she doing the right thing by not telling the truth to Ayse about her son's whereabouts? What would you have done?

#8. In the novel, two grandchildren help to bridge the gap between the families. Do you have any personal examples where this kind of thing has happened? As Rebecca points out to her husband, is it fair to blame the children for the apparent sins of their parents? Had the angel not spoken to Clayton through Sarah, do you think he would have ultimately reconciled with Daniel? Were Daniel's reactions to his father's dying wishes believable?

#9. Every location in this novel is true and authentic except for the angelic apparitions. Has anyone in the discussion group ever seen or heard of Oglethorpe University, Thornwell Jacobs or the Crypt of Civilization? What does the Crypt of Civilization symbolize in the novel? Has anyone in the discussion group ever been to Turkey or to Istanbul and, if so, how does that nation compare with the United States?

#10. How do you think Jesus Christ would have responded to the incident of 9/11? Would Christ have turned the other cheek? As Daniel asks, is the behavior of radical Islamic fundamentalists who bomb innocent civilians fundamentally different than that of radical Christians who bomb abortion clinics? Ultimately, is the behavior of a radical group like Al-Qaida a Christian or a Muslim problem? Do you believe the world's great religions are different paths up the same mountain? Is heaven non-denominational?